THE
GUILTY
GIRL

BOOKS BY PATRICIA GIBNEY

THE GUILTY GIRL

PATRICIA GIBNEY

bookouture

Published by Bookouture in 2022

An imprint of Storyfire Ltd.
Carmelite House
50 Victoria Embankment
London EC4Y 0DZ

www.bookouture.com

ISBN: 978-1-80314-251-7
eBook ISBN: 978-1-80314-252-4

For Jo Kelly and Antoinette Hegarty

PROLOGUE

Every time a punch landed on his skin, she winced and tried not to look. But she couldn't help peeking out through her fingers. Thick red streaks paid testament to the beating being meted out. It appeared particularly violent and she wasn't sure she could stomach much more.

It wasn't a street fight. It was a sparring match. Rules, timings, trainer and coach. Yet it was brutal. If this was what they did in training, how would it translate into an actual bout with a championship on the line?

She strolled around the perimeter of the raised ring. Eyes cast downwards, she listened instead. The sound of their footwork could have rivalled any *Riverdance* routine. Sweat flew through the air like a soft morning mist. Wheezing and gasping created a wordless language, as though they were engaged in a silent conversation. And then there were the intermittent slaps and punches. Groans and feet sliding, trying to remain upright. Trying to avoid hitting the deck or they might not get up again. It was imperative not to go down for the count. That could spell disaster. She knew that.

Though she was young, she felt like she'd been around this

sport forever. She never understood its attraction. But if it made him happy, she wouldn't argue.

Reaching the end of the room, she sat down heavily on a bench and waited, stealing the odd glance at the fighters in the ring.

They pirouetted, swayed, ducked and dived, neither man giving in nor giving up. One was destined to be dead within weeks. But she was not to know that as she waited. She was not to know that her actions had already started the tragic events and she still had one innocent mistake to make that would result in death.

Maybe if she'd been more tuned into the dangers of the small slice of world she occupied, she could have halted the series of events about to unfold. But she hadn't been tuned in at all, so she couldn't change destiny.

The precariously stacked deck of cards would topple, and as they came tumbling down, few would escape the fallout, least of all her.

So there she sat, oblivious, watching and waiting.

1

It was not yet four a.m. and Sean Parker hadn't slept at all. Perhaps it was the warm cider he'd had at the party. Doubt niggled at his brain, because he couldn't remember bringing home his new leather jacket. Was that why he'd been unable to sleep?

Mooching around his room, he searched again for the jacket. Anxiety took root in the pit of his stomach as he got down on his knees and looked under the bed. A pair of rolled-up dirty socks and one runner. Dust. Nothing else. He glanced around the room. His gaming chair held his new controller and the second runner. The desk was cluttered, but no jacket.

He'd have to go back.

After pulling on jeans and a clean sweatshirt, he dragged his runners onto his bare feet and rushed downstairs. In the kitchen, he poured a glass of water and stood at the window staring out at the darkness. The jacket had been a present from his mother, *an expensive one and he wasn't to come home without it*, she often reminded him. But now he had come home without it. It hadn't even crossed his mind, because of the heat at the party.

It wasn't often he ventured out, and the one time he had, he'd lost the jacket. No, not lost. Forgotten. It had to be at Lucy's house.

It was a mile trek up the country road, that was once he reached the end of the avenue at his own house. The house they called home for now. Farranstown House had apparently been in his mother's family for decades, and they were basically house-sitting the draughty old building until Uncle Leo made his decision. If she threw a hissy fit over the jacket, Sean could threaten to go live with Leo in New York. That would silence her tirade.

He turned on his phone torch and set off. Lucy might still be partying, and if she wasn't, he'd hammer the shite out of the door. Facing an angry Lucy beat facing his apoplectic mother any day of the week.

A set of headlights appeared over the brow of the narrow hill. He stepped into the ditch to avoid being mowed down. The driver never even saw him, such was their speed. Sean stared at the red tail lights as the car disappeared. He thought he recognised it. A small Fiat. Hadn't a lad arrived at the party in it? The same guy who had been serving the alcohol. Perhaps the party had just finished and the door would be open and he wouldn't have to annoy Lucy. Yes!

He walked on, thinking how the distance appeared so much further in the dark. Over the hill and down the dip and another few hundred metres and he'd be there. A soft whoosh of tyres and he watched as a bicycle with a weak lamp approached. It was just a kid. No one he knew.

'What you staring at?' the kid shouted as he passed, disappearing from sight before Sean could reply.

Eventually he saw the light spilling out from Lucy McAllister's home. Despite the house being lit up like a Christmas tree, all was quiet. Party was over.

Trudging up the shingle driveway, kicking at pebbles, he

was deciding on his best approach. He didn't want to sound childish by telling Lucy he'd forgotten his good leather jacket and his mother would kill him. He had to think of a suitable lie.

The front door stood open and the interior light spilled out into the darkness. Soon the sky would shimmer with the pinkness of dawn, but that was a few hours off yet. He weighed up what to do. He'd run in, find the jacket and leave before he was noticed. Best plan. Buoyed by his decision, he stepped inside.

He stalled, staring at the mess of party debris littering the carpet. Not his problem, but he couldn't see any coats in the hall. He had a quick look in the kitchen at the end of the hallway. Glasses and bottles stacked along the marble worktops. No sign of his jacket. He backed out and moved into the living room.

Agape, he took in the scene. As untidy as the kitchen had been, he had not been prepared for the destruction in the living room. The patio doors hung open; one had its glass smashed. Upturned chairs and ...

Shivers shook his body and he was powerless to stop the spasms. It was as if his whole skeleton was trying to break free of its barrier of muscle and skin. Before him, the wall and the floor beneath it were dotted with blood spatter. What the hell had happened here?

A sound from above broke the deathly silence. Dragging his eyes away from the blood, he glanced up at the ceiling. Footsteps padded down the stairs. Was it the injured person or whoever had caused blood to be spilled? He burst into motion and fled through the door, the one close to where the DJ had played. He moved so quickly he almost toppled head-first over a tangled cable on the floor.

Back in the kitchen, he heard muffled voices in the living room. Someone let out a cry. Then there was silence. He waited for a full minute before he dared look. The living room was empty.

Glancing at the discarded bottles and glasses spread around the kitchen, and the black bin bags full to bursting, he noticed spots of blood on the floor here too. What had happened? Maybe he should get the hell out. But he had inherited his mother's nose for sniffing out trouble, so he forced himself through another door and up a concrete staircase that led from the utility room to the upper level of the house.

Careful not to stand on the blood spatter – he was frightened but not stupid – he found himself on a carpeted landing. The smell of blood was as strong as the silence was palpable.

He crept along the landing, following the trail into a bedroom. The sheets on the bed were tangled, as if someone had tugged at them, dragging them to the floor. At the far side, he came face to face with the horror he had hoped he would not see, though subconsciously he'd known it would be bad.

The body was on the floor, arms outstretched, legs crossed. Clothing in disarray. There were many wounds, but the neck wound was the most disturbing in the sea of blood.

His stomach rumbled. A wave of nausea shot up to his throat. Clamping a hand to his mouth, he shook his head in disbelief, as if that action would rid him of the sight of the broken body on the floor. This couldn't be happening. He backed out of the room before realising that maybe he should check for signs of life.

Preparing himself, he took a deep breath outside the door before creeping inside, aware that his runners could leave imprints on the soft carpet if he wasn't careful. But he had to know if an ambulance was needed. He gagged as he tentatively put his fingers around the wrist, checking for a pulse, knowing he would not find one. Hoping all the same.

No sign of life. No hope.

Fear squeezed his heart and goose bumps rose on his skin. This wasn't a PlayStation game. This was in front of his eyes and there was nothing he could do. No way to reboot. No option to start again. No second lives. This was reality.

He remembered the voices he'd heard a few moments earlier. Were the killers still here?

He wasn't waiting to find out. Making his decision, right or wrong – probably wrong – he backed out onto the landing. Turned and fled down the main stairs. Before leaving, he glanced into the desecrated living room, as if hoping his jacket might suddenly appear. But he couldn't see it. A rucksack and a few cushions were thrown around on the couch. He couldn't go in there again. His terror was too real.

He flew out the front door. He could phone 999 anonymously, couldn't he? But first he had to get away, before the killer came for him.

2

That night, the fateful night, fifteen-year-old Jake Flood was full of how he was going to overcome all his difficulties and make something of himself. Become someone important. Someone to be reckoned with. A hero. Yeah, he wanted to be everyone's hero, but most of all, he wanted to make money.

Top of the list, he saw himself as an Olympian. A gold medal shining brightly around his neck as he stood on a podium with the Irish flag fluttering in the breeze behind him. Everyone said he could run, and he knew he had stamina. Only last week he had outrun the guards, and they'd been on bikes! That had been a great laugh. Nothing could stop Jake Flood becoming just about anything he wanted to be. He was the man! Or so he thought.

He lifted his black T-shirt, the one that had once belonged to his dad, the one with the Blizzards photo cracking from wear, that one, and sprayed Lynx Africa under his arms. He marvelled at how his abs were coming along. Nights in the gym were not wasted on Jake. The Leinster boxing championships were next week, and though he had no interest in them, he didn't want to piss off his coach, Barney. Barney had encouraged him to enter the lightweight under-sixteen competition. Jake knew he could win easily; once he put his mind to it, he could do anything. The question was, could he be bothered? Once maybe, but not any more. Sure, he wanted to be an Olympic boxer, but he also wanted to earn money.

Tucking his top into his faded black jeans with the knees torn out – he'd used a steak knife on them, even though it was blunt as shit – he decided to let it fall loose over his belt instead. Black Converse with pristine white laces completed the look. The look he strived for: namely, cool dude, like the guys on YouTube. The guys who made loads of money.

He ran his hand through his black hair and smoothed down a few errant strands around his left ear that he'd missed with the gel. He'd had the hair shaved over the right one. He winked a green eye at himself in the mirror.

'Ready to rock and roll,' he sang.

'You look like a goth, Jake.' A voice from the doorway.

'Go away, Shaz.' He shook his head slowly. Why did she have to break the spell he'd cast for himself? Sharon was the reality from which he constantly sought escape. He fought the urge to tell his ten-year-old sister, the most annoying person on the planet, to shut up and get out, but the truth was he couldn't bear her tears.

With a sigh, he turned from the mirror and caught her swinging on the door handle.

'You'll break it, Shaz.'

'Won't.'

'Will.'

'Don't care. Where you going?'

'Out.'

'Can I go with you?'

'For crying out loud, squirt, you should be in bed.'

'Duh.' Sharon rolled her eyes like she'd seen him do a thousand times and tugged at the too-short legs of the Disney pyjamas she'd got last Christmas. She'd shot up at least six inches since then. His little sister was growing up fast. That made him fearful.

'Jake, you know Mam will have a canary if you're not here when she gets home.'

He was supposed to be babysitting. How was he ever going to make something of himself with Shaz and Mam holding him back? *Stop.* None of this was Shaz's fault. He really should stay home, but he couldn't miss tonight's adventure. Time to be nice to the most annoying person in the world.

'Tell you what, Shaz, I'll bring you back a bag of chips, but you have to listen to me. It's on condition you go to bed and stay there. You can't tell Mam I went out. Promise?'

With a strand of her dark hair in her mouth, she squinted at him. 'Maybe I won't tell if you get me chicken nuggets too.'

'Deal.'

'Yes!' She ran over and hugged him before scooting out the door and into her bedroom.

In the kitchen, he noticed the key to his mother's old Fiat Punto on the table. She had walked to work that afternoon, complaining that she couldn't afford to waste money on parking fees.

He reached out his hand and paused.

No, Jake, don't.

But why not?

He imagined the gobsmacked expressions on the faces of his friends if he showed up in the small blue car. Didn't matter that it was a crock of shit, it could still move.

Biting his lip, he glanced behind him. Shaz was up in her room. He'd have the car back before Mam got home. No one would know, and it'd be so exciting with four wheels under him!

'Don't open the door for anyone, Shaz. See you later.'

He scooped up the key, closing his fist around it. Tonight he'd be king of his world. The fact that he had only driven the car once, out by the lake when his mother had given in to him, didn't faze him. He was a quick learner. Still, he hoped he could remember which pedals to press.

'Don't forget the chicken nuggets,' Sharon shouted, her voice muffled from behind her door.

'I won't forget,' he shouted, and banged the door on his way out.

The last extension was a bitch to clip into her hair, but Hannah Byrne wanted to add an extra burst of volume. She didn't need the length, as her blonde mane caressed the dip in her spine just above the belt on her tight black mini skirt.

Lucy was hosting the party to celebrate end-of-school exams and Hannah knew she was lucky to be invited. Lucy McAllister's parties were legendary in Ragmullin. Getting an invite meant you were *someone*. That worried Hannah. She felt she was a nobody.

She'd arrived at Lucy's house full of excitement and jittery with nerves. Lucy had welcomed her with a hug, albeit without touching cheeks. Hannah immediately felt a glow of happiness. She was being accepted into a new world.

Lucy's best friend, Ivy, had mimicked the hug. 'Ooh, what is that perfume you're wearing?' She made a 'yuck' sound.

'It's my mother's. A little white bottle. Don't know what it's called.' It was cheap, and Hannah felt a wobble in her stomach at being reminded how shitty it smelled. She glanced at Lucy, who smiled back sweetly.

'Probably Anaïs whatsitsname,' she said.

'That's ancient.' Ivy twirled a lock of black hair around her finger.

'We're upstairs,' Lucy said, flicking her long dark hair over her shoulder, leading the way. 'Don't worry about your clothes not being suitable for the party. I can lend you something to wear.'

'It's okay, I brought other stuff to change into,' Hannah said, looking down at her grubby jeans and old shirt. Even her trainers were 'yuck'.

'If your *stuff* is anything like your perfume, sweetie, you'll have to wear something of mine. Come on, you can use one of the guest rooms to change.'

While Hannah was undressing, Lucy and Ivy had burst in.

Ivy turned up her nose. 'Unmatched underwear? Gross, hun. Have you got a bra to fit her, Lucy?'

'Are you mad? Those fried-egg boobs are not going in any of my Wonderbras,' Lucy snorted, swallowing a laugh.

'I'm fine.' Hannah was close to tears. 'My underwear won't be seen.' How could they be so cruel?

'If you say so,' Lucy said, and handed over a skirt and top. 'You can keep these. I don't want them. I've outgrown them but you can squeeze in. The top will fit anyhow.' With that, she and Ivy doubled over laughing and ran from the room.

Staring sadly at her reflection in the floor-length mirror, Hannah tried not to wonder why Lucy was being so mean after inviting her. What was her aim? Wasn't it too late for friendship, now that they'd all be going off to different colleges in the autumn? Despite feeling humiliated, she was too soft; she vowed not to let Lucy and Ivy's behaviour dim her enthusiasm for the party. Not yet, anyhow.

She'd stripped off to try on Lucy's clothes, and she was sure someone was sniggering in the corridor. Whirling around, dressed only in her knickers, her arms crossed over her nakedness, she spotted the door slightly ajar. She whipped up her shirt and, holding it to her chest, crept over and glanced out just as the door to Lucy's room swung shut and the giggles intensified into raucous laughter.

I can't cry, she warned herself. Her make-up had taken ages to get right, so she buried her tears and got dressed.

Twirling, she made sure the short skirt didn't show off her knickers. Had Lucy intentionally given her clothes that were a size too small? She hoped not, but she had a feeling the other girl was making fun of her.

Plumping up her flat boobs in the black halter-neck with a row of shiny sequins along the hem, she had to admit the top was too tight. Lucy must have owned it when she was ten! Despite all that, the short skirt highlighted her best asset. Her legs. Legs that made her the fastest athlete at school.

It felt awkward getting ready in Lucy's house, but how else could she get away with so much make-up and these skimpy clothes. Her mother would have a grade A fit. Don't make the same mistakes I did, she'd say, and Hannah would grimace hearing the barb in the unspoken words. She meant 'don't get pregnant at seventeen like I did'. That made Hannah feel even more unwanted than she already did.

She felt a tightness in her chest then. Grades. The exams had been difficult, but she hoped she'd secure enough points for her chosen degree, sports science. Ambition motivated her, because she didn't want to spend a day longer than necessary in the one-bedroom flat she shared with her mother and little brother. She was getting out of Ragmullin.

An uneasy flutter caused her to stall. She heard more giggles coming from the room next door. The other girls were drinking vodka mixed in glass Coke bottles with straws. Hannah had had her fair share of experience dealing with people who drank, namely her mother. Perhaps that was the reason she avoided drinking herself.

Shrugging off the feeling of being unwanted, she shook out her hair, admiring the volume. It was fab, so feck Lucy and Ivy!

She straightened her shoulders as she exited the bedroom.

Hannah Byrne was about to act the part, even if her confidence was crumbling.

———

Seventeen-year-old Lucy McAllister knew she was very nearly drunk before her foot even hit the top step of the stairs. It was cool, but she really needed to be alert tonight. It was going to be a mega party. The best one she'd ever thrown. Her parties were the most talked about beforehand and, more importantly, afterwards. Everyone would be talking about this one until at least Christmas. She giggled and planted her high-heeled silver sandals on the floor, then inched up her sparkly white dress to show off a lean thigh. She knew how to make an entrance.

'Ha, you made it down the stairs in one piece, Lucy.'

'Cormac O'Flaherty! Thought the zoo was closed. Who let you in?'

Lucy had not invited red-headed, freckle-faced Cormac. She jerked her head towards the door. Noel Glennon, her PE teacher, was standing there. Good. He'd agreed to be bouncer for the night, as he often manned the door at local nightclubs. She posed him a question with her eyes. He shrugged. Of course he'd have thought Cormac was one of her friends. He looked a lot younger than twenty.

'Door was open.' Cormac shrugged and spilled his drink from the paper cup clutched in his hand. A clear stain spread across the cream carpet and he wiped it with the toe of his black runner.

'You're such a dickhead. Count yourself lucky that's not red wine, or I'd make you get down on your knees to scrub it.'

She couldn't be sure, but she thought he'd called her a slut under his breath. That was going too far. She should tell him to leave, but she liked having someone to ridicule.

'Takes one to know one,' she said as she moved by the open-mouthed Cormac, her friends trailing behind her like a procession of Vestal Virgins. She smirked. There were no virgins in her troop. Unless you counted Hannah Byrne, but no one counted sad Hannah. Despite that, Hannah was part of her brilliant plan for the night. The unforgettable party night!

Making her grand entrance into the expansive living room to whoops from the boys and jealous gasps from the girls, Lucy marvelled at the power she possessed. There must have been twenty-five teenagers already there, milling around, laughing and drinking. And more would arrive later. The more people around to witness her grand reveal, the better. Didn't matter if they'd been invited or not. She just needed to do it right.

'Shouldn't there be music?' Hannah said.

'Duh, Richie has just set up,' Lucy said. She eyed Richie Harrison, the DJ she'd hired on Noel Glennon's recommendation. He was standing behind his music system in the far corner of the room. She gave him a nod, and forced herself to return his smile as he blasted out an old Avicii number. The party had started.

'I think that's too loud,' Hannah said.

'Oh for God's sake.' Lucy donned her most ferocious expression and turned on the girl. 'If you complain once more, Hannah Byrne, I will personally escort you out the door.' Seeing the look of hurt flashing in Hannah's eyes, she sighed. 'It's a party, it's supposed to be loud. Be a good girl and get yourself a drink, one with plenty of alcohol. And fetch one for me too. Then find yourself a boyfriend.'

She watched Hannah elbow her way through the crowd and felt a moment of envy at her long, lean legs. Athlete's legs. Why hadn't she got big muscled calves if she was such a good runner? Maybe giving her the tight mini skirt had been a mistake – it made her look even taller. Lucy consoled herself with the thought that tonight's plan would knock the innocence from the girl's face.

'Why did you even invite her?' Ivy shouted into her ear. Her best friend, like forever.

Lucy shrugged. Ivy wasn't privy to everything, even if she thought she was. 'Come out to the garden. I've got a table of drinks set up there. If we're lucky, she won't find us for hours.'

Throwing back her glistening ebony hair, she did her best impression of Kim Kardashian's walk, sashaying across the floor smiling her perfect five-thousand-euro smile at her guests. It was all so exciting, she thought, giddy from the neat vodka she'd already consumed.

Tonight would be the night of her life.

4

A seething anger bubbled in the pit of Hannah's stomach. It swelled upwards, settling like a ball of wind in her chest. She wasn't stupid. She knew when she was being belittled, excluded and made fun of. Lucy had displayed utter contempt for her in that short exchange. It was obvious she wasn't wanted.

Biting back her hurt, she fought her way to the table where bottles of alcohol were being served by a bored-looking lad in a faded black T-shirt. He held out a long-neck Bulmers. He looked too young to legally drink, let alone be serving alcohol.

She shook her head. 'Can I get a Coke?'

'What'd you say?' He leaned closer and she got a whiff of Lynx. The cheap pound-shop variety. Fake stuff. As awful as her own perfume.

She flashed him a smile, realising he didn't fit in with the crowd any more than she did.

A little louder, she said, 'A Coke or water, please.'

He grinned. Cute, despite his overlapping front teeth and gelled-to-death black hair. He only came up to her shoulder.

'Alcohol only. Haven't even tonic water for the gin. I guess Lucy wants everyone paralytic drunk.'

'She wants everyone to talk about this being the best party ever, and that's not even a guess, it's the truth.'

'Don't think anyone will remember much of it.'

There was something about his eyes. Hypnotic, she concluded. In that moment, she felt alone yet not alone. 'What's your name?'

'Doesn't matter. I'm only here to hand out the drink and the crack.' He winked.

'You're here for the craic?' She strained to hear over the loud music.

'You're so wet,' he said, digging his hand into his jeans pocket and showing her the top of a plastic bag. It was rammed full of pills.

'Oh!' Hannah recoiled.

'Come back later if you want one.' He pushed the bag back into his pocket and turned to hand the bottle of cider to the next in line.

Hannah was glad he hadn't insisted, because she was morose enough to take one. She turned away and leaned against the wall, wondering if she could leave now without being noticed. Grab her rucksack from the room upstairs and call a taxi. She could disappear into the night and hope never to see Lucy McAllister again. The girl was such a fake. Why had she trusted her? Now she was thankful that school had ended and college beckoned. If she got the grades, she'd be going to Athlone Institute of Technology. Of course Lucy had picked courses at Trinity. *Only the crème de la crème get into Trinity*, she was apt to remind everyone at any opportunity.

What had Hannah been thinking of, coming to her party?

Bad move.

———

Cormac O'Flaherty was still smarting from the insults Lucy had flung at him. He needed to have a word with her. He found her outside with her posse by an egg chair swing and a large rattan table overloaded with bottles. Lanterns with tea lights lined the massive garden, adding to the party atmosphere.

'Cormac, you're like a leech,' Lucy said. 'Did anyone ever tell you that?'

He smiled his lopsided smile. 'Only you, Lucy.'

Her friends giggled and sipped their Coors Light.

'I'll tell you something for nothing, Cormac, I don't like leeches,' Lucy hissed into the warm night air. 'They're slimy and stick to your skin and suck the life out of you. So could you please fuck off. Just because you cut the grass for my dad doesn't give you a right to be here. Are you listening to me? You are not wanted.'

Cormac recoiled from her words and picked at the acne on his throbbing forehead. Lucy had not been like this the last time they'd spoken, so why was she acting the bitch now? Probably because she had an audience.

He watched as she turned to the coven huddling around her, their shoulders rocking with laughter. Clenching his hand into a fist, cracking the plastic cup into bits, he thought how he'd love to thump her.

Making his way inside, he spied one of her friends lolling against the wall. Different to the rest of the clique. He'd seen her traipsing down the stairs behind Lucy, but he'd never have clocked Hannah Byrne as a groupie. Well, what did he know?

'You're Hannah Byrne, aren't you?' Still reeling from Lucy's tirade, he joined her propping up the wall.

'I don't think we've ever talked to each other, Cormac,' she said, 'so how do you know my name?'

He had to lean in close to speak above the noise passing as music. She didn't pull away from him. He liked her scent. Soft and aromatic.

'I know a lot of people,' he said. 'You know my name too. How is that?'

'Lucy shouted at you in the hallway, but I knew who you were anyhow. Not your name, like. Just to see.'

'And where did you see me?'

'You do the gardening around our school. Saw you hanging around town too.'

Cormac felt his face burst with heat. 'Yep, everyone calls me a hanger-on. Including your friend Lucy.'

'She's not really my friend. I suppose you could call me a hanger-on as well.'

'Maybe we could "hang on" together.' He did air quotes and smiled as she turned to look at him. Gosh, she was beautiful.

'I don't think that's a good idea,' she said softly, and he had to lean in even closer.

'Give me one good reason.'

'Because ... I'm going home. I don't drink and there's only alcohol and drugs here.'

'Drugs?'

'Yeah. That boy handing out the drinks showed me a bag of pills.'

'Ah, don't mind Jake Flood. He's a fifteen-year-old dick-head. Will we call the guards to raid the place?' He nudged her with his elbow and flashed what he thought was his best grin.

Her soft lips curved upwards, lighting up her face. His heart somersaulted in his chest.

'It had crossed my mind to make the call,' she laughed, 'but I think I'd be Lucy's first suspect if the guards arrived. I couldn't be arsed giving her something else to hate me for.'

'Suppose that's as good a reason as any.' He nodded towards the drinks table. 'Like I said, I know of Jake.'

'Is that a good thing or a bad thing?'

'I didn't think he'd be one to sell drugs.'

'Maybe Lucy wants him to liven up the party.'

'Hey, listen, do you want to try one?' he asked, then grimaced as her eyes widened in horror. Shit.

'No way,' she said.

She inched away and he felt the space expand as if a physical being had pushed in between them.

'I'm sorry, Hannah. Didn't mean to offend you.' He wanted to move in closer, but decided to change the subject. 'Hey, I know that guy over there too.'

'The tall, geeky blonde dude?'

'Yeah. Sean Parker. His mother's a cop.'

'A cop? You mean, like a real guard?'

'A detective. I didn't think this was Sean's scene.'

'How do you know him?'

'We play online games.'

'What type of games?'

'Used to be FIFA, but F1 is the latest craze. He's good, too. He could be a champion gamer. He live-streams. You can subscribe to it on YouTube. Listen, why don't we get out of here and I'll tell you about it? We could grab a coffee. I'm sure the Bean Café is open late on Friday nights.'

He watched her as she glanced at her phone. Checking the time? Or looking for a way out?

'A few minutes ago I was thinking of calling a taxi to go home, but now I don't think it's such a good idea.'

'In other words, you don't want to give Lucy McAllister the satisfaction of knowing she got to you?'

She smiled. 'Something like that.'

'I'll *hang on* with you for a while, if you like.'

'I suppose there's no harm in that.'

He inched closer, a broad smile spreading across his face. He might just have been totally right to gatecrash Lucy's party.

5

The party was definitely not Sean Parker's usual scene, but a few of the lads in his year were going with the intention of getting plastered and getting a girl. Sean couldn't be bothered about either, but he'd turned seventeen in April and hadn't even celebrated. When he'd mentioned Lucy's party at home, he sensed his mother was hoping he wouldn't go. It wouldn't surprise him if she was parked across the road from Lucy's house watching to see him leave or else waiting to knock on the door at one in the morning to haul him home.

He made his way through the crowd towards the makeshift bar, where he spotted Cormac chatting up a girl.

'Hi, Sean,' Cormac said. 'Didn't think this would be your thing.'

'I'd rather be in my room playing F_1.'

'Me too.'

Big mistake, Sean thought as the pretty blonde stepped away from Cormac.

'Hi, I'm Sean.' He introduced himself, trying to rescue the situation.

'Hannah.' She kept her head turned away.

'Nice to meet you.'

She looked at him then and rolled her eyes. He felt a blush scream up his cheeks. He was as bad as Cormac, awkward as anything.

'I'll leave you two nerds to talk gaming,' she said. 'I want to see who else is here.'

Sean couldn't take his eyes off her long legs as she elbowed her way through the dancing crowd. She was a stunner.

'Thanks, bud,' Cormac said.

'For what?'

'Ruining my night. I didn't know you'd be here.'

'Trying to get one up on my mother.'

'Is she being the usual pain in the arse?'

'Something like that.'

'Want to get a drink?'

'I'm okay.' Sean tipped the bottle to his mouth and nearly gagged as the cider scalded his throat. 'It's hot in here.'

'What?'

He was leaning towards Cormac to repeat his words when he noticed the lad at the drinks table eyeing them.

'Who's the kid?'

'Jake. Hannah thinks he's a drug dealer.'

Sean stepped back, bumping into someone behind him, and felt a stream of warm liquid soak his T-shirt.

'Drugs? That's so not cool. I'm leaving before someone calls the guards. I'll be mincemeat if my mother finds out there were drugs here.'

'Get real, Sean. She has to know house parties are drug dens.'

Sean squirmed. 'I doubt if she thought Lucy McAllister would be the type of girl to have drugs at her party.'

'Lucy is exactly the type. Her parents are in Spain, so when the cat's away and all that.'

'How do you even know that?' Sean felt a shot of panic. He was surely dead if his mother found out Lucy's olds were not at home. Confined to his room for a month, maybe the whole summer.

Cormac tapped the side of his nose. Sean sipped his tepid cider and surveyed the damage being caused to the McAllisters' beautiful home.

'There will be some mess to be cleaned up in the morning,' he said. Why had he said that? Definitely time to leave.

Cormac laughed. 'Can you imagine Lucy going around with a mop and bucket? I'd pay to see that. She's not the type to break a nail to save a life, never mind lift a mop.'

'You're so right.'

'This is boring. Hold my space. I want to see what Jake has to offer.'

Sean watched as Cormac haggled with the dark-haired boy behind the table. He looked away quickly as the deal was being done. Maybe he should have a look outside to see if his mother was actually waiting for him and catch a lift home. The sanctuary of his room with his gaming gear was more inviting than a night of warm drinks being spilled on him and watching his friends getting high.

Before he could move, Cormac was back by his side with a giddy smile. 'I hope it's good stuff, because this party is shite.'

Sean sighed. How soon could he make his escape?

Later, as he edged towards the door, he saw Hannah approaching him. She might be pretty, but he really needed to get out of there. Then again, she was *very* pretty!

———

Lottie yawned and closed her eyes for a moment before shaking herself awake. It was close on midnight and she hoped Sean would leave the party soon. The music was deafening even with the car windows closed. The McAllisters were lucky they had no close neighbours, or the garda station would be flooded with complaints.

She let her eyelids droop again.

A knock on the window made her jump. She banged her knee against the steering wheel. 'What the hell?' She relaxed seeing the grinning face of her son.

He walked around the car and slid into the passenger seat.

'I knew you'd be here. Thanks, Mam.'

'You're not mad at me?'

'For once, I'm glad. It'll be impossible to get a taxi later on.'

She started the engine, hit the lights and reversed out onto the road. 'Dull party?'

'Not my thing.'

She headed away from the noisy house. 'Music sounds a bit mental. Seems to be a big crowd there. I'm sure Mrs McAllister won't be too pleased if the place gets smashed up. I'd say she's walking around flicking a duster everywhere.'

'She's not there. Shit.' Sean clamped a hand to his mouth.

'What? The adults are not at home?'

'I'm saying nothing. I'm tired. Can you drive faster?'

'I wouldn't have let you go to it if I'd known it was going to be a free-for-all.'

'It's grand. Just music and drinks. Celebrating the end of exams before everyone heads to college. I know I've another year left, but sometimes I like to have a little fun, you know. Maybe you should try it.'

His words stung. Lottie bit her tongue, holding back a retort. Sean was right. She was boring and couldn't think when she'd last had any fun. But at her stage of life, on the wrong side of forty, she supposed it was to be expected.

'I just hope they're behaving themselves,' she said, 'and no one gets hurt.'

'Why would anyone get hurt?'

'I've seen the aftermath of wild parties. Trust me, Sean, things can go belly-up very quickly. Are there drugs there?'

Her son remained silent.

6

Hannah saw Cormac palming the pills into his pocket. She rushed over to him.

'She's a bitch,' she said through gritted teeth. 'That's all there is to it.'

'What did she do to you?'

Angrily she jabbed at her phone. 'She ... Doesn't matter. I tried to talk to her about something, but she totally ignored me.'

'What do you mean?'

Swallowing her rage, she said, 'Did you see the guy at the front door acting like a bouncer? He's my athletics coach. Noel Glennon. Teaches PE at our school too. I only wanted to know why he was here.'

'Did she tell you?'

'No, but it seems weird and creepy for a teacher to be at a teen party.'

'Suppose so. And she wouldn't tell you why?'

'Nope. Lucy can be such a pain.'

'Ask him yourself, if you know him.'

'It's too embarrassing. He must be thirty or even forty years old. It's wrong. It gives me the creeps. I'm going home.'

'Wait. Don't go yet. I got you a present.'

Hannah gawked as he opened up the fingers on his fisted hand to reveal two pink pills.

'You need to lighten up a little,' he said. 'Have some fun. Take one. Just the one. You won't regret it.'

She looked doubtful. 'There could be rat poison in them.'

'Ah, come on,' Cormac insisted. 'That's just in the movies. You've got to live.'

She watched as he picked one of the pills from his palm and swallowed it.

'Look, I'm not frothing at the mouth and my eyes aren't bulging out of my head.'

'I can't,' she said, dubiously. 'I need water or something.'

'Well get some then.'

She went over to Jake.

'Hey, the girl who doesn't drink,' he said. 'I found a bottle of Coke in the kitchen.' He took the bottle from under the table, uncapped it and poured Coke into a plastic cup.

Taking it, Hannah went back to Cormac. 'This night is totally shit.'

'Try one. It'll make it better.'

Was she really about to do this? To take drugs when she was anti anything that made you lose control? 'Are you sure one won't hurt?'

'Cross my heart and hope to die.' He grinned widely and opened out his palm.

She looked at the pill for a moment, then took it from him. 'I'll keep it for later.'

'You're staying so?'

'For a while. Maybe.'

She put the little pill into the hidden pocket in her skirt. Noticing a notification on her phone screen, she tapped it open and almost let the cup fall from her other hand.

'I'm going to kill her. I swear to God, I'm going to fucking kill her.'

———

Lucy watched Hannah and Cormac from outside the patio doors, a slow smile sliding across her face. She glanced over at Jake in the corner. He gave her a thumbs-up. Richie the DJ was grinning at her like a Cheshire cat. His long dark hair was tied in a knot at the neck of his shiny red shirt. A string of coloured beads hung low on his chest. He looked like an ageing hippy, though she supposed he was only in his thirties. He gave her a sultry eye, then licked his finger and held it up to her. She giggled as a warm feeling flooded her abdomen.

'Later,' she mouthed, and turned to watch Hannah staring at her phone. The night was getting better by the minute. And she was about to make it totally awesome. She scrolled through her recent photos and got ready to hit send.

Ivy tottered up to her. 'Can I borrow your phone for a second? I need to take a selfie. Can't find mine.'

'Sure.' Lucy sipped her drink and watched Hannah and that mutt Cormac get close.

What she was doing was cruel, but it was the only way she knew to attract attention.

Someone had to suffer to get her noticed.

———

The kid on the bike leaned against a tree. He'd seen Jake arrive earlier in the ugly blue car. Jake was now their main guy to push the pills, and even though he'd been slow to take to it in the beginning, he was now fully committed. Money appealed to Jake Flood.

What would Sharon think of her big brother if she knew

what he was at? The kid sniggered into his hand. Everyone thought Jake was pure as the driven snow, but he knew different.

He settled under the branches, lush with leaves, where he was sure no one could see him. It was going to be a long night. He didn't want to mess up and he had to make sure Jake didn't either. That was his job. Watch and report back. He was good at it too.

———

I watch everyone. Taking note of all around me.

No one even notices me for who I really am when I'm in my transformed state. That was always the way.

I could stand in a brightly lit room and still the eyes would not be on me. Once upon a time it didn't bother me. Now, though, I feel personally affronted by the lack of acknowledgement. I am the reason they fulfil their youthful ambitions. I think of myself as a magpie.

The magpie is one of the most intelligent creatures on earth. Legend has it they swoop in and steal shiny objects to line their nests. Legend or not, I am good at stealing things. Like the innocence of young girls. Tonight's party is ripe with young flesh just waiting to be ravished.

First, though, I need to know what Lucy McAllister is scheming.

7

Sharon tossed and turned until 3.35, when she got up for a drink. Outside her brother's room she noticed there was no light seeping from the gap at the bottom of the door. Jake must be asleep, and she felt sad that he hadn't brought her home chicken nuggets and chips.

She crept across the tiny landing to the main bedroom. The door was slightly ajar. She pressed her nose through the slit at the jamb, trying to see into the darkness. The curtains had not been closed nor the bed slept in. Her mother had not come home.

Downstairs, the kitchen was neat and tidy. She poured herself a glass of milk and stood at the sink drinking it. She could smell something rotten coming from the plughole. Setting down her milk, she searched the cupboard and found an unopened bottle of disinfectant. Pouring a liberal amount into the sink, she inhaled the floral scent, hoping whatever was in it wasn't toxic. That was what her brother called anyone he didn't like.

'Don't talk to him, he's toxic.' Or sometimes he'd say, 'Run a mile from her, she's toxic. You don't want toxic people in your life, Shaz.'

She didn't think her brother knew – she hoped he didn't – but she had already been in close contact with very nasty people. They must be toxic. Did that make *her* toxic? Was it contagious?

She finished her milk, then rinsed the glass under the tap and left it in the sink. Her head felt woozy from the bluebell odour rising from the plughole. Maybe it would make her sleep. She hoped so, because she was shivering with the thought that her mother was still out and the toxic people might know where she lived.

8

SATURDAY

Sarah Robson loved early-morning house cleans, especially in summer. Getting up early meant she could appreciate the crisp morning air and marvel at the misty fog hanging low over the town as the sun rose. Fine weather eased her depression.

Looking up at the sky, she knew it would be a nice day, even though the weather forecast promised rain in the midlands by nightfall.

She left home with the car radio belting out a Niall Horan song. She knew someone who had taught him in school, and she'd met his father once. She smiled at that piece of useless information as she drove.

After parking at the front of the McAllister house, grandiosely called Beaumont Court – some people had notions – she unloaded her cleaning basket and hoover. She always brought her own hoover to the McAllisters', because the one they owned was a cordless piece of shit that needed to be charged after half an hour's work. Hers was an old-fashioned, slightly battered Nilfisk. She'd bought it second-hand. Best fifty euros she'd ever spent.

Twirling the awkward hose around her arm, she bent down

to scoop up the basket, before pausing. Something had subconsciously struck her as being out of place.

Was it the silence?

Beaumont Court was located over two kilometres outside Ragmullin, with no close neighbours, and this morning a deathly noiselessness hung in the foggy air. Inexplicably, she felt something was wrong.

Abandoning her equipment, she crept towards the large front door under the portico. On the step sat a crate of empty beer bottles. More bottles and glasses lined the windowsills. Had Lucy thrown a party while her parents were away?

She pushed the heavy mahogany door inwards, surprised to find it unlocked, and stuck her head around it. The lights were still on.

'Hello? Anyone home? Lucy?'

No answer, which wasn't odd in itself, because it was just gone seven a.m. She stepped inside.

The state of the carpet!

Her heart dipped at the thought of the job she'd have to do to clean it. She could see a multitude of stains and ... were those bits of pizza crushed into the deep pile? Who put cream carpet in a front hallway anyhow, with all that foot traffic? Sometimes the richest people had the poorest brains.

'Lucy? Where are you?' she called up the stairs, which stood majestically midway down the wide hallway.

She shook her head at the broken glass scattered around her feet, shattered crystals sparkling in the morning light pouring in behind her. Stepping forward, she noticed the stem of a smashed glass. A wine glass. She hoped it wasn't the Waterford crystal she was tasked with washing and shining once a month. She certainly hoped *she* wouldn't be blamed for breaking it.

Moving towards the open door to her right, she entered the massive living room.

'Christ almighty,' she cried at the scene of destruction laid bare before her.

Her first thought was: what the hell has happened here? Her second thought was the length of time it would take her to deep-clean and restore the room to its former self. Her third thought was obliterated in a flash as her eyes were drawn to what looked suspiciously like blood on the far wall and the carpet.

She froze where she stood. Who had been hurt? The McAllisters were due home from their holidays today. Lucy should be around, though, shouldn't she? The glass in one of the patio doors was broken, and she glanced into the garden. Bottles strewn around and more desecration on the lawn.

She pushed open the kitchen door and noticed the droplets leading up the back stairs. Leave now and call the guards, or take a look? If someone was hurt, she had to see if they needed help. But what if someone had been attacked and the attacker was still on the premises?

'Cop on and check it out,' she chided herself, and climbed the concrete staircase.

More red droplets.

On the large landing, with doors leading off in all directions, she followed the blood trail towards one of the guest bedrooms. Taking a deep breath, she stepped inside.

The girl was lying on the floor on the far side of the bed. Hands outstretched. Legs crossed at the ankles. Sarah couldn't tell the original colour of her dress, because it was now blood red. Staring at the gaping cut in her neck, she knew there was no one here to save. The girl had been savagely murdered.

That was when she finally released the scream she'd been trying so hard to hold in.

She screamed and screamed until her throat was raw.

———

Sean lay curled up on his bed, his eyes hurting from lack of sleep. Why hadn't he called the emergency services when he'd seen the body? Because he was a coward, that was why. Plus, he didn't want his mother to know he'd gone back to the house in the dead of night.

But he knew why his fear was real. A few years ago, he had suffered at the hands of a madman. His sister Katie's boyfriend had been killed by that murdering bastard, and she didn't even know she was pregnant with Louis at the time.

Now flashes of that awful time skidded through his brain and he shivered uncontrollably. No, he couldn't tell his mother. Not yet. He had to come to terms with what he'd seen. He hoped he hadn't left any trace evidence behind. No doubt he had. Footprints on the carpet. Fingerprints on the body when he'd checked for signs of life. Evidence that could not be explained by being a party guest.

He was in deep shit.

He needed time to think, but his brain was filled with the image of the dead girl and of his own traumatic time in the clutches of a raving murderer.

Hugging his head with his hands, he tried to blot out the sound of his sobs.

Detective Sergeant Mark Boyd sat at a small round table outside a café in the sweltering Malaga heat. Partially sheltered by the café awning, he stared at the boy sitting across from him, nicely in the shade. The boy sucked loudly on a straw, draining his chocolate milkshake. A little stranger with a milky mouth.

Boyd was still getting used to the fact that he had a son. After receiving the letter from his ex-wife, Jackie, back in April, he'd intended travelling to Spain immediately to check if she was telling the truth about the child. His plans were thwarted when Superintendent Deborah Farrell refused his leave. They'd just closed a murder investigation and the paperwork was supporting the ceiling like scaffolding. In the end, he'd escaped the first week of June on a combination of annual and unpaid leave. He'd loaded up his credit card from his savings and boarded a Ryanair flight to Malaga.

He was due to fly home Monday evening after almost a month away. And still he stared at this little stranger who was his son.

The boy must have sensed Boyd's eyes on him, because he looked up quickly. Two brown orbs flecked with hazel mirrored

Boyd's own. And if that wasn't proof enough, the boy's ears stood out at almost right angles, even more pronounced than his.

He'd carried out the DNA test to be sure, because he couldn't trust his ex-wife. He wouldn't put it past her to have had the boy undergo plastic surgery on his ears! He smiled to himself. A preposterous thought, but where his ex was concerned, anything was possible. Lottie had said the same. God, he missed her. Missed the barbs and smart comments to each other. Missed her presence, full stop.

'What are you smiling at?' Sergio said.

'You, because you're such a good boy,' Boyd said, though what he really wanted to say was that he still found it hard to believe Sergio was his son.

The kid looked heavenwards and sucked loudly on the straw. Boyd didn't even clench his teeth at the irritating sound, he was so enthralled. 'I think you're done there. We should get back to the apartment.'

'Wait.' Sergio lifted the glass to his lips, slurped the last of the liquid. Then he put his finger in and swirled it around the edge before licking it.

Boyd groaned. How was he ever going to get used to how his son behaved? His son. The word still sounded foreign to his ears. He was terrified of it. It carried the weight of responsibility.

'Will Mamá be there?'

Boyd's hands clenched into fists beneath the table. Jackie had cut loose as he'd arrived. Dumped the boy on him and left him the number of a neighbour, Señora Rodriguez, if he needed someone to babysit. Jackie was tanned and looked as high-maintenance as always. She showed him where she'd hidden Sergio's passport, with instructions to take him to Ireland if he wanted to. He wondered when she had become so cold, but he had no time to quiz her, such was the haste of her departure. He reckoned she was running from some criminal she'd crossed. With tears in her eyes, which surprised Boyd, she'd hugged her son.

Dropping the money on the table to cover the bill, Boyd stood. 'Let's find out what this glorious sunny day holds for us, Sergio.'

He wondered if he should buy more sun lotion. His pale skin had tanned lightly in the last few weeks, but because he was in remission from leukaemia, he was ultra-careful about getting too much sun.

As they turned away from the café, he bumped into Albert and Mary McAllister. They'd been holidaying in an apartment they'd bought some years ago. The first day he'd met them, they'd introduced themselves, saying they'd met Jackie a few times. Since he'd been in Malaga, Boyd had discovered that a large Irish community resided on the Costa del Sol.

He smiled. 'Thought you'd be at the airport by now.'

'Last-minute gift buying.' Albert eyed his wife and tapped his man bag sadly. 'Still can't believe how small the world is. You're not the first from Ragmullin we've met out here. It was good to see you. When are you heading home?'

'Soon,' Boyd said, not wishing to divulge his plans.

'Don't forget to look us up. We can go out for a drink. Cafferty's bar is your local, isn't it? Can't say I've ever been in there, but there's a first time for everything, as they say. Come on, Mary, or we'll miss the flight.' He patted Sergio on the head and strutted off with his wife in tow.

'You don't like him,' Sergio said.

Boyd had to give it to the lad, he was astute.

Masked, suited and booted, Detective Inspector Lottie Parker glanced around the impressive hallway. The deep-pile cream carpet was stained, saturated in spilled drink and littered with shattered glass fragments, scrunched-up paper cups and bits of food.

'No sign of forced entry,' Detective Larry Kirby said, looking back at the big heavy door.

'The cleaner said it was open,' Lottie said sharply. A late night was not good for an early morning. 'I picked Sean up from a party here last night. Must have been around midnight. Every door and window was open.' She shivered at the thought of her son having being at a party that had ended with a murder.

'Your Sean was here?' Kirby asked. 'Last night?'

'Do you have to repeat everything I say? I'm tired. I've a headache and I haven't even had a sniff of coffee yet.'

She moved away from him, treading carefully, her forensic suit crinkling with each muffled step. She recalled the report she'd received earlier. Sarah Robson, the cleaner, had been first on the scene and called 999. The two responding uniformed officers had been professional and sealed off the perimeter, standing guard awaiting the ambulance, detectives and the scenes-of-crime officers. The uniforms had taken a statement from Sarah. She'd said she arrived around seven a.m. to clean the house and stumbled into a nightmare. The parents were away and if the guards wanted more information they should talk to Ivy Jones, the deceased's best friend. Once they'd taken down her garbled statement and had her checked by a medic, she was sent home.

Lottie approached Detective Maria Lynch, suited up, standing at the foot of the staircase.

'The body is up there,' Lynch said, 'but you might want to have a look in the living room first.' She pointed to an open door to Lottie's right.

'Thanks.'

Lottie walked on the stepping plates placed on the floor to preserve any evidence that might be salvageable. She felt instantly disturbed by the scene inside the living room. Blood spatter on the walls. Blood dried into the floor. Upturned chairs and tables around the room. The glass from one of the patio doors was scattered in a thousand pieces on the ground, inside and outside. Food had been trampled underfoot and glass splinters shone in the early-morning sun streaming in. Besides the food walked into the lawn, she noted expensive-looking rattan furniture, one chair upended, a hot tub, an egg chair sans cushion, and a cabin-like structure at the end of the garden. She turned back to the living room.

'Someone lost it in here,' Kirby said.

'I agree, and we need to get the sequence of events straight,' Lottie said, trying to sound amicable.

'If the body is upstairs, why is there blood in here?'

'Whatever went on, it started here before moving on up the stairs. But I didn't notice any blood out in the hallway.'

Looking up from the job of dusting an overturned table for

fingerprints, a SOCO said, 'There's a back staircase, Inspector. Head that way, it takes you through the kitchen.'

Lottie followed his direction to a doorway located behind what seemed to have been a music station. Cables protruded from an extension lead and some equipment. A speaker, turntable and mixing dock. Shouldn't there be more equipment? She filed that for later.

To her left, another upturned table, bottles smashed on the ground. A stack of crates lined the wall, with others skewed across the floor.

She trudged through the doorway and stepped into a monstrously large open-plan kitchen diner. Drops of blood along the white floor tiles, some smudged. Despite the jumble of bottles, glasses and pizza boxes littering the countertops, there was no evidence of destruction of fixtures or fittings. The wounded person had fled this way. With someone in pursuit? She couldn't see any footprints in the blood, but SOCOs might be able to find them if they were there.

Through another door to a set of concrete steps. Each droplet was marked by a numbered plastic card. She climbed the stairs, careful not to smear anything.

Lots more activity. Outside the bedroom, she braced herself for Jim McGlynn's grouchy face. He was the SOCO team leader, but she was pleased to find Gráinne Nixon in his place.

'What have we got, Gráinne?' she said, already feeling a lot calmer. The woman was a dream to work with, unlike grumpy McGlynn.

'Based on the blood downstairs and in here, in lay terms I'd describe it as a frenzy.' The SOCO got up from her knees on the far side of the bed. 'It's worse over here.'

Lottie leaned forward. 'Hell.'

There was no other word to describe the image of the body, blood-soaked clothing ripped, skin torn and bloody, eyelids half open with the horror of it all. And a gaping wound to the neck.

Around the victim, the bed, floor and walls all had heavy blood spatter. SOCOs would map the trajectory. The girl's arms were spread out wide and her feet crossed. The image nudged something in Lottie's brain. Was that a pose sometimes used by serial killers? Surely not that!

'The poor girl,' she said. 'It's an awful waste of a young life.'

'Do you know who she is?' Gráinne asked.

'Lucy McAllister. Aged seventeen, almost eighteen.' Her words caught in her throat.

Gráinne pointed to the neck wound.

'I estimate this to be the fatal strike. There are many others, mainly superficial but deep enough for blood loss. A steak knife is missing from a knife block downstairs. It could have been the weapon used. The pathologist will be able to tell you more.' Gráinne's silvery blue eyes were clouded today. It was clear she was affected by the murder of one so young. They all were.

'There's a lot of blood spatter downstairs,' Lottie said, struggling to control her emotions. 'Why would that be?'

'I can't answer that yet.'

'Could the assailant have been wounded?'

'Possibly. Once the blood is analysed, we will know more.'

'Any sign of sexual assault?' Lottie tried to get her head around the trauma the victim had endured.

Gráinne shrugged noncommittally. 'No visible evidence, but it's possible. Post-mortem should tell you. I hear the state pathologist is in Dublin.'

'Yeah, she's preparing for a court case. I hope she can get here.'

She looked up as Kirby bustled in, breathless, his belly straining inside the protective suit. Beads of sweat and damp curls lined his brow, his hood hiding most of his bushy hair.

'Has anyone managed to contact the victim's family?' Lottie asked.

'Parents were in Spain,' he said. 'They happen to be on their way home. Flight has just departed. Due to touch down in Dublin in three hours. They own an apartment in Malaga. Funny, but if they were still there, we could've asked Boyd to inform them.'

'It's far from funny.' Lottie felt her heart rate spike at the mention of Boyd. She missed having him around, especially when faced with a serious investigation.

'Make sure we have someone to meet them at the airport,' she said, 'to escort them home.'

'What do we tell them?'

She thought for a minute. 'That there was a break-in at their home. Nothing else, for now. And keep the media away from here. We don't want the family finding out about this online when they switch their phones back on.'

'Right so.' Kirby turned and rushed off, panting loudly.

'Gráinne, I don't suppose you have any idea of time of death?'

'The pathologist will have to determine that. But I'd guess she's been dead no more than five, maybe six hours.'

'Thanks. I'll let you continue.'

Lottie stepped out of the room, the stench of death clogging her nostrils through her mask. Downstairs, she spoke to Lynch. 'Has the victim's phone been located?'

'Not yet. SOCOs are going over the place inch by inch, in a grid. But we have a laptop. It could belong to the victim.'

'Good. When you get back to the station, start interrogating Lucy's social media. See if you can find anything on the laptop. Then send it to Gary in technical. Plus, we need to track down everyone who was at the party last night.'

'It might have been a girls' night in that went haywire.'

Lottie swallowed hard, smelling death everywhere.

'It was a party. Sean was here and I picked him up shortly after midnight. The music was full on, so we are looking at some time after that. Listen, Maria, it's imperative we talk to all the young people who were here and anyone who might have been working at the party. Find out the names of Lucy's friends. Liaise with McKeown and get everyone interviewed as soon as possible. Find out what time the pizzas were delivered and talk to whoever dropped them here.'

'I'll get on to it once I can get away.'

Lottie didn't relish the task of setting up interviews with hung-over teens accompanied by their parents or guardians, but it had to be done. 'Tell me more about the woman who found the body.'

Lynch checked her notebook. 'She'd already been escorted home when I arrived. Sarah Robson. She's a cleaner. Don't know much more than what uniforms got from her initial interview.'

'I'll need to have a word with her.'

'The medic advised her to take a Valium.'

'Okay.' Lottie was thinking she could do with a Valium herself right about now. 'I'll interview her later. Hopefully she'll be fit enough to answer more detailed questions then.'

'I'll ask Garda Brennan to locate Ivy Jones for an interview. Ivy is Lucy's best friend.'

'Great, I'll begin with her then. You start with the laptop.'

Lynch looked around anxiously. 'When will reinforcements arrive?'

'When indeed?' Lottie said.

A long day beckoned.

11

Ivy Jones came to the station voluntarily, accompanied by Garda Martina Brennan. Garda Brennan had collected her from her home following Lottie's call. Ivy's mother, Rita Jones, consented to her daughter being interviewed without her presence, saying she was sorry but she had to referee an under-twelves camogie match. It was the county final and she just couldn't skip it, even though she was horrified by what had happened to Lucy. Her husband was working all weekend, preparing a presentation for a work conference.

The girl trembled uncontrollably. Garda Brennan fetched her a cup of sweet tea while they waited for Lottie to get settled.

Ivy never uttered a word, just continued to shiver.

'Garda Brennan can get you a soft drink if you don't like the tea,' Lottie said.

Shaking her head, Ivy picked at the pink polish on her long nails and kept her head studiously downward, her bunched-up dark hair flopping to one side. The girl was pretty in an understated way and it was obvious she'd worn heavy make-up the night before. There were still traces of eyeliner around her eyes and she'd missed cleansing the foundation from around her ears. Fake tan streaked her arms, her white T-shirt similarly stained. She wore blue skinny jeans and white running shoes.

'I know this must be difficult for you, Ivy, but I need you to tell me everything you can remember about last night.'

'I ... I don't remember much. I had a lot to drink. Don't tell my mum that.' She shook so much her untidy hair fell from its moorings and settled around her shoulders.

'For Lucy's sake, you have to try to remember. Think of her poor parents.' Lottie could have sworn Ivy snorted, or maybe she was just swallowing a sob. Whatever it was, it put Lottie on alert. 'Do you not like the McAllisters?'

A shoulder shrug. 'They're adults, and I don't much like anyone older than me, including my own parents. Sorry, shouldn't have said that. TMI.'

Too much information, Lottie thought. Instead of delving into that relationship, she decided time was of the essence. She needed pertinent facts. 'Tell me what you do remember.'

Another shrug. Lottie stemmed an urge to put her hands out and hold the girl still.

'It was good,' Ivy said. 'The party, like. Everyone was there. Well, everyone who mattered to Lucy. But there were a few I wouldn't have invited and then there were the ones who just turned up.'

'Who might they be?'

'Does it even matter now? Lucy is gone. She's ... was my best friend.' Loud sobs crowded the airless interview room.

Handing over a box of Lidl tissues, Lottie waited impatiently, her foot tapping the floor, her knee beating off the underside of the table.

'How long have you been friends with Lucy?'

Ivy dabbed her eyes and blew her nose, then balled up the tissue and left it on the table before pulling another from the box.

'Since junior infants. We were in the same class the whole

way through ... *hic* ... primary school. We took the same subjects in secondary. We've just ... *hic* ... finished our Leaving Cert exams and Lucy decided to throw a party to celebrate, and ...' Another balled tissue rolled onto the table.

'Take a sip of tea,' Lottie prodded.

Ivy shook her head. 'I'm okay.'

'Who was at the party?'

'Everyone. Told you that ... *hic* ... already.'

Lottie wished the girl would take a drink to stem her hiccups. 'Who was there that you felt shouldn't have been invited or who turned up uninvited.'

'It was like all parties, you know? Word gets out. Snapchat, WhatsApp groups. People turn up for the free drink and ... make a mess. God, the hot tub was swimming with vomit at one stage. Disgusting.'

Trying not to visualise that image, Lottie continued, 'I noticed pizza boxes in the kitchen. When was that delivered?'

'I don't know. Late. Maybe an hour before things finished up.'

'Had Lucy been threatened recently? Any enemies?'

'Enemies? Lucy was the most popular girl in school.'

Lottie counted to five in her head. 'Ivy, Lucy is dead and I have to gather as much information as I can as quickly as possible. We need the names of those at the party and the names of those who were there that maybe shouldn't have been. The faster we can interview them, the closer we might be to figuring out who killed Lucy.'

'I suppose you could start with Hannah Byrne.'

'Did she gatecrash?'

'She was invited, but I've no idea why. Lucy always called her the ugly duckling to us beautiful swans.' Ivy actually smiled, and Lottie held her tongue. 'She named her Little Miss Nobody, like out of the Little Miss books. Hannah was there early last night. She got changed in a guest room while we were having a few drinks and doing our make-up.'

'Was she supposed to stay overnight?'

'God, no.' Ivy's face distorted into an expression of horror. 'Lucy would never have let her stay. To be honest, I think she might have been a little jealous of her. Hannah isn't really an ugly duckling. She's pretty but acts like she doesn't know it. She's into athletics in a big way but I don't know a whole lot else about her. Oh, except her mum used to have a drink problem.'

Lottie had garnered enough to make this Hannah a person of interest, especially if there was no love lost between her and Lucy.

'Then there's Cormac O'Flaherty,' Ivy went on.

Noting the name in her notebook underneath Hannah Byrne's, Lottie said, 'Was he invited?'

'I doubt it.'

'Tell me about him.'

'He does gardening around our school. It's an all-girls' school. And he does some for Lucy's dad too. Lucy made fun of him. Not behind his back like she did with Hannah, but to his face. He didn't seem to care. Always came back for more. I actually think he had a crush on her.'

'Came back for more what?'

'Insults, I suppose.' Another shoulder shrug. Lottie saw enough shrugs at home to make her dizzy.

'Why did Lucy insult him?'

'I don't like saying negative things about my best friend, but the fact is, Lucy could be the ultimate mean girl at times. I thought it was funny, but now I'm wondering if it could have had something to do with her ... with her being murdered, you know?'

'She pushed someone to the brink, you mean?'

'Possibly. I can't believe she's gone.' Loud sniffling, and another tissue rolled onto the table.

'Did anything happen between Lucy and Cormac last night?'

'Not really. Oh, he spilled drink on the hall carpet and she said something about it. This was early on, before the party got going proper, like. Later Lucy had an argument with Hannah, and Cormac got involved.'

'What was this argument about?' Lottie glanced at Martina Brennan, pleased to see the young garda taking copious notes compared to her own minuscule offering.

'I ... I don't know. I was out in the garden and they were inside. The music stopped suddenly and I heard them shouting. But then the music started up again and that was it.'

'Did you go inside to investigate what was going on?'

'I could hardly stand up by then, so I stayed where I was. On the garden sofa.'

'What time was this?'

'I don't know.' Ivy twirled a tendril of hair around her finger. 'My head is killing me. I really need to go home and lie down.'

'Soon. What happened after that loud argument?'

Her bottom lip covered her top one as her eyes filled with tears again. 'I can't remember. I think Lucy came back outside. She was looking at something on her phone, but she wouldn't show it to me when I asked. After that it's a blur. Can I go now?'

'Were *you* supposed to sleep there last night?'

'No. Lucy's parents were due home from Spain, and she'd arranged for the cleaner to come first thing this morning.'

'What time did you leave?'

'Late. I was there for the pizzas, so sometime after they were delivered.'

'How did you get home?'

'Erm ... not sure. A taxi, maybe. Sorry, I was totally out of it.'

'Can you try to remember when the party actually ended?' Lottie pressed for a more definitive answer.

'It was late. Maybe two or three-ish?'

'Why do you think it was two or three?'

'I don't know for sure, but Lucy booked the DJ until two, so it was after that, okay?'

'Who was the DJ?'

Ivy looked up and Lottie noticed a different expression on the girl's face. It was like something had skittered across her eyes and her mouth had flatlined. Silence.

'Well, do you know his name?' Lottie prodded.

'Richie something or other. Don't know anything else about him, only that the music he played was pure shite.'

There was something else there. Lottie sensed an undercurrent but couldn't put her finger on it. Before she could ask anything else, Ivy continued.

'How ... how did Lucy die?'

'I'm sorry, but I can't reveal that just yet.'

'But someone killed her?'

'All I can say is that we are treating her death as suspicious.'

'Poor Lucy.' Tears filled Ivy's eyes and she sniffed loudly.

'Do you know of anyone who would harm your friend?'

Ivy tugged at her lip with a pink-polished nail. 'I don't know. Lucy is ... was very popular, but there's always jealous bitches around, isn't there? Especially because she was good-looking, and so brainy. And she had loads of money. She only had to ask her dad and he bought her whatever she wanted. She loved being spoiled by her dad.' A long pause. 'Hannah Byrne was the odd one out.'

'Okay. I'll talk to Hannah. Where could I get a full list of everyone who was present last night?' Lottie didn't want to have to bring Sean into the equation, but if all else failed, she knew he could give her some of the names.

'Lucy's phone, maybe. She kept everything on that. It was her life.'

'We haven't recovered that yet.' Lottie tore a page from her notebook and placed it in front of Ivy with her pen. 'Write down as many names as you can remember, then you can go home to sleep.'

'Thanks.' Ivy picked up the pen, paused it in mid-air.

'Is there anything else you want to tell me?'

'Like what?'

'Something that might have happened in the days leading up to Lucy's death. Or anything that happened at the party?'

'No, no. N-nothing. Her dad will be devastated. I am too. I can't believe she's actually dead. What am I going to do now?'

Just write the names, Lottie thought. She was getting a strange vibe about Lucy McAllister's murder and she didn't like it. Not one bit.

12

Hannah Byrne lived with her mother in a one-bed flat located above Cleanz Dry Cleaner's on Main Street. The street door opened in on a narrow staircase. A wooden affair, barely accommodating one person at a time. Lottie climbed it with Kirby wheezing behind her and knocked on the door at the top.

She had tasked Detective Sam McKeown with responsibility for allocating Ivy's list of names to a team of uniforms. Each person was to be interviewed. She hoped the teenagers could add the names of others who were present.

The door was opened by a woman Lottie knew was only in her mid thirties but looked nearer fifty. A toddler with hair to their shoulders clung to her legs. With a cross expression, she lifted the child and allowed the detectives to enter.

The room was tiny. Lottie noticed a bedroom and bathroom off the living area. Her gaze was drawn to a mattress on the floor. A teenage girl lay flat out, snoring loudly. At her feet was a dirty blue rucksack decorated with once-white daisies.

'What's this about?'

'Okay if I call you Barbara?'

'Everyone calls me Babs.'

The woman's eyes flitted about the small room as if checking for anything lying around that might get her in trouble with the guards. Lottie hastened to reassure her.

'Babs, there's nothing for you to worry about. I just need your daughter to come to the station. I have a few questions. All routine. She'll need an adult present when questioned. Can you accompany her?'

'Question my daughter? About what? You think she's done something? You must be wrong. Hannah's a good girl ...'

So Babs hadn't heard about Lucy's death. 'An incident occurred at or after a party at Lucy McAllister's house last night. Everyone who was in attendance is being interviewed. Your daughter's name came up as having been there. We need to talk to her.'

'What's happened?'

'A girl was badly assaulted. That's all I can say at the moment.'

'Hannah wouldn't hurt a fly.'

'I'm sure that's true, but she still needs to be interviewed.'

'Talk to her here.'

'I'm afraid the interview must be recorded.' Lottie's jaw hurt from her forced smile.

'She needs to sleep. It's been a long few weeks of exams.'

'What time did she get home from the party?'

'It was late. Banged the fu— bloody door behind her. Woke up Olly, her little brother.' Babs patted the child in her arms, who was struggling to be released. 'She never even turned on a light, just fell into bed and has been asleep since. I can tell you she's in for an earful when she wakes up.'

Lottie wondered how the girl wasn't already awake, with her mother's increasingly shrieking voice almost rattling the gritty window panes. It cut through Lottie's skull.

'I'd appreciate it if you could wake her now, please.'

Babs stretched out a foot and kicked at the mattress. 'Hannah, wake up. There's two detectives here to talk to you.'

The girl raised an arm over her eyes and moaned. 'Go away.'

Another kick to the mattress and she shot upright. 'Mam? Stop. I'm sick. My head is spinning.'

'If you were drinking, *I'll* make it spin, missy. Get up.'

Hannah squinted through her fingers with a groan.

Lottie donned a stern expression. 'Hannah, you have to come with us for an interview.'

'What? Where?'

'To the garda station.'

'What happened?' Hannah looked pained, as though if she attempted to raise her head it might fall off.

'We'll discuss it there. Come on.'

'This is a joke.' The girl threw off the blanket and stood up in her underwear. She wobbled, putting a hand to the wall to steady herself. 'I'm going to be sick.'

That was when Lottie noticed that her fingernails were caked with something that wasn't a million miles from dried blood. 'What happened to your hands?'

The girl leaned against the wall and held her hands up, then turned them over and stared at them in disbelief. 'I don't know.'

'It looks like blood,' Lottie said, wondering how quickly she could get her to the station to have them swabbed.

Babs mouth formed a massive O. 'No way! It's only dirt. You fell on the way home or something, didn't you, Hannah?'

Lottie wasn't buying the mother's insistence. 'Did something happen at Lucy McAllister's party?'

Hannah shrugged, continuing to stare at her outstretched hands.

'You need to shower. Go on, Hannah. Now!' Babs went to pull her at daughter, but Lottie stood in her way.

'I've a lot of interviews to get through this morning. You can wash later. Pull on some clothes. Babs, you can follow us.'

'I can't. I need someone to mind Olly.'

'I'm sorry, but I insist on Hannah coming with us. When you have a babysitter, phone this number and I'll send a car for you.' Lottie handed over a card with her details.

She kept her eyes focused on Hannah. The girl grabbed jeans from the end of the mattress and tugged them on. She slipped a partially buttoned-up blue blouse on over her head and shoved her bare feet into a pair of tatty runners. The clothing had no evidence of blood and Lottie concluded she had worn a different outfit at the party.

'Where are the clothes you wore last night?'

'I don't know. Maybe I put them in the laundry room.'

'Why would you do that?'

'I don't know.'

Lottie turned to Babs. 'Where is this room?'

'Downstairs. We share it with Krysta from the dry cleaner's. She lives in the flat next door.'

'I'll need to take those clothes.'

Lottie hoped Hannah hadn't switched on the washing machine. She recalled Ivy saying that Lucy and Hannah had had an argument. Had it turned bloody? Was it anything to do with Lucy's death? If Hannah had killed Lucy, how did she have the sense to wash her clothing but not her hands? Nothing was adding up. Evidently Hannah thought so too.

'This is so weird,' she said. 'I don't understand what's going on. I feel so sick.'

'This has never happened before,' Babs said, her voice now brittle. 'You can't take her when she's confused and ill.'

'Follow us down to the station when you can, Ms Byrne,' Kirby said.

Hannah looked totally lost. 'I'd better go with them, Mam. There's no need for you to come.'

'You can't interview her until I'm there, isn't that right?' Babs shook a finger, but a deep crease of worry appeared between her eyebrows.

'We won't start until you arrive.' Lottie turned to Kirby. 'Bring that rucksack, and fetch the clothes from the laundry room.'

With that, she took Hannah by the elbow and steered her out the door and down the stairs. She was anxious to get her into the car, where she could place two sterile bags over the girl's hands. And she hoped to God the washing machine hadn't been switched on.

13

The morning warmth had wended its way inside the station. Lottie dragged her jacket off. She untucked her sweaty white T-shirt from the waistband of her black jeans, reckoning she could do with a blast of deodorant, but she dare not let the girl out of her sight.

With steely eyes, she watched the teenager being processed. Even though she wasn't yet under arrest, Lottie felt that by the end of the interview, Hannah Byrne would be detained; at the very least, she'd be issued with an assault charge.

'We have to wait for your mother to arrive before commencing the interview,' she said, directing the teenager into the interview room.

'I don't understand.' Hannah looked down at her hands as she sat.

Lottie was glad she'd bagged them. Samples had been retrieved from beneath her nails, and the technician had confirmed it was blood. The lab staff would check if it was a match for Lucy's. Hannah's rucksack contained a bloodstained teal-coloured towel. It, along with the rucksack, were also sent to the lab for analysis.

She hadn't been able to recall the colour of the towels in Lucy's house. She'd placed a quick call to Gráinne, who confirmed the towels in all the bathrooms were teal. Bloodstains had not been found in any bathroom examined so far, but there was no way to know if a towel was missing.

'What's going on?' Hannah cried. 'Am I arrested?'

'You're just here for a chat, under caution.'

'What does that mean?'

'I'll read you your rights and ask you a few questions. You have the right to a solicitor if you want. Would you like a cup of tea? A soft drink, perhaps?'

'A solicitor? Is this serious?'

'Routine,' Lottie lied. It was anything but routine. So far she had no proof Hannah had killed Lucy, and there were many questions to be answered. Unfortunately, securing a confession might take time. The girl appeared mystified.

'I don't understand. What happened? Why were my nails scraped? It's something to do with evidence, isn't it? But I didn't do anything, I swear.' She stared at Lottie, wide-eyed.

Seeing the confusion spread across the girl's face, Lottie said, 'Hannah, you were at a party last night, weren't you? At Lucy McAllister's house?'

'Yeah, me and a million others.' Her shoulders shuddered beneath her thin shirt.

'A tragic event occurred in the early hours of this morning, and we are interviewing everyone who was at the party.'

'Why? What happened?' Hannah reached into her jeans pocket and extracted her phone.

'I think it best to leave the phone on the table. When your mother arrives, I'll explain everything to you.'

'It will take her forever to find someone to mind Olly.' Dark blue eyes pleaded with Lottie. 'Ask whatever you want now, and then can I go home?'

'I'm sorry, Hannah, you're under eighteen. I need the consent of your legal guardian.'

'This looks bad,' Hannah muttered.

Unable to contain her eagerness for information, Lottie leaned across the table. 'What does?'

The girl held up her hands. 'This ... under my nails. It's blood, isn't it? And you took a sample from me for a DNA test.'

'We have to do that with everyone who was at the party. To rule them in or out of the investigation.'

Hannah's eyes widened like china saucers, circled with remnants of black liner. Lottie could see where blonde extensions had come loose from her long hair and hung fuzzily from their clips. No scratches or cuts were visible, and she hadn't noticed anything incriminating when the girl had stood up in her underwear at home.

Despite that, things were not looking good for Hannah Byrne. The halter top and skirt that Kirby had taken from the laundry basket by the communal washing machine were spotted with a few dark stains. A simple test confirmed the presence of blood. Further analysis would prove if it was Lucy's. Sooner rather than later, Lottie hoped.

A knock on the door and Babs Byrne was ushered inside, followed by Kirby, who took a seat beside Lottie.

'I got delayed,' Babs said breathlessly, pulling out a chair to sit beside her daughter. 'It was impossible to get someone to mind Olly. Mrs Delaney is sick with the flu. I think it's only a cold, but anyway, I ended up leaving him with Krysta in the dry cleaner's. This better not take long. The fumes in that place can't be good for him.' She unbuttoned her cardigan. 'You said there was an assault last night, and Krysta told me she heard that it was Lucy McAllister. God, if it's true ... poor Lucy.'

Lottie concentrated on Hannah's reaction to this news. She appeared paler and her eyes even wider, if that was possible.

She tore at her hair until she caught a few tendrils and wrapped
them around her trembling fingers.

'What happened to Lucy?' she whispered. 'Is that why I'm
here? Please tell me. I need to know what's going on. Oh God, I
feel so sick. What's wrong with me?'

Ignoring her pleas, Lottie directed her attention to Babs.

'This interview is being recorded as evidence of our conversation. Your daughter has not been arrested at this time. We
have taken a sample of a substance from her nails to be
analysed, and a sample of her DNA. Her rucksack and clothing
are also being examined. She has been fingerprinted. At the
moment this process is in order to eliminate her from our
enquiries.'

'I never gave permission for any of that. You had no right to
—' Babs was quickly losing her composure.

Lottie cut in. 'There was visible evidence of blood on your
daughter's hands.'

'I told you it was dirt. She fell ... or something.' Babs
grabbed Hannah's hands and slapped open the palms, then
turned them over, pointed at the fingernails. 'It's just ... dirt.
What is going on here?'

Lottie nodded at Kirby, who pronounced the details of
those present and the usual wording for the recording that
preceded interviews.

'Do I need a solicitor for my daughter?' Babs nervously eyed
the light flashing on the equipment.

'That's entirely within your rights,' Lottie said.

'I don't trust you, Inspector. Nor you.' The woman pointed
at Kirby with a shaky finger before stabbing Lottie with angry
eyes. 'You'll try and pin this assault or whatever it is on my
daughter. Is Lucy dead? You have to believe me, my little girl
wouldn't hurt a—'

'Dead?' Hannah gulped loudly and a green hue crept over
her cheeks. She gagged, gulped again, and before either Lottie

or Kirby could move out of the way, a spurt of bile spewed from her mouth out across the table. Lottie grabbed for her notebook and file, rescuing them. Kirby jumped up and started mopping the pungent mess with the useless tissues.

'S-sorry,' the girl cried. 'I'm so sorry.'

'What is wrong with you?' Babs said.

'I feel like my head is going to split open. Oh God—'

'You hear that, Inspector? Hannah is ill. She has Mrs Delaney's flu. Call a doctor for her. Please.'

'I want to go home,' Hannah whined.

'You can go home soon,' Lottie said. 'Can you answer a few simple questions first?'

'I didn't do anything.' After wiping her mouth and then her eyes, Hannah said, 'Tell me, please, is Lucy dead?'

'I'm afraid so,' Kirby said as Lottie faltered. He pushed the almost empty tissue box forward as Hannah clamped a hand to her mouth.

'Wh-what happened to her?'

'We were hoping you could help us with that,' Lottie said. 'You were at the party, right?'

Hannah's entire body shook. 'I feel really weird. I can't remember much. And my head is bursting.'

'Inspector, my daughter is ill,' Babs said.

'Why do you think you can't remember?' Lottie kept her eyes on the girl.

'Don't know.'

'Did you consume a lot of alcohol?'

'Hannah doesn't drink,' Babs butted in.

Lottie raised a quizzical eyebrow.

'It's true,' Hannah said. 'I only had a Coke, but I ...' She glanced at her mother before making up her mind about which was the lesser evil. 'I took a pill. But I can't remember anything else.'

'Where did you get this pill?'

'Don't know.'

'Who gave it to you?' Lottie persisted.

Babs nudged Hannah with her elbow. 'How many times have I told you ... Oh, forget it. Tell them.'

'Erm ...' The girl hesitated, lowering her head. 'From Cormac.'

'Cormac who?' Lottie said, as Kirby tracked his finger down the list of names Ivy had provided.

'Can't remember his last name.'

'Cormac O'Flaherty?' Kirby asked.

'Could be,' Hannah said with a shrug. 'I ... I was ch-chatting to him and then I was upset and angry ...'

Feeling she might be on to a confession, Lottie kept her tone even and ploughed on. 'Why were you angry, Hannah?'

'It might've been because Lucy was mean to me, though that's nothing new.' The girl sat up straighter, as if confident that at last she could recall something of importance to get her out of the stifling room. 'Cormac scored a few pills off the boy handing out the drinks. I must have taken one. I don't know what happened after that.'

'Any adults present?'

'No. Oh, yes. Mr Glennon was there. At the front door. Maybe he was the doorman, or a bouncer. I don't know.'

'Mr Glennon? Who is he?' Lottie said, noticing Babs's mouth hanging open.

'My athletics coach. He teaches PE at my school too.'

Lottie digested this news while forming another question. Ivy Jones hadn't mentioned a Mr Glennon.

'A teacher from your school was at a teenagers' party? He was the only adult there?'

Hannah nodded. 'Think so.'

'Doesn't seem right to me,' Kirby said with a head shake.

'Well, at least there was an adult there,' Babs said, but she didn't sound convinced either.

Hannah said, 'Most of us are finished with school. Lucy said he moonlights as a bouncer at some of the nightclubs.'

'Moonlights?'

'That's what she said.'

Lottie parked that information. 'Let's back up a little. Did you and Lucy have an argument last night?'

'Well, she invited me to her party, but then she acted like she'd made a mistake or something. She made fun of me in front of her friends.'

'What happened when she made fun of you?'

Hannah ignored the question. 'How did she die?' she asked earnestly, and Lottie felt sad at the intense saucer-like eyes.

'The exact cause of death won't be confirmed until the state pathologist conducts a post-mortem. All I can say is that Lucy suffered a serious assault. It's likely she was murdered,' Lottie added for maximum effect, to see how the girl reacted. Unfair of her? She thought it was necessary or they'd be going round in circles all day.

Hannah sat stock still for a moment, before slipping from the chair in a faint. Babs was too late to catch her, and she slid under the table.

'Look what you've done to my daughter!' Babs sobbed as she knelt on the floor and held her. 'How could you be so cruel?'

While they awaited the doctor's arrival, Hannah woke up cradled in her mother's arms. Kirby had got bottled water while Lottie fetched a T-shirt from her locker for the girl to change into.

Babs glanced up at them. 'Please, give us some privacy.'

Lottie and Kirby left them alone.

'What do you think?' Lottie leaned against the wall with one foot up against it, the other taking her weight. She crossed her arms, feeling drained.

'She doesn't look strong enough to have carried out such a frenzied assault,' Kirby said, tapping his shirt pocket for a cigar that he couldn't smoke indoors. 'There was a lot of blood in the living room. Whoever killed Lucy wounded her there, then chased her through the kitchen and up the stairs, where they finished what they'd started. That takes stamina.'

'Blood spatter analysis will confirm if it's all Lucy's blood. But what if Hannah was high on whatever pill she took? She might have exceeded her normal energy levels. Plus she is an athlete.'

'If the DNA from the blood on her hands is a match to Lucy, that's game over. Drugged or not.'

Lottie shook her head thoughtfully. 'It doesn't sit well with me, Kirby. A DNA hit will only prove she was present when the assault occurred, or even afterwards. It could be from earlier in the night. It doesn't mean she actually killed her friend.'

'Do you believe they *were* friends?'

'It seems a bit of an anomaly for Lucy to invite Hannah and then treat her badly.' Lottie pushed away from the wall and paced in small circles. 'Unless Lucy wanted her there to humiliate her in front of their peers.'

'That might have caused Hannah to flip out.'

'Ivy mentioned that Hannah and Lucy had an argument. We need to get all those kids interviewed. Someone who was there has to know what actually happened.'

'If she gets a solicitor, we won't get anything else out of her.'

'We need to find out how and when she got home. She claims she can't remember much, but she dropped her clothing in the basement. Why do that if she wasn't guilty?'

'But if she was guilty, she'd have washed the clothes and the towel, or thrown them in a street bin. It's all a bit odd if you ask me, boss.'

'We need the DNA analysis fast-tracked. Get onto the lab

and impress on them that we need the results in order to arrest the murderer of a teenage girl.'

'Will do.'

'And prepare a search warrant for the Byrnes' flat. We have probable cause. We need to find rock-solid evidence. The post-mortem should help too. If Hannah really is under the influence of drugs, we can't interview her further.'

'Okay. I'll organise a drug test,' Kirby said.

'I want that Glennon man brought in.'

'Who?'

'Athletics coach, PE teacher guy. It's not sitting well with me that he was present at a teenage party, especially with the parents away. Why would he put his career in jeopardy like that?' Lottie couldn't get her head around it. 'Something smells off, Kirby. Find out who the DJ is and bring him in. And we need to talk to Cormac O'Flaherty. Get the details for me.'

'Not enough hours in—'

'I know, and I don't want to hear it.'

As Kirby waddled off down the corridor, Lottie wished for the second time that morning for Boyd's presence. He had a clear and level-headed approach to investigations that she often lacked. She thrived on chaos, while he operated in a linear fashion, helping him to see light at the end of the tunnel.

She felt she was staring into the bowels of a very narrow and dark tunnel.

14

The events of last night's party played on Richie Harrison's mind like one of his bad records. Being a DJ meant plenty of late nights, but he preferred parties to nightclubs. He swallowed a couple of paracetamol on top of the two he'd taken half an hour earlier, but still he twisted and turned, the sheets knotted around his body. He shot out his arm in frustration, knocking over a glass of water from the bedside cabinet.

'Fuck's sake!' Leaning over the edge of the bed, he watched the liquid seep into the floorboards, then flopped back on the pillow.

'Richie?' his wife shouted up the stairs. 'Was that you?'

'Who else?' he muttered. He heard the stairs creak. 'It's okay, Brontë, I just knocked over the glass.'

She was at the door then, her pregnancy bump entering the room before the rest of her. He closed his eyes to blot out her flaming red anger. He could do without another fight.

'What time of the morning did you arrive home?'

'Why are you asking when you seem to know the answer?'

She glared and clenched her hands into fists. He knew she'd wait until he told her.

'Okay, babe. After three, maybe four. I don't know. Damn kids can party like we used to.' Once upon a time, he thought, but didn't say aloud.

The expensive memory-foam mattress dipped as she sat on the bed. Everything about the house was too bloody expensive.

'I know you were with one of them. You disgust me, Richie.'

He leaned up on one elbow, catching his long hair, which had come loose from the band, a trigger of fear flipping his stomach over. 'What do you mean?'

'You were with one of those leggy, fake-tanned teenagers.' A flush of red screamed up her cheeks. 'Don't lie to me, Richie. I can smell her on you.'

No you can't, he thought. The first thing he'd done when he eventually arrived home was take a hot shower in the downstairs shower room before he'd silently climbed the stairs. Not that he had to worry about waking her, because Brontë had recently taken to sleeping in the spare room. Said he snored too loudly. He couldn't win. She didn't want him near her when he was at home and gave out when he wasn't there. Still, he needed to reassure her.

Reaching out, he rubbed her bare arm softly, squinting at the light streaming through the top of the blind. 'What time is it anyhow?'

'You can't talk your way out of this.' She stood quickly, her face twisted in fury. 'Not this time, Richie Harrison. I've had enough. Either you leave or I do.'

Tugging at the sheet, frantically trying to unwrap it from around his body, he attempted to get out of bed, but fell face-first on the damp, highly glossed floorboards. He hoped she didn't see the stain from the spilled water.

Brontë laughed then, and Richie exhaled. He might escape in one piece. This time.

Struggling to his feet, his boxer shorts low on his hips, he wrapped one arm around her and patted her bump.

'The baby is playing with your hormones. Listen, Brontë, you know I would never go off with someone else. I love you. Get rid of those silly notions.' He leaned down and kissed her brow.

She shook him off. 'Why did you take a shower at five o'clock in the morning? You never do that no matter how drunk you are, and Richie Harrison, you were *not* drunk.'

'What do you mean?' He shrank away, bumping against the wall. So she had been awake.

'I heard you come in. I went downstairs to make you a cup of hot chocolate to help you sleep. That was before I realised how late it was. I saw you. In the downstairs shower. Why? Why do you do this to me?'

'Do what?'

'Whoring around! With teenagers. And all I do for you. Do you think we would be living in this house if it wasn't for me? You need to fucking grow up! I'm this close to kicking you out on your cheating arse.'

He grabbed her arm before she could lash out at him. 'Stop it, babe. You don't know what you're saying.'

'Oh, I do. This isn't your first time and I know it won't be your last. I've had it with you.'

He tightened his grip. 'You're carrying my baby, Brontë. We're in this together and we'll stay together.'

'Stop it. You're hurting me. Richie! I mean it. Let go.'

He watched as she rubbed her arm furiously, making the red imprint of his fingers sing on her flesh. He'd gone too far.

'I'm sorry. I'm just exhausted. Believe me, I was not with anyone last night.'

'This morning then,' she said, her voice now a childish sneer. 'Where were you until five?'

'It wasn't even five, and I had to pack up some of my gear. You know how long that takes. I have to go back for the cables and some other stuff this morning. Come with me. I can sleep later on. Deal?'

'I could scream. You infuriate me so much, I don't know what to do.'

'Put the kettle on. I'll get dressed and then we can head over to the McAllisters'.'

'I'll see.' She shrugged and left the room.

Richie exhaled a long, relieved breath. He slid down the wall and cradled his head in his hands.

15

At her desk, going over her notes, Lottie tried to figure out how to proceed with Hannah Byrne. Then Kirby returned with the girl's athletics coach and deposited him in their old interview room.

Noel Glennon appeared tense and uncomfortable seated on the narrow chair. Lottie thought he was attractive, in his matching navy tracksuit bottoms and partially zipped top over a rugby shirt. His blonde hair was combed back from his forehead and cut neatly around his ears and neck. Early thirties. That was what made her uneasy. And, with Lucy's parents absent, it was further complicated by the fact that he taught at the school that most of the teens attended.

With increasing wariness, she took her time settling her file of papers, and lined up her pen and notebook like Boyd always did. Kirby started the formalities, and once done, she let silence wash over the room.

Glennon fiddled with the white collar of his green rugby shirt, then put his hands on his lap under the table. He leaned in and smiled, flashing too-white teeth in his sculpted face. 'I'm here to do all I can to help, Inspector.'

His smile looked forced. His charm was well practised, she thought.

'Thank you for coming in, Mr Glennon. Our aim is to interview everyone who was at Lucy's party,' she said casually, to give him a sense of composure and to see what he might reveal. 'It's difficult trying to trace so many teenagers.'

'I understand totally. And rest assured, I'll help if I can.' He shook his head slowly, a whisper of blonde hair fluttering across his eyes. 'Awful business. When a detective contacted me, I didn't hesitate to come in and talk to you.'

'Appreciate it, Mr Glennon.'

'Noel, please.'

'No bother. You were at Lucy McAllister's party last night?'

'I was.'

'Please don't take offence at this, Noel.' She knew she had to tread carefully. 'If you don't mind me saying, did you not think it was inappropriate for you, as a teacher and athletics coach, to attend a teenage party?'

The mask slipped slightly before he quickly recovered. 'In hindsight, I agree I should not have been there.'

'So why were you?'

'You already know I teach PE at Lucy's school, but they don't give me many hours. Being the athletics coach pulls in a little extra income, but I'm not making enough, so I sometimes work as a nightclub bouncer.' He paused, as if that was enough justification.

Lottie nodded for him to continue.

'I overheard some of the kids talking about the party and I knew Lucy's parents were away, so—'

'Excuse me, how did you know the McAllisters were away?'

'Lucy told me.'

'Why would she tell you?'

He smiled his fake white-toothed smile again and Lottie cringed. He was trying too bloody hard.

'Inspector, the kids don't see me as a teacher as such, because it's just sport and recreation. They talk to me. Lucy talked to me. She was always bringing in notes from her mother with reasons to be excused from PE. The week before the school broke up for the holidays, she was in tears. Said her parents were away and she wasn't feeling well so she couldn't get a note.'

'And what did you do?'

'I excused her.'

'Still not a valid reason to be at her party.'

'No, but she was upset and we got talking. She told me she was throwing an end-of-exams party. She knew I worked at some of the nightclubs, and because her parents were on holiday she was afraid there might be trouble. She asked if I could stand at the door to keep out troublemakers. I said of course, I'd like to help out for a few quid and—'

'Help out?' Lottie said. 'I can't understand how you thought that was okay.'

'At the time, I didn't see any harm in it. After all, most of them attend the nightclubs where I work.'

'Most of them are too young to be allowed into nightclubs.'

'Doesn't stop them. Fake IDs and all that jazz.'

'All that jazz,' Lottie muttered, trying to contain her irritation. 'The school is closed for the summer holidays. How did you make the arrangements with Lucy?'

'I needed the extra cash, so I was supervising the exams. Before her last exam, Lucy came and spoke to me.' His face took on a mournful expression. 'It's really awful what's happened. She was a lovely girl. How ... you know ... how did she die?'

Lottie ignored the question. 'You knew her well?'

'Not really. Like I said, she wasn't into sports at all. It's Hannah Byrne who's the star of the show. In the not too distant future, Hannah will represent Ireland on the international stage. She's a natural athlete.'

'Was Hannah friends with Lucy?'

'Ivy Jones is Lucy's best friend. Joined at the hip, those two. Hannah is a bit of an outsider. I was surprised to see her at the party, if I'm honest.'

'Why?'

'She doesn't move in Lucy's circle.'

'Yet she was there.'

'She was. I'm sure there were plenty who just turned up. Hard to keep a party secret nowadays, you know.'

'Did any troublemakers try to get in?'

'Everyone seemed fine to me.'

Not by the end of the night, Lottie thought. 'Did anything stand out at the party for you?'

He shook his head. 'It was just a crowd of teenagers celebrating the end of exams. For some of them it means moving on to college. A lot of drinking and dancing.'

'Any evidence of drug taking?'

'I didn't see anything like that. I'm not naive, so I'm sure it went on. You know kids of that age ...'

'Is there a drug problem at the school?'

'God, no. I'd have heard if there was.'

'Do you know Cormac O'Flaherty?'

He shook his head emphatically. 'No.'

'You sure?' She glanced at the details they had for Cormac. 'He was at the party. He's twenty years old. He's a gardener at the school. I'm told he wasn't invited but you let him in.'

'If he got in, it's because he looked young enough to be there. Can you show me his photo?'

Dismissing his half-hearted enquiry, Lottie went on. 'At the party, did you see Hannah Byrne with anyone?'

'Saw her a couple of times. Didn't notice her with anyone in particular, to be honest, but I was out front most of the night.'

'Did you come inside at any stage?'

'Went in for a drink of water and the loo, that's all. The music was loud.' He tapped his ear. 'Old age.'

'Do you know the boy who was working the bar?' Lottie wasn't falling for his bullshit. Loud music? He worked as a bouncer, for Christ's sake.

'No, I don't think so.'

She continued her quick-fire questioning. 'How did Lucy seem?'

'She was great. Knew how to throw a good party.'

'Been at any other parties she held?'

'No.'

'Had you ever been in her house before?'

'No. It's something else, isn't it? A bit different from my little apartment, anyhow.' He laughed.

Lottie detected jealousy in his tone. Or was she hearing things that were not there?

'Pizza was delivered at ...' She turned to Kirby, who shuffled through the file in front of him.

'One ten,' he said. They had the computer printout from the shop. Lucy had made the order online from her phone and paid with her own credit card.

'Did you let the delivery guy in?' Lottie asked.

'I did. He had about ten large pizza boxes. Local guy.'

'How long was he inside?'

'Maybe a minute. I showed him the kitchen. He went in, dropped the pizzas and left.'

'What time did you leave the McAllister house?'

'Whenever the music stopped. After two.'

She flicked through her notes. 'Who was the DJ?'

'DJ Rich, or Rich Discs, something like that. Don't think I know him.'

'Really? Our information says he plays at some of the night-clubs in town.'

'He might do, but I'm out on the street, not on the dance floor.'

'Did you talk to him at all?'

'No. He was inside, I was outside.' Glennon shuffled on the chair.

Lottie pressed on. 'How did you get to the party?'

'Drove.'

'Give any lifts there or back?'

'No.'

'You sure?'

'Of course I'm sure. I know how rumours start and I love my job enough not to allow any situation to be incorrectly construed.'

Lottie hid a snigger that was in danger of escaping. He had the grace to blush.

'Like I said, in hindsight, it was a mistake to be there. I'm sorry, but I did nothing wrong and I didn't see anything to make me feel uncomfortable. I definitely didn't see anyone hurt Lucy. She was fine when I left.'

'Did you speak to her then?'

'Just to say I was off. She was with Ivy. The DJ was packing up. Kids were lounging around, getting ready to leave. That's all I can tell you. I drove home. End of story.'

'Did you see Hannah Byrne then?'

'Can't say for sure.'

'Can anyone verify what time you got home?'

'I live alone.'

'To be clear, there's no one to confirm when you arrived home or whether you stayed there?'

'I don't like your insinuation.'

'I'm stating a fact.'

'I went home, got into bed and slept until eight a.m.'

She sighed. There wasn't much else she could extract from him at this point in time.

'If you think of anything else, contact us, and thanks for coming in so promptly,' she added grudgingly.

'Anything I can do to help, I'll be available. By the way, the school principal contacted me. She's organising a memorial for next week. Will I let you know the details?' He stood to leave.

'Sure, let me know. One final thing, did you happen to see anyone hanging around the house? Someone acting suspiciously during the night or when you were leaving?'

'I didn't notice anyone or anything out of the ordinary. You know how kids are. Some were leaving, others were making out, and stuff.'

The 'and stuff' was what Lottie was worried about, especially for her Sean.

Before she went to talk to Cormac O'Flaherty, Lottie grabbed two minutes at her desk.

First, she phoned Sean.

'What's up?' he said.

'I wanted to tell you something before you heard it from anyone else.'

'Tell me what?' He sounded tentative.

'There was an incident at Lucy McAllister's last night.'

'A what?'

He must be in the middle of a game, she thought. She was relieved she'd picked him up last night. Hopefully he wouldn't be involved in any part of the investigation, save for an initial interview.

'There was a serious assault. Sean, Lucy is dead. I wanted to let you know. Detective McKeown or one of the team will be talking to you. Just routine.'

'Me? Why? I didn't do anything.'

She held the phone away from her ear and looked at it, wondering why her son sounded so defensive.

'Sean, you have nothing to worry about. Just tell him I picked you up shortly after twelve. Okay?'

'When did the assault happen?'

'What do you mean?'

'What time?' he snapped.

This attitude was so unlike Sean.

Kirby appeared at the door. 'Ready, boss?'

She nodded and held up one finger. 'Is everything all right, Sean?'

'Why wouldn't it be?'

'Because you sound upset. Did you know Lucy well?'

'No. Mam, I'm in the middle of a game.'

'Okay, make sure you tell McKeown everything. If you can give him the names of who was there, that'd be great.'

'I only knew a few lads from my year.'

'Grand. See you later on. Mind yourself.' She looked at the phone. 'He hung up on me.'

'Kids,' Kirby said with a rueful shake of his head.

She followed him out to the car, a sense of disquiet taking hold between her shoulder blades.

———

Sean threw his phone on the bed and sat on the floor, biting into his knuckles. He'd been so on edge during the call with his mother that he couldn't wait to end it.

Did she know something? Was that why she'd called? If she'd known he'd been back at Lucy's house, she'd have told him, wouldn't she? She would have arrived home and dragged him into an interview room.

Now he'd have to endure a formal interview with Detective McKeown. There was no way he could lie; he'd have to tell the truth. Or should he wait to see if anything turned up to place him at Lucy's after four a.m.? He wished he could

ask Mark. But his phone credit wouldn't stretch to a call to
Spain.

And he knew in his heart that he should have told his
mother everything.

16

The one-way street was so narrow, Kirby had to pull into a tiny space behind the Chair Bar, leaving the rear of the car jutting out on the road.

'It'll do,' Lottie said.

The small terraced house, two doors down from the cycle shop, was plain and simple. It could do with a coat of paint, but who was she to criticise anyone given the state of her own place?

She waved at John Kenny, whom she knew from Sean and Boyd getting their bicycles repaired with him.

'Nice morning,' he said, ready to chat.

'It is,' Lottie replied.

'Rain later on, though.'

She kept walking and he went back into his shop.

Kirby rang the doorbell. When no one came out, Lottie leaned in by him and pressed down hard on the bell. Eventually the door was opened.

The boy standing there was thin as a rake, hungry-looking. Wary eyes, the pupils so wide they practically obliterated the colour from the irises. Cormac O'Flaherty was twenty years old, but he looked about sixteen, in his bare feet, a creased blue T-shirt and cut-off jeans showing pale freckled legs.

'Can I help you?' His short red hair stood to attention, highlighting an angry thread of acne across his forehead.

Lottie got a whiff of his sour breath. Not long out of bed. Unperturbed, she stepped over the threshold. 'Okay if we come in, Cormac?'

'Hey, you can't just waltz in. Who are you?'

She slid past him into a small kitchen. Kirby had to wait until the boy let him pass, the house was that tiny.

'I'm Detective Inspector Parker and my colleague is Detective Kirby.' She looked over her shoulder as Cormac closed the door with a shake of his head.

'Okay, but what is it you want?' he growled.

'You might need to put some shoes on. We're taking you to the station, to have a chat about last night.'

Cormac shifted from foot to foot. 'What's wrong with talking here?' He pulled out a chair but remained standing, rubbing a hand over his flaring forehead.

Lottie sat in an effort to force him to do likewise. As she did, she heard a soft hum that sounded like a washing machine. It came from behind a door close to where she sat. 'Are you doing a wash?'

'So what? It's my house.'

'You live alone?'

'With my dad.'

'And where is he?'

'Syria. Army peacekeeping. He'll be home in October. Talk to him then if you like.'

She'd had enough of this. 'Get your shoes, I haven't time to waste.'

Cormac's bluster deflated and he seemed to morph into the boy his petulance portrayed. 'Why do you want to talk to me?'

Lottie paused, considering her options. The minutes were

ticking into hours, and with each tick, she was losing precious ground on Lucy's killer.

'Sit for a minute and I'll explain.'

'What if I don't want to sit?'

Kirby stuck out his chest, shirt buttons ready to pop. 'The sooner you sit down, lad, the sooner we'll be out of your hair.'

Cormac dragged out a chair and sat.

Kirby remained standing at the head of the table. The room was so small he was still close to the front door.

'Where were you last night?' Lottie began.

'Here.'

'We know you were at Lucy McAllister's party, so I'll ask you again. Where were you last night?'

'If you know, why are you even asking me?'

She tapped a finger on the table without answering.

'Okay, okay,' he said. 'Yes, I was at Lucy's party.'

'Were you invited?'

'Yeah.'

'Cormac, I can drag your arse down to the station and lock you up in a windowless cell for twenty-four hours if you insist on being a belligerent pup.' She couldn't without it being evidence-based, but he wasn't to know that.

He played with three stale crumbs on the table, balling them up between his fingers. She thought he was about to flick them at her, but he continued rubbing them, head bowed.

'Okay, so maybe Lucy didn't invite me.' He looked up. 'But she asked everyone else. The guy on the door didn't stop me. Are you going to lock me in a cell for that?'

'Was she annoyed to see you there?'

'She was a bit smart with me, which is nothing new. She didn't really tell me to leave, so I stayed.'

'Who did you talk to last night?'

'Can't honestly remember.'

'Names.'

'Hannah Byrne, for a while.' Cormac stared hard at Lottie, then he dropped the shredded crumbs and pointed a freckled finger at her. 'I spoke to Sean Parker. Hey, you're his mother! I play F1 with him online. He's good. And he's building up his live-stream subscriptions.' He grinned, but it was half-hearted. Lottie didn't approve of the amount of time Sean spent gaming, but it seemed to keep her son calm, which suited her.

She studied Cormac and dived straight in. 'Where did you get the drugs?'

'What drugs?'

'You really don't want to piss me off, Cormac, and I'm well on the way to getting truly pissed off. Tell me the truth.'

He seemed to consider his options. 'Has something happened to Hannah?'

'Why would you think that?' Folding her arms, Lottie had an urge to scratch the back of her hands. The small house was grubby, and if she had to spend much longer in it, she thought she'd burst out in a flurry of hives.

'You're here, aren't you? Besides Sean, I really only talked to Hannah. She's a nice girl.'

'Nice enough that you filled her with drugs?'

'Hey, come on, that's not true. I don't do drugs.'

'But it is true that you gave her a pill, isn't it?'

He drummed a finger on the table, his face suddenly flushed. 'Whatever. I didn't force her.'

Reaching out, Lottie grabbed for his hand before she realised she was doing it. 'I'm warning you ...'

'Okay, okay. It was just one pill. She doesn't even drink, for God's sake.'

Lottie pulled back and wiped her hand on her jeans. 'One pill can do immense damage to someone who doesn't normally take drugs, you know?'

'I told you, I didn't force it down her neck.'

'What did you do?'

He sighed dramatically. 'The party was boring, so I bought a couple of pills. Showed them to her. I swallowed one. She took the other from me. Happy?'

'What type of drug was it? MDMA?'

'I've no idea. Told you, I don't normally do drugs.'

'Where did you get the pills?'

Cormac gulped. 'Does it matter?'

'Everything matters in a murder investigation.'

His jaw literally dropped and his face turned ashen; even his freckles took on a sickly hue. His hands shook. 'Murder? But she was okay ...'

'Who?' Lottie was in her stride now, but she wasn't enjoying undressing the boy's lies.

'Hannah. She went a bit weird after she eventually swallowed the pill. She was upset, and I think that's why she took it.'

'Why was she upset?'

He wrenched his hands into one another, twisting his fingers. 'I'd never have given it to her if I thought it would affect her so much. Swear to God.' He started to shiver.

'Hannah is fine,' Lottie said. White lie – the girl was anything but fine. She wondered if the doctor had seen her yet so that she could be formally interviewed.

Cormac swiped his sleeve under his nose and sniffed. His breathing was laboured. 'My inhaler ...'

'Where is it?'

'I'll get it.' He stood and found a blue inhaler on the shelf beside the sink. He took a few puffs before sitting down again. 'What do you want to know?'

'Who did you buy the drugs from?'

'Jake Flood.'

'Tell me more.'

'He was handing out the drinks. He's only fifteen, so I don't know why Lucy roped him in.'

'How do you know him?'

'Just know *of* him. He does boxing.'

'Know anyone else who was at the party?'

'Hannah knew the guy on the door. She said he was her coach or a teacher at her school. Then there was that creepy DJ. Richie something. Ponytail and beads round his neck, thinking he was the dude.' The words tumbled from his mouth in his hurry to unburden himself.

'Take another puff of your inhaler.' She needed him to calm down. 'Back to Jake Flood. Is he known as a drug dealer among your peers?'

'My what?'

'Your friends.'

'Don't know. Told you, I don't normally do—'

'You know his name, so you must know more.'

'All I know is that he boxes, but I've seen him with a gang of teens on bikes. BMXs, shit like that. They sell pills to the estate kids and outside the schools.'

Lottie was aware of these teenagers. They were a recent addition to Ragmullin's crime scene and renowned for terrorising kids at school gates. The garda cycling patrol unit was desperately trying to catch some of them in the act, so far without success.

'Would Lucy have had any dealings with these drug-dealing teenagers?'

He shrugged. 'She must have had. Why else was Jake at her party pushing drugs?'

'Okay. Talk to me about Hannah Byrne. Why was she upset before she took the pill?'

'I suppose you'll keep on about it if I don't tell you.'

'You're right there,' Kirby said, and Lottie nodded.

'Can I get my phone? I can show you.'

'Sure.' Lottie leaned back as he left the room, trying to get a look at what he was doing. 'What do you make of him?'

Kirby tapped his pen against his notebook filled with illegible script. Illegible to Lottie, anyhow.

'He's jumpy as hell,' he said. 'He's hiding something.'

'For sure. Look at the state of this place. Why would he have the washing machine on?' She pointed to the half-open door behind her and went to investigate. 'What teenager washes his clothes straight after a night out?'

'You're asking me? I never washed as much as a sock when I was a teenager. Even now I'm hard pressed to pick shirts up off the floor a week after I've worn them.'

Lottie sat back down and grimaced. 'Sean is the same. I'm blue in the face picking up after him. The girls aren't much better. Maybe Cormac is in this with Hannah.'

Cormac returned to the room with his phone and a charger. He plugged it into a socket and waited for the phone to chirp into life. After a few minutes of silence, he began scrolling and tapping.

'Look at this.'

Taking the phone from him, cable still attached, Lottie stared at the photograph on the screen. The girl in the picture was naked from the waist up. She was holding her blonde hair high above her head with one hand, her other hand around her waist propping up her almost non-existent breasts as she stared into a mirror, seemingly admiring her physique.

'Who is it?' she asked, though she knew the answer.

'Hannah,' Cormac said softly.

'How do you have this photo of her on your phone?' Lottie felt a slow rage burn up through her chest.

'Lucy shared it on Snapchat and WhatsApped it to absolutely everyone, including Hannah. Hannah was so upset. I asked her to send it to me because I wanted to find out what was going on.'

'Did she send it to Hannah intentionally?'

'Erm ... you'd have to ask her that.'

Impossible, Lottie thought as she tried to quell the fire in her belly. 'When was it shared?'

Cormac glanced at the time on the message. 'Twelve thirty-four last night ... this morning. Whatever.'

'What did Hannah do about it? How did she react?'

He pressed a finger to his brow, thinking. 'Phones started vibrating with the message. She was just standing there with everyone staring at her. She stormed around giving out yards about Lucy. That's when she took the pill.'

Lottie tutted. 'And after that?'

'We danced.'

'And?'

'Yeah, that's all.'

She didn't believe him. To wrongfoot him, she said, 'Why are you washing your clothes?'

He blushed. 'Not a crime, is it?'

'It is if you're trying to wash away evidence.'

'What do you mean? I did nothing wrong. I admit I gave Hannah the pill, but she took it and totally chilled.'

'Our forensic team will want your clothes from last night, even if you've washed them.' If Cormac or Hannah had committed the crime of murder, either together or alone, she hoped SOCOs would be able to find something to analyse on their clothing.

'Don't you need a warrant for that?' He looked even more uneasy. 'If you tell me what I'm supposed to have done, maybe I could help you.' He ran his hands up and down his bare arms, and dry skin fluttered in the air.

'How did you get home from the party?'

'My car. Heap of shite.'

'Where is it?'

'Parked in the harbour car park. I'll need to put a ticket on it or I'll get a fine.'

'What time did you leave?'

'Late.'

Lottie despaired of anyone knowing the time of day any more. 'Did you give anyone a lift? Hannah maybe?'

'I don't understand what this is about.'

That was when she realised he'd never asked her who was dead. Keeping her eyes firmly locked on his, she said, 'Lucy McAllister was murdered last night.'

Cormac's jaw slackened and he averted his eyes towards a spot on the wall behind her. 'That can't be true. It can't be.'

'Believe me, I wouldn't be wasting my time with you if it was untrue.'

'Shite. Jesus. Fuck.' He paused his incantations and rubbed his forehead furiously. 'Holy crap. Her father will be devastated.'

'Do you know Lucy's parents?'

'No. I mean, I do gardening for them. The few times I was there, it was obvious Lucy and her mother didn't get on. But her dad never stopped talking about her.'

'When exactly did you last see Lucy?'

That was when Cormac clamped his mouth shut and refused to say another word.

———

The detectives left with the lad in the car, and the kid on the bike sent the text. Then he pushed the bike out from behind the steps that led towards the shopping centre car park and rode down the narrow street.

'Hey, you there! You owe me for fixing your brakes last week. Come back here.'

The boy stood up on the pedals and with one hand gave the bike shop man the finger. No way was he paying for getting his poxy brakes fixed. The man could shout all he liked. No one was listening to him.

He pedalled fast, trying to catch sight of the unmarked car, relieved to see it turn up towards the garda station. Now maybe he'd have time to have a piss and something to eat.

———

I, the Magpie, am on edge and I don't like that. I thought I could easily slip from my everyday reality into my avian persona, but it's difficult.

The exhilarating feeling died fairly quickly after I'd left. I thought I'd be able to fly high on my imaginary wings, but my feet remain rooted to the ground. Stuck. This isn't good.

What can raise me up again?

I need to take something young and shiny for myself. My very own treasure.

That motivates me.

Now that I have started my quest, there will be no stopping me. I feel I might fly as my mind conjures up the image of young, tender untouched flesh, soft and supple beneath my fingers. I imagine caressing the skin, teasing open a quivering mouth and staring into terrified, questioning eyes.

I know what I have to do. Someone needs to suffer to restore my euphoria.

So be it.

17

Hannah had never felt so rotten in her life. Her head throbbed and her body shook all over. She was hot and cold simultaneously. She'd told the detectives Cormac's name because they'd have found out about him anyhow. But the blood under her nails ... what did that mean? How could Lucy be dead? And why was her memory so blank?

'You don't have to say anything,' her mother urged. 'You did nothing wrong, pet.'

She couldn't even if she wanted to. 'I can't remember anything. This looks bad, doesn't it, Mam?'

'Yes, so please keep your mouth shut.'

'I want to go home.'

'They say a doctor has to examine you and take blood to see if you were drugged. They mentioned a psychiatric evaluation, so you've to wait for that too.'

'Do you think I need a solicitor?' Hannah felt close to tears again.

'Please, Hannah, I'm trying to think of a way around this.'

'Free legal aid is for people who can't afford a solicitor.'

'Shut up. I'm thinking.'

Hannah recoiled from her mother and watched her walking up and down behind the table in the small, suffocating room they'd been moved to. Suddenly her brain flashed with a horrific memory. She slammed her fist into her mouth to keep from crying aloud.

There'd been a photo, hadn't there?

Squeezing her eyes shut, she tried to recall it. Some kind of half-naked photo that everyone had seen. She ran her fingers in and out of her hair, desperate to remember. Had Lucy sent it? Or Ivy? Who was in the photo? Breasts on show? Was it a flat chest? Hers? God, no, please don't let it have been me, she silently pleaded. It might ruin her athletics career before it started. And what would it do to her mam?

Why was she even thinking of some random photo when she couldn't remember anything to help herself? She pressed her knuckles either side of her temple as if willing a truth to make itself known.

A faint thread was there, if only she could catch it. She dropped her hands as a sliver of truth slowly wended its way from her mind's eye to nestle like thorns in her brain.

What had she done?

18

Sharon Flood woke up and felt the emptiness in the house. She jumped out of bed and slipped into Jake's room. Scratching her head sleepily, she scrunched up her eyes and wondered why her brother wasn't there. He always slept in, even on school mornings, but this was holiday time and today was Saturday.

She looked out of the window, craning her neck, but her mother's car wasn't parked on the road. Checked her mother's room. Empty. Opened the bathroom door. Also empty. After peeing, washing her hands and face and brushing her teeth, she headed downstairs.

The small sitting room was deserted, as was the kitchen. Where was everyone? As she traipsed back up the stairs, she heard a key turn in the front door lock. Standing on the top step, she watched her mother creep into the hall and hang up her black gilet on the hook behind the door.

'Mam, where were you?'

'Jesus Lord almighty, Shaz, you frightened the living daylights out of me. Be a star and put the kettle on while I jump under the shower.'

'Were you working late?' Sharon knew the hotel bar officially closed at 11.30, and even though it sometimes took another hour or two to clear up, there was no way her mother was there all night.

'I had to help Gino do a stock-take. Went on for hours. I'm gasping for a cup of tea.'

As her mother passed her on the landing, Sharon said, 'Jake isn't home, Mam.'

'What do you mean, he isn't home? He was minding you last night.'

She didn't want to rat out her brother, but she was worried. Was he with the toxic people? She bit the corner of her thumb.

'Well, he went out.' Once she started talking, she couldn't stop. 'I woke up and thought he was in bed, but I think he took your car and he didn't come home. He promised me a bag of chips and chicken nuggets. Where is he, Mam?'

'What are you talking about? Took my car? Shaz, don't be silly, my car is outside.'

Liz Flood hurried down the stairs and out the front door, but before she reached the front path, she turned and ran back inside, banging the door.

'I'll ground the little shit for life.'

Following her into the kitchen, Sharon said, 'Will we call the guards?'

'They'd throw his thieving arse in jail.' Liz filled and flicked on the kettle. 'Did he say where he was going?'

Sharon shook her head. 'He said he'd bring me back chips and—'

'I'll give him chips and bloody chicken nuggets!' Liz shouted, and Sharon nearly had to put her hands over her ears. 'What time did he go out?'

'Don't know.'

'He knows he isn't supposed to leave you on your own.' Liz marched up and down the narrow kitchen. 'Did anyone call for him or ring him before he went out?'

Sharon felt dizzy watching her mother. 'Mam, I don't know. I went to bed when he went out. I dreamt about chicken nuggets and Jake wasn't here when I woke up this morning, and that's all I know.' She stopped to catch her breath as Liz phoned Jake. She should have thought of doing that.

'Little fecker has his phone switched off.' Liz took a mug from the cupboard, ran a tea towel around the rim and dropped a used tea bag into it. She stood with her hands flat on the countertop. Deep breaths. 'This is my own fault for trusting him.'

'Maybe he crashed the car. He might be in hospital. The guards—'

'Shush, Shaz. I need to think. Get dressed, then go knock on his friends' doors. If he was out drinking, I'll kill him. He's probably somewhere sleeping off a hangover. I'll tell you this for nothing, Jake Flood won't sleep for a month when I get my hands on him.'

'Maybe the car was stolen. He might be afraid to come home, or—'

'Are you still here? I told you to get dressed! Does no one in this house listen to me any more?'

Sharon slunk out of the kitchen as her mother poured partially boiled water from the kettle into the mug. She was acting weirder than normal, Sharon thought. Where had she been last night, anyway?

And where the hell was Jake?

The doorbell blared just as Sharon came back down the stairs in her ripped blue jeans, black tee and stained pink runners. Only one runner had a lace in it. Jake must have swiped the other lace, as well as taking their mother's car. He was so stupid.

Maybe it was Jake at the door. But he'd have a key, wouldn't he? Unless he'd lost it. Maybe he'd lost the car too. Yeah, Jake wasn't so clever after all.

As her mother opened the door, Sharon stalled on the curve of the narrow stairs. Hunkering down, she gripped her knees and peered under the handrail through two posts that needed a fresh coat of paint. Mam had bought the paint and given Jake the job, but he still hadn't done it. If Daddy was here, Sharon thought, the stairs would be painted by now. A lump formed in her throat and she tried desperately not to cry. Crying set Mam off, and Sharon knew she wouldn't be able to cope with that on top of everything else this morning.

Two people stood on the step. A man and a woman. They looked like guards. If Jake was here, he'd know who they were. He was good at figuring out what people worked at. And then she did let out a cry. Were they here to tell them Jake was dead? No!

She watched as her mother stood back to bring them inside. The woman, wearing a grubby-looking T-shirt and holding a folded-up jacket and a creased leather bag under her arm, smiled. Sharon raised her hand to wave, but stalled it mid-air as her mother shot her a warning look.

Definitely the guards.

————

Lottie and Kirby had deposited Cormac O'Flaherty at the station for a DNA sample and fingerprints to be taken in order to rule him in or out of their investigation. She had mentioned the name Jake Flood in the incident room, and Garda Lei, a member of the cycling unit, knew of him and where he lived.

The estate was broken into various roads and avenues, as if the developer had tried to give the impression it was comprised of individual areas. But there was no getting away from the fact that whether you lived in Brinsley Terrace, Brinsley Road or Brinsley Avenue, it was still a web of closely built, similarly designed houses. A haven for poverty, antisocial behaviour and illegal dumping, and a breeding ground for gangs.

They were looking for 16 Brinsley Terrace to interview Jake Flood. At this stage, Lottie had Hannah Byrne firmly in the cross hairs for Lucy McAllister's murder, but the fact that the girl might have been under the influence of an illicit substance caused her to have doubts about it being a cut-and-dried case. And then there was Cormac O'Flaherty. She couldn't get a handle on him. First, though, she had to find the little scumbag drug dealer.

Once they were admitted inside the Flood house, she found herself pleasantly surprised. The kitchen was small, but neat and tidy. She inhaled and admired a floral smell, so unlike Cormac O'Flaherty's fusty abode. Kirby pulled out a chair at the tiny round table and sat. Liz Flood busied herself filling the kettle, even though the detectives had refused her offer of tea.

'I need one myself,' she said, emptying an already half-full mug into the sink and rinsing it under the tap, hands visibly shaking. She eventually ceased fussing, dried her hands and leaned back against the counter. 'How can I help you?'

'We're sorry to disturb you on a Saturday morning, but we'd like to have a quick word with Jake.'

'Jake?' The thin, drawn woman sat. Her face looked like someone had drained all the blood from her body. 'Why? What has he done?'

'Not sure, to be honest, that's why we want to talk to him,' Kirby said, making himself look important by placing his tattered notebook and pen on the table.

'Jake isn't here.'

'Where might we find him?' Lottie said, her stomach gnawing away with hunger. She hadn't eaten a thing all morning. Hopefully she'd have time to grab a coffee and sandwich on the way back to the station.

'I ... I don't know.' Liz faltered and the kettle squealed. She stood and switched it off. 'Can you come back? He'll be home later.'

'I'm afraid it's urgent.' Kirby tapped his pen noisily against the table leg.

A young girl, dressed in torn jeans, a ribbed black top and grubby pink runners – one without laces – walked into the kitchen. Hands on hips, a brazen look spread across her face. 'What's going on, Mam?'

'Go up to your room, Shaz. It's nothing to do with you.'

'Why are you looking for Jake?' Sharon said, not budging an inch.

Lottie hadn't time to engage with the youngster; she wanted to talk to Jake. 'Mrs Flood, we really need to find your son. You must have some idea where he is.'

'He's ... out.'

Time to change direction. 'Do you know about a gang of teenagers who cycle around selling drugs? I believe they operate on this estate.'

'Never heard of anything like that,' Liz said, stony-faced, but the little girl twisted her head, looking up at her mother.

'You have, haven't you, Shaz?' Lottie said.

'Have not. And I'm Sharon to you.' The girl put her hands on her hips again, trying to be cool, Lottie suspected, but she just looked lost.

'I think you know something. I could tell by your face when I mentioned it. What age are you, Sharon?'

'Ten.'

'You seem to be really clever for ten. It's very important that you tell me what you know.'

'Well ...'

'If you know something,' Liz said, a puzzled look furrowing her brow, 'tell them.'

'I heard about them. But Jake has nothing to do with them.'

'Where do they hang out?' Lottie pressed.

'How would I know?'

'Manners, Shaz,' Liz said.

'It's okay,' Lottie said. 'If Jake is involved with them, we need to know.'

Liz shoved her daughter out of the way and leaned both hands on the table. 'My son is a good boy. He's had it tough, and so has Sharon. Their dad died last year and I'm working every hour I can to keep food on the table and books in their school bags. Whatever you think he's involved in, well, it's not true. Outside of school, Jake lives for his boxing, so I think you're barking up the wrong bloody tree.'

'Which boxing club does he belong to?' Kirby asked.

'Why do you want to know that?'

'Please, Mrs Flood, we need to know.' Lottie felt impatience growl along with the hunger in the pit of her stomach.

'And I need to know why you're asking about Jake.'

The woman was going to hear about it soon enough, so Lottie said, 'A teenage girl was assaulted last night after Lucy McAllister's house party. We believe Jake was present during the evening. The girl is dead.'

'A house party?' Liz looked from Lottie to Kirby before settling her gaze on Lottie. 'You're mistaken. Jake is only fifteen. He wouldn't be at a house party.'

'I have witnesses who confirm he was at one last night. Are you sure you don't know where he is this morning?'

'He's out. Like I already told you.' The woman was trying to sound angry, but Lottie noticed her chin trembling, her hands continuing to shake.

'Was he at home last night at all?'

Liz glanced at her daughter, as if wishing the girl was anywhere but standing there open-mouthed looking up at her. 'I was working late. I ... I only got home this morning.'

'Where do you work?'

'In the Brook Hotel bar. It was very busy last night. Always is on a Friday.'

'And you were working until this morning?'

'Erm, yeah.'

Lottie didn't believe it. 'What time did you arrive home?'

'Look, whatever time I arrived home has nothing to do with you or with where Jake is.'

'The thing is, it might have something to do with establishing whether your son was home last night or at the party. If he is involved with a gang of kids selling drugs, he might be in trouble.'

'Jake wouldn't hurt anyone,' Sharon blurted.

'Were you here last night, Sharon?' Lottie turned her attention to the child.

'Yeah.'

'And Jake?'

Sharon glanced up at her mother as if silently asking for permission. But Liz was staring straight ahead, wringing her hands. At last she broke the silence.

'I'm not long home,' she said, defeat in her tone. 'Jake was supposed to be here. I'd never leave Shaz on her own, but she tells me Jake went out last night and wasn't here when she woke up this morning. I'm sorry about before, but I'm worried about him.'

'He took Mam's car,' Sharon added.

Lottie stood at this news, trying to keep the shock and anger from registering on her face. She rounded on Liz. 'When were you going to tell me that your fifteen-year-old son took your car?'

Liz shook her head and sat down heavily, her expression one of bewilderment. 'I didn't know until a few minutes ago. You have to find him.'

'I'll need the registration number,' Kirby said.

She recited the details.

'Make and colour?' he prompted.

'Fiat Punto. Blue. You don't honestly think Jake had something to do with this murder, do you?'

'I just need to talk to him. Which boxing club is he affiliated to?'

'Ragmullin Goldstars. They use a gym in the old squash club. Jake goes there three times a week to train.'

'He's good, too,' Shaz said.

'Who runs the club?'

'I'm not sure, but I can find out,' Liz said, frowning, as if suddenly realising there was a lot about her son she didn't know.

'Leave it to us.'

'You know Lucy's dad is an agent for professional boxers?'

Lottie glanced at Kirby, who shrugged a shoulder. 'Okay. We'll put out an alert for your car and for Jake. I need a photograph of him.'

Sharon took a battered iPhone with a cracked screen from her jeans pocket. 'I can send you one.'

Lottie handed over a card with her details. She glanced at the photo of Jake that the girl had opened on her phone. His front teeth overlapped slightly and his skin was pale against his dark hair, which was shaved on one side. Sad but sweet. Not the image you'd have of a young drug dealer, or even a murderer. But Lottie knew murderers often didn't fit the perceived mould.

She followed Kirby out of the kitchen, Liz and Sharon close behind.

'When Jake comes home,' she said, 'contact me immediately.'

She closed the door on the silence.

———

The boy sheltered in the gloom of the alley, hands on the brakes, ready to pedal off if he needed to make a quick exit.

He'd seen the two detectives go into the house. He'd taken a piss against the wall but still hadn't had time to eat, and he was fucking starving.

They'd been in there a long time and he wondered if Sharon had opened her big mouth. There was no way you could trust kids. They'd say anything. He didn't think of himself as a kid. He was fifteen, same as Jake, but Sharon was only ten. And she was a girl. Ugh!

As the detectives came out of the house, he watched the leggy one with the scuffed handbag talk to the small fat guy across the roof of the car before they got in and drove off.

With his mobile phone in his hand, he tapped another text and sent it. Jake was in big trouble now. When his phone pinged with the reply, he pedalled away to his next mission.

———

Jake felt the blood seep from his side. It had happened so fast, he'd hardly had time to react, except to try and hide. It proved how much of a coward he was outside the ring.

He thought of Shaz waiting all night for her chips and nuggets. A strangled screech caught in his throat. Here he was, tied up, not knowing whether he would live or die, and he was thinking about his little sister not getting her food. He groaned and the pain increased. He had no idea where he was, but the ground beneath him was cold concrete.

How long had he been knocked out? A good few hours, he thought, because he could see a little daylight through the jamb of the door. The ache in his back was excruciating, the wound in his side unbearable, and his mind magnified his fear a thousand times.

A door creaked inwards and the space filled with brightness, blinding him. He raised his bound hands to shield his eyes. A human shape loomed towards him. Jake's eyes were badly bruised and almost closed, but he was able to make out a chain wrapped around a hand.

'Please don't kill me,' he whimpered. He realised then that he was gagged and the sound was smothered by the rag.

His captor flicked the chain. Jake wondered why he had been so stupid. The toxic people he'd warned Shaz about had got him. He curled his body as best he could despite his restraints as the first lash cut through his skin.

'I'm sorry,' he said, knowing that no one who mattered could hear him.

He feared no one would hear his voice ever again.

They swung round by the DJ's house after sourcing Richie Harrison's address. It was a new-build, semi-detached, located on the upmarket side of town. Lottie marvelled at the comparison with Liz Flood's house. Richie Harrison's place was straight out of *House and Home* magazine.

'This is like somebody's wet dream,' Kirby said.

'How can he afford it?'

'Not on his DJ earnings anyhow. The wife must have a good job.'

There was no car or van outside, and no one answered her incessant knocking.

Heading back to the station, Lottie received word that the McAllisters' plane had landed and they would soon be on their way to Ragmullin under escort. Time to sort out somewhere to break the terrible news. She shivered at the thought of telling them that their only child was dead.

At the station, she learned that the duty doctor had attended Hannah Byrne. He'd taken blood and urine samples to test for the presence of drugs and alcohol in her system. The girl was awaiting the psych evaluation. All time being wasted when Lottie could be taking a statement, though she had to admit Hannah was unwell.

She'd just stowed her bag under her desk and had her purse in her hand to go for food when Garda Martina Brennan arrived.

'Cormac O'Flaherty, Inspector, I put him in an interview room. He's being a pain.'

'He refused to give the samples?' Lottie asked.

'Yeah.'

'Walk with me,' she said, despairing of getting a bite to eat. 'I'll have a word with Cormac. We have a missing boy. Fifteen-year-old Jake Flood. Kirby will fill you in. Check if we have eyes on the mother's car. The little shit stole it. And get someone to chase up the whereabouts of Richie Harrison, the DJ.'

'Will do.'

'While you're at it, talk to Kirby and see what you can find out about the Goldstars boxing club. Jake's a member and Lucy's dad is involved in boxing too. It's based in the old squash club down in the industrial estate. Find someone who might know where the lad is.'

'Boxing in a squash club?'

'And have a chat with Garda Lei. He knows about the lads selling drugs. He might have information about them.'

'Grand.'

Lottie watched Martina walk down the corridor repeating the instructions to herself. She had no idea what Jake Flood being missing or being a member of a boxing club had to do with anything, but his facilitation of drugs at Lucy's party bothered her. First, though, she had the Cormac O'Flaherty problem to deal with.

'I want a solicitor.' Cormac was leaning against the wall, inhaler in one hand, a bottle of Lucozade Sport in the other. He had scratched his forehead and his spots were raw, one bleeding.

'Why do you need a solicitor?'

'I'm here, aren't I? You want to take samples from me, so I'm thinking you believe I did something wrong. And if that's the case, then I understand I need representation.'

Representation? He was having a laugh, surely?

'It's routine to take samples for elimination purposes. Nothing for you to worry about, unless you think we're going to match your DNA to samples we get from Lucy's body?'

He bit down on his lip and sat. She thought he was about to shut up shop like he'd done at his house, but as he traced a line in the condensation on the bottle, he began to speak. His was voice so low, she had to crane her neck towards him to hear his words.

'I think it might have been Hannah.'

'What might have been Hannah?' She dared not take her eyes off him as he continued to fiddle with the bottle.

'She might have done something to Lucy.'

'Why do you say that?' She wondered if this was self-preservation or whether he honestly believed Hannah had committed a murder.

'The photograph. Hannah was so upset over it, and she was mad at Lucy. They were arguing and it wasn't cool.'

'Not cool?'

He squinted out from under his ginger lashes. 'They were screaming at each other. The DJ guy ... he helped me separate them.'

'What happened after that?'

'Lucy ran upstairs. She must have been fixing her make-up, because a few minutes later she waltzed down the stairs like nothing had happened. Not a mark on her. All fake smiles.'

'And Hannah?'

'She was so upset. Frantic. But then she started to chill.'

'In what way was she chilled?'

'Kind of … out of it. Dancing around all floppy. I don't know how to describe it.'

'Was it because of what you gave her?'

'I took one exactly the same and I wasn't acting like that. Maybe she'd taken something else before she attacked Lucy. She said she was drinking Coke. There could've been something mixed in it.'

Lottie wondered about that. 'Could Jake or someone else have slipped something into her drink?'

He shrugged. 'Maybe. I wasn't with her all the time.'

'Tell me more about the row.'

'When she attacked Lucy, I tried to restrain her, before the DJ got involved, and she scratched my stomach with those long nails of hers. So if you find blood on her, some of it could be mine from when I separated them.'

The young man was talking nineteen to the dozen. Lottie was finding it hard to keep up. He twisted around in the chair and lifted his shirt, and she visually examined the raw scrapes criss-crossing his torso. 'What were you wearing?'

'A belly top?' Kirby snorted.

'It's not funny.' Cormac leaned over the table.

'Murder is definitely not funny.' Lottie glared at Kirby.

'My T-shirt was loose and I'd my hands up trying to stop her when she scraped me.'

Lottie wondered if this was the reason why Hannah had blood under her fingernails. She needed that DNA analysis fast-tracked.

'Cormac, we have to take samples from your injuries, and photograph them. Okay?'

'They're just a few scrapes, but yeah, it's cool. It might prove how unhinged Hannah was.'

Unhinged?

'After Lucy escaped upstairs to fix her make-up, what did Hannah do?'

'The DJ calmed her down, got her a drink. Like I said, she was spaced out. It was as if she didn't know what was going on around her. She probably doesn't even know what she did.'

'You're remembering an awful lot all of a sudden. What's changed?'

He shifted on the chair and picked at his thumb. 'I didn't want to snitch on Hannah, but with Lucy dead, it changes everything. Sorry I lied earlier. I still want a solicitor.'

'Right.' Lottie stifled a groan. 'I'll try to arrange it. The guy on the door, Noel Glennon, the athletics coach, PE teacher, whatever he is, have you managed to remember anything about him?' She failed to hide her cynicism.

'I'd never seen him before last night.'

'Really? He taught at Hannah and Lucy's school. You're a gardener there, aren't you?'

'I call it landscaping. I still don't know him.'

She wasn't sure whether to believe him or not. Was Cormac someone who found lying easy and omitting the truth even easier?

Leaving the room, she wondered which version he was telling her. The truth, lies, or fiction with an element of truth? She needed to talk to the DJ, Richie Harrison, wherever the hell he was. And when Hannah was deemed fit and passed the psych examination, she was in for a grilling.

But what about the photograph? Why had Lucy shared it? Maybe Maria Lynch would find something on the laptop. What Lottie needed was the dead girl's phone.

20

Kirby pinned Jake Flood's photo to the board in the incident room.

'Looks like butter wouldn't melt,' Garda Brennan said.

'Oh, there you are, Martina. We have a missing teenager and a stolen car, as well as the murder investigation.'

'What's the story with the missing kid?'

'Fifteen-year-old Jake Flood. Lives at 16 Brinsley Terrace with his mother, Elizabeth, known as Liz, and ten-year-old sister, Sharon, fondly called Shaz.' Kirby stopped to take a breath. 'Jake is implicated in selling drugs at Lucy McAllister's party. Hearsay for now, but probably true. Stole his mother's car last night. An ancient Fiat Punto. Bright blue, if you don't mind. He's involved with a boxing club, Ragmullin Goldstars. Lucy's dad, Albert McAllister, is a boxing promoter. But it seems Jake may have a connection to a gang of youths on bikes who sell drugs. A right mish-mash of information.' He tapped his cigar shirt pocket in frustration.

'We should get Garda Lei in here,' Martina said. 'He's had more punctures than you've had Happy Meals, trying to catch those lads.'

'Give him a shout for me, please.'

When Martina went off to find Garda Lei, Kirby tried to breathe normally. He liked her, and he knew she liked him – as an older brother. He figured it would remain like that as long as Detective Sam McKeown was around. Despite a major eruption when McKeown's wife received a mysterious phone call telling her that her husband was conducting an affair with Martina, he seemed to have weathered that particular storm. Maybe it was time for another phone call.

Before he could think about it further, a shadow fell over the room as the sun cut around the side of the building.

'You wanted me?' Garda Lei hurried in.

Lei was the newest recruit to Ragmullin station. He was as short as Kirby, but the similarities ended there. Lei was lean without being skinny, though he could give Boyd a run for his money in that department. He was also fresh-faced and eager, whereas Kirby was flabby, flushed and faltering in his enthusiasm for the job. As far as Kirby knew, Garda Lei had been born and bred in nearby Longford, where his mother hailed from. His father was second-generation Chinese. Kirby pitied the young man being assigned to the bicycle unit. The abuse he must get didn't bear thinking about. Kirby himself had been ridiculed for his weight and appearance, so God knows what verbal taunts Lei had thrown at him.

'Garda Brennan tells me you might know about Jake Flood and the drug-dealing teenagers on bikes. What can you tell me?'

Lei studied Jake's photo. 'He can move, so he can. He left me for dead a while ago.'

'Was he with the gang at the time?'

'A few of them were causing a ruckus outside the girls' school. I followed them. All I got was a blistered arse for my trouble.'

'Did you talk to Jake at all?'

'No.'

'Know anything about him?'

'I keep my ear to the ground. He's a more recent recruit. I heard his dad died last year and he's been acting out ever since. He's not your usual scumbag. I have the feeling the kid took a wrong turn in life; eventually he'll find his way back.'

'Can't wait that long.' Kirby gave Lei a rueful smile. 'Jake's been missing since last night and we need to find him.' He filled him in on what they had learned so far.

'I'll ask around,' Lei said. 'Someone must know where he is. He's definitely not at home then?'

'No, only his mother and sister are there. His phone's switched off. Follow up on the car. Make sure the usual missing person notifications are sent out, and run everything by me first.' Not that he didn't trust Lei to do the job, but he couldn't risk Lottie chewing his arse if something went public that shouldn't.

'He's keen,' Garda Brennan said, returning as Lei left.

'Implying I'm not?'

'Not at all, but you have to admit, you can't beat the flow of fresh blood running through the station.'

'You've just planted a horrible image in my brain.'

She laughed. 'Sorry. I've to go help Garda Furey on the checkpoint near the McAllister house. I'll give Lei a hand later.' She turned to leave.

'Martina?'

'Yes?' She glanced over her shoulder.

'Fancy a drink after work?'

'Can't, sorry. Another time, maybe?'

He could have sworn she blushed as she left.

Damn you, McKeown.

21

Richie Harrison stopped half a mile from the McAllister property. A tape ran the width of the narrow road and a uniformed garda held up her hand and halted him. He squirmed in the seat while doing his best to remain calm. Brontë was spooked enough without adding fuel to that particular fire.

'I'm afraid you'll have to turn around,' the guard said. 'The road's closed up ahead.'

'What's wrong?' Richie nervously threaded his fingers around the beads hanging from his neck.

'An incident further up. You'll have to go back.'

'I've to collect equipment from the McAllisters' house. I left it there last night. I'll be ten minutes.'

'Hold on.' She turned and spoke into her radio. He couldn't hear what was being said.

'Why won't they let us through?' Brontë said.

'Fucked if I know.'

'You never know anything.'

Before he could reply, the garda was back. 'What's your name, sir?'

'Richie Harrison.'

'What do you work at?'

'I'm a DJ.'

'And you played at Lucy McAllister's party?'

'Erm ... yeah. I've another gig tonight. I need my gear.'

'Would you mind stepping out of the vehicle, please, sir?'

'I'm in a bit of a rush.' This was not good.

'Sir, please step out of the vehicle. You too, miss.'

'It's *Mrs* Harrison,' Brontë said spikily.

Feeling he had little choice, Richie jumped out. 'What is this about?'

Another garda arrived. Both stared at him, tight-lipped.

On the far side of the van, Brontë let out a yell. Richie raced around, the two guards following him.

'My baby!' she cried, clutching her tummy, bent in two. 'I think ... Oh God ... it's coming.'

Putting an arm around Brontë, helping her upright, Richie said, 'We need to get her to the hospital.'

'Garda Furey will accompany you to town,' said the stocky female, who seemed weighed down with heavy equipment on her belt.

Richie couldn't help noticing her soft, clear skin. She was quite good-looking, he had to admit, for a guard.

'Thanks,' he said. The baby wasn't due for another five weeks at least. He hoped everything was okay.

He got Brontë into the van. She threw him a knowing look, but he couldn't figure out what it meant. He pulled the seat belt around her girth and leaned over to snap it closed.

'Act the worried father,' she whispered.

'What do—?'

'Shh. Get in the van and shut up.'

He closed the door and sat in the driver's seat.

'Follow me,' Garda Furey said, and began to walk to the squad car.

'What's going on?' Richie asked. Brontë gave him a hard dig in the ribs with her elbow.

'There was a serious incident at the McAllister property. A young girl was found dead there this morning. Probably murder. Now let's get this lady to the hospital.'

As Richie reversed the van, stalling it on the grassy verge before succeeding in turning it around, he noticed the good-looking guard write down the registration number. What was her problem? That was when the other guard's words hit home and he nearly threw up in his lap.

A murder at the McAllisters' house.

And the guards were all over it. Shit.

The squad car sped along the back lanes before screeching onto the main road, blue and white strobe lights flashing on the roof and grille. Richie found it difficult to keep up. His van belched out diesel fumes when he pressed hard on the accelerator. Brontë was being a bitch about giving him the money for a service. Now, though, he had more pressing things to worry about.

'Are you okay?' He glanced over at his wife to find her staring straight ahead, her mouth set in a firm line. 'Brontë?'

'I'm fine.'

'Any more pain?' He was used to her moods, but she seemed to be entering a new sphere altogether.

'Duh, there wasn't any pain in the first place,' she said, and he nearly slammed on the brakes. She added angrily, 'Keep fucking driving.'

Gulping loudly, he tried to regain a modicum of composure. 'Why the act, then?'

'I had to get you away from them. That guard might have been pretty, but she wasn't buying your faux charisma. That must only work on teenage girls, because she looked at you like you were a ... I don't know, a pervert? Or a suspect, maybe.'

'For Christ's sake, a suspect for what?' His knuckles turned white as he grasped the steering wheel tighter. It never helped to lose his temper with Brontë. 'You don't honestly think I had anything to do with the death of that girl, do you?'

'I don't know what to think.'

'Are you serious? I haven't a notion about what's going on, babe.'

'You sure about that, *babe*?' She turned to him then, eyes black pools of anger.

He wanted to curl into himself like a cornered animal. He knew what she was like once she started.

'I wonder who it is,' he whispered.

'Listen here, Richie, you need to get real for a minute. Keep close to the squad car and start acting like an anxious first-time dad. God knows you've been doing nothing but acting since I told you I was pregnant.'

'Ah, don't say that. It's way below the belt.' He flicked on the indicator and swung left at the roundabout, staying as close as he could manage behind the squad car.

'Admit it, Richie, and for once in your pathetic little life be honest. You view a baby as an encumbrance to your lifestyle.'

'What lifestyle?' He shook his head, totally puzzled.

'The lifestyle you live after dark. The one where you act the sexy stud while playing your crappy music. All that late-night flirting and whatever else you get up to will be curtailed once our son is born. And I get the feeling ... no, I'm sure you resent this baby. You won't know what's hit you when he arrives.'

He didn't reply, but his stomach dived. Her words cut through him because they were true. Brontë was on to him in a big way, and he hoped to Christ she had no idea about what had happened last night.

'You're not denying it, are you?' She gently rubbed her bump.

Silence might be the best option – he didn't want to incriminate himself in front of his highly intelligent, eagle-eyed wife. That argument was for another day. Instead, he tried to figure out what, if anything, she knew. If she was aware of even a little, he was in deep shit. He was beginning to think she knew too much already.

Lottie had grabbed a coffee and sandwich from the Bean Café and was sitting at her desk chewing away when her mobile rang. Sean. What now?

'Sean, I'm busy. What's up?'

'Granny rang. She doesn't sound good. A cold, I think. She asked me to buy her milk and bread and drop them over to her.'

'Okay.' She'd have to call to her mother after work. 'Can you go on your bike?'

'Sure. Mam, that's not really why I—'

'I'm busy, Sean. I'm investigating a murder.'

'Yeah, you told me, and it's shocking. You see, the thing I wanted to know about ... Erm ... when am I going to be interviewed?'

'Sometime today. It will probably be Detective McKeown.'

'Will you be taken off the case? Because I was there?'

She saw where he was headed. 'Don't worry, I won't. I picked you up around midnight. Lucy's death occurred hours later, though I've yet to get anything near an exact time. Just tell what you saw or heard, and give the names of anyone you knew there. Okay?'

A long pause. She could hear him breathing while she sipped her coffee.

Eventually he said, 'Okay.'

He didn't sound too sure. 'Is there something else?'

'Well ... I mean, I don't think so. Will I have to tell ... everything?'

'Yes.' She paused. 'You have nothing to hide, Sean, have you?'

'I better go and get Granny's stuff. Chat later.'

Lottie stared at the phone in her hand as her son killed the call. What could be wrong with him? She'd picked him up shortly after midnight and he was home in his bed not long after. Maybe he had seen the half-naked photograph of Hannah. She should have asked him about that. McKeown would.

Then she wondered if he had taken one of those pills like Hannah and Cormac had. He wouldn't have, would he? She'd kill him if he had. She was about to ring him back when she was alerted by raised voices in the general office outside her door.

Eat first, then see what's going on.

She swallowed a mouthful of coffee and took a bite of her sandwich, readying herself for whatever would hit her next.

———

Oppressive heat clogged the office air. Lynch abandoned her jacket and cardigan and rolled up her shirtsleeves. Only for McKeown being there, she'd have kicked off her shoes. Scrolling on Lucy's laptop, she furrowed her brow and scratched her head with the end of her pen.

'This is so frustrating.'

'Is Ben not giving you enough rides?'

'Shut up, McKeown. I'll report you for sexual harassment.'

'Like you told my wife about me and Martina. You're a right little snitch.'

She scowled and pursed her lips. Fucked if she was going to discuss anything with him.

'Go on,' he said. 'I know you're dying to tell what you've discovered.'

Bloody hell, but she had to talk to someone. 'Lucy made plans to be away with someone last weekend.'

'The weekend before her party?'

'Yeah. It looks like whoever she was emailing was using one of those anonymous accounts. I've asked Gary to see if he can trace the address.'

'Why don't you just email it and see who replies?' McKeown said, stretching his arms above his head and yawning.

'And spook them? No way.' But she gave his suggestion some thought. 'I could ask Gary to set me up with a fake account and VPN.'

'See, I'm not just a pretty face.'

Lynch groaned. 'Why don't you do what you're supposed to be doing and get back to interviewing the teenagers from the party?'

'I can multitask, unlike some I know.'

'Prick.'

She had little time for McKeown since the row at the station over his affair. If she was honest, it was more to do with the fact that he had boldly continued carrying on with Garda Brennan. Men! They led with their dicks. She shook her head furiously.

'Careful there, or it'll fly off,' he said.

'Twat,' she muttered.

'You're so childish. For the record, it's none of your business what I do with my private life, or who I do it with. Lighten up.'

'Arsehole.' She slapped the laptop shut, stowed it under her arm and marched into Lottie's office, closing the door behind her with a bang.

———

'Sorry, boss,' Lynch said. 'I didn't mean to slam the door. Well, I did, but not on you.'

'Take a seat.' Lottie scrunched up the sandwich wrapper and dumped it in the bin. She wiped the crumbs from the desk to the floor. 'You look like a storm about to blow. What's going on out there?'

'Just McKeown being ... bull-headed.'

'Being a dick, you mean?'

'Exactly.'

'Try to keep the peace. I'll have a word with the super about transferring him back to Athlone once this investigation is over. I'm well aware that the office atmosphere isn't great ...'

'That's an understatement.'

'... but we need all the personnel we can get and—'

'It's fine.' Lynch held up a hand in surrender. 'I can handle him.'

'You sure?'

'Honestly, it's okay.'

'Good to hear.' Lottie wasn't sure how long Lynch could keep control for, but she couldn't afford to lose McKeown yet. He had skills that others on her team hadn't, so it was imperative to keep things calm until they found Lucy McAllister's killer. 'Did you get into Lucy's laptop?'

'Gary broke the password for me.'

'And?' Lottie couldn't hide her impatience. She had to meet Lucy's parents soon, and she'd love to have something positive to report to them at a time of inevitable shock and grief.

'I'm trawling through her social media accounts. So help me, if I see another selfie, I'll cry. That girl loved herself.'

'They all do at that age,' Lottie said, thinking of her daughters, though she didn't think it held true for Hannah Byrne. 'Any clues as to why someone might want Lucy dead?'

'No, but I found something in her emails. It seems she'd planned to meet someone last weekend. Don't know who. Gary is trying to trace the email user. It's a bit weird.'

'Explain.'

'It says, "Meet at Lagh Café, 19.00, Saturday. Bring a sexy nightie." That location doesn't exist, and whoever she was conversing with used an anonymous account. Someone who feared discovery, perhaps?'

'Damn. Did Lucy reply?'

'Just to say "I'll be there."'

'Wherever *there* is. Have a word with Ivy Jones. She's Lucy's best friend and she might know about this.'

'Will do.'

'Print out the email for me, and any others you find like that one. I'm expecting the McAllisters back any minute.'

'Rather you than me.'

'Thanks a bunch,' Lottie said drily.

23

Lottie checked in on Hannah and was surprised to find her mother absent. A uniformed officer was standing guard outside the door, so there was no way the girl could make a run for it. Not that she seemed to be in any fit state to walk, let alone run.

'Apologies for the psychiatrist's delay,' Lottie said. 'Outside my control. We can't continue until the evaluation deems you fit for interview.'

'Why do I even need it?'

'The doctor has taken blood samples, which should determine if you were drugged with ...' She paused. She didn't want to frighten the girl. 'The psychiatrist needs to find out if your faculties are impaired from whatever drug you took.'

Hannah chipped away at her cracked nails. 'And if I'm unfit for questioning, what happens then?'

'You may have to go into hospital for observation.'

'I just want to go home. I feel rotten.'

'Where is your mother?'

'She went to check on Olly. She'll be back as soon as she can.'

'Do you want anything to eat or drink?'

'Someone brought me a bottle of water.'

'Do you need to use the bathroom?'

'No.'

'Knock on the door if you need to go.'

'Whatever.' Hannah stared at her hands. 'Why don't you just ask me what it is you want to ask?'

'Because you were ill, there are certain procedures to be followed.' Much as Lottie would love to ask about the photograph and the incident Cormac had revealed, she couldn't. It must be done properly. She also knew she couldn't detain the girl indefinitely.

'I've been trying to remember stuff. Bits and pieces are coming back to me, but it's all so fuzzy. I'm sure Jake must have slipped something into my drink. Can't you talk to him?'

'We're having trouble locating him.'

'Did you speak to Cormac? He'd know.'

'I did.'

'What did he say?'

'Sorry, Hannah, I can't tell you that.'

'Well then you have to find Jake. He poured a Coke for me. It has to be his fault. I'm an athlete and I care about what I put in my body. It's not my fault if someone drugged me.' Hannah's shoulders slumped as all the fight left her body, and she wrapped her arms around herself, as if that could fend off the trouble she was in. In her sorry state, she looked about seven rather than seventeen.

'I'm sorry, Hannah. As much as I want to discuss the events of last night with you, you're a minor and my hands are tied until you're passed fit for questioning. Sit tight, and I'll see what the issue is with the doctor. If you need anything, just ask.'

'All I want is to go home, shower and sleep.'

You and me both, Lottie thought.

24

Sean pedalled as slowly as he could without falling off his bike. He needed to get his story straight before being interviewed. The longer it went on without him telling his mother that he'd gone back to Lucy's last night, that he'd seen the body and heard someone talking, the harder it was going to be. He was sure she would be taken off the investigation.

Shifting the rucksack on his back with his granny's groceries, he tried to rid his mind of the image of Lucy's broken body. Impossible. It remained behind every blink of his eyes, tormenting him. Who could have been that vicious? And who had he heard talking? The killers? He nearly fell off the bike. Could his evidence shift the direction of the investigation? He'd ask Granny Rose for advice.

He propped his bike against the side wall and entered through the back door into the kitchen, resolved, knowing his granny would tell him how to handle it.

'There you are, Sean. I don't know what I'd do without you. You're a saint on a bike.'

He forced a smile, because if he didn't, he thought he might cry. He began to put away the groceries.

'You don't look well, Gran. Have you a cold?'

'I look a lot better than you, son. Not sleeping? A glass of warm milk before bed does the trick. Or hot cocoa. I have a tin somewhere. I'll get it for you.'

She got up from her wing-backed chair and fussed around, opening and closing cupboards.

'It's okay, Gran.'

'Oh, here it is. Now a spoon of that in hot milk and you'll sleep like a baby.'

Sean stared at the tin. He hadn't the heart to tell her it was Bisto gravy. 'Thanks. I'll try it tonight, but I won't be partying again for a while.'

'Partying? I'm glad you're getting out and about. All those computer machine yokes aren't good for you. It's time you got yourself a little woman.' She sat back in her chair by the fire and pulled a blanket up over her knees. 'Do you have a girlfriend? Or maybe a boyfriend? I'm not as narrow-minded as your mother would have you believe.'

Sean sat in front of her. 'I'm in a spot of trouble, Gran.'

'She's not pregnant, is she? Don't tell your mother.'

'I don't have a girlfriend, or a boyfriend.'

'Oh, that's good. I mean about no one being pregnant, not about not having a boyfriend, though I don't know what your mother would think of it. She can be prudish at times.'

'Gran,' Sean moved closer, 'is it always better to tell the whole truth or is it okay to be economical with it?'

'Oh.' That was all she said, then she closed her eyes.

This was a waste of time, he thought.

Her eyes flashed open and she leaned forward. 'Sean, I lived with a lie for over forty years, and when the truth came out, it almost destroyed me and your mother. You might think it's better to lie, but no matter how clever you believe you are, the truth eventually makes itself known.'

'That's what I thought. Thanks, Gran.'

'Do you want to tell me what it's about?'

'It's better not to involve you.'

'I hope you're not in any danger.'

'So do I.'

'Whatever you decide, be careful.' Her eyes seemed to cloud over. 'Before you go, will you go out to the boiler house and turn up the thermostat? It's freezing in here.'

It was roasting in the kitchen, but Sean did as he was asked. When he returned, his granny was snoring softly, her head resting awkwardly on her shoulder. He fixed her blanket, closed the stove door and left her there while he mentally wrestled with his dilemma.

———

Trying to plan a memorial for Lucy McAllister, with most of the teachers already abroad sunning themselves, was next to impossible. Noel Glennon escaped the meeting as soon as he could without appearing rude and without revealing that he'd worked at Lucy's party. He knew it would come out at some stage and fuck up his life. No question about it.

Taking a detour through the town park on the walk back to his apartment, he mulled over his earlier interview with the detectives, word for word. Had he inadvertently said the wrong thing? Something that would cast suspicion his way? More suspicion than his stupidity had already aroused?

It had been a mistake to help Lucy out. Hadn't been his call, had it? He had been told it was an opportunity to keep a close eye on the teenagers. The lure of the hundred euros she'd promised had blinded him. Now he would never get it.

He had to admit he was lucky that most of the kids at the party had already finished school, or he could be in even bigger trouble when the truth was revealed. Then he thought of the small number of teenagers who'd be returning after the holidays. Kids loved getting teachers in trouble. That meant he might not have a job.

He sat on a bench and watched a duck trying to paddle across the pond. The whole thing had been a huge miscalculation. And now he was being dragged into a murder inquiry.

'Lucy McAllister is dead,' he muttered. There was no getting away from that fact. That beautiful, troubled girl was no more. She could not reveal the truth.

He knew things he could never tell. He'd been bribed into secrecy, and that secret now rested with him. Like a concrete block pressing on his chest, it suffocated him. Why had he allowed himself to get dragged into it, when he wanted nothing other than peace in his life? And money.

He curled his hand into a fist and slammed it down on the iron bench. Immense pain rushed up his hand and arm, like a cruise missile blasting off. He tried to straighten out his fingers, but the agony prevented him.

A mistake. He'd made a few mistakes, but now a girl had lost her life.

If everything came out, shit, he could end up in jail.

He had to do something about it now.

But what?

He nursed his painful hand for a moment longer, made up his mind and left the park, his steps slow and measured.

————

Cormac had been struggling to breathe in the claustrophobic interview room, so in the end, he allowed them to take their samples. He reckoned he'd have to provide them at some stage. His hands shook so badly that his fingerprints had to be taken twice. He wondered about the logic of taking prints when so many people had trampled through Lucy's house. He hoped the guards knew what they were doing.

Out in the fresh air, a warning not to leave town ringing in his ears, he felt he'd been cooped up inside the station walls for days. Don't leave town? Like he even had somewhere to go, besides dead-end Ragmullin.

He walked quickly, gulping fresh air, attempting to fill his brain with the sights and sounds of the town on a busy Saturday. It was an effort to dislodge the image of a half-naked Hannah clogging every square inch of space in his skull. There were other images too, but it was dangerous to go there.

He passed the Bean Café. He loved their coffee, and the smell of it followed him like a shadow. He was starving, but he walked on. With forced purpose, his steps propelled him down Gaol Street and across the road. He skirted around the outside of the park until he found himself at the path leading to the canal. He hoped he could find space to think by the water.

Though it was quieter here, he still heard the hum of traffic and the screech of brakes. He sat on the reedy bank, crossing his legs at the ankles, tucking his hands beneath his knees as he stared into the murky water and thought about throwing himself in. Genuinely.

He was totally fucked up. This whole thing was sick. He would never be able to forget that photo of Hannah. How could Lucy have been so cruel? He'd been mortified for Hannah, so why had he opened his mouth to the detective? Why hadn't he told the truth? The whole truth? Instead, he'd thrown Hannah to the guards to deflect attention from himself. Did he even know the whole truth?

At the time, he'd felt like killing Lucy over that photo. That thought caused him to lose his breath. Was it in him to kill someone? Lucy had had a mouth on her and she'd given him stick, but it had never really bothered him. Not until last night, when she'd targeted sweet Hannah.

Did he feel this intense emotion against Lucy because of what had happened the week before she died? Or was it because she'd called him out in Hannah's presence? He liked Hannah and hadn't wanted to appear like a wet rag in front of her. Was it the effect of the drug he'd taken? What had Jake actually sold him?

And then there were the bloodstains on his clothing. The guards would get a warrant for them. Even though he'd washed them, maybe he should burn them? No, that would make him look guilty, and he had nothing to be guilty about, had he?

He realised he was crying, his breath catching in his throat with each sob. He dug around in his pocket for his inhaler and realised he'd left it at the station. He tried to stop crying. Tried to breathe.

How could he have dropped Hannah right into the mess? She was as much a victim of Lucy's sharp tongue as he was. The tears fell in a rush and he sensed what was coming, unable to stop it.

Fast and furious, panic rose like a wrecking ball in his chest and its long, searching fingers clamped around his lungs in a vice-like grip. He could no longer catch his breath. He tried to get air in and out of his nose, but the tsunami refused to let up, twisting tighter and tighter. He had to ride it out. It always passed. In the throes of the attack, a thought streaked across his brain. What had Hannah told the guards?

As the air around him was sucked away he thought he saw a kid on a bike coming towards him.

He got up quickly and stumbled home without a backwards glance.

25

With his hands tightly bound, Jake was powerless to stop the lashing of the chain against his skin. He cried and screamed into the gag, choking himself with bile rising from his stomach. He had no idea if his attacker was male or female because their face was covered in a ski mask. He couldn't understand why it was happening. He'd done what he'd been asked. Except for one slip-up, and that didn't warrant the intensity of the beating, which was tearing great lumps of flesh from his body.

His little sister appeared before him, pleading with his attacker to stop hurting her big brother. The image faded to red as blood filled his eye sockets. His little sister, the most annoying person on the planet, was at risk. He loved her, despite how much she irritated him, and he had put her in terrible danger with no way to save her.

'Shaz!' He thought he'd screamed her name, but the only sound was the links of the chain clinking as his attacker drew back before landing another agonising blow. He'd already been weakened by what had happened in Lucy's house, but now he felt himself fading away.

Tears mingled with his blood in the dark space where he

was unable to see whoever was wielding the chain with such cruel force.

He felt the life leave his defenceless body, and his last thought before his world turned dark was: who would save his little sister?

26

It was going to be a heart-wrenching encounter with the McAllisters, and Lottie's stomach was tied up in knots. She could do with a swig of Gaviscon. Or vodka.

Lucy's parents had been discreetly escorted from the arrivals hall in Dublin airport. A uniformed garda had elicited the car park information from Albert McAllister and, taking the keys, had headed off with a heap of expensive luggage to fetch the vehicle and drive it to Ragmullin. The couple were then placed in an unmarked garda car and whisked away. Their frantic questions were deftly handled. The only reply was that this was on the instructions of Inspector Lottie Parker from Ragmullin garda station.

Lottie had arranged for them to be brought to an apartment in the Brook Hotel. She didn't think it would be fair to break the news of their daughter's murder in the garda station, and they couldn't go home. Their house was still being forensically examined by SOCOs.

Before she made her way up to the apartment, she checked with the bar manager about Liz Flood's work hours the previous night. She wasn't surprised to hear that the woman had clocked out at fifteen minutes past midnight. So where had she been from then until she'd arrived home this morning?

The boutique apartment was compact and clean. Lottie sat on a chair opposite the two anxious faces while Kirby stood by the door.

Albert spoke immediately. 'I read on my news app about an assault close to our house. The driver refused to bring us there. Who was assaulted? Where is Lucy? What's going on?' His mahogany skin creased like her old leather handbag and his brown eyes flashed anger.

He'd stood when Lottie sat. To cast a superior shadow over her? Feck that. He was around five eight in height, and if she stood up, she'd no longer be overshadowed by him, but now wasn't the time for role play. She remained seated.

They were neighbours of sorts, though she'd never met them before now. His navy chinos were crumpled from the flight, his white linen shirt creased and sweat-stained, the top two buttons undone. From a background check earlier, she'd learned he was forty-five.

Mary McAllister teetered on the edge of the couch, twisting her tanned diamond-clad fingers into knots. 'I need to go home. I'm worried about Lucy. She hasn't returned my calls.'

The opening Lottie needed.

'When did you last speak with your daughter, Mrs McAllister?' She ignored Albert pacing behind the couch, but was distracted by Mary's long blonde curls. They somehow looked unnatural on a forty-year-old woman.

'Around five o'clock yesterday afternoon. Well, it was five o'clock in Spain, so it must have been four o'clock here. Or maybe six. I can never figure out which way the time difference works. Albert?'

'It would've been four here,' he said impatiently. His hair, highlighted by the sun, looked like straw and fell in a mess around his face. 'Why are we even here? I want to see Lucy.'

There was no easy way to do this, there never was, so she just said it. 'I'm so sorry to be the bearer of tragic news. I'm afraid your daughter Lucy was found dead at your home this morning.'

Albert's face flashed red-hot with anger. 'Don't be ridiculous. Mary talked to her yesterday. Lucy is fine. There's been a horrible mistake.' Then he stopped and slumped down beside his wife.

'Unfortunately there's no mistake.'

He must have caught the sincerity in Lottie's expression, because his skin blanched, and he fell back into the plush cushions.

'What do you mean?' Mary's voice was brittle. 'I want to see my daughter.' She made to stand, but Lottie stayed her with a raised hand in the space between them.

'This is absolute bullshit,' Albert said before she could speak, slapping his knees, his pre-eminence resurfacing with a vengeance.

Lottie focused on his wife. 'Mrs McAllister, can you—'

'Oh for God's sake, call me Mary.'

She straightened her back and placed both hands on her knees, leaning forward slightly. 'I'm truly sorry. This is horrific news and it will take time to process. I apologise for being blunt, but you need to know that your daughter was murdered. Who did it and why is something we don't know yet, but I need your help to find out. I appreciate it's heartbreaking, a shock, but time is crucial and I want you both to work with me to find who did this to your beautiful daughter.' She felt like a bitch talking to grieving parents this way, but sometimes she just couldn't avoid having to be cruel to be kind.

'I still don't understand. Our Lucy? She can't be dead ...' Mary's lips trembled like jelly.

'I think it's true.' Albert's voice was a low whisper and his eyes looked everywhere but at Lottie. His fingers fumbled on his phone, and after a few seconds he turned the screen to his wife so she could look at whatever news app he had tapped. 'Says here a teenage girl was found dead ... at Beaumont Court ... Dear God, it's our address.'

'It can't be true. Don't tell me my little girl is dead, please don't do that to me.' Mary slumped, her face crumpled, hands twisting into knots.

'It says it's rumoured that the parents left their seventeen-year-old daughter home alone for over three weeks. How the hell did reporters get that information?' Albert turned a pair of blazing brown eyes on Lottie. She was used to anger before grief.

'I assure you it did not come from us, but I'll check it out.' Her heart bled for them as she thought of how she would feel if anything happened to her own children. 'I can't begin to understand what you are going through, but time is so important in murder cases. Please help me.'

'Lucy is our only child. She can't be dead. She's all we've got.' Mary seemed to fold into herself, her tanned complexion several shades paler. It was as if she was shedding her outer skin in shock. Then she glanced up, her eyes suddenly full of hope. 'How do you know it's her? We haven't identified a ... b-body. You might have made a mistake. Perhaps it's not Lucy at all.'

'There's no mistake. I'm so sorry.'

'How ... how did she die?' Albert asked. The fight had left him.

Lottie avoided his question. 'There will be a post-mortem, but I can arrange for you both to view your daughter's body.'

'Was she shot?' Renewed energy crept back into his voice. 'Stabbed? Beaten? Jesus, I want to know what happened to our little girl. Tell us. Don't sugar-coat it.'

Breathe, Lottie warned herself, as she mentally counted in her head to retain her composure. 'Lucy was the victim of a knife attack. She died from her wounds.'

'Oh dear God in heaven, my little girl,' Mary wailed, her hair flying around her like a curly halo.

Albert brought her head to his chest, stroking it as if she were a child.

'What do you want to know?' he asked, subdued again.

'Can you think of any reason why someone would kill your daughter?'

He shook his head slowly. 'Of course not. She was only seventeen. This is horrific. Our Lucy, she was a good child. Great at school. A dream at home. We never had a minute's trouble with her, did we, Mary? She was an absolute treasure, loved by us and by her friends. I've never once heard a bad word said about my little girl.'

Lottie wondered if maybe his own words were a little too forced.

'Did she have a boyfriend?'

'She was dating someone last year. Brad or Bud or something. She broke up with him because she was heading into her final year.'

Listening to Kirby scribbling, Lottie said, 'Surname?'

'No idea. It wasn't serious.'

Mary lifted her head from her husband's shoulder. 'His name was Bradley Curran. He lived somewhere on the north side of Ragmullin. He's moved to Australia with his family.'

'Okay. Do you know who might have been at the party last night?'

'What party?' the McAllisters said simultaneously.

'Lucy threw a party last night to celebrate the end of exams. There was quite a crowd there. Did you not know about it?'

Mary looked at her husband. Both shook their heads.

'You're mistaken,' Albert said. 'She would have asked us for permission. When Mary spoke with her yesterday, nothing was said about any party. Are you sure?'

'Quite sure,' Lottie said. 'Who normally has access to your property? Keys to the house, that kind of thing.'

'We have a cleaner who comes in twice a week. She has a key. Sarah Robson. She used to teach in Lucy's school at one time. Salt of the earth.'

This was the first Lottie had heard Sarah used to be a teacher. She parked the information. 'Sarah arrived to clean your home this morning and she was the one who made the sad discovery. What about gardeners, handymen? It's quite a size-able property.'

'A young lad cuts the lawn for us. Cormac O'Flaherty. He doesn't have keys or anything. I'm usually there with him. No one has private access apart from Sarah.'

And the killer, Lottie thought. Though there had been a crowd in the house last night, so a large pool of people had gained entry. 'Did Lucy have much interaction with Sarah?'

Mary said, 'She was normally at school when Sarah cleaned. But they probably had conversations while we were away. Oh Albert, we should never have left her alone.'

'I'll need a list of Lucy's friends and acquaintances and their contact details.'

'They'd be on her phone,' Albert said.

'Okay.' SOCOs hadn't found it yet.

'Ivy Jones is her best friend,' Mary offered. 'She'll help you.'

'I've already spoken with Ivy, thanks. Do you know Noel Glennon?'

'Who is he?' Albert said.

Lottie glanced at Mary, but the woman merely shrugged.

'He's the PE teacher at Lucy's school. He was at the party last night.'

'A grown man mixing with teenagers outside of school time?' Albert said. 'I don't know him, but I'll be reporting him to the school principal and the Department of Education.'

'What about Richie Harrison? Heard of him?'

He squinted as if trying to place the name. 'Can't say that I have. Mary?'

'Is he another teacher?'

'He's a DJ. Played at the party last night. What about Jake Flood?' Lottie was trying to find a connection.

Mary shook her head, but Albert looked up. 'I know of *him*. He's one of the kids at Goldstars. The boxing club. Why are you asking about him?'

'He was at the party.'

'He can't be more than fifteen.'

'I'm aware that you are a boxing agent and promoter, Mr McAllister. Are you involved with the Goldstars club too?'

'Not directly. I helped set it up, and I provide funds from time to time. I only know about Jake because I've been told he's one to watch for the future.'

'This is hard for you, I know, but did Lucy ever dabble in drugs?'

He turned on her then, his face ready to explode. 'How dare you! Lucy was an upstanding girl. The very mention of drugs in the same sentence as her name is ridiculous. You are way out of line, Inspector.'

She hurried on. 'Can I move on to yourselves? You're a stay-at-home mum, Mary, is that right?'

'Yes.'

'And Albert, what exactly does your work entail?' Lottie thought that if she could get him to relax, she might be able to elicit something to give her a lead.

'I represent Terry Starr. I've represented big names in the past, but he's one of my main clients now.'

Lottie had heard the name. Hadn't he won some big fight? 'What age is he?'

'Thirty. He won gold at the European Championships a couple of years ago and turned professional. Late to the game.

My job is to get him good fights. He'll be a world champion one day.'

Echoing what he'd said about Jake Flood, Lottie thought. Deciding she could find out more about this later, she said, 'Is there anyone you know who might have a grudge against you? Someone who would hurt your daughter to get at you?'

Albert closed his eyes for a moment, and when he opened them, they were like black buttons on a leather coat. 'No, I can't think of anyone who would want to harm my family.'

'If you do think of anyone, please let me know.'

'I will.'

'Can you tell me why were you in Spain for three weeks? It seems a long time to leave a seventeen-year-old alone in that big house, especially with her final exams and—'

'Don't you dare judge us,' Albert spat, shoving his wife away from him as he got up from the low couch. He moved like a man possessed to stand in front of Lottie. 'Lucy always comes first in our lives ... Came first ... Oh God, how could you begin to understand?' His shoulders slumped and he moved over to the window.

'I'm trying very hard to understand, and I'd appreciate it if you could sit back down, Mr McAllister. I won't be much longer.'

He kept his back to her. 'Lucy was our world. Everything we did, we did for her, to secure her future. Now all that is meaningless. My poor little girl.'

Not to be thwarted, Lottie said, 'Why did you go away then, at such a stressful time for a teenager sitting her exams?'

'We own an apartment in Spain. Mary was ... a little depressed and we decided a few weeks in the sunshine would do her the world of good. Lucy was happy enough with the arrangement. She said she studied better when we weren't around. She was a very capable young woman. We often headed off to the sun and she was happy to stay at home.'

Lottie thought how she wouldn't leave her kids home alone for a weekend, let alone three weeks. They'd be living on take-aways and the house would be like a tip. Then again, that scenario wasn't a million miles from the state of affairs every time she got stuck into a big investigation.

'Had you business to attend to in Spain while you were there?'

'I continued with my work. Technology is wonderful at times, a curse at others.'

Running out of questions, she stood. 'I'm truly sorry for your loss. I'll get back to you once I hear from the state pathologist.'

'We just want to see our daughter,' Mary said sadly.

'As soon as I can arrange it. I promise.'

Leaving them alone with their grief, Lottie wondered despondently whether if any of her children were to suffer a death like Lucy had, she would want to see their bruised and battered body. Probably. Yes. And then she'd want to crucify the killer.

27

They were sitting on two sun chairs on the apartment roof terrace. A canopy cast a shadow over them, but being super careful, Boyd had plastered a second layer of sun cream over Sergio's tanned arms and legs, then wiped away the greasy stains the bottle had left on the glass-topped table.

'Mark, does your apartment have a rooftop terrace like this?' Sergio asked, taking out one of his earbuds.

He was listening to an audio book. At that age? In Boyd's day, the only entertainment available was hitting a sliotar against a wall, or reading a second-hand *Beano*.

'No, it doesn't.' He hadn't even a window with decent light.

Sergio looked over, a furrow between his eyes. 'Where do you go to sit in the sun?'

'No time for sunbathing. My job takes up a lot of my time.'

The boy considered him for a moment, cocking his head to one side, his dark hair flopping over his eyebrows. 'Is it even sunny where you live?'

'Sometimes.' Boyd realised Sergio was in for a shock when he arrived in Ragmullin.

'Mamá told me it rains all the time there, that's why she likes living here. When will she be back?'

That same question, asked multiple times a day. Boyd had opened his mouth to reply when the shrill tone of his phone cut through the air.

He went over and leaned on the balustrade, tutting at the dust smudged along the railing. Looking out over the rooftops, he watched a cruise liner slipping into Malaga port, remembering when he and Lottie had been here interviewing a crime lord in connection with an investigation. So much had happened since then.

'Hello, Lottie Parker! I was just thinking of you.'

'And here I was believing you were thinking of me all the time. I'm disappointed in you, Boyd.' She laughed, and he felt a warm fuzziness in his chest.

'You're never out of my mind. I'm delighted you rang. I'm really missing you.' Damn, he said that every time.

'What's the weather like?'

'Raining,' he said. 'All the time.'

'Liar.' That soft, caressing laugh again and Boyd felt his cheeks flush. She continued, 'I need a favour.'

Of course there was a catch, but it was still good to hear her voice. 'A new case?'

'A teenage girl was murdered after a party in her home last night, early this morning. Her parents were on a three-week break in Malaga. They own an apartment in the city. I know you're staying in an area popular with Irish residents. I'm wondering if you can do a little digging for me. I have the address.'

'I'll do what I can, but I have to watch Sergio too.'

'How are you getting on with him?'

'Fine. He's here with me now, soaking up the rays. Listen, why don't you grab a couple of days and join us in the sun before I head home?'

'You know very well I can't do that, especially with this new investigation.' She paused, and he listened to her breathing, wishing he could be there with her. 'Anyway, aren't you coming home on Monday?'

'Barring you-know-who reappearing. Tell me more about this favour.'

'Like I said, a seventeen-year-old girl was found dead in her home this morning. She had multiple stab wounds. I'm waiting for the post-mortem to see if there was also a sexual assault. The thing is, her parents flew back from Malaga as planned this morning, without any knowledge of what had happened to their daughter.'

Boyd felt a flutter of unease. 'Go on.'

'The girl's name is Lucy and her parents are Mary and Albert McAllister.'

'Bloody hell. I was only talking to them this morning, just before they left.'

'You were? That's so weird. I never thought for a moment you'd actually know them.'

'I don't know them as such. Bumped into them a few times. You're right, they own an apartment not too far from where I am now. God almighty, they'll be devastated.'

'I've spoken with them. It never gets easy, does it?'

'No.'

'Will you find out what you can? I'm trying to cover all eventualities. McAllister said he's an agent for a boxer called Terry Starr. Lucy's murder probably has nothing to do with her father's work, but I can't help feeling uneasy about them leaving her home alone during exam time. Do you think Albert was up to something dodgy in Spain?'

'We both know there's an underbelly of Irish criminals residing on the Costa del Sol,' Boyd mused. 'You hardly have to lift a mat to find them crawling underneath. Is that what you're getting at? You think Albert is involved in something shady and it got his daughter killed?'

'It's possible Lucy was murdered for something her parents might have been involved in. I just need to tick that box and move on.'

'I'll see what I can find out. Have you any suspects?'

'There's one girl who had dried blood under her fingernails when we picked her up. I'm not sure how she is involved because she has no memory of anything relevant. She took some sort of narcotic, so anything is possible.'

'Sounds cut and dried,' he said.

'The thing is, Sean was at the party too. I brought him home early, but do you think I should tell Superintendent Farrell?'

'Jesus, she'll chew you up and won't even wait to spit you out. She'll swallow you and your career. You have to tell her straight away.'

'But won't I make it worse if I mention it now?'

'Up to you, but she needs to be told.'

'I'll see. Will you ask a few questions out there? You know the drill.'

'Yeah, I'll see what I can find out and let you know.'

'You're a star.'

'As long as I'm *your* star, that's all that matters to me.'

'I'll text you the full address.'

'I miss you, Lottie.'

'Miss you too.'

'Love you.'

'Me too.'

He hung up and stared at the phone. Why did she find it so hard to verbalise her feelings? He turned around. Sergio was standing right behind him.

'Who was that?' the boy said.

'My boss.'

'You *love* your boss?'

Boyd laughed and gathered him in a warm hug.

'Ugh, let me down,' Sergio said. 'I'm not a baby.'

'Right you are.' Boyd's phone pinged with the McAllisters' address. 'Fancy a little walk?'

'It's thirty degrees. We should have a siesta.'

Boyd grinned. Sergio reminded him of his sister Grace in more ways than one, and he still couldn't get over the fact that he spoke like an adult. Despite his misgivings about his ex-wife, she'd done a good job rearing the boy. But as he picked up their towels, he worried about Jackie reappearing to prevent him taking Sergio to Ireland.

'Fancy being a *policía* for a few hours?'

'Like real detective work? Wow!'

'You're my son, so I think you'll have a nose for sniffing out the bad guys.'

'Sure thing, Papá.'

That was the first time Sergio had called him Papá.

Boyd followed his son down the narrow winding staircase into the apartment with a smile etched so deep on his face he could feel it tugging his cheek muscles.

28

After leaving the stunned and grieving McAllisters, Lottie and Kirby headed across town to see Sarah Robson, the cleaner who had discovered Lucy's body.

Sarah lived in an apartment located in the refurbished staff quarters of the abandoned St Declan's asylum. The main building had been closed and neglected for years, but some of its surrounding land had been sold for housing developments and apartments.

She guided the detectives into her living room. Compact, cluttered and stuffy, Lottie noted.

'It's such a shock,' she said, tearing a tissue into shreds as she sat on an armchair, her small frame propped up by a multitude of matching cushions. Copper hair hung limp around her face, with a severe fringe lining her eyebrows. Fleecy red pyjamas, the front emblazoned with a Christmas tree, hung from her shivering frame. Lottie had to remind herself it was nearing the end of June rather than December.

Sitting on the couch, she shooed away a black cat, which then sat on the window ledge behind her. Kirby leaned against the door jamb. She noted how quiet he was today. She'd have to have a chat with him.

'Sarah ... Is it okay if I call you Sarah?'

'Yes.'

She was in her early thirties but looked older. Perhaps it was from the shock of discovering a particularly bloody crime scene. At times like this, Lottie wondered if she herself was becoming immune to the horrors of murder. She often found herself surprised at how violent deaths affected those who did not encounter crimes on a regular basis. Maybe she was just tired.

'You provided my colleagues with a preliminary statement, and I know this must be awful hard for you, but I need to go over everything with you again. You okay with that?'

'Yes.'

She hoped the interview wasn't going to be one of mono-syllables.

'Were you due to be at the McAllister house today?'

Sarah swallowed hard. 'Saturdays are not on my usual rota. Lucy called me yesterday afternoon and asked if I could do an early-morning clean. She wanted the house shining before her parents returned home.'

'How did she sound?'

'Chirpy. A bit hyper, now that I think of it.'

'Did she say anything about her party?'

'Not a word.'

'Did you talk about anything other than cleaning the house this morning?'

'Just about payment. I agreed to be there by seven thirty at the latest and she said she'd pay me herself. Between the lines I assumed she didn't want her parents to know about it. But I could be wrong.'

'How long have you been working for the McAllisters?'

'A few years.'

'Did you have much interaction with the family?'

'Just to say hello to Albert. At times I had to discuss my tasks with Mary. Never had reason to become chatting buddies.'

'How often did you clean there?'

'I had a set routine. Tuesdays and Fridays. Three hours. Sometimes Mary would give me additional work. Like cleaning the crystal once a month. I didn't mind that. They paid me well.'

'Had you been cleaning the house while they were in Spain?'

'Mary told me Tuesdays would do while they were away, so I thought it was unusual for Lucy to ask me to clean on a Saturday, but I need the money so I wasn't about to argue.'

'How are you normally paid?'

'My wages are transferred to my bank account. All above board. No cash under the counter, if that's what you're getting at.'

Catching an undertone of distrust, Lottie said, 'Sarah, I'm trying to get a picture of what the family was like. The fact is, Lucy was murdered in her own home while her parents were away. Understanding the family dynamic might help us clarify what happened and why. I need to establish as many facts as possible in order to conduct a thorough investigation into her death.'

'Sorry. I'm still in shock.' Sarah looked up from the shredded tissue on her knee.

'Tell me about Lucy. You must have had some personal interaction with her while her parents were away. What was she like?'

'I don't like speaking ill of the dead.'

Interesting, Lottie thought. 'Lucy can't hear you now. And you might have witnessed or overheard something pertinent in the weeks leading to her death that can help bring her killer to justice.'

'I got the impression she was Albert's perfect princess.'

'I also got that impression from speaking with him earlier,' Lottie said.

'She could do no wrong in his eyes, though her mother saw through the doting daughter facade.'

'Do you mean Mary didn't spoil her like Albert did?'

'Suppose so.'

'What was Lucy like?'

'I'd have to describe her as domineering, spiteful, spoiled. She could be a bully.'

The words, spoken so softly and calmly, left Lottie dumbfounded.

'Listen, Inspector, I'm not saying she got what she deserved. Not at all. But she was like a prima donna. I didn't particularly like her, but she was popular. She had a lot of friends.'

'Tell me more.'

'Behind the outwardly confident persona, I honestly think she was a sad girl.'

'Sad? In what way?'

'I'm not sure. I just got an odd feeling about her.' Sarah scrunched her eyebrows into a frown. 'It was like everything she did and said was an act, while inside her spirit was dying. I believe the prima donna act was just that. An act.'

Lottie filed the observation in her brain. 'Did you ever meet any of her friends?'

'While her parents were away, she had her friend Ivy over at least once. They were eating breakfast in the kitchen with school books on the table and I had to clean around them. I didn't see any boys there. But that doesn't mean they weren't around at other times.'

'Anything else stand out for you?'

'Not really. They seemed to be genuinely studying. And the house wasn't a mess, like it was today. I can't get the image of all that blood out of my head.'

'The image will fade with time,' Lottie said. 'However, it won't negate the horror of what you witnessed.'

'I need a cup of tea.' Sarah stood shakily.

'Before that, can you tell me more about yourself.' Lottie wanted to find out what made the woman tick. She'd been first on the scene. She had regular access to the house. She had to be added to the suspect list. 'I believe you taught in the school Lucy attended.'

Sarah sat again, eyeing the door as if she wanted to escape.

'Yeah, I used to teach. I don't do cleaning work to supplement my income, I do it because I have to pay the rent somehow.'

Lottie wondered why she was no longer teaching. 'What subjects?'

'Why do you need to know that?'

She smiled sweetly. 'I like to be thorough.'

'I taught business and geography. I also covered the PE classes when I was needed.'

'So you must know Noel Glennon. He's the PE teacher and athletics coach.'

Sarah's hand shook and the tissue fluttered like snow to the floor. When she looked over at Lottie, her eyes were hard as lead.

'Noel Glennon is the reason I gave up my job.'

'What happened?' Lottie inched to the edge of the couch in case she missed anything crucial.

'It's not relevant to your investigation.'

'We don't know what's relevant at this stage. Noel Glennon was working at Lucy's last night.'

'That really disturbs me.' Sarah paled.

'Why?'

'Others might tell you he can do no wrong, but I don't believe that for a minute.'

Lottie perked up at this snippet of information. 'Please, Sarah, tell me what happened.'

'I accused him of stalking a student. She had come to me in confidence. Told me how she thought he was watching her. Hanging around the changing rooms. That type of thing. She was distraught. I handled it all wrong.'

'How did you handle it?'

'I tried to deal with it myself when I should have reported it to the principal and informed her parents. The whole thing blew up in my face.' Sarah found another tissue under a cushion and blew her nose loudly.

Lottie remained silent. Best way to let the woman reveal her story.

'You see, I confronted Noel. First mistake. He laughed in my face. Such an awful man.'

Silence ensued, so Lottie said, 'What happened?'

'He got to the principal before I did and twisted everything. He made out that I was the one harassing students. The thing is, I previously had a problem with alcohol, and I'd already had a warning against me. I was fragile at that time and my defence got lost in the myriad of accusations he flung my way. My job became untenable. I had to leave before I literally cracked up.'

'The school couldn't dismiss you without a proper investigation, surely?'

'I couldn't take it. Not with a previous warning hanging over me. I lost my confidence in one fell swoop. I quit.' She looked up at Lottie, her eyes a blaze of burning rage.

'Do you mind telling me who brought you the original allegation of stalking?'

'I can't break her confidence.'

'A seventeen-year-old girl has been murdered. Noel Glennon was present at her party. It is imperative that I know who he was stalking.'

Sarah's eyes dulled as she lost her fight. 'It was Ivy Jones.'

'Thank you for telling me.'

The revelation worried Lottie. She needed to dig deep on Noel Glennon before she hauled him in again. She'd have to talk to Ivy about it, and that meant breaking a confidence.

'Ivy never pursued her allegations. Please don't tell her about this conversation.'

'I can't promise you that. Did you hear from Glennon again?'

'No, and I don't want to either.'

'I appreciate you being honest with me.'

Sarah glanced over at Kirby and back again like a scared rabbit. Was she hiding something? Lottie wondered.

'Would either of you like a drink? Tea, water? I really need a cup.'

'No thanks,' Lottie said, though she'd kill for a coffee. She had the feeling the woman was stalling.

'Right. Okay. I have to tell you this.' Sarah paused as if weighing up what she was about to reveal – or conceal. I'm just too suspicious of everyone, Lottie thought.

'Noel Glennon threatened me and it scared me. He knew I was still sneaking drinks at school and I couldn't face the humiliation if he reported me. That's the real reason why I left. I was terrified to be in the same room as him, even with others around. I have no idea if he killed Lucy, but I think it's possible. That poor girl. I will never forget the sight of her lying there, like Jesus on the cross.'

The words prompted Lottie's mind to focus on the image of Lucy in death. Had the killer posed her body? 'Why do you use that analogy, Sarah?'

'That's what she looked like. Arms spread out and ankles crossed. All that was missing were nails through her hands and feet. She suffered, like Jesus did.'

'Suffered for her sins, you think?'

'I ... I don't know what to think.'

'Anything else to add?'

'Don't think so.'

'Thanks for your time. If we need to speak to you again ...'

'You know where I live.'

Lottie moved to the door and the cat jumped from the window ledge back to his spot on the couch.

At the car, she said, 'We need to find out more about who Lucy McAllister really was and if she'd been hiding something that might have got her killed.'

'Like what?' Kirby asked.

'I don't know, but something was going on in her life, because now she's dead.'

'It's getting complicated.' He thrust the car out onto the main road, cutting between two vehicles in a line heading back to town.

Holding the dashboard, Lottie said, 'Delve into Noel Glennon's background. I want something solid before I bring him in again.'

'Sarah has certainly stirred up the suspect pot.'

'And we need to find out more about her too.'

––––––

The kid on the bike munched a Mars bar while he waited. He'd swiped two bars from the corner shop and this was the second he'd had in quick succession, trying to fill his belly.

The job he'd been given wasn't cool any more. His legs were tired from all the cycling around after the two detectives. And he was bored.

He didn't like being close to the old asylum. It gave him the creeps. He shivered as he looked up at the narrow windows and the multiple chimney stacks. It could fall on top of him any minute.

When the car pulled out onto the main road, he sent the text. Zipping his jacket up to his neck, he pedalled away as if the devil himself was on his heels.

He refused to look back.

Scary old buildings gave him the runs.

29

Boyd hadn't realised the walk would take so long, but Sergio was slow and hot, and he had to adjust his stride to match the child's. Maybe he should have left him with Señora Rodriguez, the neighbour Jackie had depended on, but it felt good to have his son's sweaty hand in his own.

They turned left down by the dry riverbed, and just before he reached the giant mural, he looked up at the building containing the McAllister apartment. It didn't seem particularly inviting, from the outside at least. A double-height wooden door, with a myriad of intercom buttons lining the portal. Boyd had an uneasy feeling that someone was watching him. He looked around quickly. It might just have been the sweat trickling down the nape of his neck.

He stood aside as the door creaked inwards and a suited man brandishing a briefcase and phone shot out. Reaching out his hand, Boyd kept the door open and ushered Sergio inside. Breathing the cool air with relief, he was amazed at the expansive tiled hallway with its high ceiling. An old steel lift stood in the middle of the floor. He might strike lucky and get to talk to a neighbour. But he felt a little nervous involving his son. Maybe it wasn't such a good idea after all.

'Let's see how fast this is.'

He slid the accordion-like door to the side and walked in after Sergio. The air smelled of expensive aftershave, probably from the man who'd just left, overriding an oily odour. He pressed for the fourth floor and the door slid shut. A creak and a squeal, and to his surprise the closed-in box rose upwards quickly.

They stepped onto a narrow landing with four doors branching from it. He checked Lottie's text. The McAllisters' apartment was 4.4. He knocked, not expecting anyone to answer. The couple had already left, so why was he even here? To talk to the neighbours. He was about to turn away, his hand still on the door, when it opened slightly.

Cautiously he put his finger to his lips and moved Sergio over beside the neighbouring apartment. Then he leaned against the door and listened. A hint of a sound perhaps? He debated whether to just leave, but curiosity won out. The McAllisters had left so why was the door open? Sergio would be okay as long as he stayed put.

Inside, he heard a noise like the flow of water into a sink or bath. He took another step forward. The narrow hall led into an open-plan living room with floor-to-ceiling windows, a view of the port to the left and the city to the right. Directly in front of him was a landscape of rooftops.

Glancing around, he failed to pinpoint the source of the water. He turned left to the open-plan kitchen. Ultra-modern monochrome decor with stainless-steel appliances. Backing out, he made his way down another corridor, wider than the one at the front door. Three bedrooms. All immaculately decorated. Two had beds made up and clear of clutter. The third had a cabin-sized suitcase open on the floor. He ignored it for the moment and walked to the next door. The sound of water grew louder. The bathroom.

He depressed the silver-plated handle and pushed the door inwards.

The room was steamy and the shower occupied. The male occupant thrust his head around the glass door.

'What the fuck? Who are you?' he barked, his accent distinctly Irish.

'Sorry to disturb you,' Boyd said. 'The door was open. I was looking for the McAllisters.'

Once he'd switched off the shower, the man grabbed a towel and wrapped it around his waist, then stepped onto the marbled floor. 'Who the fuck are you?'

'I was about to ask you the same question.' Boyd tottered on the wet ground as the man pushed past him. Once he'd regained his footing, he followed.

'And who are you, kid?' the man growled as he entered the living room.

'Don't touch him,' Boyd said, his voice quivering. He had not anticipated finding anyone here. What had happened to 'expect the unexpected'? He pulled Sergio close, placing a protective hand on his shoulder. Why hadn't the boy stayed outside? He supposed at eight years of age, curiosity overcame any fear he might have. Like father, like son.

'You're Terry Starr,' Sergio said, surprising Boyd.

'Yeah, I am, son.'

'I'm not your son. I'm his.' Sergio pointed his chin up at Boyd.

'Are you going to tell me why you've barged in, or do I call the police?'

Boyd felt almost hypnotised under the man's black gaze and bruised right eye. His ribs looked black and blue too. Terry Starr, he thought, the boxer Lottie had mentioned.

'The door was open,' Sergio said.

'You have no right to be here.'

'The door was open.' Boyd repeated Sergio's words.

'Must've left it off the latch.'

'I'd like a chat with you.'

'I'll get dressed first.'

Boyd watched Starr stroll down the corridor and took his hand from Sergio's shoulder. 'I told you to stay outside.'

'Sorry.'

'It's okay, but we should leave.' Boyd didn't relish getting into a sparring match with a professional boxer. 'By the way, how do you know who he is?'

'Mama watches his fights. He's good.'

'Is he?' Boyd said, not knowing the first thing about boxing.

'Undefeated light-heavyweight European champion.'

'Yes, I am.' Starr returned kitted out in khaki Bermudas, his feet shod in brown leather loafers Boyd knew he himself could never afford. He tore off a price label from a white T-shirt with a Tommy Hilfiger motif and pulled it over his head before busying himself at a monster coffee machine. 'Care for an espresso?'

'No thanks,' Boyd said, trying to figure out why the man was so easy with a stranger in his apartment. Not even his apartment.

He watched open-mouthed as Sergio flopped down on a massive white leather chair and began fiddling with a remote control. A flat-screen television, at least sixty-five inches, slid up from the floor.

'Wow! This is cool.' The boy's eyes widened in wonderment.

Boyd supposed his son was safe sitting in front of the TV.

'This is Albert McAllister's apartment, isn't it?' He slid onto a high stool at the breakfast bar, his attention now firmly on the boxer.

'Yeah. Whenever I visit the Costa del Sol I stay here. Plus I like the view.'

'When you're not in this region, where do you live?'

'I take it you're some sort of a cop with all the questions.'

'I'm on leave at the moment, but I know Albert and Mary.'

The machine spurted tar-like coffee into a miniature white china cup.

Terry faced Boyd. 'Doesn't stop you asking questions, does it? Why are you here?'

Boyd carefully considered what he was about to say. There was no knowing how close Terry was to the McAllisters or the real reason for him being present in their apartment. He figured honesty was the best policy to avoid getting caught out in a lie later on.

'When I'm on duty I'm Detective Sergeant Mark Boyd at Ragmullin garda station. A colleague suggested I make some enquiries. Albert and Mary arrived home to some terrible news. Have you heard anything about that?'

'What news?' When Boyd didn't reply, Terry said, 'I only got here about twenty minutes before you.'

'Where did you come from?'

'First you need to tell me about the disturbing news.'

'I'm afraid their daughter was murdered within the last twelve hours or so.'

'Lucy?' The cup clattered onto the quartz counter. Terry's skin took on an ashen hue. 'I don't believe it.'

'Their only child. Sad.'

'Oh God, Albert will be devastated. He adored Lucy. What happened to her? Do you know why, or who ...?'

'I've no further information at present,' Boyd said, automatically slipping into professional mode. 'I note you mentioned Albert being devastated but not Mary. Did Mary and Lucy not get on?'

'I didn't mean anything by it,' Terry said hurriedly. 'I just know Albert better.'

'I don't think you meant that at all,' Boyd said, his tone measured. 'I'd appreciate it if you told me the truth.'

'You're certain you don't want a coffee? I sure as hell need another.' Terry turned his back on Boyd and pulled levers on the machine. He put a larger mug under the spout this time.

'A glass of water would be good, and one for my son.' Boyd glanced over to see Sergio engrossed in a Spanish-language news programme.

'Is he really your son?'

'Yeah. Long story.'

'Aren't they all?'

30

Detective Sam McKeown was less than impressed with Lottie's house. One of her daughters, he had no idea which one, led him into the sitting room.

'Tea or coffee?'

'No thanks.'

'That's great, because I used the last tea bag and the coffee is rock hard in the bottom of the jar. I'll call Sean down for you. Hope he hasn't been a bold boy.' She winked. That made him feel awkward.

She went off to find her brother and McKeown glanced around the cold, cavernous room. He sniffed the air and found it fusty. The furniture would look better in a museum. In the hallway he'd feared the old chandelier was about to crash on top of his head if he didn't move out from underneath it.

Standing by the fireplace, he watched Sean Parker enter the room. The boy was tall and lean, his eyes ringed with black circles. Someone didn't get much sleep last night.

'Hello, Sean. I'm Detective Sam McKeown. Call me Sam.'

Sean eyed him from under his long lashes, probably seeing right through the faux-friendly introduction. Not that

McKeown cared. He was looking forward to grilling Lottie's son.

'Chloe told me you were here.' The kid was tapping his knee. Nervous or impatient? Time to find out.

'You were at Lucy McAllister's party, weren't you?'

'You know I was there, so why are you asking me?'

Spiky, like his mother. 'No need to get your back up. Are you okay?'

'I'm fine, thanks.'

Down to business then. 'What time did you get to Lucy's house?'

'Around nine o'clock.' A steady stare. Still unrattled.

'How much did you have to drink?'

'A couple of bottles of warm cider. I don't touch anything else, so there was no way I was drunk if that's what you're implying.'

McKeown ignored the dig. 'Drugs?'

'Pardon?'

'Did you take any drugs at the party? Uppers or downers. Crack, cocaine, MDMA, skunk. You take anything like that?'

'Are you joking? I don't do that stuff. Mam would murder me.'

'But she wasn't there, was she?'

'No, but she collected me and drove me home.'

Was this six-foot tall teenager still a mammy's boy? McKeown hid a smile. 'Time?'

'Sorry?'

'What time did you leave the party?'

'Around twelve. Ask my mother. She'll tell you.'

'Don't worry, I intend to.' That made the lad's head snap upwards. Was he naive enough to think this conversation was private? Tough luck, kid. 'Tell me about the party.'

'What about it?'

If he didn't stop tapping, McKeown thought he might actually grab Sean's hand and slap a pair of handcuffs on him. 'Who was there? What went on? Any shagging, rows, drug taking? Anything stand out as unusual?'

'I don't go to many parties, so I wouldn't know what's unusual. There was a good crowd there. I didn't know many. I left early. It was too warm, the drink was shite and I was hungry.'

'No food? I heard a ton of pizzas were delivered.'

'That must have been later on.'

'Who were you there with?'

'A couple of lads from school. After a while I bumped into Cormac O'Flaherty. I play online games with him and I've met up with him in town a few times. We talked for a while. He was hanging out with Hannah Byrne. I didn't really talk to anyone else.'

'What was their relationship like? Cormac and Hannah?'

'How would I know? She went off outside for a while and I chatted to Cormac.' The tapping stopped.

'Were they taking drugs?'

Sean bit his lip. Making a decision, probably. Would it be a lie or the truth? McKeown hoped it'd be a lie, and oh how he'd bask in bringing his mother down to earth when it was revealed.

'I think Cormac bought a few pills.'

The truth. McKeown was disappointed. 'What type of pills were they?'

'I don't do that stuff, so I don't know.'

'Did you see Cormac or Hannah take the pills?'

'I left shortly after meeting up with them.'

Not a direct answer to the question. 'Did you witness any fights or arguments?'

'Witness?'

'Sean, you're an intelligent boy, so stop acting like you're stupid. It's wearing thin, and if I'm honest, I don't like being made a fool of.'

'No.' Sean gave him a side-eye. Cheeky bugger.

'No what?'

'I didn't see any arguments.'

'A fight between Lucy and Hannah maybe?'

'I didn't *witness* anything like that.' Air quotes. Now he was really taking the piss.

'You said your mother picked you up. What did you do after that?'

'I made a sandwich and brought it up to my room. I was starving.'

'And after you ate your sandwich?'

'What are you getting at?' The tapping resumed.

McKeown paced up and down in front of the fireplace. The kid was nervous about something. 'How did you get to the party?'

'I walked.'

'Alone?'

'I was with two friends. Nigel and Barry. You can check with them.'

'I will. So you abandoned your friends and went home with Mammy. Were they annoyed with you?'

'Why would my friends be annoyed? They're not seven years old.'

'What time did they leave?'

'How would I know?'

'Maybe they were still there when Lucy was murdered.'

'They weren't, she was killed later on.'

McKeown stopped pacing and stared at Sean, whose cheeks had suddenly flared. 'Sean, how do you know when she was killed?'

'I ... I ... don't know.'

'It seems to me that you do. Tell me before your mother finds out from someone else.'

'Oh shit.' Sean sat down on the lumpy-looking couch. 'Shouldn't I have an adult with me for this?'

'I can phone your mother if you want.'

He shook his head. 'I went back.'

McKeown lit on him. 'Back where?'

'To Lucy's. I'd gone home without my new leather jacket. I couldn't sleep because I was sure Mam would go mental if she found out I'd left it behind. So I walked back to Lucy's. There was no one around. The door was open. And I saw her ... I saw her body. Oh God, she was dead.'

McKeown ran a hand over his shaved head, working hard to keep his jaw from dropping. Despite his aim to make Lottie look foolish, he felt sympathy for the boy. He sat on an armchair and folded his arms.

'Sean, you'd better tell me everything.'

31

Kirby sourced the registration number for Richie Harrison's van from the National Vehicle and Driver File and circulated it. A report came in from Garda Furey stating that he'd logged the same vehicle attempting to gain entry to the McAllister property earlier in the day.

Kirby relayed the news to Lottie. 'Furey says Harrison's wife started having contractions so he escorted them to the hospital. I phoned the hospital and Brontë Harrison is still there for observation. Wouldn't tell me anything else.'

'Good work. Let's see what Mr Harrison has to say for himself.'

─────

Lottie unbuckled her seat belt outside Harrison's house. Sarah Robson's revelations were still cartwheeling around her brain. Noel Glennon had catapulted to the top of the suspect list, but Hannah was the one with the bloody hands. And she was sure Sarah knew more. A clear head was needed to work it out.

'How is McKeown's team getting on with interviewing the partygoers?'

'Slowly, so I heard.' Kirby tugged at his trouser belt, loosening it a notch.

'He'd better smarten up. Right, let's get this one done, then we can move on.'

She marched to the front door and rang the bell. Richie Harrison's red van was an eyesore parked outside his designer house on the executive estate.

'Must have pumped all their money into the mortgage,' Kirby noted, 'to be still driving this heap of shite.'

'Does his wife work? They must have another income source.'

'I doubt there's much to be made being a DJ nowadays. I thought all music was online anyhow.'

'Ibiza is all about the DJs, according to Chloe.' Her daughter was forever begging for money to travel, even though she was earning a wage working in Fallon's bar. She glanced at the van, then back to the pristine black door with its chrome finishes. 'I'd say the wife must have a decent-paying job.'

'Or maybe Richie is involved in something more lucrative to supplement his income.'

'We shall see.' She rang the bell again.

The man who opened the door squinted in the sunlight, his face as tired as the creased, red T-shirt stretched tight across his chest, where a string of coloured beads hung from his neck. Blue jeans, white socks, no shoes completed the look.

'Mr Harrison, is it?' Lottie showed him her ID badge. 'We'd like a word. May we come in?'

'Is this about what happened at the McAllisters'?' He kept his hand tight to the door, his taut body in the gap.

'We'd like to discuss it inside, if you don't mind.'

He paused, then opened the door wide.

Lottie wasn't sure if she was required to take off her shoes, but she wiped her feet on the mat and followed him into a sitting room. It was so minimalist it was almost bare.

Stark white walls. A low blue L-shaped couch, one matching armchair placed opposite. The glass coffee table was without a book or magazine, let alone a coffee stain. The almost white carpet made her glance at her shoes to ensure she hadn't walked dirt in. A massive television was fixed to the wall above an insert fireplace. Everything was modern and expensive.

'Nice house,' she said, more than a little jealous.

'I'm sure you're not here to admire my home.' Harrison swiped up his long hair and tied it back with a band from his wrist. His skin was smooth and his fingers long. She noticed his nails cut short. Clean.

'You're right,' she said, sitting on the couch, her legs too long to be comfortable. Harrison sat on the armchair. There wasn't even a wedding photograph on the walls. She'd have liked a look at Mrs Harrison. 'What do you know about the incident at the McAllisters' house?'

He tightened an arm around his waist, coiled like a spring, she thought. 'Nothing at all.'

'Why were you trying to gain access to the house earlier today?'

'I had to pick up equipment I'd left behind last night. A guard stopped me at a checkpoint. And then Brontë had to be rushed to the hospital. She's pregnant. They're monitoring her. What's this about?'

'I'd like you to tell me that.'

He appeared mystified, uncoiling his arm and throwing up his hands. 'I don't know anything. The guard wouldn't let me pass. He mentioned that someone had been killed. Was it a robbery gone wrong or what?'

'Why would you think it was a robbery?' Lottie had the feeling he was trying hard not to let something slip.

'All that garda presence. Albert McAllister is a big knob.

House must be worth a fortune, not to mention all the fancy shit he has in it.'

'You've been in the house?'

'I was working there last night, as you know.'

'Tell me about the party. I want chapter and verse.'

'Definitely wasn't any murder when I was there.'

She wasn't sure if he was making fun of her, but she pressed on. 'Richie, you were in a position to view what was going on. You could be a crucial witness.' *Dickhead*, she added in her head.

'Witness? Right. Okay.' He picked at a non-existent spot on his jeans, his hands shaking. 'I got there about eight, to set up, you know, before the crowd arrived. Lucy let me in.'

'Was she alone?'

'There were a few girls with her.'

'What was the mood like?'

'Typical schoolgirls. Giggling and messing. Make-up and glitter everywhere. Nothing out of the ordinary, though what would I know about that? It's been a few years since I was a teenager.' He tried to laugh, but it came out like a groan.

Lottie knew he was thirty years old from his driving licence data. 'Go on.'

'Lucy showed me where she wanted the decks set up, then she went upstairs. I didn't see her again until the bell started leaping off the front door.'

'Anyone on the door?'

'No. Oh, wait. There was a guy there.'

'Know him?'

'Erm, don't think so, but I didn't see much of him.'

'You sure?'

'I was inside and he was outside. So yes, I'm sure.'

'How many were present during the course of the night? An estimate will do.'

'I don't know. Kids were coming and going. Might have

been thirty-five or so by the end of the night. Most were out in the garden. The patio doors were open so the music filtered out there.'

'Was there much drinking going on?'

'Ah come on, what do you think? They were teenagers at a party with free booze.'

'Drugs too, I suppose?' She maintained what she hoped was a neutral expression.

He hesitated. 'Probably. Not that I saw anything like that.'

'I believe you were set up beside the bar area. The lad doling out the drink was selling something more potent than Smarties. Tell me about that.'

He tugged at his beaded necklace. 'I don't want to get the kid in trouble.'

'Richie, we know all about it. I'd like you to confirm what he was up to.' She thought his beads were about to snap, he was twisting them so hard.

'Yeah, all right. He was selling pills. Not my house. Not my party. I just wanted to do my job, get paid and get home to my pregnant wife.'

'And is that where you went once you'd finished up?'

'What?'

'Did you go home after the party?'

'Of course I did. Where else would I be going?' He released the beads and ran a finger along the neck of his T-shirt, his face bright red.

Liar, Lottie thought. He wasn't going to admit to anything at this juncture, though, so she parked it with the intention of returning to it later.

'Did anything out of the ordinary happen at the party? Besides youngsters having a good time on booze and drugs.'

'No, nothing.'

'Patio door was smashed. Did you see how that happened?'

'It was fine when I left. Wide open. Some kids were still in the garden.'

'I heard there was a row between Lucy McAllister and another girl.'

'Oh, *that*. Handbag stuff.'

'Explain.'

'Some blonde girl had a right go at Lucy. A shouting match. I calmed them down with the help of another lad. No blood spilled.'

'Curious phrase.' Lottie threw Kirby a look, and gathered he thought so too.

'What?' Richie looked from one to the other.

'"No blood spilled", you said, which is an odd turn of phrase for something you called handbag stuff.'

He blanched. 'I ... I don't know what you mean.'

'Any other incidents you care to tell us about?'

'Nothing else happened while I was there.' He stood up, then sat back again.

'How did Lucy hire you?'

'She called me a week ago to book me.'

'So she had your number?'

'My details are on my Facebook page. She probably got it there.'

'You're sure about that?'

'Yes, I'm bloody sure. And I'm not saying anything else until you tell me what this is about. Did Lucy or Ivy send you to talk to me?'

'Ivy Jones? How do you know her?'

'I don't. I mean ... I only met her last night. She was hanging off Lucy like a shadow. She ... she introduced herself to me. Asked me to play some song or other. That's all I know about her.'

'Anything else you can remember? Like what time Jake Flood went home?'

'Who?'

'The young guy selling the drugs. He's missing.'

'Missing? I know nothing about that.'

'Did you see him leave?'

'I don't think so. He was probably still there when I left. I gathered up most of my equipment and put it in the van, and Lucy said to call back today for the rest of it and my money. She said I was traipsing in and out too much. That's it.'

'What time did you leave?'

'Could have been two thirty, maybe three o'clock.'

'And your wife will confirm you were home shortly after that, will she?'

He chewed on his lip, hard, and his hand found the beads again. 'Brontë was asleep when I got in. She won't be able to tell you the exact time. I don't want you bothering her. She has only a few weeks to go before our son is born, and I really have to get back to the hospital. I came home to pick up a few things for her.'

'What does your wife work at?'

'What has that to do with anything?'

'Humour me.'

'She's a PA. For Bright Side Home Furnishings.'

'She must be paid well.'

'We manage.'

'I'm curious as to how you can afford this lovely home. Do you do any other work besides being a DJ?'

'What are you suggesting?'

'Answer the question.'

'No, I don't work anywhere else at the moment.' He looked at the floor. 'I was let go from a building site about two months ago. Job finished. It's tough at the moment, but I'll get something else soon.'

'Where was this job?'

'In Dublin. The construction of the new Coyle Plaza Hotel.'

'Okay. Where were you last weekend?' Lottie wondered if he could have been Lucy's mystery email contact.

'Last weekend? What has that got to do—' He caught her dagger look. 'I was here. At home. We'd bought a cot in IKEA and it took me the guts of two days to make the blasted thing. Flat-pack is a pain in the hole, and me in the building trade.'

'The guy doing security at Lucy's, are you sure you don't know him?'

'I don't think so.'

'His name is Noel Glennon. He's a teacher at Lucy's school and the athletics coach. Ring any bells?'

He shook his head. The beaded necklace was wound tight around his fingers.

'Was he still there when you left?'

'There was no one on the door, if that's what you mean. He could have been in the garden, or the toilet. I don't know.'

'Did you see anyone hanging around who maybe shouldn't have been there?'

'It was just a crowd of teenagers letting their hair down, having a good time.'

Lottie caught his tone. Insinuating that she couldn't have a good time, or maybe she needed to let her hair down. Well fuck you, Richie Harrison.

'Call into the station today to make a formal statement. We need all the help we can get. Are you willing to do that?'

'Sure, if you insist. But Lucy can back up everything I've told you. Ask her.'

'Unfortunately, I can't ask her anything,' Lottie said.

Kirby added, 'You see, Richie, Lucy McAllister was murdered sometime during the night. And I may as well tell you, a lot of blood was spilled.'

They left him sitting there with his mouth hanging open.

———

Ivy slid down in the driver's seat of her mother's SUV as the two detectives left Richie's house. She'd parked at the end of the cul-de-sac, partially hidden by a cherry tree, its blossom long since scattered in the wind.

She didn't like that they were talking to him. He was liable to say anything. Richie was a gobshite. Gullible. All the clichés she could think of. Just like that creepy teacher Mr Glennon. She shivered thinking of him. She'd nearly died when she'd seen him at the party, and had said as much to Lucy, who'd just laughed it off.

After the detectives had left, she contemplated whether to knock on Richie's door. His wife might be home. If so, what story could she come up with? She had to talk to him.

She palmed her phone and was about to send him a text when the door opened again and Richie rushed out, holding a bulging plastic bag, which he threw into the van. Before she could leave the car to stop him, he had reversed and chugged up the narrow road, exhaust fumes trailing behind.

'Damn you, Richie.'

She yawned and turned the key in the ignition.

It was so tiring keeping a secret.

———

What was *she* doing here?

The kid on the bike spied Ivy in the SUV as the detectives left the fancy house. He'd sheltered by the gable end on the opposite row.

Really, like! What was she doing? He kept staring. Once the DJ drove off in his van, she waited a few more minutes before following him.

This was interesting, but he wasn't sure if it was important enough to report her being in the same place as the cops. Maybe he'd leave that detail out of his report.

He wrote the text and sent it, without mentioning Ivy.

If anyone knew about her being here, he could always say he hadn't seen her. But as he took off on his bike, he had an uneasy feeling that he'd made his first mistake.

32

Once he'd taken a long drink of cold water, Boyd kept one eye on Sergio to ensure he didn't end up watching something he shouldn't while also scrutinising Terry Starr. It was difficult to marry the well-spoken, friendly man with what Boyd had seen of him boxing in the ring on television. You live and learn, he supposed.

Terry leaned against the counter, blew on his coffee and took a sip. 'I love the coffee out here. Tastes expensive without costing the earth.'

Boyd said, 'So where are you from, Terry?'

'Tullamore originally, but I have a pad in Kensington – that's in London – and another on Dublin's Southside. I can't believe Lucy's dead.'

'You said you've only just arrived here. Early flight?'

'Yes. First of the morning from Dublin.'

'Where were you prior to taking the flight?'

'At home.'

'In Tullamore?'

'No, that's my parents' place. My Dublin apartment.'

'You arrived here after the McAllisters had flown home, though?'

'Yes.'

'Do you have any idea why they were out here for three weeks?'

'Albert said he was organising a fight with a big payday. I should contact him to see if he's had any success.' Terry's hand stalled the mug halfway to his mouth. 'Shit, forgot. He has other things on his mind now.'

'How well did you know Lucy?'

'Not that well. Saw her a few times when I was over at Albert's. Hovering.'

'What do you mean by that?'

'I'm not blowing my own trumpet here, but Lucy was in awe of me.'

'Really? How did that go down with her parents?'

'Albert thought it was hilarious, but Mary ... I don't know much about these things, but she seemed uneasy. I think she was jealous of Lucy.'

'Interesting. How did this jealousy manifest itself?'

'Well, maybe it was the way Mary always acted, but she'd shout at Lucy any time I was there, telling her to go to her room and study.'

Boyd thought this was normal enough. 'When did you last see Lucy?'

'Couple of weeks ago.'

'When her parents were away?'

Terry slammed the mug on the counter. 'I don't like what you're insinuating.'

'I asked a perfectly reasonable question.'

'You've no authority to ask me anything.'

'True, but the fact is, the daughter of your agent was murdered, and it seems by your own admission that you met her while her parents were out of the country. Why were you at her home?'

Terry ran his tongue around his teeth, as if he'd found something distasteful lurking there. At last he spoke. 'I called out to the house last Tuesday week, I think, to pick up a file Albert had left for me. Tax stuff for my accountant. Lucy happened to be there, studying at the kitchen table with her friend. She let me in, I picked up what I'd come for and left. End of.'

'Tax returns are not due in until October. Why the urgency?'

'My accountant asked for it. Jeremy Stokes. Based in Dublin.'

Boyd made a mental note to tell Lottie to check with Terry's accountant. Might be nothing, might be something.

'Could it not have been emailed?'

'I just did what I was asked.'

Taking a punt on his next statement, Boyd said, 'Because you were in the McAllister house recently, you'll need to volunteer a DNA sample. For elimination purposes.'

'No problem, I'll be home next week. Friday.'

'Are you staying here until then?'

'Yep.'

'Does Albert know this?'

'I have a key. They trust me not to trash the place.' He laughed. Half-heartedly, Boyd thought.

'You might want to ensure you close the door properly next time.' Boyd stood and pushed the stool in. 'Can I have your number in case the inspector needs to contact you?'

'In case you think of something to accuse me of, is that it?'

Sergio switched off the television and strolled over. 'Can I have another glass of water?'

'Sure.'

As Terry filled the glass, Sergio said, 'May I use the bathroom before we go?'

'It's at the end of the corridor.' Terry placed the glass on the counter and looked pointedly at Boyd. 'I hope you get whoever did this to Lucy. She didn't deserve to die at the hands of a murderer.'

'No one does,' Boyd said.

'Listen, I know you detectives will find some people who will be only too happy to speak ill of Lucy McAllister – even her own mother. Albert told me Lucy was troubled. I saw something of myself in her the few times I met her. The younger me. Don't be too quick to judge her character.'

Boyd shivered under the black stare and was about to press Terry further when Sergio breezed back into the room.

'Can we go now?' the boy said.

'Yes.' He'd try to follow up with Terry about Lucy again.

'Nice to meet you, Mr Starr,' Sergio said.

'You too,' Terry said. He gave Boyd a half-smile. 'He's a bright kid.'

'He is that.'

Boyd followed his son, with Terry behind them. On the landing, he waited until he heard the door click shut.

Stepping outside into the searing heat, he wondered if he'd missed an opportunity to learn something significant. But he was off duty and there was only so much he could ask with his son around. He put out his hand for Sergio's.

'What have you got under your T-shirt, squirt?'

The boy smiled brightly, his teeth worthy of a Colgate advert. He lifted his shirt and extracted a toothbrush from his waistband. 'You can get DNA from this.'

Boyd was dumbfounded. 'You can't just steal it. You need a warrant, or permission from the owner.'

'But Terry would never give you permission.' Sergio smiled from ear to ear. 'I'll make a good detective. I might even be better than you, Papá.'

'How do you know this is Terry's?'

'It was in a bag with his electric razor.'

Boyd took the toothbrush from the small outstretched hand. First thought, should he go back with it? Second thought, where could he quickly find a bag to store it? Third and most stressful thought, if he had anything to do with Sergio's future, there was no way on earth he'd allow the boy to follow in his footsteps. Then again, it might be a better option than following in his mother's, wherever the hell she'd taken herself. He had to admit, he really didn't want to know anything about her.

Walking hand in hand with his son, he couldn't shake off the feeling he'd had earlier.

Someone was watching him.

———

Feathers keep birds warm, and I am suffocating. My black and white world is no longer a comfort. I need something softer and newer to soothe me. I touched her with my claws and drew the skin from the flesh, taking away the part of me that she had stolen. I hadn't believed I could feel so elated, but I need to be sated once again. I crave the glow of the untouched. I want to be the first to suck the life from it.

I have decided who will be next, and once I am done, I will savour the memory for a long time. I want to conquer the innocent flesh and keep it for myself.

Tired but refreshed, I want to fly up high to capture and protect what will be mine.

No one is watching me.

No one is watching my prey.

I am free to take it all as my own.

33

After pulling on forensic clothing, Lottie entered the cutting room. She'd taken the call as she and Kirby arrived back at the station after meeting Richie Harrison. Kirby had cried off attending the post-mortem, so she'd headed to Tullamore alone.

'Hi, Jane,' she said, fixing her face mask.

'Lottie.'

Jane Dore, the state pathologist, was probably one of the few people, apart from Boyd, that Lottie could count on. The woman was tiny in physical stature but a powerhouse in her field.

She adjusted her spectacles on her prim nose, precise and professional. 'I carried out a precursory examination of Lucy McAllister's body before you arrived. If I was to step into psychology mode, which I rarely do, I'd say intense anger was behind the final wound.'

'Why would that be?'

'I don't like to speculate. The victim tried to protect herself. She sustained defensive wounds to her hands and both arms. The cut to her neck was the last act of the assault.'

'You mentioned anger; could it be jealousy?'

'Maybe. I've seen the scene. Lucy was initially attacked downstairs and further assaulted as she hid behind the bed upstairs. The assailant chased her to complete the job.'

'Could it be a female assailant?'

'Possibly. Why?'

'My person of interest is a teenage girl.'

'Mmm. If I was a jealous female on the rampage, I'd have gone for the face.'

'Okay,' Lottie said, pondering whether Hannah was even strong enough for the ruthless attack. She was athletic, so anything was possible. 'Any clue as to what the weapon might have been?'

'I don't know for sure. I'll take measurements, but from what I can see with the naked eye, I'd say a knife with a five-inch serrated blade.'

'A steak knife?'

'Did you find it at the scene?'

'Nothing recovered so far, but Gráinne thought the same as you, and the kitchen knife block has a steak knife missing. Anything else that could help me?' Lottie moved closer to the table.

'I should be able to gather DNA if she made contact with her killer as she tried to defend herself.'

'Good.'

'And I'll carry out the usual screening for drugs and alcohol.'

'My guess is that you'll find evidence of those in her bloodstream. She'd thrown a party for her friends that evening. Any sign of sexual assault?'

'I haven't commenced the full post-mortem yet, and her clothing is at the lab for analysis.'

'Can you tell me anything at this stage?'

'I'm doing my best, Lottie. I got out of that court case to be here.' Jane walked around the body. 'Okay. Let's see what I have from the prelim. Visible vaginal bruising, so it's probable she had penetrative sexual intercourse shortly before she died. I will swab for semen, but if a condom was used, I may not find sufficient evidence.' She paused. 'Whether it was consensual or not I can't say until I do further examination, and even then it won't be conclusive.'

'If she's so badly bruised that it's visible, it would point in the direction of the sexual intercourse not being consensual, wouldn't it?'

'Could be rough sex. I'll take the swabs. We might get lucky with a DNA sample to match to a suspect, though that in itself won't tell you if the person she had sex with actually killed her.'

'I know, but at the very least it'd give me another witness. Any clue on time of death?'

'Pending further tests, I'd say she'd been dead between three and four hours when she was found.'

'The cleaner made the call at seven ten a.m. So that would put the death before four a.m.'

'Say between three and four. I'll know better later,' Jane said.

'The amount of blood spatter in the living room bothers me. Could Lucy have lost that much blood from superficial wounds if the final stabbing occurred upstairs?'

'I was about to mention that. It's unlikely she lost that amount of blood downstairs.'

Blowing out her cheeks, Lottie let out a low whistle. 'You think someone else was assaulted there?'

'I'll leave that up to you.'

'We have a missing fifteen-year-old boy.' She pictured the scene in her mind. 'If someone fell through a patio door and the glass shattered, could that have caused the blood spatter?'

'Enough speculation, Lottie. Allow the scene to be fully processed and the evidence tested and analysed; only then might you get the answer.'

'Fair enough.'

Jane called in her assistant and picked up a scalpel. 'Are you staying to observe?'

'I haven't time, but please send me your report as soon as you have it. Day or night. Even a prelim would be a huge help.'

'Sure. That coffee we were to have—'

'I know, I'm terrible. Soon, Jane, I promise.'

'You break my heart, Lottie Parker.'

'I think Boyd would agree with you there.' Lottie smiled, once again thinking she could do with Boyd by her side offering his controlled judgement and assessment. 'See you soon.' She headed for the door.

'Wait a minute,' Jane said. 'Meant to tell you about this. Take a look.' She lifted Lucy's arm.

Lottie's heart palpitated. She had tried to view the body as a means of gathering evidence to convict a murderer, but the closer she got to the table, the more she saw Lucy as a young girl with her life viciously snuffed out. Who would take a life so brutally from one who had yet to live it?

'What have you found?' she asked tentatively as she looked at the girl's dark hair spread over the slab of steel propping up her head.

'See this area here? Side of her chest, under her right arm.'

'What am I looking for?' Lottie struggled to make out anything because of the stab wounds on the girl's torso.

Jane pointed with the scalpel. 'A section of skin has been cut away on the upper right side of her rib cage. It was done shortly before death occurred.'

Lottie stared at the wound, her earlier hastily eaten sandwich and coffee curdling in her stomach. 'I'm not sure, but has it a particular shape?'

'I'll photograph it and zoom in, but to the naked eye it appears to be a crudely shaped heart.'

'Shit, that's what I thought.'

'Shit is right,' Jane said, surprising Lottie. The pathologist rarely swore.

Not normally squeamish, Lottie sensed nausea bubbling in her stomach. She made her escape before she had to witness the pathologist cutting into Lucy's body. She didn't want to embarrass herself by emptying her stomach contents on the sterile tiled floor.

She held onto it until she reached the car park.

34

On the motorway, driving back to Ragmullin, Lottie's phone rang on the hands-free set.

'Gráinne, please tell me you have good news.'

'Can you meet me at the crime scene, Inspector? I've something you need to see.'

'I've a team meeting in twenty minutes and I've just left the state pathologist. Make sure all the blood spatter in the living room is analysed. Jane seems to think it might not all have come from Lucy. And the glass shards from the patio doors need to be examined for blood. You know the drill.'

'It's being taken care of. I'd appreciate it if you could call round. It's important.'

Lottie looked at the time on the dashboard. The meeting would have to be delayed. She floored the accelerator. 'Can you email it to me?'

'You need to see this before anyone else is made aware of it. It concerns your son.'

'Shit. On my way.'

Disconnecting the call, Lottie pressed the speed-dial for Sean. It rang out. She swung up the slip road, driving off the motorway. Once she was on the Ragmullin road, she never let her foot up off the accelerator. All the while her mind was churning over what Gráinne could have found.

She had a bad feeling about it.

Gráinne's demeanour had dulled with tiredness in the hours since Lottie had left the crime scene. She was standing in the living room, where most of the destruction had occurred.

'Gráinne, what's so urgent?'

'There was a bundle of jackets, sweaters and cardigans behind the couch. Clothing the kids went home without.'

'Right.'

'I found a black leather jacket.' Gráinne's eyes were penetrating as she waited for Lottie to twig.

She was at a loss as to what the SOCO meant. 'I'm sorry, but what's the relevance? Does it belong to the killer, perhaps?'

'It's your son's.'

'Show me.'

Gráinne opened a large paper evidence bag. Lottie peered in.

'Gloves first,' the SOCO ordered.

She pulled on a pair and extracted the jacket. It was Sean's. After all she'd said, he'd still bloody left it behind him.

'How do you know it belongs to my son?'

'His school ID badge was in the inside pocket.'

Lottie's tongue stuck to her roof of her mouth, her throat dry. She had been transparent about him being at the party – well, semi-transparent, because she hadn't informed Superintendent Farrell. She'd made it clear to her team that she'd picked him up just after twelve. Now she'd definitely have to tell the superintendent.

She caught Gráinne staring. 'What? Is there something else?'

'I'm not sure how to ...'

'Spit it out.' Her temper was rising, though she knew it was misplaced. Gráinne was only doing her job.

'There was a box of condoms in the inside pocket. One is missing.'

'I thought for a minute there you were about to tell me you'd found the murder weapon in my son's pocket.'

Gráinne bent down to pick up another evidence bag. 'I also found a knife.'

'You what?' Lottie could feel the blood physically draining from her face.

'A Swiss Army knife.' The SOCO held up the bag. 'The good news is, it can't be the murder weapon. Blade is three inches, so it's too small.'

'Oh, that,' Lottie said, her shoulders sagging as the tension left her body. 'His dad gave it to him. It's old. I told him not to carry it around, but obviously he does. Sean was kidnapped a few years ago.'

Her spine shuddered at the memory. Sean had been traumatised, and he still carried within himself the stress and horror of what had happened.

'It'll have to be logged and tested,' Gráinne said, 'for blood and DNA. Protocol.'

'Test and log away. You won't find anything on it.' Lottie was totally confident on that score. Her son was not a killer. But it bothered her that he was still scared enough to carry his father's knife.

———

Hannah had been moved to one of the cells, given a scratchy blanket and told to rest. She'd curled up on the hard bench and slept fitfully until the psychiatrist arrived.

He'd been young and chatty. Her one thought was that he

would let her go home. Instead, he'd recommended she be admitted to hospital for comprehensive tests, citing dehydration, possibly from whatever narcotics she'd ingested.

Now she lay on a bed with a rubbery mattress in Ragmullin hospital. Additional bloods had been extracted and she was currently under observation until the psychiatrist returned to assess her further.

She wanted to go home. She missed her little brother. She even missed her mother. Babs had promised to call in if she got someone to babysit Olly, otherwise she'd said she'd phone. So far it was radio silence.

Lying there becoming more uncomfortable by the minute, Hannah wondered about Cormac and what he'd told the detectives. She was sure he'd been questioned. Ivy would have made it her business to rat them out.

Thinking of Ivy automatically shot her thoughts straight to Lucy. Someone had killed her. Hannah herself had had blood on her hands. Her memory was full of blanks. What had happened? She needed to talk to Cormac. But she was stuck in hospital without her phone. She had to convince the doctors she was okay, and then she'd answer all questions, even to say no comment. They'd have to let her go. After that, she'd find Cormac and maybe uncover the blanks in her memory.

She should have felt better once she'd made this decision, but she felt worse. For some reason she was scared of what Cormac might tell her. Why? What had she done? What had *he* done?

Shoving her face into the lumpy pillow, she sobbed until she fell asleep.

35

Half an hour late for the already delayed team meeting, Lottie swept into the incident room, handbag trailing off her arm, her bad mood evident to those gathered there without her opening her mouth. She dumped the bag on the floor and kicked it under the desk as she tore off her jacket, rolling it in a ball. It suffered the same fate as the handbag.

The chatter in the room ceased, everyone on high alert. The air was stuffy from body odour and a sickening floral perfume. It smelled like something her mother would spray liberally on her wrists. That thought prompted her to recall Sean's earlier phone call about buying groceries for his granny, which in turn spiked her irritability. Her son was in for an inquisition when she got home.

Without preamble, she launched straight into the meeting, setting the grim tone.

'Seventeen-year-old Lucy McAllister died following a sustained and frenzied knife attack. She suffered several stab wounds to her torso; the fatal wound according to the pathologist was the one to her throat. The other wounds may have weakened her by the time she'd dragged herself up the back stairs to the room where she was found this morning. The pathologist suggests the weapon could be as simple as a steak knife. One such knife is missing from the kitchen. It has yet to be found and extensive searches are continuing at the McAllister property.'

'Probably thrown into the canal,' McKeown muttered, keeping his shaved head bent and tapping his iPad idly.

Lottie ignored him, fighting a battle to keep her anger under wraps. It was reasonable to suspect McKeown had already spoken to Sean, so she had to tread carefully.

'There are signs Lucy was sexually active ... erm ... prior to her death.' She stumbled over her words as she recalled Gráinne mentioning the box of condoms in Sean's pocket. *Get a bloody grip, woman.* She coughed, masking her hesitancy. 'If intercourse did occur, there's still no proof the same person killed her. We await the full post-mortem results, but one interesting—'

'Could have been a sexual assault,' McKeown interrupted. 'First he raped her, then he tried to cover it up by killing her.'

Lottie silently counted to five before continuing. 'My information is only preliminary, so we don't know anything else about it.' She took a few breaths to calm her racing heart. 'It will take time, but the DNA will be analysed against samples taken from any suspects we bring in. Noel Glennon is currently top of that list, plus Cormac O'Flaherty and possibly Richie Harrison.'

'A lot of other red-blooded young males were there too, and what about Hannah Byrne? Is it the victim's blood on her hands?' McKeown was now verging on belligerence. 'Where is she anyhow?'

Digging her nails into her palms, Lottie took a deep breath, her thoughts scrambled by his constant interruptions. 'Hannah has been moved to hospital for precautionary tests. I hope she'll be well enough for interview tomorrow.'

McKeown stayed quiet. Good.

'What is the motive for Lucy's murder? Why would Hannah assault her? We have the photo Cormac O'Flaherty said was shared with everyone at the party. I'm reluctant to put it on the board because I don't want to subject the unfortunate girl to further voyeurism. One gruesome fact emerged from the preliminary post-mortem. A section of skin was incised from Lucy's torso.' She paused as a collective groan went up from the assembly. 'Under her arm, on her ribcage. Here's a photograph of it.'

She pinned up the photo of the wound that Jane had emailed.

'Is it shaped like a heart?' Kirby enquired, leaning his head sideways, squinting at the image.

'Could be. But why would the killer, who seemed to have been in a frenzy, have taken the time to do that?' Silence greeted her question. 'Any bright ideas? What about you, Detective McKeown?'

He kept his mouth zipped.

Garda Brennan put up her hand as if in a classroom. 'It's possible Lucy had a tattoo that might have identified her attacker. His initials in a heart? Something like that ... Sorry, that's stupid.'

Lottie leaned forward. 'No, that's good. I'll ask Lucy's parents about it.'

'But,' Garda Brennan said, 'when you look at where it was situated, it seems it was meant to be hidden. They might not know about it. I'd ask her friends ... if I was you, I mean.'

Lottie wondered why the young guard was so nervous, and quickly concluded it was to do with McKeown.

'That's good, Martina. Ivy Jones was her best friend. Check with her. Has anyone found Lucy's ex-boyfriend?'

Kirby said, 'Bradley Curran. He's in Australia. I can put a call through and ask him if Lucy had a tattoo.'

'And find out anything else he might know to help us deconstruct Lucy's life. So far we've only heard that she was a bully, prone to ridicule her peers. According to the cleaner, Sarah Robson, she was also a sad girl behind the facade. Why did Sarah think that? We need to know more about Lucy.'

'What did the toxicology report say?' Kirby asked. 'Any drugs?'

'No results yet. Tomorrow hopefully.'

'Good luck with that,' McKeown said. 'It's Sunday tomorrow.'

'I'm well aware of the days of the week,' Lottie snapped, though she had totally forgotten.

'Hannah says she can't remember a thing,' Kirby said. 'She might have been slipped a date rape drug. Is it too late to test for that?'

'I requested the blood test. We all know that GHB only stays in the bloodstream for up to eight hours after being administered. If that's what Hannah was given, it might already be flushed from her system and may not be detected. But I agree, there's a strong possibility her drink was spiked. We have to wait and see what comes back from the lab.'

She turned to McKeown. 'I want you to dig into all the relevant persons' backgrounds. See if they have any skeletons knocking to get out of cupboards. Put Noel Glennon top of your list. I want to know everything about him before I bring him in for questioning again. I'm worried that he had an ulterior motive for being at a teenage party.'

Relating what Sarah Robson had said about the PE teacher, she added, 'While you're at it, dig into Sarah's background. How are you getting on with the interviews with the partygoers?' She had the words out of her mouth before she realised what she was saying. Shit and double shit.

'Glad you asked,' he said with a smirk.

I bet you are, Lottie thought, mentally kicking herself for giving him the opening.

'I've gone through the list provided by Ivy Jones. Every last one of them was *totally wasted*. Their words, not mine. A few recalled the altercation between Hannah and Lucy. No one remembers anything out of the ordinary other than that snippet of excitement. I've had a look at the photos on their phones and social media. Found nothing to help us.'

Once she had started the conversation, she couldn't row back. 'Did you hear any names of those who were there but are not on Ivy's list?'

'A few. Most of the kids were vague, as you can imagine, based on their alcohol consumption.'

'Not to mention their consumption of the drugs sold by Jake Flood,' Kirby added, tapping his pocket for the cigar he normally kept there. 'He hasn't been seen since the party. Alerts are out for him and his mother's car, but so far without success.'

'I spoke with your son too, Inspector,' McKeown said, a serious but forced expression clouding his face. 'I can discuss it with you in private.'

Heads turned towards him, and back to Lottie. He was a bastard. He could have come to her afterwards. But she had provided him with the opening, and if she hadn't been late, she could have spoken with him before the meeting. Time to move on.

'Fair enough.' She smiled pleasantly. 'As Detective Kirby mentioned, we also have a missing boy. Fifteen-year-old Jake Flood. He was dealing drugs at the party. We need to establish why he was there. Did Lucy invite him for that purpose? And the big question, where is he now? He stole his mother's blue Fiat Punto. Details have been circulated and alerts issued for the car and the boy. Anything we can learn about him is crucial to the investigation, based on our supposition that Hannah was drugged. Cormac O'Flaherty isn't saying much, and what he does say I'm taking with a huge grain of salt. Did any of Lucy's pals have information on Jake?'

McKeown shook his head. 'I'd interviewed most of them by the time I learned the kid was missing, but the remainder were tight-lipped.'

Garda Lei spoke up. 'Jake's dad died last year and it seems to have set off a downward decline. I believe the boy is part of a gang of thugs who cycle around town snaring kids into a drug habit.'

'Follow up that angle,' Lottie said. 'Who is in the gang? Who is their leader? Who's pulling their strings? And in particular, what is Jake's role in the gang and why was he at Lucy's party? You know the drill.'

'Sure thing. Of course. I'll get straight to it.' Lei flashed a wide smile and stood to leave.

She admired his awkward enthusiasm. 'Wait until after the meeting. One interesting fact is that Albert McAllister is a boxing agent and Jake trained at a boxing club, Ragmullin Goldstars, funded by Albert. I'll follow up at the club and see what I can discover. I want to be the first to know of any reported sightings of Jake or the car.'

'Like the murder weapon, the car's probably been dumped by now,' McKeown muttered.

He was really getting to her. 'Detective McKeown, I want a report on what you learned from the party guests. What they drank or took at the party. If they noticed anything unusual, saw anyone acting suspiciously, the time they left and their insight into what was going on in Lucy's life. No matter how out there it may sound to you, I want it in your report.'

'Got it.' He tapped something into his iPad.

'There's no harm having a look at Liz Flood, Jake's mother. She arrived home early this morning saying she'd been working all night, but the bar manager at the hotel says she clocked out at twelve fifteen a.m. Where was she after that? We need to tick that box. Anyone got anything else to offer?'

Mumbled muttering greeted her question.

'Is everyone clear on what you have to do?'

A series of nods greeted the question. It was time to wrap it up before Superintendent Farrell made an unwelcome appearance.

'Perhaps Hannah Byrne killed Lucy, but we need to eliminate all other suspects. If someone outside of the party group murdered her, how did they gain access to the property? How did they leave? How long was Noel Glennon manning the door? Security cameras were not switched on at the house last night, so find the nearest property with them and check the footage. CCTV in this town leaves a lot to be desired, but keep searching. Scrutinise the traffic cams for the blue Punto.'

'Should we put out an appeal for dashcam footage?' Kirby asked.

'We don't have a definitive timeline, but see what you can get. And put out another appeal for anyone who was in the area after midnight to come forward. Sometimes people see things they think are irrelevant but might provide an unexpected lead.'

'It's a lot of back-breaking, mainly worthless work,' McKeown muttered.

She pretended she hadn't heard him.

'By the way, Detective Lynch, any update on Lucy's emails? I need to know who she had planned to spend last weekend with and if she went through with it.'

'Gary is still working on the email address. He said something about a Tor browser and Guerrilla Mail, whatever they are.'

'Tell him to work harder and quicker. We're losing valuable time.'

'The email might be nothing.'

'And it might be everything. Did you talk to Ivy about who sent it to Lucy or where this rendezvous might have been?'

'Ivy claims she didn't see Lucy last weekend and she heard

nothing about Lucy planning to be away. I can't put my finger
on it, but I have a feeling she's withholding something.'

'Keep on her back.'

'Will do.'

'Any sign of Lucy's phone?'

'Not yet.'

'What's the story with the McAllisters?' Lottie said. 'Did
they refuse a family liaison officer?'

'Yeah. Said they wanted to grieve in peace.'

'We really need to keep a close eye on them. Why did they
go to Spain for three weeks? I'm not buying the tale of Mary
being depressed. Is there some scandal brewing with Albert's
business that he had to try and sort out? I need to know more
about that boxer, Terry Starr, too. Take a nosy around their
financials. See if there's anything suspicious.'

Lynch raised an eyebrow. 'What exactly am I looking for?'

'I haven't a clue, but you'll know if you find it.'

'Sure,' Lynch said, not sounding sure at all.

'I was just thinking ...' Kirby said.

'That's a dangerous activity for someone with no brain,'
McKeown sneered.

Sniggers echoed around the room.

Kirby glared. 'What if the killer didn't know that Lucy had
asked Sarah to clean the house this morning? They might have
wanted the parents to discover their daughter's body. A message
of sorts.'

'Surely they would have been aware that someone else
might find the body. I take your point, though. There's no harm
in keeping it in mind as we press forward.'

Lottie racked her brain to see what else needed doing, but
she knew she was only delaying the inevitable conversation
with McKeown. She couldn't put it off any longer.

'Right, that's it for today. Detective McKeown, my office.'

36

Sitting heavily on her chair, Lottie scowled as she waited for McKeown. He was taking his damn time. She wanted to ring Boyd to find out if he'd learned anything at his end. She needed to know what Albert and Mary had been doing in Malaga that was so important they'd left their daughter home alone for three weeks.

Before she could make the call, McKeown strode in with his iPad, all business. Fuck him.

'Take a seat,' she said with a fake sweet smile. She could see he wasn't buying it.

'Thanks.'

'What have you to tell me that I don't already know?'

'What *do* you know?' He raised an eyebrow.

'I'm asking the questions.' She unfurled her clenched fists and placed her hands on the desk, out of trouble. 'Tell me what you learned from Sean.'

McKeown scrolled his screen, then looked up with forced seriousness. 'I established that your son left the party shortly after midnight. You picked him up. He found it hard to sleep.

Warm cider at fault, he said. He denied having taken any drugs.'

'Fair enough.'

'During the night, he realised he'd left his new jacket at Lucy's. Because he couldn't sleep worrying about it, he left home around four a.m. He's not sure of the exact time. He walked the mile or so back to the party house.'

'I'm sure the party was long over by then.' She couldn't wait to get home to Sean, because she was itching to wring his neck. Metaphorically speaking. Why hadn't he told her this?

'The door was open. He assumed everyone had left because there was no sign of anyone around. Not at that stage.'

Lottie braced herself for the mic drop she felt he was building up to. He was in his element. A sly grin curved his lips as he delivered his news.

'He entered the living room where he'd last seen his jacket and stumbled into the crime scene.'

'He should have told me.' Lottie was glad she was sitting; she felt weak.

'Said he forgot all about looking for his jacket then because he heard someone coming down the stairs. He fled to the kitchen, where he noticed drops of blood. He must have your nosy gene, because he went up the back stairs and found Lucy's body.'

A wave of nausea surged from her stomach and she held a hand to her mouth. 'Good God. You're telling me my son stumbled on Lucy's body and never reported it?'

'Yep.'

'This is a nightmare.' Then a thought struck her. 'The killer could still have been on the premises at that stage.'

'That depends on one simple fact.'

'What might that be?'

'That your son is not the murderer.' Another sly grin slid across his face and she wanted to slap it off. Then she remembered the knife that Gráinne had found in Sean's pocket. It wasn't the murder weapon because the blade was too short, but it was a mercy McKeown didn't know about it or he'd milk it for all it was worth.

She tried to keep the conversation professional while a migraine threatened to explode. 'You said Sean heard someone coming down the stairs. If that person was the murderer, it ties in with the rough time of death Jane gave me.'

'He thinks he heard two people talking.'

'Thanks for not revealing this to the whole team,' she said grudgingly. He could have made a holy show of her.

'You do realise, Inspector, that I've had to log Sean's interview.'

'Of course.' She barely heard him. She was thinking of her only son and his near escape.

McKeown stood, snapping his iPad closed. 'And I informed Superintendent Farrell.'

'You what? Are you trying to get me thrown off the case? There was no need to do that, no need at all. Christ on a bike.'

Before she could fully register the smug smile widening on McKeown's face, the door flew inwards. Superintendent Farrell stood there, with a bulging, inflamed face.

'I'm not Christ on a bike, but you might be wishing that I was, Inspector Parker. My office.'

'I've to finish up with Detective McKeown.'

'Are you deaf as well as incompetent? Now!'

Lottie pushed out past McKeown. He had a triumphant smirk plastered to his face and she had no time to focus on how best to handle the super.

After knocking politely on Farrell's door, she entered the office when instructed to do so. Inside, she blinked. Every piece of furniture had been moved around. She had to twist on the balls of her feet to locate Farrell seated at her desk to the right.

'You moved the ...' Lottie waved a hand but quickly shut up. None of her business.

'Therapy. Relieves my anxiety.' Arms folded. Face verging on purple.

Lottie reckoned that if she adopted the super's version of therapy in her house, the furniture would be in perpetual motion. She tried to concentrate while figuring out her strategy.

The super was still speaking. 'And I can tell you this for nothing, Inspector Parker, my anxiety has gone through the roof since I came to Ragmullin. My blood pressure is so high my doctor has me wearing a monitor for the next twenty-four hours. Can you guess the cause of my high blood pressure?'

'No, boss.'

A loud snort from Farrell and Lottie shuffled her weight from one foot to the other. Wrong thing to say.

'You!' A wagging finger pointed at her and Lottie silently groaned. 'I can see how poor Superintendent Corrigan met an early grave.'

'That's not fair. He had cancer. May I sit?' For some unfathomable reason she felt vulnerable while standing with her boss seated.

'You may not, because you won't be here long enough.' Farrell twiddled her clip-on tie until it broke free so that she could open the top button of her creased white shirt. 'Explain to me in less than thirty seconds about this mess you've got yourself into.'

'Lucy McAllister's body was only discovered this morning, so I don't understand what you mean.' Fingers crossed behind her back.

'Your son. His jacket. Knife in the pocket. Not reporting that he was at the scene of the crime in the middle of the night. Finding the body. Do you want me to draw you a diagram?'

Shit, how did Farrell know about the knife? 'Oh, that's what you mean. It's nothing to worry about. Just a misunderstanding.'

'A mis-under-standing?' Farrell drew out the word. 'Enlighten me.'

Quickly Lottie explained what Gráinne had found and repeated what McKeown had told her. 'I've yet to speak with my son, so it's just hearsay at the moment.'

'Listen carefully, Inspector. That is not hearsay. It's straight from the horse's mouth. You are off the case.'

'You can't do that.'

'I just did.'

'Please! You think I'm compromised because of this, but I'm not. Sean is not involved in the case. The facts as I know them are that I picked him up shortly after midnight. True, he went back around four in the morning to look for his jacket. He left straight away without it. Lucy was already dead by the time he went back there.'

'And you can prove this?'

'At the very least I need a chance to talk to my son before you take me off the case.'

Farrell shook her head and Lottie thought she heard the blood pressure monitor bleep. The super tapped a finger on her desk. Probably counting to calm herself down and avoid throwing a punch.

'You make the wrong choices all the time. You almost got Detective Sergeant Boyd killed in an explosion a while back. There's dissent in your camp, and affairs happening left, right and centre. You've lost control.'

So now she was being blamed for McKeown's affair on top of everything else.

'You can't deny that I bring in results. All I ask is that you let me talk to Sean. Once I've done that, I will report back to you. I know I can find Lucy's killer. One chance, that's all I ask.'

After considering it, Farrell eventually spoke. 'You have

until the morning. And I don't want to arrive in here with another victim's face stuck on the incident board. Got it?'

'Loud and clear.' Relief flooded through Lottie and her legs felt like jelly. Time to escape.

As an afterthought, she remembered her manners. 'Thank you, Superintendent.'

37

Ivy was so annoyed about Richie ignoring her that she drove aimlessly around town. She checked the time on the dash. Another half-hour before she was due home with the car. She knew she'd be looking at her mother's sour puss for the rest of the evening if she was late.

Her hangover was relentless. She needed a Chinese take-away, Lucy's go-to cure. But Lucy was dead. The realisation left a hollow in her stomach. She felt totally lost without her friend.

She drove up and down Main Street, circling the round-about twice. There wasn't a vacant parking space to be found close to the restaurant.

No way was she going to park in a car park and walk all the way back with her head thumping. Maybe she could sneak some of her dad's vodka at home. She'd heard him call it *the hair of the dog*. Might not beat Chinese food, but she was willing to try anything to get rid of the headache that was threatening to blind her.

She fired off another text to Richie, knowing he wouldn't reply, like he hadn't replied to the dozen earlier ones. She'd have to leave it until tomorrow. Then she would march up to his house, ring the bell and keep ringing it until he opened the door. If his wife was there, bad luck.

Ivy was long past caring.

―――――

Cormac changed into his jeans and went to stuff his cut-offs into the washing machine. The forensic guys had taken the clothes he'd been washing that morning. He found it hard to believe it was still the same day.

The nagging feeling tearing away at the base of his skull wouldn't let go. Should he have told the truth about what had really happened? He wondered if Hannah had talked. Or was she so badly affected by the drug that she had no recollection of the remainder of the night? She'd scared him badly. He couldn't understand it. Hadn't he taken the same type of pill and it had had little or no effect? Perhaps it was because she was a narcotic virgin. It must be that.

Maybe he shouldn't have shown the detectives the photo. It provided a motive for Hannah to attack Lucy and took the pressure off him. Hannah was a sweet girl and didn't deserve all this. Despite everything, he liked her.

It was such a fucking mess.

A panic attack began to take root in his chest and he struggled to control his erratic breathing. There was a spare inhaler somewhere in the house, but he ransacked every drawer without success.

He shivered violently as his chest constricted again.

In the cupboard under the sink, he found a folded-up paper bag. Flapping it, he made a funnel to breathe into. It was the only thing he could do to normalise his breathing.

At last the rasping eased.

No matter what he'd done, Cormac wasn't ready to die.

Maybe it was time to tell the truth.

When Babs arrived at the hospital, the look on her face told Hannah she'd been expecting to see her daughter in a straitjacket.

'I can't understand why you're here.' Babs pulled a chair to the bed and sat.

'The doctor thinks it's possible my drink was spiked, despite inconclusive test results. He said too much time had passed before the test was done, but I had all the symptoms. I've to stay in overnight attached to these monitors.'

'I hope I haven't to pay for all this – we don't have health insurance.'

'Would you rather that detective charged me with murder?'

'Not at all, but I can't understand how you had that blood on your—'

'Neither can I, Mam, because I can't remember. I think Inspector Parker was right to agree that I come here to be checked over.'

'She can pay the bill then. I heard it's like five hundred euros a day.'

'It's a public hospital, Mam.'

'They'll try to screw us.' Babs folded her arms.

'I don't care.' Hannah noticed that her mother hadn't even asked how she was, and that filled her with a huge sense of loneliness.

'You should come home with me now. Where are your clothes?'

'I want to go home, but I don't want to be arrested and I still feel sick. I'd better stay.'

'I have to leave. Mrs Delaney is sitting with Olly, and if he catches her flu, you can mind him.'

'Mam, where's my phone?'

'At the garda station. They wanted to examine it.'

'Can they do that?'

'They can do anything they bloody like.'

As Babs swept out of the ward, Hannah wished she'd pulled the curtain around the bed. The other women were staring at her.

Yeah, she thought, I have a stressed mother, but I know she cares for me.

No phone.

No way to contact Cormac.

And then she realised she didn't even have his number.

―――

It was beginning to spit rain as Noel Glennon pulled on a clean tracksuit to go for a run. He decided to sit out on his decking in the drizzle to smoke a cigarette instead. It felt like he was doing something, even though all he was doing was damaging his health.

He rang the number again, but there was still no answer. He had to find out if he'd slipped up anywhere. His head was thumping and he pulled deeply on the cigarette. There was one ace he could play. He didn't want to do it, but he was left with no choice.

Tomorrow Richie Harrison could yell at him, but now was the time to plan.

―――

Brontë Harrison listened to her baby's heartbeat while Richie sat by her bed.

'You need to tell my father I'm here,' she said.

'You'll be home by morning. No point in worrying him.'

'My father worries about no one other than himself.'

'Why tell him, then?'

'I hate it when you insist on being a fucking idiot. Forget it.'

'There's something I have to tell you, Brontë, and you're not going to be pleased.'

'What have you done now?' She bunched up the sheet, her fingers turning white.

'Nothing, I swear. But the thing is, two detectives called to the house and interviewed me about last night's party at the McAllister house.'

'They what?' She sat up in the bed and the monitor slipped from her tummy. The room dipped into silence without the baby's heartbeat echoing in the air. Brontë soon filled the silence. 'You can't be interviewed without a solicitor. I hope you didn't tell them anything.'

'Of course I didn't. There's nothing to tell.'

'You are so full of shit, Richie Harrison.'

A nurse arrived to strap the monitor back on her tummy, saving Richie from a tongue-lashing.

———

Magpie, that's me. I am glorious and magnificent. I hide but I want everyone to know me. But that's not possible.

Standing at the window I stare out at the fading evening light. I hear the birds twittering in the branches and wonder what it would be like to sleep in a tree.

Daft thoughts.

I turn back to my laptop and stare at the clock in the top corner. I have time to view a few more video clips before I must wipe the device clean. It's crucial that I leave no trace of my work online. I've been careful, but have I been careful enough?

But I can't help having a final look at my beautiful, profitable work.

38

It was beginning to rain as Lottie unlocked her mother's front
door and walked into stifling heat. Rattled after the confrontation with Superintendent Farrell, she'd decided to call on Rose
before heading home to have it out with Sean. She didn't want
to be in attack mode when she talked to him.

'What temperature have you the heat at? It's like the Sahara
in here.'

Without waiting for a reply, she went outside to check the
boiler. It was humming away with the thermostat clipping
ninety degrees. She turned down the gauge and went back
inside.

Rose was sitting by the stove with the door open, a blazing
fire burning in the grate.

'It's the middle of summer,' Lottie said.

'I'm perished with the cold.' Rose pulled a multicoloured
fleece blanket up to her chin.

'Maybe you've caught the flu.'

'There's no flu this time of the year.'

Lottie could never win where Rose was concerned. She
busied herself by rinsing a cup and plate under running

scalding water. It was unlike her mother to leave dirty dishes lying around, but at least it proved she had eaten something.

'I've a pain in my ear,' Rose said. 'Need my ear plug. Can you get it for me?'

'You don't have any ear plugs.'

'Of course I do. On the dresser in my bedroom. Small bottle. It's still in the box.'

'Oh, you mean ear drops.'

'That's what I told you.'

Not wanting to argue, Lottie said, 'Do you want to come over to mine for dinner?'

'I had my dinner. Sean brought me groceries. He's a good boy. More than I can say for my own daughter.'

'What did you eat?' Lottie bristled at Rose's pointed barb.

'A sandwich.'

She looked over her shoulder, hands dripping water onto the floor. 'A sandwich? For your dinner?'

'What about it?'

'Nothing.' She grabbed a tea towel and placed the dried mug on the counter.

'Don't leave it there.'

Opening a cupboard door, she wished she was in Malaga with Boyd.

'Not that one, the one beside it. Are you stupid?'

Lottie stared at Rose.

'Don't look at me like that. For God's sake, why can't anyone do what I want and do it right?'

Drying her hands, she concluded that her mother didn't look well. 'I think I'll call your doctor.'

'Why would you do that? Anyway, it's after hours and he doesn't make house calls.'

'I'll leave a message requesting an appointment for you.'

'Stop fussing. I'll be fine. It's just a cold.'

'All the same, I'll organise an appointment.' In the hall, she found her mother's coat. 'Put this on. You're coming home with me.'

'In your dreams,' Rose scoffed, before doubling up, coughing. 'If I'm going to die, I'll die in my own house.' She folded her arms over the lurid blanket, and her grumpy, resolute face defied Lottie to cross her.

When Rose was in this mood, it was torture to argue with her. But she wasn't well and Lottie knew she couldn't leave her alone.

'I'll pack some clothes for you. You're staying with me for a few days.'

'Over my dead body.'

'Mother, you'll be better off with me. I'll look after you.' She had no idea how that would work out and thought that perhaps it wasn't one of her better ideas.

'You? Look after me?' Rose was on a roll. 'Don't make me laugh.'

'Sean has school holidays, and little Louis loves you.' Even if you make life difficult for everyone, Lottie added in her mind. 'Tomorrow is Sunday, so Katie won't be working.' Sunday! Shit, she wouldn't get a doctor's appointment until Monday.

'I've been on my own this long. I can manage another few months, then I'll be out of your hair for good.'

'Don't talk rubbish.' She had never before heard Rose being so fatalistic. Today was not a good day for this conversation, with her ears still ringing from Farrell's fury.

'Just go home, Lottie.' Rose doubled up in another coughing fit. It was a moment before she caught her breath. 'I didn't ask you to call round. I can manage.'

It didn't look like she was managing very well at all.

'Hard luck, Mother, because I insist.'

'You're good at that,' Rose said.

'What?'

'Giving orders.'

Lottie threw her hands in the air. 'Right. You know, it'd be a whole lot easier for me to leave you here.' Belatedly she tried to reel in her tantrum. 'But you raised me to care about people. I might not always show it, but I do care for you, Mother. Okay?'

'Never.'

'What?'

'You never show me you care.' Rose sulked and coughed. Lottie noticed tears gathering in her eyes. 'Okay, have it your way. One night. That's all. I'm not an invalid.' She made to stand, wobbled beneath the blanket then sat down again. 'Maybe you could help me get my coat on.'

Lottie hated to admit it, but she'd been half hoping Rose would refuse to leave. I'm going straight to hell, she thought as she tugged the coat around her mother's bony shoulders, then wondered what, if anything, there was at home to cook for dinner.

And she still had to talk to Sean.

Why was her life so bloody complicated?

Never a dull moment.

After Sean had brought down blankets and pillows from upstairs to the cold sitting room, Lottie stripped her own bed and dressed it with fresh sheets. She hadn't got around to furnishing a guest bedroom. She could only find one clean duvet cover and that wasn't even ironed. In her mind, she heard Rose's rebuke about her lack of household skills.

'Tough,' she muttered, struggling to get the cover over the unwieldy king-size duvet. 'It's my house and I don't have to iron if I don't want to.'

'It's fine, Lottie.'

She froze. She hadn't heard her mother come up the stairs.

'I'm tired,' Rose said. 'I can sleep on the couch rather than uprooting you.' She suddenly looked old and frail.

'I brought your nightdress. Are you okay to put it on … to undress yourself?'

'Stop fussing.' Rose sat on top of the half-covered duvet. 'I should have stayed in my own house.'

Lottie hadn't the heart to ask her mother to move so that she could close the final buttons on the duvet cover. 'Get yourself ready for bed and I'll bring up some food when it's cooked.'

Rose took the nightdress from her hastily packed bag. 'This is not the right one.'

Of course it's not. Lottie groaned silently. 'It'll do for tonight. I'll get more of your clothes in the morning. Are you okay up here on your own while I put on the dinner?'

'I'll be back at home tomorrow, so there's no need to fuss. And I'm not hungry. Didn't I tell you I'd had my dinner?'

'Please don't make this more difficult than it is. I'm trying to help you.' Lottie felt close to tears. Maybe it was Lucy's murder, or the fact that Boyd was away, or that she still had to have it out with Sean, not to mention McKeown with his smug grin after he'd landed her in it with the super. Or maybe, just maybe, it was because she'd never seen her mother look so vulnerable.

'I'm sorry,' Rose said quietly. 'I know I'm not the easiest person to like, and by God you have reason more than most to dislike me, but—'

'I don't dislike you. For God's sake—'

'Let me finish what I'm saying. I appreciate you looking after me tonight. But I'm going home tomorrow. I've never been a burden on you, and I'm not about to start. I've lived a lot of my life alone and I think I'm qualified to know that I can still manage.'

'Not when you're ill, though.'

'Go and cook that dinner. We can argue about it later. Did you bring a nightdress for me? I told you to pack one.'

Lottie sighed as she stared at her mother holding the night-dress, a vacant look in her eyes.

39

Colette Ennis loved bringing her dog for a walk in the evening, even after rain.

With the black Labrador straining on his leash, she jogged along the canal towpath. The evenings were long and there had been a hint of summer in the air earlier, but it wasn't quite there yet. She eyed the black clouds gliding across the sky, thinking it looked like a stealthy cat about to pounce on a mouse. The mouse being the dipping sun. She undid the leash to let Jasper run freely.

Just before she reached Piper's Lane, she passed a couple of disappointed fishermen packing up their kitbags. She ran on, but slowed for a moment to gaze at the small bronze famine monument depicting a child's shoes. She'd passed them regularly but had never looked properly. How sad, she thought, and quickened her steps again.

The canal was a muddy brown. The earlier shower had caused the silt to rise. She didn't think the fishermen had caught anything, and if they had, the fish were most likely already dead. The canal looked like a watery grave. That thought caused her to shiver.

She realised then that her dog had stopped somewhere behind her.

'Ah come on, Jasper, I'm recording *Coronation Street* while I'm out and I want to watch it before bed.' The dog was nuzzling the reeds at the canal bank. 'You'd better not be disturbing rats, or I'm leaving you there.'

Jasper barked.

'What is it, boy?'

Colette bent down beside her dog, unfurling the leash from her fingers, ready to snap it onto his collar. He barked again, a howl disturbing the stillness of the evening. That was when she saw what had made him nuzzle the reeds and bark like a banshee.

A thin white arm extended upwards, a rope around the wrist.

Holding a hand to her mouth so as not to throw up, Colette grabbed Jasper's collar and hauled him back to the path. He was wet and slippery and it took three tries to snap on the leash.

She looked around for help, but the fishermen had disappeared off home. She was all alone. The first drops of a fresh shower hit her skin. Taking her phone from the hip pocket of her tracksuit, she glanced once more at the lonely arm reaching for the sky. It looked like it was pleading for someone to rescue it.

Then she punched in 999 and waited as the rain fell in a torrent.

She didn't even feel it.

40

Katie and Chloe told Lottie to fix up the bed in the sitting room and they would make something for their late dinner.

'There's a first time for everything,' she quipped. Tiredness seeped through her bones.

'Don't push it, Mam,' Katie said, stirring a pot of soup with little Louis hanging off her jeans.

'Sean is lighting the fire for you. That room is freezing cold,' Chloe said, taking the ladle from Katie.

'Fine. Shout if you need anything.'

'A takeaway would be nice.' Chloe winked. 'Go on. I've no work tonight or tomorrow. I'll get up early to help with Granny.'

'Me too,' Katie said. 'I'm off until Monday.'

'Me too,' Louis said, taking the crust of buttered bread Katie had given him to bribe his hands off her jeans.

In the big old draughty sitting room, Sean was down on his haunches, fanning a reluctant flame with a sheet of newspaper. Her bed was made up on the couch. A bit haphazard. At least he'd tried.

'Sean? Come here for a minute. We need to talk.' Lottie sat

on the couch, determined to keep her eyes open and her anger closed tight.

He continued to fan the fire. It was now blazing.

'No need to set the house on fire.'

'Is it insured?'

'Funny.'

'Feels odd to have a fire lit this time of year,' he said. At last he folded up the newspaper and stuffed it in the coal bucket.

'You should have seen the blaze in your Granny's stove and the heat of the house.'

'I turned up the thermostat. She said she was freezing.'

'Really? She'll be fine after a few days' rest.'

'Rest, here? I wish her luck with Louis around.' Sean sat beside her. 'I haven't had one lie-in yet.'

'You love him all the same.'

'Of course I do. Just like you love Granny Rose even though you give out about her.'

'Point taken.'

Sean shifted uncomfortably. 'I'm sorry for not telling you I went back to Lucy's.'

'Superintendent Farrell threatened to take me off the case.'

'I couldn't lie to Detective McKeown.'

'You should have told me.'

'I tried. I called you earlier today, but you said you were busy. You're always busy.'

'I might have some free time soon, if McKeown and the super have their way.'

'Sorry.'

Lottie straightened up. 'Tell me all.'

'I will, if you stop being a cop and just be my mam for a few minutes.'

She caught his grin. 'This is my mam face. Go on.'

Sean relaxed. 'When I was walking back to Lucy's, it was pitch dark. I hate the countryside for that reason, but anyway, I used the torch on my phone. A car sped by, weaving across the road. I couldn't see who was driving, but I think it was the same car Jake Flood had. He's the guy Cormac said was selling drugs. I saw the appeal, his photo and a description of the car on Facebook.'

'And this was around four a.m.?'

'Yeah. Then a few minutes after that, a kid on a bicycle rode by in a huge hurry.'

'Did you see this cyclist at the party?'

'No. But cycling at four in the morning? That was weird.'

He had Lottie's full attention.

'What happened when you reached the house?'

'Door was open. I went in. Lights were on. Living room was a mess, and all that blood. The patio door was smashed, as if someone had been pushed or had fallen through the glass. I wanted to get the hell out of there, and then I thought I heard footsteps on the stairs.'

'Did you hear anything else?'

He dropped his eyes. Hiding something? 'Like what?'

'Like someone talking?'

'Yeah. There might have been two of them.'

'Male or female?'

'I'm not sure.'

'Go on.'

'I hid in the kitchen. Then I heard a screech. Sounded like a girl, but I was scared shitless, so I'm not sure. After that, it went quiet. There were drops of blood on the kitchen floor, and even though I was terrified, I had an urge to go up the back stairs. That's ... that's when I saw what had happened to Lucy.'

'Did you touch her body or anything in the room?'

'I hadn't gloves on, if that's what you mean. I knew she was dead, but I felt her wrist for a pulse anyhow. Then I thought, what if the killer was still in the house? I got the hell out of there as fast as I could.'

'Why didn't you call the emergency services?'

'Mam, she was dead. I didn't want to get in trouble. I legged it.'

She couldn't believe he had been so stupid. 'Right. Okay. Do you know Hannah Byrne?'

'She was with Cormac. Only talked to them for a few minutes.'

'You didn't see her arguing with Lucy?'

'No. It must have been after I left.'

'Sean, are you disturbed by all of this?'

'Disturbed?'

'Troubled or anxious. Will I call your therapist?'

'If I need to talk to anyone, I can phone.'

Lottie could see how difficult it was for him not to cry in front of her. 'I'm sorry I'm not here for you when you need me.'

'I love you, Mam, but you can be so frustrating.'

'You're not the first to say that. My boss is wearing a blood pressure monitor because of me.'

Sean laughed, and the joyous sound warmed Lottie's heart.

'I'm not surprised,' he said, tears rolling down his cheeks. From the laughter? She hoped so.

'She moved all the furniture around in her office. Said it helps relieve her anxiety. I think I'll take up that kind of therapy.'

'If you started moving things around here, this ancient stuff would crumble.'

'We could use it for firewood. Save a fortune on fuel.' They both laughed, and Lottie felt the closest she had to him in a long time, maybe since Adam had died.

Louis rushed into the room. 'Nana Lottie, Uncle Sean. Dinner's ready.'

'That's great, Louis. We'll be there in a minute.'

'Mammy! Nana be there in a minute!' Louis roared, running back out.

220 PATRICIA GIBNEY

Moving to the edge of the sofa, Lottie faced her son and took his hand in hers, relieved when he didn't withdraw it or flinch. 'Sean, I don't want you to tell anyone else what you've just told me.'

'I told Detective McKeown most of it.'

'I'll ask him to keep a lid on it.'

'But I didn't see anything.'

'I know that, but the killer doesn't.'

She watched the weak blaze from the fire settle on Sean's face as his eyes widened.

'You mean if they find out I was at the house while they were still there, they might come after me?'

'That's exactly what I mean.'

'I only saw the car and the kid on the bike ...'

'You heard voices and footsteps and some sort of scream or cry. It's crucial we keep this out of circulation. It might give us an advantage in catching the killer.'

'You need to be careful too, Mam.'

'My middle name is careful.' She laughed.

'Yeah, and everyone believes that. Not.'

'Hey, I'm starving. Let's see what the girls have ready to poison us with.'

They stood to leave. Lottie felt a warm glow, and not from the struggling fire. Sean had put his arm through hers and leaned his head on her shoulder for a moment. It meant more to her than anything. She had to do everything in her power to protect her loved ones. No way was she going to allow anyone to target her family. It had happened before, but never again, she vowed.

She'd just sat at the table when Kirby rang.

'Boss, we found another body.'

41

The boy's body had been removed from the water and placed on plastic sheeting by the time Lottie arrived on the scene.

Kirby shook his head and wiped raindrops from his hair before pulling forward the hood of his forensic suit. The promised shower had turned into a deluge. Typical.

'The poor lad's body is a bit of a mess,' he said. 'Badly beaten. Welts all over. Gráinne says he was stabbed too. We're waiting for the state pathologist to arrive. Hopefully she can confirm time and cause of death.'

Lottie nodded. 'This rain will hamper the preservation of evidence.'

'Doesn't really matter. He's been in the canal a good few hours, according to the experts.' He pointed to the ghost-like figures of the SOCOs.

Sidestepping Kirby's bulk, she made her way up the final few feet of the incline.

'He's just a kid,' Gráinne said. Her eyes looked strained above her mask, their colour dulled to grey with exhaustion.

Hunkering down, Lottie shook her head as she looked at the boy. 'He's only fifteen. Damn.'

'Your missing boy?'

'Yeah, Jake Flood. He was dishing out drugs and drink at Lucy's party last night and now he's dead.'

'He got a right going-over. I did a visual check. The marks on his body are unusual. They might have been made with a bicycle chain. Even though he was in the water, I noticed a black oily substance embedded in the wounds.'

Lottie glanced out over the canal, its surface dancing with pinpricks of piercing rain. 'Could he have fallen in after being beaten, and then he drowned?'

'The post-mortem will confirm if there's any water in his lungs, but he was helped on his way. Look, his hands were tied at some point.' Gráinne pointed to the frayed rope around one wrist. 'It's just twine. Rats might have gnawed it.'

'That quickly?'

'Perhaps it was already weakened or rotting.'

'Do you think it's possible he was still alive when he was thrown into the water and he tore at the rope trying to free himself?' Lottie shivered at the thought of the drowning boy feverishly attempting to escape.

'Stop, Inspector. You'll only eat yourself up with anxiety. Wait until everything is forensically examined.'

'You're correct, of course. The canal bed will need to be searched. I'll call the Water Unit over from Athlone. Hopefully they can get here first thing, and I'll have a team ready to search along the bank. The entire area will have to be cordoned off.'

'Do you think this is related to Lucy McAllister's murder?'

'If it's not, it's a very strange coincidence,' Lottie said. 'Coincidences can happen from time to time, but this stinks of something else entirely. Is there any sign that he might have fallen through the patio doors at the McAllister house?'

'Quite possible. His back has tiny cuts. I'll mention it to the pathologist when she arrives.'

Lottie nodded. 'It's been a long day, Gráinne. Thanks for all your work.'

'Just doing my job.'

The wind gathered pace and the rain dwindled to a soft drizzle. Lottie stared down at Jake Flood's face. He appeared serene, but she knew he had died violently. Poor kid. She groaned at the thought of having to deliver the bad news to his mother and little sister.

About to tell Kirby to widen and secure the perimeter of the scene, she felt eyes on her back. She swung around, searching through the gathering darkness for the source of her unease. All she saw were huddled SOCOs and uniformed gardaí working in silence as the night folded in around them.

Walking down the narrow slope, she was certain there had been eyes on her. And that spooked the life out of her.

———

Had she seen him?

The boy hung back under the railway bridge, against the mossy wall. She'd glanced all around as if looking for someone. He wanted to get away, but he had a job to do.

After he'd heard the sirens, he'd followed the sound and skirted around by the main road to enter the canal path via the railway. On arrival, he'd kept a safe distance. He didn't like what he was seeing. It sure looked like Jake that they'd pulled out of the canal. A cold shiver of fear travelled the length of his spine and he shuddered.

He sat up straighter on the saddle, leaning one hand against the wet bricks. One foot on the pedal, the other on the ground.

He didn't like this and he wasn't sure if he should send a text or not. He honestly didn't know what to do.

Watching the tall, leggy detective talking to one of the forensic people, who looked like Casper the ghost in the dying light, he wondered what had gone wrong. Was this because of Lucy? Could it mean that Jake's little sister was in danger too? Uneasiness pumped goose bumps up on his arms under his thin wet jacket. He didn't like this at all.

He slipped the phone back into his pocket, telling himself there'd be time enough later on to send the text. Or maybe tomorrow.

As he turned the bike, a slimy fat rat came up from the reeds and ran across his path. He nearly fucking screamed his head off. Stopped himself just in time by jamming his hand into his mouth.

Then, like the rat, the kid slunk off as quickly as he could through the darkness.

42

The rain had stopped and the last of the evening light had disappeared as Lottie shrugged on her jacket and made her way to the front door of 16 Brinsley Terrace, Jake Flood's home. She'd left Kirby at the scene – proper protocol to have a senior member of her team there to meet the state pathologist – and rushed to the station, where she'd commandeered Garda Lei, who'd been on his way out after an extended shift. He'd readily agreed to accompany her.

'Try it again,' she told him after he'd received no reply. The interior hall light was on, and she stepped back, checking the upstairs rooms.

'Maybe they're out searching for Jake or the car,' he said.

'The car is either burned out or in a ditch in another county by now. We'll find it and hopefully be able to lift some evidence from it.' If Sean had been honest from the get-go about his four-in-the-morning trek, when he'd seen the car fly by him, would things have turned out differently? Would they have found Jake alive? But it was no use speculating. Deal with the facts. That was her job. Jake was dead and her immediate task was to break the news to his family.

Lei pressed the doorbell again while knocking on the glass pane. Opening the letter box, he bent down and shouted, 'Mrs Flood? It's Garda Lei with Inspector Parker. Please open the door.'

As he straightened, a shadow appeared behind the door. Too small to be Liz.

Lottie held her breath, trying to align words in the correct order before she'd have to utter them. She heard a chain being pulled back. The door opened a fraction and two frightened green eyes stared out.

'Sharon, remember me? I spoke with you and your mum earlier today.'

'I'm not stupid.'

'I know you're not. Is your mum here?'

'No. What do you want?'

'Where is she?'

'Out. Looking for Jake. Did you find him?' Her eyes brightened momentarily.

The door opened another fraction and Lottie saw glitter sparkling on Sharon's Disney princess pyjamas. It could be Belle or Elsa; she wasn't sure which and it didn't matter. She was about to destroy a little girl's world.

'Can we come in, Sharon? We'll phone your mum.' Lottie wondered at Liz leaving her daughter alone. Was it a regular occurrence? In normal circumstances she could report her to child services, but this was anything but normal.

'Where's Jake?' Sharon opened the door fully, her face gleaming with hope as she peered around Lottie. 'Did you bring him home?'

Lottie put an arm around the girl's shoulders. 'Why don't we go inside? Garda Lei will contact your mum.'

Sharon resisted. 'You're going to tell us Jake's dead. I know you are.' With that, she screamed and fled up the stairs.

'Phone her mother and get her back here quickly.'

'Are you going upstairs?' Lei asked dubiously.

'I am.'

'But what about ... you know ...' He stalled as if unsure he was in any position to question a superior. 'Think about child protection protocols.'

'I don't care, to be honest. That little girl is about to have her heart broken all over again. I need to comfort her.'

'Again?'

'You're already aware her daddy died last year, and I know what that can do to a child. Get busy and find her mother.'

Lottie knocked on the open door and peered round. 'Okay if I come in, Sharon?'

The girl was sitting in the middle of her bed, a pillow clutched to her chest, her head buried in the softness. Another princess adorned the duvet. Snow White this time.

'Can I sit beside you?'

'Don't care,' she sobbed.

Lottie sat on the end of the bed, thinking how Boyd would be better able for this. He had a way with kids that she hadn't, even though she was the mother of three, and up until a few weeks ago, Boyd had believed he was the father of none. Manifesting his calm and soothing spirit, she reached out her hand and laid it on Sharon's tear-stained arm.

The child continued to sob. 'Jake said he'd bring home chicken nuggets and chips for me, but he never came home and I promised not to tell Mam he'd gone out.'

'It's okay.'

'It's all my fault.'

'No, it's not. No one is blaming you for anything, Shaz.' Lottie inched along the bed and raised the girl's chin with her finger so that she could look into her tear-filled eyes. 'Did Jake ever do anything like that before?'

'He wouldn't go off and leave me and not come back. He just wouldn't.'

Lottie heard the front door open and slam. Voices downstairs.

'Mam's home.' Sharon leapt off the bed and scuttled out the door.

By the time Lottie reached the kitchen, Liz was standing by the kettle, her hand smoothing Sharon's hair, throwing dagger stares at Garda Lei. He was shifting from foot to foot, clearly at a loss in the situation.

'Liz,' Lottie said, 'I think you should sit down for this.'

'Don't give me orders in my own house. The two of you shouldn't be alone with a ten-year-old child. There must be rules against that. It's not right.'

And you shouldn't have left her alone, Lottie thought. Avoiding Garda Lei's uncomfortable shuffling, she pinned the woman with her gaze.

'I have news about Jake and I'd prefer it if you'd sit down. Garda Lei can make you a cup of tea.'

Dragging her daughter by the arm, Liz marched towards her. 'I don't want a fucking cup of tea. I want my son. Have you found him? Why aren't you out looking for him like I was? I've tried his friends, scoured the town, but he's nowhere to be found.'

As she ran out of steam, Lottie pulled out a chair and guided the distraught woman to it. Sharon stood by her mother's side. Liz held her close.

'I'm so sorry,' Lottie said, 'but I have very bad news. Jake—'

A strangled wail escaped from Liz's mouth. She kept shaking her head. 'No. No. No! I don't want to hear it. Sharon doesn't want to hear it. Stop.' She clamped her hands over her ears.

'I'm afraid we found him a short time ago. I'm truly sorry, but your son is dead.'

In that moment, Lottie felt an uncontrollable hatred for her job. No mother should have to tell another that she'd no longer be able to hug her son, to kiss his hair, praise or even chastise him. It broke her heart over and over again, and sometimes she just wanted to run away. But someone had to do it.

She worked at controlling her emotions and allowed Liz a few moments to digest her horrible words.

'We will have questions for you, but that can wait until tomorrow. Is there anyone I can call to stay with you?' She wondered if she could pull in Lynch to act as FLO. Failing that, she'd ask Garda Brennan to sit with them.

'How? Where? My poor boy.' Liz wiped her nose with the back of her hand. Sharon had moved away and was taking mugs from the cupboard. Keeping busy. Like an adult.

'We found his body ...' What could she say? 'In the canal.'

'He couldn't have drowned. He's a good swimmer. It's not him.'

'I'm afraid it's definitely Jake.'

'Did he fall in? Did anyone see him?'

'The post-mortem will determine how he died, but we are treating his death as suspicious.'

'Someone killed my little boy? Is that what you're telling me?' Liz's manic eyes bored into Lottie's soul, then she cried out again in grief and slapped her hand over her mouth to stop her scream escaping.

'It's an awful shock, I know,' Lottie said.

'*You* know? How the hell would you know?' Liz's voice rose in pitch with each word. 'No one murdered your son. No one took your husband away from you after he'd battled cancer. No one—'

'Believe me, I do know. I've been through a similar heartache.' She wasn't about to fill Liz in on her grief over Adam's death. She still felt like she was floundering, rudderless.

'I'm sorry,' Liz said, contrition in her tone now, her voice reduced to a whisper. 'I didn't mean any harm. I just can't believe my Jake is never coming home again.'

'You need to rest. I'll get somebody to stay with you for the night.'

'We can manage on our own.' Sharon placed a mug of tea in front of her mother. Lottie hadn't even heard the kettle boil.

'Is there a neighbour who can come here until I get an officer round?'

'We're fine with each other,' Liz said, placing a hand on her daughter's. 'We don't need anyone else.'

'I insist.'

'I can stay,' Garda Lei said. 'Mrs Flood, Liz, I really think you should have someone with you. The media will be hammering down your door before morning. I can deal with everything while you get some rest.'

'I'd give anything to have Jake back. I'd swap places with my son right this minute if it would bring him back.'

'I know,' Garda Lei said. 'I still want to stay.'

'Sure,' Liz said. 'If you're going to be a bollix about it, you might as well.'

43

Lottie plugged her phone in to charge and stretched out on the lumpy old couch, listening to the wind moaning against the single-glazed windows. They rattled like hell during a February storm, but tonight it was like the wind was attempting to soothe her to sleep. Difficult task, considering her feet were hanging over the end of the couch. The fire had gone out and the room was cold.

Her family were all home and settled in for the night. Katie had taken Louis into her bed after he threw a tantrum wanting to sleep with Granny Rose. Chloe had busied herself deep-cleaning the kitchen. That had shocked Lottie more than anything. Normally the girl was more interested in deep-cleansing her face.

Sean was probably still on his PlayStation. He needed to sleep. *She* needed to sleep. It refused to come. Maybe it was the adrenaline coursing through her veins from seeing Jake's body. Or was it the heartache of informing his family? Whatever the cause, sleep was floating too far off on the horizon to be reeled in.

Glancing at her phone, she noticed three missed calls from

Boyd. Damn. She'd put it on silent at the canal, forgetting to switch it back.

She flung off the duvet and swung her legs to the floor, then pulled her old sweatshirt – Katie's really – over her head and walked barefoot into the chilly kitchen. At least it was sparkling clean. The lights flickered and she silently prayed, because she didn't fancy a trip to the basement to check the fuse box.

After she'd filled the kettle and put a tea bag in a mug, she phoned Boyd.

'Hi,' he said. 'All okay?'

'Yeah. Sorry I missed your calls. Phone was on silent and I forgot—'

'Thank God. I was worried when I saw your name flash up there. Do you know what time it is here?'

'Shit, Boyd, I forgot about the time difference. How are things? Sergio doing okay?'

'He wants to be a detective. Over my dead body and if he isn't banged up for theft before that.'

Lottie laughed. 'What did he do?'

She made her tea as she listened to Boyd's tale, comforted by his voice. A softness settled in her stomach. From the milky tea, or something else entirely?

'So what had Terry Starr to say about Lucy?'

'Not a lot. Said she didn't get on with her mother.'

'I'll follow that up with the McAllisters.' She settled herself at the table. 'What did you make of Terry Starr?'

'Nice enough. He mentioned that he'd felt lost when he was Lucy's age and he recognised it in her. He had the start of a black eye. Probably from training. Might be no harm to run a background check on him. And confirm which flight he took over here. Just to be sure.'

'I'll put Kirby on that.'

'Sergio said Jackie likes Terry. Wonder what that's all about.'

'You still don't know where she is?'

'I'd say she's living the high life somewhere on the Costa. Probably with a criminal gang leader.'

'You really have no faith in your ex-wife, Boyd.'

'She put me through too much hardship for me to ever trust her. Wait until you meet Sergio, though, you'll love him. He's a great kid, and that's why I can't understand how she could abandon him and just disappear.'

Lottie felt nervous. How was this new dynamic going to work out? A blended family, or would she lose Boyd?

'Jackie knew you'd care for him; that you'd never deny your own flesh and blood.'

'She's too bloody clever.'

She laughed. 'Maybe you should try to reach out to her before you come home.'

'She can fuck right off.'

'Boyd, stop.'

'You're right. Tell me about your day and how the investigation is progressing. I miss all that.'

Lottie updated him on Lucy's case and Jake Flood, then filled him in about Rose. 'You know my mother, Boyd, it'll take a lot more than a cold or flu to finish her off.'

'You were worried enough to bring her to your house. I wish I was there with you.'

'Me too. Rose would do anything for you without complaint. But I have to take the brunt of her sharp tongue and bow to her demands.'

'Give her a chance.'

'I'm just tired.'

'Sergio wanted a siesta when we came back this afternoon and I swear I slept for two hours.'

'You're settling into fatherhood despite yourself, Boyd.'

'Don't know about that. I miss you, and in a few more days I'll be home.'

'Looking forward to it.'

'I'll ask around tomorrow about Terry Starr and the McAllisters.'

'Really appreciate that.' She finished her tea. 'Jake Flood, the boy we found dead this evening, trained for a local boxing club. Ask Terry about that if you conveniently bump into him.'

'I will. Had this Jake any connection to Lucy McAllister?'

'He was dealing at her party and I'd love to get hold of his supplier.' She rinsed her mug, holding the phone between chin and shoulder. 'We have a suspect, Hannah Byrne, with blood under her nails, but there's also a cryptic email on Lucy's laptop. Seems she was secretly planning a few days away last weekend. I still have to get to the bottom of that.'

'You will.'

'First I'd better try to get some sleep, despite the couch cramping my style. Keep in touch.'

'Goodnight, Lottie. Love you and miss you.' He blew a kiss down the phone and she felt her cheeks heat up.

She paused, listened to him breathing softly. Eventually she said, 'Miss you too.'

After the call ended, she stared into her empty mug. Why hadn't she told him about Sean?

In the sitting room, the wind continued to moan deep into the night. When Lottie eventually fell asleep, she dreamed of a boy bleeding, screaming and drowning in thick green water.

The boy in her dream wasn't Jake, though.

It was Sean.

44

SUNDAY

Lottie's eyes felt as if they were weighed down with two bags of coal. She pulled out the chair and sat heavily at her desk. Garda Thornton put his head around the door.

'Car belonging to Liz Flood has been found.'

'Where?' Lottie stifled a yawn. It was a while since she'd worked on a Sunday and subconsciously her brain was telling her she should be off.

'On the waste ground near the fire station. That's the good news.' Thornton paused, hand on door as if ready to escape once he'd delivered the bad news.

Lottie steadied herself. 'Hit me with it.'

'It's burned to a crisp.'

Thornton hadn't been wrong, Lottie thought as she approached the burned-out remains of the Fiat Punto. By the time the fire brigade had been alerted earlier that morning, it was too late to salvage anything worthwhile that might reasonably be used as evidence. SOCOs might find a clue, though. No harm in hoping.

With Kirby trailing behind her, she walked slowly around the blackened steel trying to avoid inhaling the fumes.

'I doubt even our best forensic expert will get anything from that ash pile.' He caught up with her, zipping his jacket against the morning drizzle.

'You never know. Are we sure it's Liz's car?'

'Yeah, even though the licence plates are scorched beyond recognition, it has to be hers. The chassis number will confirm it.'

'Jake couldn't have burned it. His body was found before the car was set ablaze. Another blind alley we've walked into. What am I missing here, Kirby?'

'Motive?'

'Exactly.'

'With traffic and dash cams, I can work backwards from the time it was found to trace its movements.'

'Work on it with McKeown.'

Kirby groaned and puffed out his cheeks, ready to launch into a criticism of his colleague.

She'd heard it all before. Holding up a hand to shush him, she said, 'See what you can find out without killing each other. I've enough of that carry-on with my girls at home. But first we're going to the boxing club. No better time to see what Jake got up to with Ragmullin Goldstars.'

The boxing club was located in what had once been a gym in the defunct squash club building.

Kirby strolled in her wake. 'This place is in shocking condition.'

She scuffed her shoes through the weeds sprouting between the cracks on the pavement. 'It could certainly do with an over-haul. I heard it's earmarked for houses.'

'It's such a small site, but I suppose developers would have us living in matchboxes if they could make a quick euro. Heard they're after the old army barracks too.'

Lottie stopped outside the door, noticing the cracked paint and the natural wood poking through. 'I need you to concentrate.'

'Sure, boss.'

Inside, she located the gym. The air was stale and smelled of sweat. The high, narrow windows allowed in little light, and fluorescent tubes hung from chains high overhead. The centre of the floor was taken up with a boxing ring, and three punch-bags swung from hooks secured to the ceiling. A series of weights lined the floor to their right. A couple of lads sat on benches in a corner. A man in baggy grey tracksuit bottoms and a shiny blue basketball vest marched up and down in front of them, shouting.

'Hello,' Lottie said, flashing her ID. 'Can I have a word?'

The youngsters seemed relieved as their tormentor turned to face her.

'You've just ballsed up an intense training session.'

'Sorry about that.' She wasn't. 'What's your name, sir?'

'Barney Reynolds. I coach these wastes of space. How can I help you?'

He grabbed a towel from the bench, twisting it around his thick neck, his greying hair damp from perspiration. The muscles on his upper arms protruded like taut ropes. A crooked nose, obviously broken a number of times, accentuated a scar from his ear to his mouth. It gave him a perpetual unnatural smile.

'Anywhere private we can talk?' she asked.

Reynolds sighed. 'The office. Follow me.'

The office turned out to be a room so small it must have been originally a cupboard.

'It says inspector on your ID. What brings someone as

important as yourself here?' Reynolds' voice was husky; probably a damaged larynx. She estimated he was in his fifties.

'I'm enquiring about Jake Flood,' she said, keeping it vague,
and leaned against the only filing cabinet in the room.

'Jake?' Barney said, his face unmoving. 'Haven't seen him
since Friday.'

'What can you tell me about him?' She wondered if he
knew the boy was dead.

'Jake is a talented kid. Likes to win. He's not perfect, but
he's getting there. If only ...' He seemed to think better of what
he was about to say and pressed his lips in a tight line.

'If only what?'

He shook his head. 'Nah, I don't want to get the kid into
trouble.'

'I doubt you will now.'

'Oh?'

Lottie kept her gaze fixed on him. He sat on the edge of the
tiny desk.

'We're trying to trace Jake's movements. Was he training
here yesterday?'

Reynolds threaded his knobbly fingers along his stubbled
chin. 'Is he in trouble?'

'Just answer the question,' Kirby said.

'No, Jake wasn't training yesterday. Saw him Friday. He
was here from two till four.'

'Do you have any idea where he was Friday night or yesterday?' Lottie pressed.

The scarred smile never wavered, and though his hands
ceased stroking his jaw, Reynolds' gaze refused to meet hers. 'I
don't have a clue.'

She couldn't be certain, but she thought his eyes were
shifty. 'Are you aware of any link between this club and a group
of youngsters who go round on bikes pushing drugs?' It was a
long shot, but what the hell.

Even though his smile remained fixed, Reynold's ruddy complexion deepened in colour. 'Jake has nothing to do with them wasters.'

Lottie pushed on. 'I have reason to believe he was selling drugs for this gang. Know anything about that?'

'Jake's ambitious. He wouldn't get caught up with that crowd. No way.' Reynolds was incandescent.

'Are any of those kids involved in the club?'

He seethed, knuckles whitening as he grasped the edge of the desk behind him. She thought he would surely crack the light timber.

'I'd never allow that scum to be associated with my club. If it turns out Jake is involved with them, he's out on his ear.'

Changing direction, Lottie asked, 'Do you know a girl called Lucy McAllister?'

'Of course I do. Her father funded this place to get it up and running. Terry Starr pumped in a few quid too. He's a champion boxer.'

'Lucy ever show up here?'

'You're joking me, right?'

'I'm conducting a murder investigation, so no, Mr Reynolds, I'm not joking.'

'Murder?'

'That's right.'

'You're really confusing me now.'

'Lucy McAllister was found murdered at her home yesterday morning. I can't be any clearer than that.'

'You're taking the piss.' He swallowed hard, his Adam's apple bouncing under the skin. 'You're not, are you?'

'I'm deadly serious.'

'Poor Albert. Why did no one tell me? I'll have to ring him. Christ, where's my phone?'

'Is this the first you've heard of it?'

'Yeah, yeah. I've been flat out. We have the Leinster championship next week. I never heard a dicky bird. Shit. This is bad.'

'Yes, it's bad.' It's even worse, Lottie thought. She still had to break the news to him about Jake. 'What can you tell me about Lucy?'

'I only know her to see.'

'Do you train girls as well as boys at this club?'

'Sure. You have to realise the majority of the kids here are from the Brinsley estate. They find their true worth inside these mouldy old walls. I do my best. I really do. Of course some slip through the net ...'

'Who do you mean?' She was trying to keep track as he jumped from one thing to the next.

'Maybe you're right about Jake. Maybe he is mixed up with the wrong crowd.'

'How do you come to that conclusion all of a sudden?' Frustration chewed at her and she clenched her hands into fists. Initially he knew nothing, now he knew it all. It was difficult to get a proper handle on him.

'Jake's been a bit on edge lately. Jumpy whenever I shouted at him. And believe me, shouting is what gets them to listen. Some of these kids live in environments where only a yell will make them pay attention. It's not drugs, though. I'd recognise the signs.'

'You know his father died a year ago?'

'Sure, but Jake changed more recently. Can't put my finger on it.'

'Are you positive you don't know what was bothering him?'

Reynolds shook his head. 'No idea at all. I'll have a chat with him. He's our best hope of a medal.' His cheeks lost their heightened colour. 'Please don't tell me you're looking for Jake in connection with the girl's death.'

Time to break the news that his prodigy was no longer around to win any medals.

'I'm really sorry to be the one to tell you this, Mr Reynolds, but we pulled a body from the canal late yesterday evening. We believe it to be Jake Flood.'

The same unnatural smile remained plastered to the man's face.

'Don't you have anything to say?' she asked.

'I ... I can't believe it. It must be a mistake.'

'There's no mistake.'

He leaned against the desk, shaking his head. 'Why would he do that?'

'Do what?'

'Do away with himself.'

'We believe he was murdered.' She had no confirmation yet, but it was obvious Jake hadn't beaten himself, tied his own hands and thrown himself into the canal.

'You mean ... you can't mean ... There's two murders?'

'Yes, and both have connections to this club.'

'I'm in complete and utter shock. I'll have to close the gym. Mark of respect. Who am I going to get to fill in for Jake next week? This is a godawful nightmare.'

'It is indeed. Especially for his mother and sister.' People were grieving and Reynolds was worried about getting someone to replace Jake in a boxing competition. Human nature confounded her at times. 'I need you to tell me the names of Jake's friends. Or enemies.'

'Never saw him with anyone.' He wiped his face with the towel, and with the movement of his arms, his acrid body odour clouded the air.

She readied herself to leave. 'I want you to think carefully about anything that might be relevant to my investigations. When you come up with something, call me.' She handed over her card. 'By the way, are you any relation to Brontë Harrison?' Lottie recalled the DJ's wife's maiden name from their checks.

'She's my daughter.'

That brought her up sharp. 'Really? She's married to Richie, the DJ?'

'My Brontë could've had the pick of anyone, but no, she goes and marries a loser.'

'No love lost there, then?'

'I love my daughter dearly. That's all I have to say on the matter.' He slipped his phone out of his pocket. 'Now if you're finished, I've calls to make.'

'I'll let you get on with it,' Lottie said, thinking she was far from finished.

She'd need to be armed with more than suspicion to take it any further. However, Barney Reynolds, his daughter and her husband had all slotted into the cross hairs of her investigation.

———

I am all a-flap. Worried.

That little fecker's death is all over the news. His body was found too soon after Lucy's. I need to speed up if I am to claim the ultimate prize for myself. Magpies can swoop in and plunder a nest without fear, so why have I waited this long? I need to flap my majestic wings and grab her for myself. Young and untouched until my hands caress her soft flesh. To inhale her youthful scent. To send me into wild oblivion. But the scent is never enough, like when I found photos were no longer enough to satisfy me. Videos sufficed for a time, but then they too waned in their appeal. I might be a voyeur, but I'm also a thief. A thief watches, makes sure the coast is clear and then dives in and steals the treasure. Like the magpie.

And I am the magpie. A plunderer of nests. Once my eyes latch on to a treasure, I snatch it for myself without delay.

With that thought my worry flies away, leaving me with a solid conviction. It is my time.

Beware, pretty one, I am swooping in low and fierce. For you.

45

Hannah's mother had booked a taxi to bring her home from the hospital because she couldn't get out that early with Olly. She'd been discharged at seven a.m. They needed the beds, the nurse had told her, and the gardaí said it was okay to go home and stay there, for now.

'They won't give me the results of the blood tests,' she told Babs once she was inside the door.

The apartment felt smaller, even though she'd only been in hospital for one night. Was it because she'd been in a clean, sterile ward that made her detest the state of her home? She still felt nauseous and disorientated.

'Once the hospital have your results, the guards will get them,' Babs said, clattering dishes and banging cutlery against the edge of the sink.

'Surely there's data protection or something. I have a right to get my own results.'

'You have a right to absolutely nothing at the moment. They are out to charge you with Lucy's murder, so you better come up with a better defence than data bloody protection.'

Hannah hadn't seen her mother this angry or nervy since

she'd started AA a year ago. She moved closer to the sink, where Babs was torturing her hands under hot water, and sniffed.

Babs swung around, water flying everywhere. 'And you needn't be at that. I wasn't drinking, though I was this close.'

Hannah knew her mother was desperately trying not to cry. Olly obliged with a scream and threw his Thomas engine against the wall.

'Amuse him, Hannah. I can't cope with him today.'

Hannah knelt on the floor and played trains with her little brother, keeping her eyes fixed to her mother's back. It was obvious Babs thought she had killed Lucy.

If her mother didn't believe in her, what hope did she have?

46

Lottie took Garda Brennan with her to Jake Flood's house.

She'd dropped Kirby off at the station, telling him to liaise with Lei when the garda returned, and to investigate the kids dealing drugs. She needed to know if there was anything on the radar linking them to the youth boxing club. Hannah had been sent home from the hospital, but there was still no word on what drugs had been in her system. Lottie would have to check on her once she was finished with Liz Flood.

Sharon opened the door. 'Mam is asleep. She cried all night. Don't wake her.'

'Where is she?'

'In the sitting room.'

Sharon led them into the kitchen, still wearing her Disney pyjamas. Today Lottie thought the little girl was more like a big girl in child's clothing.

Garda Lei was sitting at the table.

'Did you get any sleep?' Lottie asked.

'A little.'

'Detective Kirby needs a hand at the station.' Seeing the

fatigue in his eyes, she added, 'If you want to catch a few hours' rest first, that's fine.'

'It's no bother.'

'You'll have to walk,' Lottie said.

'The fresh air will blow the cobwebs off. See you later, Shaz.'

Sharon gave him a slow wave and stood awkwardly, biting her lip.

Lottie said, 'I wonder if I can take a look around Jake's room?'

'I should ask Mam, but I suppose it's okay.'

'I'll be as quiet as a mouse. This is Martina. You can stay down here with her, or come up with me if you'd prefer?'

'I'd like to go with you.'

Following the child up the stairs, Lottie felt her heart tug at the sight of Sharon's thin little ankles. Such a torment that had been visited upon this family. It wasn't fair.

Jake's bedroom was no more than a box room. A large poster of a local band, the Blizzards, was pinned above the single bed. It covered most of the wall.

'Dad liked them,' Sharon said. 'That's why Jake has the poster and Dad's T-shirts.'

Lottie checked out the bed. Plain blue cotton sheets. A three-legged wooden stool in place of a bedside cabinet, with a lamp, an empty Coke can and an opened packet of Haribos. The scuffed floorboards were littered with T-shirts. A pair of inside-out jeans lay on the bed.

'Did Jake have a phone?'

'Yeah. Mam says he has it glued to his hand.'

It's in the bottom of the canal or burned in the car, Lottie thought. 'Any laptop?'

'Just his PlayStation. It's connected to the telly in the sitting room and you're not going in there to wake Mam.'

'I won't.'

The single wardrobe held very little clothing. A school uniform hung there, the shirt collar and underarms sweat-stained. Sharon went over and held the shirt to her nose.

'It smells just like him. He sprayed himself in Lynx before he went out. I like Jake's smell.' She let the shirt drop back, life-less on the hanger, and this broke Lottie's heart a little bit more.

'You loved your brother, didn't you?'

Sharon sat on the bed, tongue stuck to the inside of her cheek, trying hard not to cry. She pulled the jeans onto her knee. 'He was the best brother in the world.'

'Did he buy you nice things? You know, for your birthday and Christmas?'

'He had no money. He used to say, "We have nothing but we have each other." He sometimes brought me home a bag of chips when he went out. And chicken nuggets if I begged him.'

'He was a good brother to you. Did he often go out at night?'

'Suppose so.'

'Every night?'

'Only when Mam was working late. The weekends and that.'

'Did he tell you where he used to go?' Lottie was thinking that the chips and nuggets were a bribe to keep Sharon quiet about his escapades.

The girl shook her head slowly, tears now running silently down her cheeks.

'Sharon, if you know, you have to tell me.'

'I promised.'

'You're not breaking a promise, sweetheart. You'll be helping me find the bad person who took Jake away from you.'

'I'm no snitch.' She gathered her brother's jeans into a ball and caressed the hard denim. 'Jake's good. He's not friends with bad people.'

'Do you know any of the bad people?'

She shook her head vigorously. 'They'll come and kill me

and Mam, like they killed Jake. I'm not a snitch,' she repeated tearfully.

'Sharon, no one will hurt you.'

'Yes they will, so they will. They hurt Jake and he was their best asset.'

Strange vocabulary for a ten-year-old to use. 'Is that what Jake told you?'

A series of silent nods.

Lottie knelt on the floor, trying to get the girl to look at her. 'Sharon, you must tell me who these people are. If I know about them, I can protect you and your mother.'

'I don't know them. I don't.' Sharon shook her head so hard, her tears flew into Lottie's face.

'Have these bad people anything to do with the gang on bikes, maybe?'

Was that an imperceptible nod?

The door burst inwards and Liz stormed over to envelop her little girl in her arms. 'What do you think you're doing? Terrorising my child. It's child abuse, you hear me, child abuse!'

Lottie stood. There was no point in arguing with the distressed mother, but she tried to placate her. 'I'm sorry, Liz, but time is critical in murder investigations. I need to know everything Jake might have told you or Sharon about who he was meeting on the nights he was out.'

'What do you mean? Out? He wasn't out and he wasn't meeting anyone. He was a fifteen-year-old kid.'

Not wanting to betray Sharon's trust, she said, 'Jake stole your car, Liz. We found it burned out on waste ground. I know he couldn't have set it alight, so it's likely he was involved with someone else, maybe a gang.'

'Burned out? No.' Liz held her daughter even tighter.

'Your insurance should cover malicious damage,' Lottie said, though the fact that her uninsured and underage son had stolen it might mean she'd get nothing.

'It won't ... I couldn't afford ... Oh forget it. It's just a heap of rust. I hardly used it. Can you leave us alone now?'

'Martina will stay with you.'

'We're fine on our own. Just go.'

About to leave, Lottie noticed a nail head sticking up from the floorboards near the leg of the bed. There was a rough edge to the board and it was slightly raised. She decided to lift it without asking permission, because in Liz's current mood it would surely be denied.

'Just a minute, what are you doing?' Liz said as Lottie knelt down.

Undaunted, she tugged at the nail. The board lifted easily, revealing a cavity between the floor and the ceiling of the room below.

'I don't understand,' Liz said, her voice quivering.

Lottie reached in.

Lying in its underfloor grave was a clear plastic bag. Inside it were at least half a dozen vials containing a bluish liquid. If she wasn't mistaken, this was GHB, commonly known as the date rape drug.

She held up the bag, questioning Liz with her eyes.

'I had no idea,' the woman whispered, shaking her head incredulously.

Lottie believed her.

———

Sharon couldn't bear to watch her mother crying any longer. After she let the detective out the front door, she was surprised that the other guard remained standing in their kitchen.

'Why aren't you leaving too?'

'My name is Martina.'

'I know that.'

'I'm here for you and your mother.'

'We don't need you.'

'I want to keep you both safe and keep the reporters away.'

'What's that supposed to mean?'

'When word gets out about Jake, they will try to talk to your mother.'

'What word? Jake didn't do anything wrong. That stuff hidden in his room, it's not his.'

'Don't worry. Everything will be sorted out.'

Sharon turned away. With Jake gone, who would mind her when Mam was at work? No one, that was who. The pretty guard wouldn't be around forever.

Gulping down a sob, she twisted the bottom of her pyjama top into a knot. What if the bad man who'd killed her big brother came for her next? Was he a toxic man? Poisonous and dangerous? Yes, he was.

'Hey, sweetie, don't cry.'

The pretty guard was holding out a tissue.

Sharon took it and blew her nose. 'It's not fair, so it's not.'

'You loved your brother very much, didn't you?'

'Yeah, and I loved my daddy and he's gone too. I hope my mam doesn't die …'

She felt an arm slip around her shoulders.

'I won't let anything happen to her. Want to help me make breakfast?'

'Not hungry. I've to get dressed because I want to call round to my friend Charlene.'

'I'll boil the kettle in case your mother wants tea.'

Upstairs, Sharon found her mam fast asleep on Jake's bed, his jeans cradled in her arms the way you'd hold a baby. The gap in the floor where he'd hidden his secret was still there. Sharon wasn't stupid. Whoever Jake was keeping the little bottles for might know he'd had them in the house. What would happen when they came looking for them? No matter how nice Martina was, there was no way she could save Sharon and her mother when the bad men knocked on the door. They probably wouldn't even knock.

She had to find them first and tell them the guards took the stuff. Then she had an idea. She emptied her money box into a sweet bag. Dressing quickly, she crept down the stairs and out the front door, tugging it ever so softly so as not to alert pretty Martina.

Without a backward glance, she ran down the terrace and through the tunnel under the canal.

She had to stop them before someone else died.

———

When Boyd raised the blinds, letting in the morning sunshine, he noticed a man sitting at the tiny table outside the café across the street. He was drinking an espresso, gazing up at the apartment.

Boyd moved out of the direct light. Was there something familiar about the man? The way he slouched his shoulders? He wasn't sure, but he was certain it wasn't the first time he'd seen him.

Sergio was in his room, asleep. He'd be fine for a few minutes, wouldn't he?

Making his decision, Boyd put on his shoes and a light sweater over his shirt. Then he slipped out of the apartment and crossed the road.

47

Lottie ran along the corridor hoping not to bump into Superintendent Farrell. In her office, she slipped off her jacket and shoved her bag under the desk. She photographed the vials before making arrangements for them to be entered as evidence and dispatched to the lab for forensic examination.

In the incident room, she greeted her team. She was glad McKeown had dropped his sly smirk. She had to concentrate on the case. Hopefully he saw it that way too.

'Why had Jake Flood got vials of a drug hidden under the floorboards of his bedroom? If they turn out to be GHB, he had enough to knock out a busy nightclub.' Lottie paced, scratching her head, trying to get a straight-line thought going.

'I've got a lead on the young lads on the bikes.' Garda Lei burst into the room. The door banged into the wall behind him. 'Oh, sorry. Didn't mean ... You know, sorry, the door.'

'What have you got?' Lottie asked, hoping he'd soon learn to embrace composure.

'I called into the bicycle shop on my way back here earlier. It's down the road where Cormac O'Flaherty lives ...'

'Breathe, then tell us.' Lottie wheeled over a chair, indicating for him to sit.

He took a few deep breaths as instructed, and continued.

'Yeah, well, Mr Kenny, he fixes the bikes for our bicycle unit. You wouldn't believe the amount of punctures ... Not relevant. Sorry.' He held up a hand in apology. 'Anyway, I asked him if he ever repaired bikes for teenage lads. Lads that come in with their own money. And he says, are you asking about the youngsters going around who might be selling drugs? Well, you could blow me over with a ...'

McKeown sniggered. Lottie glared at him. Garda Lei waved his notebook in the air.

'Mr Kenny was suspicious of these lads, but never had proof of any wrongdoing to report them. I got the names and addresses, phone numbers too, of three members of the gang. He said he saw another one of them yesterday after you left Cormac O'Flaherty's house.'

'Great work,' Lottie said. 'I've to call to Albert and Mary McAllister, then see Hannah Byrne. She's been discharged from hospital. When I get back, you can come with me to have a chat with the youngsters, Garda Lei. McKeown, I want everything you can find on that PE teacher, Noel Glennon. I need to know if there's any truth in what Sarah Robson alleged, that he was stalking a girl in the school and if so, was that girl Ivy Jones? I need it yesterday.'

———

Noel Glennon hated Sundays, hated days he didn't have to work or train. Work kept him busy. Training kept his mind occupied. It figured then that school holidays were the most boring time for him, especially this year. He hadn't saved enough to travel, so he'd had to abandon his trip to Thailand.

Here he was stuck in his apartment, and the one night he ventured out, a girl was murdered.

Sitting on the damp wooden patio chair, he lit a cigarette, with a second ready to light before the first one even hit the water in the ashtray. Bad for his health, but he didn't give a damn any more.

Scrolling through his phone, he wondered if there'd been any arrests for Lucy's murder. He read that a teenage girl was helping with enquiries. He knew that meant she was a suspect. Hopefully it wasn't Ivy. She was liable to say anything – maybe everything. He couldn't risk that happening.

He'd noticed Ivy's intense jealousy a long time ago. Could she be the reason Lucy had developed scruples in place of her normal cocksure confidence?

He had all their numbers saved in his phone. It had been easy to find them on the school's computerised register. His finger hovered over the one name that might have the answers. Could he? Was he really that stupid? He'd saved her number under 'Vine'. A deadly vine of poisonous ivy. He grinned. Maybe he should have been an English teacher. The way things were turning out, he wouldn't be any kind of a teacher much longer.

Before he could tap the number, he stopped. It was too dangerous to make the call. He lit a third cigarette, then scrolled through his contacts once more. Lucy's number was under 'Snapdragon', a name for one who concealed things, a deceitful person. She'd epitomised deception and now she was dead.

Scrolling again, he came to Hannah Byrne. He had her number saved under 'Jasmine', because of her delicate beauty. Should he call her? Would she even answer him? Could she be the person being questioned?

He needed to be one step ahead of the guards. His freedom depended on knowing everything relevant to the case. But he was at a disadvantage. He couldn't talk to anyone without raising suspicion. In other words, if anyone talked, or the guards found what was buried as deep as the dark web, he was basically fucked.

He blew smoke rings into the sky. Maybe he should pretend to come clean. Try to secure immunity for himself if he became a witness. But he knew if he said anything, he wouldn't live long enough to concoct evidence against anyone.

Lucy McAllister's death was testament to how far some were prepared to go to protect themselves. And he was part of it.

As he watched the smoke ring dissolve, his phone rang.

When he saw the caller ID, he dropped the cigarette and nearly puked into the ashtray.

His past was catching up with him.

Yes, he was well and truly fucked.

48

The Brook Hotel apartment being used by the McAllisters had lost the neatness of the day before. The smell of fried food hung in the air and the table was littered with takeout boxes. Cardboard tubs of congealed rice with what looked like a chicken curry floating in a grease-topped sauce.

When Lottie arrived, Detective Maria Lynch informed her that Albert had left.

Mary McAllister indicated with a wave of her hand for Lottie to sit on a chair close to her. They were facing the window, which looked out over the playground in the town park.

'Children playing on swings and slides,' Mary said. 'Their mothers engrossed in idle chit-chat. Little do they know the anguish and torment ahead of them.' Her voice was a monotone, and Lottie wondered if she'd taken a sedative.

'I'm so sorry this has happened to Lucy.'

'I'm not talking about murder. I'm talking about the act of raising a child through their teenage years to adulthood.' She whirled around so fast Lottie leaned back, expecting a blow. But it was as if Mary had punched her with two dark blue orbs. 'Lucy was not an easy child.'

'What do you mean?'

'I've been thinking all night. She changed after her tenth birthday. It was as if the terrible twos resumed at ten and carried on into the terrible teens. We fought and argued non-stop. She threw tantrums and I let myself down by shouting back at her, making her angrier. Now, when it's too late, I regret all those times I lost control.'

'Life is full of regrets. Don't let this awful act tarnish the good times you had with your daughter.'

'Don't you see? That's just it. I can't think of many good times. We were on a collision course from the day she was born.'

'Why was that?'

'She never took to me. Refused my milk. I had to bottle-feed her when all my friends were breastfeeding theirs. When she took her first steps, she toddled to her dad, not me. When she started school, she wanted him to drive her, not me. It eased for a few years, but then after her tenth birthday it was a downward spiral between us. Albert could do no wrong and I could do no right.'

'Girls and their daddies.' Lottie tried a wry smile, recalling how her children had idolised Adam.

'He bought her everything she coveted. As she grew older, toys became devices. The newest and most expensive on the market – iPads, phones, laptops. Lucy had the best of bloody everything. And she appreciated nothing. Albert still doted on her.'

Lottie saw the simmering resentment straining for release. Mary's face was flushed, hands clenched so hard her knuckles turned white, but her eyes were dry. Was she jealous of Lucy stealing her husband's attention? Or was it something more sinister?

'I spoke to a few people,' Lottie said, struggling to find words to calm the woman. 'From what I can gather, they seem to think Lucy was a sad girl. Do you agree with that sentiment?'

'Sad?' Mary stared at her before turning away to resume her vigil at the window. 'I don't understand what you mean.'

Following her gaze, tracking the squealing kids in the playground, Lottie said, 'I think what they meant was that she was hiding how she really felt.'

'Don't be fooled. I knew her better than anyone. Lucy was the consummate actress. She switched it on and off depending on whether she wanted to impress or ridicule. But she was my daughter. I loved her, and in her own awkward way she loved me too.' Mary turned to look at Lottie. 'This may seem odd to you, Inspector, but I'm going to miss the noise she carried with her through the house. The stomping of feet on the stairs, the tirades of abuse she hurled at me, the mugs she broke against the wall. I'd take all that in a heartbeat if I could have her back again.'

'Why do you think she was so angry with you?'

She shook her head slowly. 'I truly don't know.'

Lottie remained silent, listening to the woman's inhalations and exhalations. Had something extremely dark been going on under the surface of Lucy's life? For all that anger to be directed at her mother, there had to be a reason. Was it an unanswered cry for help? She sat up straighter. Could there have been something dangerous going on that Lucy couldn't verbalise, and this was her way of getting attention?

'Mary, did you ever get your daughter into therapy?'

'I suggested it.' The broken mother shrugged a shoulder. 'She laughed at me. Said I was the one who needed therapy. Little did she know I've been seeing a therapist for most of her life.'

Lottie decided to discuss Lucy's behaviour later with her father. She changed the subject.

'Do you know Hannah Byrne?'

'Was she a friend of Lucy's?'

'She was invited to her party.'

'I'm not sure I've ever met her. I still can't believe Lucy held a party in our house with us away. Then again, maybe I can. She might have wanted to annoy me by leaving a mess for me to face when I walked through the door.'

'Not true. She had organised for Sarah to come in first thing yesterday morning to clean up.'

'I don't ever want to go back to that house.' Mary fixed her lips in a defiant flat line.

'I can understand that. Do you know if Lucy was in a new relationship?'

Another shrug. 'There's so much about my daughter I don't know. Why do you ask?'

'We discovered emails on her laptop that look like she was arranging to be away with someone last weekend. We don't know anything else at the moment.'

'Ask Ivy.'

'She said she doesn't know anything about it.'

'She's probably covering for Lucy. I'll have a word with her.'

'No, it's fine. Where can I find Albert?'

'That man will work himself into an early grave. He said he had important stuff to attend to. He left for the office earlier. He's a workaholic. Even in Spain he was on the phone and computer night and day.'

Lottie wondered how he could concentrate on work after viewing his daughter's lifeless body. Then again, he probably needed to inject some normality into his life in the face of such distress. She knew all about that.

'I'll catch up with him later. I've a few questions for him.'

'He'll paint a different picture of Lucy. She could do no wrong in his eyes.'

'Can you tell me if Lucy was right-handed or left?'

After thinking for a moment, Mary said, 'Right. Why? You don't think she killed herself, do you?'

'Not at all. Did she have any tattoos?'

'No. Why do you ask?

'Just following up on queries from the pathologist.' There was no point in worrying Mary any further by talking about the heart-shaped piece of flesh that had been sheared from her daughter's body.

'Was there anything else, Inspector?'

'Can you tell me any more about your gardener, Cormac O'Flaherty?'

'No, sorry. Ask Albert.' Mary looked out the window again.

'I mentioned Jake Flood yesterday. He was at the party selling drugs. Do you—'

'Drugs in my house?' Mary whipped around and stood up, fire shooting from her eyes like arrows. 'I'd kill Lucy myself if she wasn't already ...' Her voice trailed off with the realisation of what she'd said. She sat down again. 'I'm sorry. A figure of speech.'

'I understand.'

'It's just that Albert is anti-drugs because of the scandals surrounding drugs in sport.' She fixed Lottie with a more lucid gaze.

'Can I ask why Albert would be involved in a local boxing club now that he's an agent for big stars?'

'He said he had to put something back into the community. Philanthropy, he calls it.'

Lottie stood and placed a hand on Mary's shoulder. 'Don't be too hard on yourself. I have two daughters and a teenage son, and more often than not we're at loggerheads. It's all part of the growing-up process. Hating their parents.'

'The difference being, Lucy has no more growing up to do.' A soft sob escaped Mary's throat. 'But thanks for your kind words, Inspector.'

Lottie left the apartment with a heavy heart. No mother should have to suffer like that, and she more than anyone was well aware that regrets could eat you up for the rest of your life, no matter what anyone said.

Sad. Too bloody sad.

Lynch was standing outside the apartment eating a brown-bread salmon sandwich.

'The food here is to die for,' she said with her mouth full.

Lottie attempted to shake off the melancholy roosting on her shoulders. 'Kirby would enjoy a stint here.'

'He's welcome to it. I'd rather be stuck into real detecting than babysitting where I'm not wanted. How did you get on with Mrs Stony Face?'

'She's broken inside. Full of regrets. The main thing I took away is that Lucy was a handful and fought with her mother regularly.'

'If Mary hadn't been in Spain when Lucy died, she'd be my number one suspect,' Lynch said, licking mayonnaise from her lips.

'Why do you say that?'

'She comes across as cold as ice. Not a word of comfort for her husband, and he's crying constantly. Poor man.'

'Don't jump to any conclusions just yet.'

'You have to suspect her. I know this sounds ridiculous, but if things were as bad with her daughter as she said, maybe she hired a hit man.'

'That's far-fetched.'

'Not really.' Lynch was digging her heels in while deciding where next to take a bite out of her delicious-looking sandwich.

'Arranging to have her own daughter killed? I don't buy it. Anyway, Hannah Byrne is still our main suspect. I'm waiting for toxicology and detailed forensic reports before I interview her again. Though even if she is responsible for Lucy's death because of the photo, what reason had she to kill Jake Flood? I have to figure out Jake's role in it all.'

'Well, there's no way Hannah was involved in burning the car. She was in hospital.'

'But Cormac O'Flaherty wasn't. Nor any of the other suspects.' Lottie felt her phone vibrating in her bag. She checked the caller ID before answering. 'Hi, Gráinne. Hope it's good news.'

She listened and gave Lynch a thumbs-up as she ended the call.

'They found Lucy's phone in the McAllisters' garden. Don't tell them yet.'

'My lips are sealed,' Lynch said. 'Or they will be once I finish this sandwich.'

'I'd better talk to Albert, then I'll see what Lucy's phone gives us. Still no word on who sent her the email?'

'Soon as Gary figures it out, I'll contact you. Oh, there was nothing of interest on Hannah's phone.'

'Okay.'

'By the way, Superintendent Farrell was looking for you early this morning.'

'You never saw me.'

Lottie fled down the stairs, knowing she had to act fast to keep ahead of her boss.

49

Albert wasn't at his office. His PA told Lottie he'd left for the Goldstars boxing club shortly after he'd taken a call from the coach, Barney Reynolds.

Lottie scratched her head. What was so urgent the day after his daughter's murder that he had to visit a junior boxing coach?

She drove back to the club feeling like she was going round in circles. The chock-a-block traffic punctured the excitement she'd felt about Lucy's phone being found.

She parked, slammed the door shut and placed her hand on the bonnet of a white Mercedes. Warm. Inside, raised voices echoed from the miniature office; otherwise there was no one about. She walked in just as Albert punched the filing cabinet with his fist.

'Sorry to interrupt, boys.'

'What do you want?' Albert said, then faltered realising who he was talking to. 'Oh, it's you, Inspector.'

'Back so soon?' Reynolds said, seated behind the excuse for a desk.

'What's the row about?' Lottie said.

'No row.' Albert nursed his fist in his other hand.

She leaned against the door jamb. Waiting them out. Hoping one or the other would reveal what was going on. Chance would be a fine thing. They watched her in silence.

'Albert, can you spare me a few minutes?'

'Sure, sure. Barney, make yourself scarce.'

Reynolds squeezed out of the tight space. 'I'll be in the gym if you need me for anything.'

Once they were alone, Albert took the chair. 'I'm sorry you had to walk in on that. Barney panics too easily. He told me about Jake. Do you think the boy is connected to my daughter's death?'

'Early days,' Lottie said.

'What happened to him?'

'I'm working through the events. Need to ask you a few questions.'

'Go ahead.'

'Did Lucy know Jake?'

'She might've heard me talking about him. I doubt she knew him personally.'

'The truth of the matter is that Jake was dealing drugs at her party.'

'What? There's no way she'd have allowed that. Lucy knows ... knew my stance on drugs.'

'Still, Jake was there, and now he's dead. Were you or Barney aware that he was involved in drug pushing?'

'Barney would've thrown him out of here in a flash, no matter how good a boxer he was. Drugs have tainted sport for so long, I have no tolerance for them.'

Time to change direction. 'Tell me about Terry Starr.'

'What about him?'

'He's your main client, isn't he?'

'Yes. He won amateur medals, then turned professional. He's about to become major box-office material.'

'When did you last speak with him?'

'Yesterday afternoon. He rang to offer his condolences.'

'He stays at your Malaga apartment?'

'From time to time.'

'Why is he out there?'

'I don't know.'

'Were you expecting him to be there?'

'He has a key.'

Not an answer. 'But you weren't expecting him?'

'No.'

Kirby had checked and confirmed Terry had been on the first flight to Malaga yesterday morning. But when had it been booked? she wondered.

'You trust him with your apartment?'

'Yes.'

'Like you trusted your daughter to be alone for three weeks?'

'I don't like what you are implying, Inspector.'

'Why did you go to Malaga, Albert? Three weeks was a long time to leave Lucy home alone.'

'We thought she was able to look after herself. We were wrong.'

'This was coming up to and during her exams. Seems heartless to me.'

He picked at a notebook on the desk, turning over page corners. 'It's complicated.'

'Tell me.'

'I received a threat to do with my business. I believed it originated in Spain. I went over to sort it out.'

'What threat?'

'I can't say.'

'Your daughter and a fifteen-year-old boy have been murdered, and you don't want to tell me about a threat you received? Come on, Albert.'

'It's not relevant to Lucy or Jake. It was to do with my work.'

'Let me judge what's relevant and what's not.'

He seemed to be considering his options, because it was a few moments before he spoke again. 'I received an email. I don't know who from, but whoever it was, they were going to expose me for fixing fights and my clients for substance abuse. I was to pay them five hundred thousand euros or they were going to ruin my business. And for the record, I don't fix matches.'

'Did you talk to Terry about this allegation?'

'He flatly denied drug use.'

'Did you take that at face value?'

'I believed him. He's clean. And if you knew Terry you'd believe him too. He gives his time and energy to his sport, even helps the youngsters.'

'And you got this email from someone in Spain?'

'I thought so. I went over there to check with my business associates. I wanted to look them in the eye and see their reactions.'

'Why didn't you report the matter to the gardaí? We have people who could have traced the sender.' Though she wasn't so sure about that. Gary was still having trouble with Lucy's mystery email.

'I was warned not to go to the guards.'

'Right. Did you pay up?'

'No. It takes time to access that amount of money.'

'So you left your seventeen-year-old daughter at home for three weeks with a threat hanging over you? From what I've heard, you doted on Lucy, so that makes no sense to me.' She shook her head emphatically. Albert's actions defied logic.

'The threat was not against my family; it was a threat to my business. They said they'd post the claim on the internet, and once something is online, people judge you without bothering to discover the facts. Mud sticks. It sticks for ever, even after everything is proven to be incorrect.'

'I want to see that email.'

'I'll forward it to you.'

'I want it in the next hour. You should have informed me of this threat yesterday.'

Albert buried his face in his hands, sobbing loudly. 'My baby girl is dead, and now I don't know if it's because I'm a thick-headed bastard whose pride in my work was stronger than my loyalty to my family. You have to find out who killed her.'

His tears made Lottie uncomfortable. She felt in her gut that he still wasn't giving her the whole picture. But with him so upset, there was no point in continuing the conversation.

Too little too late, my friend, she thought. Too little too late.

50

She left the incoherent Albert fruitlessly trying to stem a dam of guilt.

She found it hard to believe that someone would resort to killing his daughter rather than following through on their threat to expose him. It didn't make sense. Techie Gary had better come good with tracing the sender of the emails.

At the McAllister house, Gráinne Nixon was outside by the hot tub.

Breathing in the fresh air, Lottie walked through to the garden, pulling on gloves. The area was expansive. Perfectly cut grass beneath the recent mess. The shrubs lining the perimeter might have been trimmed with nail scissors they were so precisely pruned. Could Cormac O'Flaherty be that gifted?

Even though the air was cleaner than inside, there was no mistaking that the party had spilled outside. Glass, crisps, peanuts and pizza crusts crunched underfoot as she circled the hot tub to face the lead SOCO.

'Where exactly did you find Lucy's phone?' she asked.

'Behind that hedge.' Gráinne pointed towards the symmetrical greenery at the left of the tub.

Inspecting the area, Lottie noted how thoroughly the woman had performed her task. Dry earth had been brushed away from the roots of the bushes.

'Was it buried?'

'Not as such. It was in a little bit, face down like it had been flung or hidden there. I had photos taken before I removed it.'

'Where is it now?'

'Inside. Bagged and tagged.'

'Any sign of the murder weapon?'

'Still searching.'

'Anything suspicious in the tub?'

'It's rank, but no evidence of blood. I'm just being thorough and professional.'

'I like thorough and professional. Good work, Gráinne.'

'Thanks. The shattered glass from the patio door has been sent to the lab for analysis. There's blood on some shards. I'll let you know as soon as we get a match. It's more than possible it's Jake Flood's. The state pathologist confirmed that the wounds to his back were consistent with having been pushed through glass. She extracted fragments embedded deep in the skin of his lumbar region. She'll call you once she has a prelim report.'

Inside the house, Lottie located the phone and signed for it. When she pressed the activate button, the screen flashed on. PIN required. 2% battery. Hopefully she would find clues here to reveal the real Lucy McAllister. But she needed the PIN to unlock it. Another job for the technical team.

She placed the evidence bag containing the phone into her bottomless pit of a handbag. Then, feeling the need to have another look around the house, she climbed the stairs. She wanted to get a sense of Lucy's family life.

After a cursory look in the main bedroom, she made her way into Lucy's room. It was clear that SOCOs had been in. Lucy had been murdered in one of the guest bedrooms at the

end of the landing and her own room bore no evidence of the
bleeding, dying girl having been hurt in it.

It was a typical teenager's room. Lucy had had the luxury of
a queen-sized bed with white linen bedding. Streaks of fake tan
were evident where she and her friends had sat while it dried.
Running her hands under the pillow and mattress, Lottie came
up empty. On the bedside cabinet there was a lamp and a
crystal glass three quarters full of clear liquid. She dipped a
finger in and tasted it. Vodka. She turned up her nose at the
memory of her old habit that she'd overcome. On the dressing
table there was an overcrowded assortment of cosmetics and the
kind of jewellery only a teenager could love.

Opening each of the drawers, she failed to find a diary, and
there were no photos stuck to the mirror. Not unusual – all that
stuff was now kept on phones and the cloud. On her hands and
knees, she looked under the bed. Not even a speck of dust.
Sarah Robson seemed to be more thorough here than in her
own home.

There were no obvious hiding places like she'd discovered
in Jake Flood's room. Though what Lucy might have wanted to
hide, she had no idea.

The en suite resembled a disaster area. Streaks of tan and a
multitude of fingerprints smudged the walls, sink and mirror.
All checked by SOCOs. The towels were teal in colour. Exactly
like the one covered in blood found in Hannah's bag.

An unzipped rucksack lying under the sink bore the name
Ivy Jones. Lottie teased open the flaps. Cosmetics, two tins of
dark tanning mousse and a stained tanning glove. Jeans,
sweater, shirt and underwear. A pair of canvas runners – Lottie
recognised the designer motif. Hardly worn if the soles were
anything to go by. Rich girls. But what about Hannah?

She made her way to the bedroom next door.

The bed was made up; nothing on the dressing table.
Though forensics had been through the room, she glanced

under the bed. Clean and clear. Opened drawers. All empty. On the bedside cabinet she noted a small bottle of perfume, an inexpensive eyeshadow palette and a tube of Primark mascara. Was this the room Hannah had been allocated to get changed in? The cheap cosmetics pointed to that being the case. It made Lottie feel sad for Hannah. The girl had been denied the pre-party fun with the others. Had they treated her as an outcast? If so, it was cruel. Was it motive for murder though?

Seeing nothing else of significance, she sighed. She'd have to wait for the SOCO report. They were still working in the room where Lucy had been found. The phone offered her the best hope of a clue as to why the girl had been murdered.

As she made her way back to her car, she wondered if Sean might be able to remember anything else about his four a.m. visit to the house.

It was worth a try.

And she should really check in on her mother.

51

On her way back from the McAllisters' property, Lottie drove round by her own house.

She was greeted by raised voices coming from the kitchen. *Should have kept on driving.*

Katie and Chloe were standing on either side of the table, feet apart, hands on hips, screaming at each other.

'What's going on?' Lottie had to shout it twice before the girls noticed her in the doorway.

'Oh, you're home,' Chloe said, folding her arms defensively.

'Is something wrong, Mam?' Katie picked up a cloth and began wiping down the table.

'What's the argument about?' Did she even want to know?

'She started it,' Katie said, pointing the damp cloth in her sister's direction.

'Did not.'

'Girls! When did you regress to your childhood? Granny Rose is sick and you're shouting like a pair of fishwives. Act your age. You're supposed to be looking after her. Is she up yet?'

'Not a peep out of her,' Katie said sulkily.

'Did you even check if she wanted a cup of tea and a slice of toast?'

'Thought it best to let her rest.' Katie balled up the cloth and threw it into the sink.

'Hey!' Chloe yelled. 'I spent an hour yesterday cleaning that mangy sink!'

Katie ignored her. 'I'm going upstairs for Louis. He's probably cracking Sean up.'

'Tell your brother I want to talk to him.'

'If he's still alive after an hour of Louis pestering him to play Mario on his Nintendo.'

At least she didn't bang the door as she left.

Lottie sighed, and a headache flared behind her eyes. 'Can't you be civil to each other for a few hours?'

'She's a pain in the arse.' Chloe kept her back to her mother and scrubbed the sink vigorously.

'I could do without this drama.'

'Go back to work then,' Chloe snapped, 'where no one fights.'

'I wish.'

She was saved from being subjected to further snipes from her tetchy daughter when Sean walked in. His blonde hair stood on end and he was wearing a creased T-shirt and boxers slung low on his hips. He appeared to have had little sleep. Or maybe it was the Louis effect. Her grandson was full of energy.

'Get dressed, Sean. I want you to come to the station with me.'

'Oh oh,' Chloe sang. 'Was the good little son a bold boy? Is Mama Bear going to lock you up?'

'Shut up, Chloe,' Sean said. 'Have I time for a quick shower, Mam?'

'Not really. Won't take long. I'll get someone to drop you straight home.'

She followed him up the stairs and heard Katie in her room

placating an upset Louis. Glancing into her own bedroom, she found Rose fast asleep. She placed her hand on her mother's forehead. Clammy.

She debated her options. Rose needed to be seen by a doctor. How was she going to manage it? Why did life insist on throwing her curveballs when she was up to her eyes with work?

Downstairs, she approached Chloe. 'I need you to phone the doctor for Granny. She's spiking a temperature.'

'I didn't realise she was that sick. But there's not much point calling the doctor. It's Sunday.'

'Try MIDOC.' The out-of-hours service was based at the hospital.

'Might it be better to bring her to A&E? I can call an ambulance.'

And suffer the wrath of an indignant Rose? No way. 'No. Phone MIDOC. See what they say and let me know.'

'Okay. Should I bring her up a bowl of soup?'

'Not if it's the vegetable concoction Katie made last night.'

'I wouldn't give that to a cat. Don't worry, I'll make it fresh. Granny swears by chicken soup.'

'You're an angel, Chloe. If she's still asleep, leave her be, but keep an eye on her.'

'I will.'

'Why don't you phone Outback and get a Sunday lunch takeaway. Your granny likes their roast beef.'

'Sure, but I'll need your bank card.'

As Lottie rooted around in her bag, she noticed Lucy's phone in its evidence bag and realised how much she had to do. Eventually she found her credit card at the bottom, a lollipop stuck to it. God only knew where she'd find her debit card.

'This is for the restaurant use only. Are we clear?'

'Got it.' Chloe smirked.

When Sean was ready, Lottie was glad to leave her warring

daughters behind, but she was worried about Rose. She felt torn at having to return to work, unable to stay at home to care for her mother.

Her headache increased in intensity.

At the station, she rushed Sean up the stairs, physically pushing him along the corridor until they were safely in her office.

'What was that all about?' he said.

'I'm hiding from Superintendent Farrell.'

'Because of me?'

'Don't worry about it. Sit there while I load these photos.'

'What photos?'

'Give me a minute.' Once she had the relevant crime-scene photo open on the computer desktop, she said, 'Before I show you this, I want to try something. You game?'

'Sure.'

'Good. Close your eyes for a moment.' She waited for him to object, but he acquiesced to her request without complaint. There was no way either of her girls would be so compliant. They'd have to have an argument about it first.

This was something she'd read about but had never tried. Or maybe she'd seen it on Netflix. Whatever, God loved a trier.

'This is like a therapy session,' Sean said.

'Good. Take yourself back to four a.m. yesterday. Visualise yourself walking through the doorway of Lucy's house.'

'Okay.'

'Tell me everything you see as you go in to search for your jacket.'

'I told you this already, but if it helps ...' Sean's body relaxed, legs crossed at the ankles, arms loose on his knees. 'The hall carpet is a mess. There's no jackets or coats hanging up. I move to the kitchen. Bottles and glasses everywhere. No sign of my jacket. I go into the living room. The state of the place. One of the patio doors is smashed. That's when I notice the wall and the floor and the blood. It scares the shite out of me.' He paused, his breathing shallow.

'Did you look around? Search for your jacket? Do you see anything out of place?'

'I don't see my jacket. That's when I hear a noise on the stairs.'

'What does it sound like?'

'Footsteps.'

'Anything else at all?'

'Voices, but I don't wait to find out. I cut my stick and run into the kitchen.' Sean opened his eyes. 'That's it. I've no idea who it was, but I definitely heard voices.'

'Male or female?'

'I heard something that might have been a girl screeching. I think there was a male voice too.' He shook his head. 'But I don't know. I went up the back stairs and found Lucy. That's it.'

Selfishly, she wanted more from him. 'Did you go back into the living room?'

'I glanced in. There were cushions on the couch and a ruck-sack. No jacket.'

'Tell me about the rucksack. Can you recall what it was like?'

He closed his eyes again. 'Blue. It was bright blue. Covered in white daisies. A bit grubby-looking.'

Lottie was glad her son was so perceptive. She was certain it was Hannah's rucksack. She tapped the keyboard to awaken the screen. 'I'm going to show you a photo of the living room. You okay to look at it?'

'Yeah.'

'Right. Now, I want you to point out where you saw that rucksack.'

Sean leaned his elbows on the bundle of files piled on the edge of her desk and studied the image. 'It looks much the same as when I went in. But the rucksack is missing. I saw it on the couch, there.' He pointed to the screen. 'Did the forensic guys remove it?'

'No.'

'So who did?'

'I believe I know who removed it, but what I want to discover is how and when. Thanks, Sean. This is a great help. I'll get someone to drive you home.' She was satisfied that it was Hannah's rucksack Sean had seen shortly after four a.m. in Lucy's house, and a few hours later it was at the foot of Hannah's bed.

'I'll walk. I need the fresh air after reliving those awful images.'

'I'm sorry about all this, Sean.'

'Should have told you earlier. I hope you don't get in trouble with your boss.'

'I can handle Superintendent Farrell. You just need to be careful.'

'You too.'

'Let me know how Granny Rose is. And make sure Chloe calls MIDOC.'

'Stop fussing. Gran will be fine. As long as Katie and Chloe don't kill each other, we can manage. See you later on.'

As her son left her office, Lottie watched him stop and chat briefly with Kirby before he disappeared.

'Kirby, I think it's time we had another word with Hannah Byrne.'

52

'You better not be here to question my defenceless child again,' Babs said. 'Hannah's not well, and for your information, she never hurt that Lucy girl.' She turned away from the door.

Lottie entered the claustrophobic room. Hannah was seated on the mattress, her legs crossed in a yoga pose, hands on her knees, eyes closed. Her hair fell in damp tendrils all around her, like a Tibetan goddess.

'I didn't kill Lucy.' Her voice was as deadpan as her expression.

'I want to ask you about your rucksack,' Lottie said. 'It was on the end of your bed yesterday, before we took it into evidence.'

Hannah's eyes flew open. 'What about it?'

'When did you bring it home?'

'I don't know what you're talking about.' Her words bled into each other as she became more flustered.

'You had your rucksack with you at Lucy's house. It was seen on the couch in her living room at four a.m., but it was gone when forensics took the crime-scene photos later that morning. Now do you understand what I mean?'

Hannah glanced quickly at her mother, silently pleading for help, but Babs was at the small table, shovelling a spoonful of baked beans into Olly's mouth.

She jumped up. 'You shouldn't have taken my property without my permission. Shouldn't you have had a warrant or something?'

Lottie felt sorry for her. She looked so frail and frightened. Was she in the house when Lucy was murdered? Did she leave afterwards with her bag, or did someone else take it and bring it to her? The bloodied towel and the blood under her fingernails pointed to her being present, but Lottie needed something more to arrest her.

'Do you drive?'

'No. Haven't even done a theory test yet.'

'Tell me what you know about Jake Flood.' Lottie knew it was impossible for Hannah to have disposed of Jake's body, because she was in the hospital yesterday until seven this morning. Sean had seen what was probably Jake's car on the road before he reached Lucy's house. Was Jake driving while injured after falling through the patio door? If so, where had he gone and who had killed him? The post-mortem would provide an approximate time of death, but Lottie was certain someone else had to be involved.

Hannah said, 'I swear I never saw him before Friday night.'

Shaking her head, Lottie found she was unable to line up the sequence of events. Just what had gone on in the early hours of the morning that had resulted in two dead teenagers?

'What time did you leave the McAllister house?'

'I told you I can't remember. I must've been drugged. It's the only explanation I have. They took loads of samples at the hospital. Can't you find out the results?'

'Everything will be analysed when we receive them.' Lottie didn't hold out much hope. Too much time had elapsed to identify whether Hannah had been drugged with GHB. 'I want you to come to the station for a few more questions.'

The girl folded her arms defiantly.

'If you refuse, I've no option but to arrest you on suspicion of Lucy McAllister's murder.' She hadn't enough unequivocal evidence to make the charge stick and she might be jeopardising custody time limits, but she needed Hannah to talk.

A crash sounded behind her. Lottie swung around. Babs was standing with a spoon in her hand, the bowl smashed on the floor. Baked beans were scattered everywhere.

'Arrest her? Are you mad? Look at her. Do you honestly believe she could murder someone? Hannah lives for her sport, the only good thing in her life apart from her little brother ...'

'Babs, I just need to question her again, under caution. I don't want to arrest her.' Not yet, Lottie thought. She needed solid evidence without having to rely on suspicion and circumstance.

Babs's face drooped as she fetched a cloth from the sink. 'Hannah, you'd better go with them. I'll find someone to watch Olly and follow on after you.'

'I didn't kill anyone.' Hannah pleaded with Lottie. 'Please, I don't understand why you're fixated on me and my rucksack. Why?' Tears were now streaming down her cheeks, and as the fight left her body, she sagged like a hastily discarded rag doll.

Lottie felt the need to convince her of the gravity of what she faced. 'You have to see this from my point of view. A bloody towel was found in your bag, and blood that we believe belongs to Lucy McAllister was under your fingernails. Your bag was at the victim's house around four a.m., but it was here a few hours later. You need to explain it.'

Hannah's face turned porcelain white, and Lottie had to grip her elbow to steady her as she struggled to get her feet into her runners. Was she purposely wasting time? Lottie felt her patience stretch like a frayed elastic band, ready to snap any second.

Once she had her runners on, Hannah grabbed an oversized white sweatshirt from the back of a chair and kissed her little brother on the top of his head. He held out a hand covered in tomato sauce and smeared the arm of her sweatshirt. She didn't appear to notice.

They left the tiny apartment to the sound of Babs sobbing as she cleaned baked beans from the floor.

53

Boyd ordered a coffee inside the café before making his way back out to the pavement. Without any enquiry, he sat down opposite the man who'd been watching the apartment. He estimated he was in his forties, though it was hard to tell. His fair hair and the sweat on his forehead might indicate he wasn't Spanish, but what did he know?

With a flicker of surprise, the sweaty man raised his sunglasses, settling them on top of his head. He eyed Boyd coldly before fixing a stern expression on his face.

'Who are you and why are you watching me?' Boyd asked without preamble. A waiter placed his mug of steaming coffee on the small blue-tiled table and disappeared.

'You don't need to know who I am. I'm not here to harm you or the boy.' He spoke with an accent. A Spaniard after all.

'You'd better come up with a better explanation, or I'm phoning the police.' Boyd stared him down.

Eventually the man raised his hands in surrender. 'Okay, Señor Boyd. My name is Diego Lopez. Malaga Policía.'

To hide his surprise, Boyd swallowed a mouthful of coffee,

burning the roof of his mouth. He grimaced, and Lopez filled a glass with water for him from a jug.

Boyd drank quickly. '*Gracias*.'

'I have English. Do you speak any Spanish?'

'Very little.' Once he'd regained his composure, Boyd was at a loss to understand why a detective had been tasked with following him and Sergio. Then it dawned on him. Bloody Jackie! 'If this is to do with my ex-wife, I may as well tell you I don't know where she is or what she's done. She disappeared without a word, leaving our son behind.'

'Sergio is your son?'

'You know all about him if you've been tailing me.'

'Tailing?'

'Following me.'

'I should not tell you, but you are right. I follow you.'

'Why?' Boyd glared.

'Okay, okay.' Lopez flapped his hands in the air like a startled bird. 'It is how you say, something to do with your ex-wife. Please do not ask.'

'If you don't tell me, I'm heading to the nearest police station to report you for harassing me.'

'Please, *señor*, I cannot tell.'

Boyd pushed back his chair and stood. Lopez put out a hand, gesturing for him to stay.

Relenting, Boyd sat and blew on his coffee. He hoped Sergio didn't wake up, but he couldn't leave until the Spanish detective gave him an explanation.

'Okay. I tell you.'

'Go on.'

'We do not know where Señora Jackie is. We think you might lead us to her or she will come back for the boy.'

'And why are you interested in her?' Boyd sipped the cooled coffee and wondered just how much Jackie had dirtied her bib in Spain. The sky was her limit, and even then he knew she'd find a way to fly higher while fucking someone over.

'Señora Jackie, she help the *policía*. Her information is good and we catch criminals. But now she is gone. Where? We do not know.'

Boyd found it hard to believe. But then she had helped him with a recent investigation into illegal human organ harvesting. Had she permanently turned over a new leaf? If so, why couldn't she be honest with him? And why had it taken her so long to inform him of Sergio's existence?

The picture began to clear. Could Jackie be in trouble? Was she using him to get Sergio out of the country? Then, when she felt safe enough, she'd send for him or travel to Ireland and take him back. Boyd knew that was something a selfish woman like Jackie would do.

'Señor Boyd, I see you are angry. But it is not what you think.'

'How in God's name do you know what I'm thinking? That woman only does what benefits herself. No matter what you think you know, she's in the game for what she can get out of it.'

'Can I ask you a question?'

'Sure.'

'Did you meet Señora Jackie here when you arrived from Ireland?'

'Briefly. She left once I arrived. I don't know where she is now and I don't understand what's going on. You'd better explain.'

'I speak to my superior officers. I will inform you what they say. But you must tell me what you know about Señor McAllister and Señor Starr. You were in Señor McAllister's apartment. I need to know why.'

Boyd decided to tell him the truth, which wasn't a whole lot.

'My inspector, Lottie Parker, phoned me from Ireland. The

daughter of Albert and Mary McAllister was found murdered. I was trying to discover what I could about them and why they'd just spent three weeks here.'

'What did you discover?'

'Nothing.'

'You were a long time inside their apartment. Why?'

'Terry Starr was there. We chatted about nothing, and then I left. I don't know anything else. Your turn.'

'My turn?'

'Tell me what this is about, and what Jackie has to do with the McAllisters. And don't mention superior officers again, because I'm gone past accepting that crock of shit.'

A rocky silence descended, and Boyd was sure Lopez was about to answer with 'no comment' when at last he spoke.

'What I said is true. My superior ... I was told to keep eyes on you at all times. We need to find Señora Jackie.'

Boyd glanced across at the apartment building. He should get back to Sergio. 'Lopez, I'm done here. Stop following me. If I hear from Jackie, I'll contact you. Give me your card.' He shoved the cup of now cold coffee into the centre of the table and stood.

'This Terry Starr has returned to Ireland. He only stay a few hours in Malaga. Now he is gone. My boss, he is not happy.'

'Why? Tell me what Terry Starr has got to do with anything.'

A single shoulder shrug. 'His name come up a lot. When we talk with your wife.'

'Ex-wife. What did she say?'

'Señor Boyd, I cannot tell you that.'

'Until you decide to tell me, you can piss off back to your *superior officers* and let me enjoy my last full day in Malaga with my son.'

'No, no. You cannot go. If you leave with the boy, Señora Jackie not come back. You must stay.'

His pleading wrecked Boyd's head, as did any thought of Jackie returning to deny him access to his son.

'I'm going back to the apartment. You know where I am if you want to tell me the whole truth.'

Much as he wanted to pump the detective for more information, he was anxious to check on Sergio. Anything Jackie got involved with was rarely resolved without bloodshed. There was no way Boyd would allow his son to become a pawn in the Spanish police's game.

Nor in Jackie's.

———

Terry Starr sat slumped in his plush armchair with what seemed like two hundred cushions, though in reality there were only twelve. Reality. What he needed was twelve rounds in a ring, even though he liked to knock out his opponent earlier than that.

Tapping his knee with one hand, he checked his phone again. Still nothing from Albert. They'd talked yesterday when he'd still been in Malaga and that conversation had made his mind up for him. He had to come back. Lucy was dead and Albert was grieving.

When he'd arrived in Dublin, he realised he couldn't meet Albert at his home, so he found himself holed up in his executive Dublin apartment for the time being.

The triple-glazed faux-sash windows excluded all sound from the outside and he felt like he was sitting in a silent vacuum. The lid could pop any second. He was pumped. He needed to go to the gym. A proper gym, not the one he'd constructed in the basement of the Georgian building. He should have stayed in Spain.

He picked up a blue velour cushion and threw it across the room. It knocked a Waterford crystal trophy off the sideboard, and he watched stonily as it smashed into a hundred pieces on the cold marble-tiled floor.

He bit at a stray piece of nail on his thumb. The manicurist was shit at her job. He needed to find a new one. One who wouldn't rat him out as a pussy to the macho boxing world. The least of his worries, he supposed.

His phone rang and he glanced at the caller ID. He let it ring. No way did he want to talk to Noel fucking Glennon.

54

Having picked the pink acrylic gel from her nails, Ivy sat in her mother's SUV filing them. Parked on Main Street, she had a clear view of the dingy little apartment located over the dry cleaner's across the road. Hannah Byrne lived in that hovel with her snotty-nosed brother and her alcoholic mother. Was the kid even her brother? Maybe she should start a rumour that he was Hannah's son. That would be class.

Ivy knew she wouldn't be caught dead in a grotty, rat-infested kip like that. There was even a tattoo parlour next door. What kind of people lived in these dumps?

Looking at the tattoo place made her wonder about the conversation she'd had with that detective. It was true, Lucy had got a tattoo without telling her. She'd have stopped her if she'd known, because it had turned out awful. Why had she lied to the detective? Now the stupid guards wanted *her* to come in for a formal interview. They could fuck right off.

She put away the nail file and drummed the steering wheel. The circulation of the half-naked photo of Hannah had been so cool, until Hannah had fought with Lucy. That photo had unleashed a side of her that had shocked Ivy. And then Lucy had died. Murdered. Sad. Yes, Ivy thought, very sad. Lucy was her best friend. Would the darling of the athletics track pay for the crime? Itching with impatience, she fervently hoped Hannah Byrne would rot in prison.

The passenger door opened and she turned to her visitor. 'You took your time.'

'Give me a break. My wife could be in labour and I'm supposed to be in Tesco, shopping, so I can't delay.' Richie slid in, sitting on her cosmetic purse. Shifting, he threw it on the dash.

'Shouldn't you be holding her hand or something? Helping to squeeze the little brat out of her hole?' Ivy idly picked a non-existent hair from the seam of her sheer white top, which revealed her expensive red lingerie.

'For fuck's sake, Ivy, you don't have to be so gross.'

'It's true.' She smirked, relishing her talent for making people lose their cool. He was even shivering, like he was stuck in a snowstorm in the dead of winter. Grow up.

He refused to look at her. 'You know I don't like texts. Brontë might see them. Don't do it again.'

'Oh, so now you're worried? You weren't that concerned when you were poking me with your limp excuse for a dick on Friday night.'

He shook his head vehemently. 'You're insane. I'm out of here.'

She laughed as he opened the door, ready to flee.

'Fine by me. I only wanted to show you a selection of photos from Friday night. I think they'd look good on Instagram or TikTok, or ...' she paused for effect, hunching up one shoulder, 'maybe Brontë would be interested in seeing them.'

She waited as he stalled with one foot outside the car, a hand on the door, his back to her. Then he turned ever so slightly, eyeing her. She had him.

'I honestly think these photos are so gross I might have to

figure out a way of putting them on the dark web. That's if you keep acting the prick.' Smiling, she relaxed as he closed the door again and sank back into the cream leather seat.

'What do you want?' he asked, each word curled into a snarl.

'That tone makes you so ugly.'

'Why are we sitting in the middle of town where everyone can see us?'

'All good crime books tell you that the best place to meet is in plain sight. That way, people don't give you a second glance. Clever me.'

'I asked you what you want from me.'

'A cuddle would be nice. Then I can show you what I've got here.'

He turned to her, his cheeks red, spittle at the corners of his mouth. 'If you so much as threaten me or my wife again, I'll kill you. Do you hear me, I will kill you.'

'Oh really? Tried it before, have you? Practice makes perfect and all that.'

'You are a bitch, Ivy Jones. A slithery fucking snake in the grass.' His face had taken on a sinister hue. She felt like grabbing his stupid beaded necklace and choking him with it. He swiped her phone from the central console, where it was held by a magnet.

For a moment she felt a surge of unease, but she quickly capped it with what she hoped was a sinister expression of her own. 'Everything is backed up to the cloud, just in case you think I'm stupid enough to store my photos solely on my phone.'

He let it drop back to its resting place. Now that she had his attention, she told him her plan.

When Richie got out of the car, he slammed the door so hard her phone fell from the magnet to the footwell. She picked it up, then fetched her cosmetic purse from the dash and applied a swipe of lip gloss. It was then that she noticed the shake in her fingers. She hoped he hadn't seen it. She had to present as being fully in control, displaying no sign of weakness. Richie Harrison might be easy to manipulate, but she reckoned he could be dangerous when mad. But she needed him to do what she wanted. Then she would be free at last.

55

Noel Glennon parked his car outside the semi-detached new-build. Despite himself, he admired the impressive house. Way out of his league. He knew he shouldn't have come, but he had to talk to Richie before he gave himself a heart attack.

He checked that the buttons on his white shirt were closed, except for the one at the collar so that he could breathe. He despaired at the creased cotton. It looked like he'd slept in it. He was sniffing his armpit when the door was flung open.

A flush-faced Brontë Harrison stood there, barefoot, a long, floaty black dress thing wrapping around her legs and baby bump in the breeze. He tried to mask his surprise, but judging by the look of disdain blazing his way, he wasn't succeeding. He lowered his head, unable to keep eye contact.

'I was looking for Richie. Is he in?'

'No, he's gone into town. He should have been back by now. I can tell him you called, but I'll need to know your name.'

He thought by the look she threw him that she might know who he was.

'Tell him Noel Glennon needs a quick word. Won't keep him long.'

'Do you want to come in and wait?'

Richie would rage at him for darkening his doorstep, but they needed to talk. And soon.

'Sure.' He walked in past her, noticing her bare feet again. 'Should I take off ...?' He pointed to his black Nikes, hoping she'd say no, because he hadn't put on socks and his feet were sweaty. He was unable to control his hot cheeks.

'You're grand, no need. Would you like a coffee, Noel?' She closed the door and squeezed past him.

'That'd be great.' He had an uneasy feeling she'd brushed against him purposely.

'Kitchen is this way.'

Calm down, make small talk, appear normal. 'When is the baby due?'

'Another few weeks, but he's getting impatient. I spent most of yesterday in the hospital.'

'Everything okay?'

'The doctor says all is good, and who am I to argue with the experts? Decaf or regular?'

'Whole hog, please. I need it.'

'What's up?'

She kept her back to him, busying herself with the fancy coffee machine. Richie had fallen on his feet with this woman, Noel thought.

'Just the shock of Lucy McAllister's death.' He didn't know why he'd said that, but he had to tell someone. 'She went to the school where I teach.'

'I heard the guards are treating it as murder,' she said over her shoulder.

'Makes it all the more terrible. When do you think Richie will be back?' He thought it would look rude to check the time on his phone. Then he remembered he could check it on his Fitbit. His nerves were more frayed than he'd thought.

'He should be home any minute.' She raised her voice above

the noise of the coffee percolating. 'What do you teach?' She placed a plain white mug on the table by his hand, her fingers lightly brushing his.

'PE, and I train junior athletics.'

'You must be so fit. Sounds like too much work for me.' She worked another mug of coffee from the machine. 'How do you know Richie?'

'Erm, met him a couple of years ago, actually.'

'That's odd. He's never mentioned you, and I don't think Richie ever ran more than ten metres in his life.'

A nervous giggle escaped and he mentally reminded himself to act his age. 'My meeting Richie had nothing to do with the school or sports.'

He felt like a little boy in her beautiful, confident presence. But there was something about her that bothered him. Should he be able to identify that look at the corners of her eyes? Was it fury? He shook himself to get real.

'The thing is, I also work as a bouncer – you know, in town, at some of the nightclubs where he DJs. Met him one night.'

Brontë turned around so quickly the coffee sloshed over the rim of her mug. 'Milk?'

He physically backed his chair against the wall. Her solicitousness belied the ominous expression on her face. What was her problem? Did she think Richie was cheating with some girl he'd met at a club? Probably. With good reason.

'No thanks. I'm grand.' He stood, and the chair scraped against her pristine white wall. Fuck. And he was certain they were her walls, not Richie's. 'I think I should head off. I'll catch up with Richie another time.'

'You haven't had your coffee. Sit.'

He sat. 'Sorry about the wall, I think the chair scratched it.'

'Oh, don't worry. Richie can touch it up. You met him at a nightclub, you say?'

'Er, yeah.' His feet were definitely swimming in his runners now, keeping pace with the perspiration gluing his shirt to his spine. He felt anxious being alone with this heavily pregnant woman.

'Are you okay?' she said. 'You've turned an awful colour.'

'I-I'm fine. I really have to go. Tell Richie to give me a call.'

He was attempting to extricate himself from the chair without doing further damage to the paintwork when he heard the front door open, then shut.

'The wanderer returns.' Brontë's face was sweet again. 'What took you so long?'

'There was a queue for the checkout. Thought I'd never get out of there.'

'On a Sunday?'

'Yeah. Who'd believe it?'

'You could have used the self-scan.' Her mouth twisted slightly.

Noel really wanted to escape.

'Didn't think of it,' Richie said.

Looking from one to the other, Noel coughed.

Richie turned round and dropped the shopping bag on the table, his eyes widening.

'What are you doing here?'

On guard now, Noel said, 'Just wanted a quick word.'

'You could have phoned.'

'I could have, but I ... I was in the area. You know what? I can't even remember what I wanted to discuss. I'd better be off.'

'What happened to the wall?' Richie said as Noel shuffled out of the chair.

'My fault, sorry.' There was so much unspoken stuff going on that he felt like an extra in a tense Shakespearean drama. One where he might end up being dumped into a cauldron of boiling oil.

'There's no need to rush,' Brontë said. 'Make yourself a coffee, Richie.'

As she sat at the table, Noel tried to catch Richie's eye over her shoulder, but he had turned away, pressing buttons on the coffee machine.

'Don't forget the mug,' Brontë said.

He fumbled along the cupboards and placed a mug under the spout just as the coffee started to flow.

'He makes stupid mistakes when he's stressed.' She laughed bitterly. 'You'd think he was the one about to give birth.'

'I'm sure it's a tense time for you both, and with Lucy McAllister's murder, it must be even ...' Noel halted as Richie's eyes flashed daggers behind his wife.

'Do you know anything about it?' she said. 'They aren't giving much detail on the news.'

'Not a thing. Really, that's the truth.' Fuck, he was sounding defensive.

'You were there Friday night, same as I was,' Richie said to no one in particular. 'Must have happened later on.'

'Yeah, I wanted to go over a few things with you. You know, for the interviews with the guards,' Noel said, glancing towards Brontë, hoping Richie understood that he wanted to talk in private.

'Oh, don't mind me,' Brontë said. 'You boys go ahead and talk. I've baby things to check out on Instagram.'

She whipped out her phone from the deep folds of her dress and made a show of scrolling. She had no intention of moving. Noel brought his mug to the sink and leaned close to Richie.

'We need to talk,' he whispered. Then, a little louder, 'Thank you for the coffee, but I have to run. Give me a call.' He turned to Bronte. 'Good luck with the baby.'

As he made his escape, he felt the pair of them tracking him with their eyes. Escape? No, he had nowhere to escape to. He couldn't outrun his conscience, and he'd been unable to discuss his dilemma with Richie. He had to talk to someone or he might end up jumping into the canal in the hope that the reeds would swiftly throttle the last breath of air out of his lungs.

He'd never be so lucky as to have a quick death.

He'd have to pay for his sins first.

56

Lottie's phone pinged with a text from Boyd as she was climbing the stairs to the office. She'd left Kirby to settle Hannah in the interview room to await her mother's arrival. She glanced around to make sure Superintendent Farrell wasn't lurking before she read the message.

Boyd's words were interesting, she thought as she pocketed the phone. Terry Starr had returned to Ireland, having spent less than a day in Malaga. Good to know, but why had he been in Spain in the first place? Had he known Lucy was dead when he left Ireland? If so, was there something about the girl's murder that had caused him to flee? But then why had he come back?

She parked her questions and moved quickly to her office to examine Lucy's phone. After a call to Mary McAllister, she stared at the selection of numbers she'd written down, crossing her fingers that one of them might unlock the phone. She didn't want to waste time sending it upstairs to the tech team.

She had fetched a spare charger from lost and found, and with the phone plugged in, she thought her luck might be changing for the better when the second combination worked:

Albert's date of birth – month and year. Feeling pumped, she began.

A multitude of apps appeared on the home screen, but she went directly to the photograph icon and tapped it open. The series of selfies confirmed, as Lynch had discovered, Lucy's obsession with herself. Pouted lips. Demure eyes, shaded by false lashes. Hand on chin. Hand holding hair high above her head. Lucy and Ivy, cheek to cheek. Their hands raised in peace signs above their heads. Two pretty girls. They seemed to be joined at the hip.

She scanned a selection of selfies taken at the fateful party. Was there a time in the day when either of the girls appeared without make-up? It felt like such hard work. Lottie herself struggled to find time to shower and brush her teeth in the mornings, never mind lash on foundation.

Concentrating on the job at hand, she scrolled backwards.

The photos taken before the most recent batch of selfies caused her breath to stall in her throat. She could make out the edge of a door jamb. The photos appeared to have been snapped though a gap in the partially open door. All were of Hannah Byrne. Dressed in jeans and sweater. Undressed. Knickers and bra. Simple mismatched underwear. Lottie doubted Lucy and Ivy would ever commit such a fashion misstep, and she admired Hannah for seemingly disregarding conformity, though she reckoned the girl would never have been able to afford the luxurious underwear evident in some of the photos of the other two girls.

It was clear that Hannah had been getting ready for the party in the guest bedroom situated between Lucy's room and the room where her body was discovered. Scrutinising each photograph, Lottie shifted on the chair, becoming more uncom-fortable as she scrolled through the images. They constituted unadulterated voyeurism. All taken on Lucy's phone; all taken without Hannah's knowledge. Had they been snapped for mischief or malice?

She tugged at her ear, as if it could help her see what she was missing. Why had Lucy shared Hannah's image? Opening WhatsApp, she found twelve groups. Lucy was a busy girl. She'd sent the most revealing photo of Hannah, the one Cormac had shown her, to eleven of the groups. The names in each group would have to be cross-referenced.

It was easy to see how, in a state of excitement at shaming Hannah, she had not thought to exclude her prey. What could she gain by sending out the image? Notoriety? Attention? Hannah's humiliation and isolation? Lottie had a feeling something much more ominous was at play. And why had Lucy listed Hannah in one of her WhatsApp groups if she wasn't a friend?

Glaring at the offending photo, Lottie was filled with mortification and shame for Hannah, who had been exposed in such a manner. Then rage set in. The photo showed Hannah staring in the mirror trying unsuccessfully to pout, one hand holding her hair in a haphazard topknot. She had removed her bra and discarded it on the bed behind her. Her body was lean and athletic, but her chest was almost flat. Was this what Lucy had hoped to ridicule her for?

There was a time when Lottie couldn't imagine why a seventeen-year-old girl would do such a thing to another person, but over the years, experience had broadened her imagination to the point where very little shocked her. That was too sad.

The only WhatsApp group that hadn't been sent the image consisted of Lucy's parents. She'd titled the group 'The Olds'.

Kirby walked into the office, jacket draped over his arm, shirt unbuttoned at his collar, tie askew. 'Some dope has the heating on in the building. What is the point?'

'I wondered why it was so warm.'

'We freeze our balls off during the worst of the winter

weather, and when the sun shows half its face, the heat comes on miraculously.'

'Is that right?'

'Sorry, boss. I don't mean you have balls ... Oh, you know what I mean.'

'It's okay, Kirby.' Lottie stretched her hands over her head, conscious of the strain in her back from leaning over the desk. 'How is Hannah?'

'She's fine. Told her I'd fetch a McD's meal for her.'

'Have you or McKeown finished going through the traffic cams for Liz Flood's Punto? We need to know where that car was between the party and when it was found burned out this morning.' She didn't like being interrupted. She needed to focus her attention on the photo of Hannah. It might have been the catalyst for Lucy's murder. Or it might have had absolutely nothing to do with it. She still had to work through the conundrum of Hannah's rucksack.

'Do you think we have enough to charge Hannah?'

'Not really. We need the results of the analysis of the blood found on her hands, and I want the results on Cormac's clothes that we took from his washing machine. It will take the lab an age to get back to us, and it's Sunday.'

'I've good news for you. Martina Brennan used to date a guy who heads up the forensic lab in the Phoenix Park. She soft-talked him into pushing our request to the top of the pile.'

'How did she manage that?'

'She cried down the phone about this beautiful teenager who'd been savagely murdered in her own home and how important the DNA test results would be in securing a conviction.'

'She didn't?'

'She did.'

'And what do the results tell us?'

He checked over a page in his hand. 'Even though Cormac's

clothes were washed, they were able to extract a viable DNA sample from the shirt threads.'

'Go on.' Lottie straightened her back as Kirby stuck out his chest, full of the important news he was bringing her.

'It's a match for Lucy McAllister's DNA. And the samples taken from Hannah's hands had traces of Cormac's DNA and ... Lucy's.'

'Wow!'

'It proves they killed her,' Kirby concluded.

'Hold on a minute,' Lottie said, her excitement waning. 'It only tells us that both Hannah and Cormac were in close proximity to Lucy before, during or after the girl died. We could do with finding the murder weapon with one or both sets of prints. What about the scratches on Cormac's torso?'

'No results on those yet.'

'We have to factor in the argument between Hannah and Lucy. Lucy's blood might have transferred then.'

'Nothing in the post-mortem to indicate that. But boss, I thought you'd be ecstatic with these results.' Kirby's chest deflated, releasing the strain on the buttons, and his pudgy face seemed to fold in on itself. Anxiously he scratched his head of bushy hair.

'I have a mixture of emotions, Kirby, but the truth is, I need a confession, and I want Hannah to be innocent.'

'Why?'

'The photo Lucy shared with all and sundry was emotional abuse; a destructive act to humiliate a young girl who couldn't afford matching underwear.'

'What's her underwear got to do with anything?'

Lottie blew out her cheeks, angry at the world, annoyed with Kirby and sorry for Hannah.

'Boss?' Kirby brought her back up for air. 'No matter what the trigger was, it doesn't excuse the brutality of Lucy's murder.'

'I know that. There are too many unanswered questions. I

still want to know who Lucy had sexual intercourse with in the hours before her death. And that skin taken from her side? What's that all about? The photo might have set things off, but is it enough for a motive? I want to look Hannah in the eye when I show it to her.'

'I'm with you on that one.'

'Get her the food.'

As Kirby ambled off, Lottie leaned back in the chair and rubbed her eyes. Lethargy was dangerously close to taking hold. She jumped up. Gary could work on the rest of whatever was on Lucy's phone while she worked on Hannah.

57

Lottie left her office with the intention of dropping Lucy's phone upstairs. Lynch was at her desk, hunched over the monitor, tapping a pen on the desk to some silent rhythm.

'Have the McAllisters kicked you out?' Lottie asked.

'It was obvious they didn't want me there, but at least I got a decent bite to eat before I left.'

'I want to interview Terry Starr. Can you locate him for me?'

'I thought he was abroad.'

'Not any more. He's back.'

'I'll trace his whereabouts and let you know.'

'How are you getting on with Lucy's social media accounts?'

'Painful.' Lynch rolled her eyes. 'I'm glad my kids aren't teenagers yet. I'd go crazy trying to monitor their online footprints.'

'All ahead of you. I'm bringing Lucy's phone up to Gary. Some of the photos on it are disturbing.'

'What type of photos?'

'Body-shaming at its worst.'

'I'll say it again, I dread my kids becoming teenagers.'

'You'll be better equipped than most to deal with them by then. As for my lot ...' Lottie shook her head.

'I'll swap you mine if you want?'

She smiled, releasing some of the tension seizing her shoulders and knotting up her muscles. 'No can do. The devil you know and all that.'

'I wanted to talk to you,' Lynch said. 'I found something.'

A surge of hope powered through Lottie as she sat against the edge of the desk.

Lynch scrunched up the side of her mouth, tutting. 'Might not help much, but it clears up one thing.' She tapped the keyboard, zooming in on a photograph. 'Lucy had a fake Instagram account. They call it a Finsta. On her main Instagram account she has a few hundred followers, but on this Finsta she has about a dozen.'

'That's a new one on me.' Lottie wondered if her kids did this sort of thing. Probably. 'Explain.'

'These accounts are used mainly by teens and young adults to share their more candid photos with a select few. Take a look at this one.'

In the photograph, Lucy, dressed in white jeans and a black camisole, low at the front and even lower at the sides, seemed to be dancing, one hand raised holding a bottle.

'A nightclub?' Lottie wondered.

'I'll find out, but look closer.'

Lottie squinted. Lucy was holding her other arm aloft, phone in hand. She thought she saw what had excited Lynch. 'Zoom in.'

The image pixelated, became fuzzy.

Lynch zoomed back out a little. 'Do you see it now?'

'I do. A small tattoo in the exact spot the skin was excised.' Lottie closed one eye as she tried to decipher the tattoo. 'Is it a heart?'

'There's something written inside, but it's too blurry.'

'Did you notice it on any other photos?'

'Not yet.'

'Keep at it. Good work, Maria.'

Lynch beamed. 'I'll send the image to Gary's team. They should be able to enhance it.'

'Anything else of interest on this Finsta?'

'I've only just found it.'

'Okay. Any developments with that email that was sent to Lucy?'

'Not yet.'

'Albert was to forward the threatening email he received.' She filled Lynch in as she checked her phone for it. 'Nothing.'

She'd give him an hour and then, grieving father or not, she was going after Albert McAllister.

———

When Lottie drifted away to bring Lucy's phone to Gary, Lynch got back to business. She parked the job of trawling Lucy's social media and instead concentrated on finding out more about Terry Starr. She accessed his Instagram account. It consisted of boxing tips and triumphs. She kept digging and was rewarded when she found he too had a Finsta account. She made a call to the tech team, and within five minutes she had access.

Terry Starr hadn't posted as much as Lucy had on Finsta, and Lynch scrolled through his photos scrutinising each image.

Was she imagining it? Seeing something that wasn't there? Was her tired brain concocting a scenario from her imagination? No, she thought, it was there on the screen. About ninety per cent of the images she'd looked at so far were of teenage girls. And they all looked younger than eighteen.

If Terry had been a pop star or a famous footballer, it might have made more sense, but boxing? She didn't know what to think.

She scratched her head with the end of her Bic pen and glanced around the office for someone to nab. She needed a brain to pick. Kirby had returned from town and appeared to be half asleep at his desk as he mechanically dipped his hand in and out of a McDonald's carton.

'Kirby, come here and take a look at this.'

'Give me a minute. There's a piece of chicken stuck in my teeth.' He was working at it with the corner of a sheet of paper.

Lynch glared.

He held up his hand in surrender and slouched over to her desk. As he leaned over her shoulder, she wondered when he'd last had a shower.

'What age does that girl look?' she asked.

'There's a lot of girls there. Give me a hint.'

'For the love of God!' She zoomed in and bit her lip.

'Oh,' Kirby said.

'Oh is right.' She stared at the young girl to the right of the image of Terry surrounded by a posse of teenagers. 'She looks about thirteen, don't you think?'

'What site is that on?'

Lynch explained Finsta once again. 'I'll have to dig deeper.'

'This is sick, you know.'

'The more I delve into this case, the more it makes me want to throw up. And vital pieces of the jigsaw are missing.'

Kirby laid a hand on her shoulder before returning to his depleted box of cold nuggets and fries, digging in like it was a condemned man's last meal.

Lynch scrolled until she came to another, more disturbing image. Terry Starr was sitting with an even younger girl perched on his knee. She had fear in her eyes. The light was bad but Lynch could tell the girl was no more than a child.

Lynch felt her stomach contents liquefy. She rushed to the

bathroom, where she fell to her knees in front of the toilet and dry-retched into the bowl.

Wiping her mouth, she flushed the toilet, then turned on a tap and splashed cold water on her face. She stared into the rusted mirror above the sink with wide eyes. If that had been one of her children sitting on Terry's knee, she'd kill the bastard with her bare hands. What in God's name had she stumbled on here? Whatever it was appeared to have been conducted in plain sight.

Back at her desk, she tried to reach Lottie but the call went unanswered.

Kirby stood and wiped his greasy hands on the legs of his trousers. She almost gagged again.

'Don't look at me like that, Lynch. It won't stain.'

She wanted to throw a barb back at him, but she couldn't find any words. She hoped she was wrong about the photo, but she didn't think so.

58

Hannah Byrne was alone in the interview room when Lottie eventually entered. Kirby had pleaded the need to eat, so she'd got McKeown to join her. The food Kirby had bought for the girl remained untouched on the table.

She had skimmed through the psychological evaluation that had been conducted on the distraught teenager. The report stated that there was a strong possibility Hannah was suffering from stress or trauma amnesia. Otherwise she was deemed in possession of her faculties.

The medical report stated that the lab was unable to detect GHB drugs in her system as too much time had elapsed, but MDMA was detected in her blood and urine. The girl had taken Ecstasy. Lottie thought it was likely something else had been slipped into her drink. But had it been enough to render her amnesiac?

'Your mother not arrived yet?' She pulled out a chair, asking a simple question to engage the girl in communication.

Hannah shrugged, lashes shielding her downcast eyes. 'I don't even know why I'm here. I'm tired, sick and hungry.'

'Why don't you eat the food we bought for you?'

'You call that food? Too many unknown additives.'

Lottie refrained from pointing out the obvious. The girl had been happy enough to swallow an unknown drug. Give me strength, she thought.

Fixing what she thought was her motherly face in place, she said, 'Hannah, I got the DNA analysis results and it's not looking good for you. I need your mother here, and I advise you get a solicitor.'

Hannah looked up, her expression fractured, haunted eyes ringed black. 'Why couldn't you talk to me at home? This place scares me. I still feel awful and my head is pounding.'

You and me both, Lottie thought.

'I'll check to see where her mother is.' McKeown left the room.

Lottie considered the teenager sitting with her arms crossed tightly around her waist, her blonde hair sticking to her sweaty brow. Exhaustion was written in every pore on her skin. Her heart filled with pity for the youngster and she wondered why.

They had evidence, mostly circumstantial, but the dead girl's blood under Hannah's fingernails seemed conclusive. However, they also had to consider the earlier argument with Lucy at the party. The bloodied towel could have been planted in the rucksack. That begged the question: when had Hannah fetched the rucksack from Lucy's house? Despite all that, it was the body-shaming photos that stuck in Lottie's craw.

Babs Byrne rushed in in a fog of cheap perfume, McKeown behind her. Without even glancing at her daughter, she sat down.

McKeown conducted the formalities for the recording and Lottie asked if Hannah wanted a solicitor. 'You might be entitled to free legal aid.'

'My daughter has done nothing wrong,' Babs said, red sauce clogged in one eyebrow, 'and we don't need a *charity* solicitor. We are not a *charity* case. Okay?'

Lottie opened up the thin file folder in front of her and slid across a glossy reproduction of the photo Lucy had shared on the night of her party.

'This is you, Hannah,' she stated.

No denial, only the tightening of Hannah's lips into a thin line.

Babs erupted. 'What the hell? Why are you bandying about a half-naked photo of my daughter?'

'This image was circulated to dozens of people on the night Lucy was murdered. Many of the recipients were at the party. It was also sent to you, Hannah, either by accident or intentionally. Witnesses say you reacted violently towards Lucy and the two of you ended up in a physical altercation. Can you elaborate?'

'Elaborate?' Babs spat, her hand banging the table, the photograph shimmering with each thump. 'If what you say is true, that stuck-up bitch humiliated my daughter and Hannah had every right to confront her.'

'Babs, please,' Lottie said. 'It was more than a confrontation, it was assault. Two different things.'

'Don't you dare patronise me.' Babs's face glowed red with fury. 'I am not stupid!'

'I apologise.' Lottie had to restore calm in order to secure a confession. At the moment, she was making a complete balls of it. 'I didn't intend to be patronising. The truth is, I have witnesses who say Hannah assaulted Lucy.'

'What witnesses?' Babs demanded.

'I can't divulge that information.' Lottie turned her attention to the girl. 'Have you any memory of that altercation? I need you to tell me what really happened at the party.'

'Your *witnesses* can say what they like.' Babs flung the words across the table, spittle flying. 'Hannah was totally within her rights to defend herself.' She folded her arms, defying Lottie to contradict her.

'A young man says he gave you a pill, Hannah. Do you remember that?'

Hannah shrugged. 'Maybe.'

'Do you recall anything about the incident after Lucy sent the photo?'

She shook her head, and Lottie waited. Eventually the girl said, 'It's hazy. I don't know. I already told you to ask Cormac.'

'The samples we took from under your nails match Lucy McAllister's DNA. Can you explain that?'

Hannah gasped, and Babs shot up, slamming her chair against the wall. 'This is a bald-faced set-up. Just because that crowd have money and we don't, you think you can stitch up my daughter. You are pathetic. Come on, Hannah, we're out of here.' She grabbed the girl by the arm and hauled her to her feet.

Lottie thought Hannah looked like a reluctant marionette, her mother pulling her strings.

'Sit down, please,' she said, calmly but emphatically. 'Hannah isn't going anywhere. We are preparing a file to send to the DPP on foot of forensic evidence. I already advised you to get a solicitor, advice you declined to follow. If Hannah doesn't cooperate with us, I will have little option but to hold her for twenty-four hours.'

Babs was stunned into silence. Hannah bowed her head, her hair falling like a veil covering her face.

'If you have something you want to tell me, Hannah, now is the time,' Lottie said.

'I don't remember. I wish I could, but I can't remember anything after I took the pill. I had a drink of Coke. That's all. Little bits of memory come and go. Please, please ask Cormac, he'll tell you.' A solitary tear slid down her nose, hovering on the tip before dropping silently to the table.

'Did you and Cormac murder Lucy?'

Babs found her voice. 'Hannah might have stood up for

herself over that disgusting photograph, but murder? Find another scapegoat, Inspector, because my girl is innocent.'

Had the woman not heard her? Lottie forced her voice to an even pitch. 'We have DNA evidence that proves Hannah had Lucy's blood under her fingernails. She had a bloodied towel from the house in her rucksack and—'

'Someone put it there.' Babs was incandescent. 'You have to see sense.'

'When did you fetch your rucksack to bring it home, Hannah?' Lottie directed her attention to the girl.

'I don't know,' Hannah sobbed.

'That rucksack was in Lucy's living room around four a.m. and then it was in your home. I have a witness who—'

'You and your witnesses,' Babs spat. 'Liars, the lot of them. The cheek of you, targeting a poor innocent girl just because she hasn't a pot to piss in, while that ... that rich bitch swanned around town as if her shit didn't smell. Let me tell you this, something smells rotten about this whole scenario.' She sniffed loudly and covered her nose as if the air in the room suddenly reeked of rotten eggs. 'And if you don't fucking mind, we're getting a solicitor.' She glanced at Hannah and lowered her voice. 'Charity or not, you need it.'

Lottie sighed. Babs Byrne was only now waking up to the horror story starring her daughter as the principal actor.

'Hannah? Can you recall at all when you fetched your rucksack?' She slid across the table a photograph of the blue rucksack adorned with grubby white daisies. 'The towel had Lucy's blood on it.'

Hannah stared at her bag in the photo as if it was the first time she'd seen it. She shook her head slowly. 'I ... I have no explanation.' She looked up, eyes pleading, but Lottie thought she saw a glimmer of fear. 'Does it mean I was still at the house when Lucy ... died?'

'I was hoping you could tell me.'

She shook her head slowly. 'I c-can't.'

'Can't remember or can't say?'

Hannah shrugged.

Lottie placed another photo in front of the girl. 'Recognise this lad?'

'That's the guy with the pills. Cormac bought them from him. Ask Cormac. Please.'

'Hannah, Jake Flood was fifteen years old. We took his body from the canal last night.'

'He's dead?' Hannah's eyes widened, the dark rings circling them sagging. 'I-I ... I d-don't understand. What's going on?' She bit her lip, then drew her hand under her nose and sniffed loudly.

There were other characters in this drama shady enough to count as suspects, but Lottie couldn't ignore the fact that all the evidence, circumstantial or not, was pointing directly at the shattered girl in front of her.

'Have you anything else to add?' she asked.

'No.' Hannah began to sob.

'Okay. I'm going to request a detention order to keep you here for twenty-four hours.'

McKeown recited the legal details, adding, 'Interview suspended.'

Gathering her folder, Lottie followed him to the door. He had remained unusually silent throughout the interview. Turning back, she looked from the mother to the teenager.

'You need to use this time to try and remember, Hannah. The evidence against you is damning.'

Babs broke out of her reverie. 'Will you stop that? You're upsetting her. Beating her into a corner, me along with her. You are so wrong, because this is someone else's war to be fought, not ours.'

'I'm not your enemy,' Lottie said softly, and left the room.

Walking along the corridor, she wondered who she was

fooling. Of course she was the enemy of a woman who was only trying to keep her daughter out of prison.

Her footsteps felt like cement had dried inside her shoes, and her heart was just as heavy. It was distressing to know you might be the person instrumental in sending a teenage girl to prison, especially if that girl had no recollection whatsoever of the events.

She badly needed a coffee.

59

Back in the office, she watched as McKeown got busy with his iPad.

'Anything new before I head out?'

'We now have confirmation that two DNA matches were found on Cormac O'Flaherty's shirt and torso. Lucy McAllister and Hannah Byrne.'

Lottie paced in small circles. 'Does it mean he was present when Lucy was murdered or just at the argument? If he killed Lucy, is he now trying to pin the blame on Hannah, or are they both involved?'

'Where does Jake Flood fit in?'

'Too many questions, McKeown. I'm going out for a decent coffee to recharge my brain.'

'Garda Brennan was in the Bean Café a few minutes ago. She said Cormac O'Flaherty was there.'

Lottie patted the back pocket of her jeans, feeling for her bank card. 'I'll be back in ten, if anyone's looking for me.'

'And if the super asks?'

'I'm sure you'll think of something, seeing as you're so friendly with her.'

'You can't keep hiding from her.'

'Watch me.'

She shoved her file and notebook into McKeown's hand so forcefully he nearly dropped his precious iPad. Then she turned on her heel and was down the stairs before he could utter a word.

———

Sitting in the Bean Café nursing a coffee long gone cold, Cormac O'Flaherty studied the scratched wooden table rather than look around him. The Bean was the closest café to the station, a popular spot for gardaí to congregate. Why then had he picked it for his coffee? Was he setting himself up as a sitting duck?

His question was answered when the door opened and in stepped the tall detective, the mouthy one who had tricked him into snitching on Hannah's row with Lucy. He shouldn't have told her about the photo, but she would have found out at some stage and that would have made him look worse.

Big mistake. Sitting duck. All that and more.

A cool breeze swept towards him with the opening of the door, and he zipped his hoodie to his throat, preparing to escape the second her back was turned. Too late. She caught sight of him as his leg knocked against the edge of the chair, rattling it in his haste to flee.

'Cormac O'Flaherty, I'd like a word with you. Another coffee?' She was smiling, but he wasn't falling for it. Her eyes were like chunks of granite. Cold and hard. Shit.

'Ah, you're grand. I was leaving. I've to be—'

'I insist.' She stepped forward, blocking his exit in the narrow space between the counter and the door.

Trapped. Reluctantly he tugged at his chair and sat back down.

'Two coffees, Adrian,' she said, 'when you're ready.'

Her smile was so sweet, Cormac thought he might develop diabetes. It put him on the highest alert.

She sat after taking a bank card from her jeans pocket. He envied her in her light top. He was beginning to sweat in his zipped-up hoodie. *Concentrate. Don't open your mouth.*

She tapped the table idly with the card and he noticed that her nails were bitten down unevenly. Her eyes were tired and her hair was an untidy mess. She didn't look like a senior detective. But her image didn't fool Cormac. He'd read up about her on news stories on the web after his experience in the station yesterday. Detective Inspector Parker was unorthodox, but also one smart cookie, with a track record for catching murderers.

'I really have to be somewhere else,' he said, fidgeting.

'Just two minutes. Bumping into you is opportune. You were on my list.'

'What list?' His hands slipped in and out of each other as he sweated buckets.

'My never-ending to-do list.' She paused as Adrian placed two coffees on the table, a plastic-wrapped biscuit on each saucer. When he was back behind the counter, she continued. 'I've further questions about Jake Flood.' She rolled up her sleeves, all business now. Matter-of-fact. No accusation. Or was there? Cormac found it increasingly difficult to read her.

'Jake?' He let a slow breath escape between his teeth.

'Yes, the boy who sold you the drugs at Lucy's party.'

Her voice was too harsh, too loud. He glanced around, afraid they might now be the centre of attention. But the ambient chatter didn't fluctuate. No heads turned to stare.

'What about him?' His breath snagged the words as his anxiety heightened.

'His body was found in the canal last night.'

'No way!'

'We're treating his death as suspicious.'

'Oh.'

'*Oh* is right, Cormac. When did you last see him?'

'At the party.'

'Any idea where he might have gone afterwards?'

'How would I know?' That sounded like smart-arse talk. He had to keep calm. He hoped his expression was neutral. Impossible. Trying to master a steady tone, he added, 'I honestly didn't know him. You have to believe me.' So much for neutral and steady; he was positively pleading.

'I don't have to believe you, Cormac, I only need to prove it. So tell me again, when and where did you last see Jake Flood?'

She sipped her coffee, then unwrapped the biscuit, her eyes never leaving his. It was like he was caught in a dentist's chair, a laser beamed at him. The crunch was coming and he tried not to squirm.

'At the party.'

'When at the party?'

'When he sold me the ... when I got the ... you know.' Fucking hell.

'What time was that, when you purchased drugs from him?' She had raised her voice.

'I don't know. I'd had a few vodkas by then.'

'Did you see him after Hannah's altercation with Lucy?'

'I wouldn't swear to it. Not on a bible, like.'

'Time enough for swearing on bibles in court, Cormac. Tell me, did you return to him for more "you know"?'

Now she was mocking him. He sat on his hands to still them. He reckoned if he was a cartoon character, his eyes would be popping out of his head on springs. Keep the fuck calm, he warned himself.

'The only thing I did after the fight was help Hannah get cleaned up. And everyone saw that.'

'Where did Hannah clean up?'

'In the bathroom.'

'Which bathroom?'

'Beside the kitchen.' How many frigging bathrooms were there in Lucy's house? Any time he'd worked there, he'd rarely seen the inside of the house. Had had to piss into the rose bush by the back wall. No need to tell her that.

'Was there much blood?' She was relentless.

'I don't think there was any blood.'

'Really?'

'It's the truth.' He racked his brain, trying to remember. No. There had been no blood. Not then, though.

'Why did she need to get "cleaned up", as you say?'

'Her make-up was all over the place. She looked like she was possessed. They were just clawing at each other, pulling at their clothes. That's all.'

'Mmm. You see, Cormac, if that's true and there was no blood at that time, it makes me wonder ...' Her voice trailed off.

'Wonder what?' he couldn't resist asking.

'We found blood under Hannah's fingernails. We also forensically examined a towel found in her rucksack.'

'What does that mean?' *Cool, be cool, man.* But it was difficult with rivers of sweat trickling down his spine, pooling in the small of his back. He was finding it harder still to act his twenty years.

She looked at him as if he were dense, and took another sip of coffee before carefully replacing the cup on the saucer. 'Here's the kicker, Cormac. We found traces of Lucy's DNA on your shirt. The DNA of an innocent seventeen-year-old kid.'

'Kid?'

'Anyone under eighteen.'

'You think Lucy was an innocent kid?'

'Wasn't she?'

'Maybe.' He tried a nonchalant shrug, but he knew she wasn't buying it.

'Do you see what I'm getting at, Cormac? About the DNA evidence?'

'Yeah, I do.' He did see, and he didn't like what he saw coming next. The panic built in his chest and he wished he had his inhaler. 'The lab might have mixed up a test or something.' He fought the growing nausea constricting his stomach into a knot.

'Believe me, the lab technicians did everything correctly. Drink your coffee. You have to make a new statement. I'm sure we'll get to the bottom of it in no time at all.'

'I ... I can't go now, I have to meet someone.' He didn't like the way she was smiling, like a fucking cheetah about to pounce.

'Text them. Say you'll be late. Very late. Maybe twenty years late?' Her insincere smile mocked him.

This was bad, so fucking bad. 'Should I look for a solicitor?'

The smile died on her lips. 'That would be a very good idea, Cormac.'

Maybe the time for lies was over.

60

Sharon Flood found it difficult to breathe as she ran. She had sat by the harbour for ages, thinking of her big brother. She wondered what exactly had happened to him. Coming to the conclusion that it was all her fault, she'd got up and started to run. Now she stopped and leaned over with her hands on her knees, trying to get some normality into her breathing. In and out. In and out. And then she was running again, her shoe without the lace flopping. She was in danger of losing it.

On reaching the main gate of the old army barracks, she scooted inside without meeting anyone.

As she moved along the interior perimeter wall with the large courtyard to her left, she glanced up at the buildings to her right. The office blocks rose four storeys high. She'd overheard Jake mention the barracks on his phone when she'd been listening outside his bedroom door. She'd often earwigged. He'd even caught her once and given out to her. She'd hated him then. Not really hated, she reminded herself. And now she was the reason he was dead.

She headed down to the building at the end of the court-yard and stared at the weather-beaten door in front of her.

She put a hand to it, but it seemed to be either locked or stuck. She gave it a shove with both hands and it moved inwards.

Stepping over the threshold, she retched at the awful smell. Scattered around her feet she could see lots of rotting rubbish. She froze, hand to her mouth. Were some of the fast-food wrappers and cartons actually moving? Or was it from the breeze behind her? That was what she hoped anyhow, and she turned to shut the door.

With her eyes partially shuttered to the state of the place, a hand to her nose to block the vile odours, she glanced into the rooms on the ground floor. All empty. Hadn't she heard Jake mention something about their den being here somewhere? It had to be upstairs.

She ran upwards on her tippy-toes so as not to make too much noise. It seemed like no one was around, but she wasn't taking any chances.

She must find the person Jake had been storing the drugs for. She had the coins from her money box wrapped up tightly in a Haribo bag in her knickers. Five euros and fifty-five cents. She hoped it was enough to keep herself and her mam from being murdered like Jake.

The building seemed to be empty. She felt her heart grow heavy. At the end of the corridor she noticed a narrower wooden staircase. Up she went to the third floor. Nothing. Sinking to her knees on the roughly hewn floorboards, her body flooded with disappointment. Then she heard a sound.

A noise downstairs?

She dared not breathe.

A door banged. A breeze fluttered up the stairs, rattling the wires hanging from the ceiling. Sharon wondered if it was the person she wanted to talk to. The person who could tell her why her big brother was dead and why he had had a bag of liquid drugs hidden in his bedroom. Whoever it was, she needed them to know the guards now had the drugs, so they would leave her and her mother alone.

She moved over to the window, the glass panes cracked and shattered.

Waited.

Something whistling through the door behind her caused her to turn around.

A shadow spread across the opening. An ominous shadow.

She clasped a hand to her mouth, stilling the fear that was rising at speed from the pit of her stomach. The menacing shadow was followed by a hand holding something glinting in the thin light from the window.

A knife.

The shadow morphed into a body and slid into the room, snake-like. His mouth opened and words slipped out, fuelling the air with something like rat poison.

'Ah, Sharon, were you expecting to find someone else here?'

One step after another, he moved further into the room, until he was close enough to hold the knife under her chin, nicking her soft skin. Such was her terror that she felt the warmth on her leg before she realised with mortification that she had wet herself. The bag of change felt like a ton of wet bricks, sticking to her belly.

'Ah, the baby needs a nappy,' he scoffed. 'Have you lost your tongue as well?' The mouth curved downwards, the face twisted in a sneer. 'How about I cut it out? That way you can never tell lies like your stupid brother.'

The smell of his breath was overwhelming, but her fear of the knife beneath her chin overrode all else. She thought of her mam at home without Jake; now she'd be without her too.

He must have seen something in her eyes, because he lowered the knife and eyed her quizzically.

That was when she screamed. But such was her terror, only a strangled squeak came out of her mouth.

My wings are fluffed up and preened. I feel so good at having
snared this treasure at last. The knife in my hand is gleaming like
the North Star, lighting up the fetid room. I laugh at her childlike
scream. She sounds like a chicken squawking. I advance as she
backs up against the wall and slides to the floor, her thin shoulders shaking.

'Don't cry,' I say. 'It makes your face so ugly.'

'Go away.'

'Jake cried. He even screamed. Bad boy.'

'Piss off and leave me alone.'

'Oh, I have a fighter on my hands. That's so cute.' I walk
around the dirty floor, my nose wrinkling at the smell of her piss.
That makes me angry. I had wanted to swoop in and take what
was mine. To relish her innocent charm and fly away with her
under my wing. I had plans for her, but now I am not so sure.

'Dirty little girl. You disgust me. Pissing all over yourself.
Not nice.'

She is struggling to unbutton her jeans. She sticks her hand
down inside and I am about to tell her to stop because I have to
take a photo first when she drags out a revolting plastic bag.

'Take this for the drugs Jake had and please leave my
mammy and me alone. Please.'

I shake my head and kick the bag out of her hand. Silver
coins roll across the floor and settle somewhere among the
detritus.

'I don't want your money. I want you.' I take my phone out
then and hold it up, smiling as she cowers behind her elbow.

'Now be a good girl and smile for the camera.'

61

Lottie deposited an increasingly agitated Cormac in a cell to wait for a solicitor. She contacted the army liaison officer for troops abroad on peacekeeping duties, who promised to get a message to Cormac's dad. She gave the lad his inhaler that he'd left behind yesterday and made her way to her office.

She asked Garda Thornton to organise a duty solicitor for Cormac until they had word from his dad, and was told there would be a few hours' delay. She reckoned the delay might suit the boy. He needed time to think about telling her the truth. DNA evidence didn't lie, but there were three plausible reasons for Lucy's blood being on his shirt.

One, Cormac had killed Lucy and drugged Hannah so she would have no memory to dispute his version. Two, Cormac and Hannah had killed Lucy together. Or three, Hannah had killed Lucy, and Cormac had helped her clean up and escape afterwards. But there was also a fourth option. Neither of them had had anything to do with the murder but they had stumbled upon Lucy's body while her blood was still wet. Like Sean had.

At her desk, she got a message informing her that a knife had been found in the canal by the divers searching for anything to do with Jake's death. She rested her chin on her hand. How did Jake Flood fit into any of her scenarios? And what about the threat against Albert McAllister's business – to expose him for fight fixing and his clients for drug use – was it even relevant? And then there was the question of who had had sexual intercourse with Lucy prior to her death. No one had come forward. No lab results yet.

Her head was spinning with permutations.

She decided Cormac could stew until his solicitor arrived; Hannah likewise. She was trying to get her head straight on how best to conduct both interviews when her computer pinged with an email from Jane Dore. The pathologist's preliminary report on Jake Flood.

After reading it, she decided it was time for a quick team meeting. She'd seen Superintendent Farrell get into her car a few minutes earlier, so the coast was clear.

The incident room was taking on the usual hectic day two shape. The boards were filling up and the room hummed with activity as detectives and uniforms tried to find a spare chair.

Lottie suddenly had a spike of anxiety about her sick mother. She should have checked in with Chloe, but hadn't she told Sean to keep her up to date? He hadn't phoned yet. That was a good sign. Wasn't it? She paused, wondering if this was how the McAllisters had operated with Lucy. A phone call, rather than being present when needed?

With no time to berate herself over her empathy or lack thereof, she parked her guilt, pledging to be home early to tend to Rose.

'Listen up,' she said. 'I want everyone to hit the ground running, so let's make this meeting quick but productive.'

When the murmur of chatter died away, she began.

'Last night, the body of fifteen-year-old Jake Flood was

removed from the canal at Piper's Lane. The car he'd stolen
from his mother was found burned out this morning. Based on
the preliminary post-mortem report, Jake's death is officially
upgraded to murder. Slivers of glass were embedded in his back
and are being analysed against the shattered glass found at
Lucy's house. We believe the boy fell or was pushed through
the patio door. Blood analysis should prove that to be the case.
He was also beaten with a chain, then tied up and thrown into
the canal. No water found in his lungs. He was dead before he
was dumped in the water. The pathologist estimates he died
about eight hours before his body was found. Further analysis of
the blood in the McAllisters' living room proves Jake's was also
present. We have two murder investigations linked to Lucy's
party on Friday night.'

She paused as the group muttered, and waited until the
hum slid to a stop.

'To recap on the first murder, seventeen-year-old Lucy
McAllister sustained a knife attack, suffering seven stab wounds
to her torso. The fatal wound was to her throat. Blood analysis
proves that the initial assault occurred in the living room, before
she managed to drag herself up the back stairs to the room
where she eventually died.'

She pointed to the post-mortem photos. 'You don't need me
to tell you that it was a particularly brutal assault. The state
pathologist estimates that Lucy was killed between three and
four on the morning her body was discovered.'

'That time frame suggests ...' McKeown began. Lottie threw
him a dagger stare. He seemed to receive the message.

'The pathologist is also of the opinion that the weapon was
a steak knife. One is missing from the McAllister house, and
this morning divers discovered a knife in the area of the canal
where Jake's body was found. It will be examined and—'

'The little fecker killed Lucy,' McKeown said, keeping his
shaved head down, tapping his iPad. Lottie knew he was mad at

having to withhold information about Sean that proved Lucy was dead before four a.m.

'That *fecker*, as you call him, has a name, a mother, a little sister, and a father who died within the last year,' Lottie said firmly. 'Show some respect.'

He waved a hand in mock remorse, but he wasn't surrendering just yet. 'If it's the knife from Lucy's house, that means it wasn't premeditated murder. Something happened to provoke the killer. I think Jake Flood killed Lucy and then ...' Glancing up, he must have seen the rage flitting across Lottie's face.

'He didn't kill himself, Detective McKeown, if that's what you were going to say.'

'We have to keep all options on the table.' He eyeballed her.

What was his problem? She'd already told the meeting that the results she'd received were preliminary. He was being purposely obtuse.

'Back to Lucy,' she said. 'There are signs she was sexually active prior to her death. The final report indicates that a condom was used, but a trace of semen was discovered on her inner thigh. We don't yet know whose semen it is, but it is possible that whoever she had sex with is the same person who killed her. The semen DNA will be analysed against the database and against samples taken from every male suspect we bring in. Cormac O'Flaherty, Richie Harrison and Noel Glennon are currently top of that list. Comparative analysis is being run as we speak. Clothing taken from O'Flaherty's house has traces of Lucy McAllister and Hannah Byrne's DNA. Nothing was found in the search of Hannah's home, but she had blood on her hands, confirmed as a match to Lucy. I have a witness who can place Hannah's rucksack in the living room shortly after four a.m. That bag was on Hannah's bed yesterday morning when I arrived with Detective Kirby to interview her.'

'Slam dunk.' McKeown slapped the table.

'We need to confirm how and when Hannah got her rucksack from the McAllister property. That's a job for you, Detective McKeown.' She needed to pile him up with work to keep him out of her hair. 'I can accept that Hannah and Cormac or one or the other killed Lucy because of the photo of Hannah that she shared, but why remove a section of skin from the victim's upper right side?'

She pointed to the post-mortem photo of the wound on the board. Beside it was the photo from Lucy's social media.

'You can see that where the skin was removed, Lucy had a tattoo. A heart shape. I'm getting the photo forensically examined to see if we can find out what was written inside the heart. Initials, maybe?'

'I followed up with Ivy Jones, Lucy's friend,' Lynch said. 'She said she didn't know anything about a tattoo, but she must have done.'

'I want her formally interviewed under caution,' Lottie said. 'Did you locate Terry Starr? We need his DNA too.'

'Not yet.'

Kirby said, 'I spoke with Bradley Curran in Australia. He's Lucy's ex. He has no recollection of Lucy having a tattoo. They split up a year ago, so she must have got it inked sometime after they split.'

'Did he have anything to add about Lucy?'

'He said she was, and I quote, "hard work". He remembered that she constantly fought with her mother and was a daddy's girl.'

'Okay. We need to know more about Lucy and who she'd been secretly emailing.'

'Gary is working hard on it.' Lynch searched her notes. 'He says it's a fake email account buried under a Tor browser. It could be GuerrillaMail or ProtonMail. Apparently it makes the user anonymous. Gary is confident he can crack it.'

'Hope so. Ivy must know more than she's telling us.'

'I'll keep at her. Boss, there's something else I want—'

'Let me finish before I lose my train of thought. I'll come back to you.' Lottie checked her notes, already floundering under the amount of disparate information giving her no clear direction to advance either case.

'I want to talk more about Jake Flood. At his home this morning, under the floorboards of his bedroom, I found a bag of vials containing a bluish liquid. The vials are with the lab, but I believe the liquid is GHB.'

'The little shite,' McKeown said.

'Was Jake killed over drugs he was siphoning off from his supplier? Did he owe money? Was he involved in Lucy's murder? It's imperative that we establish the sequence of events now that we have a definite time frame for when the girl died.'

She paused, thinking about Sean. He'd seen the Fiat Punto as he walked towards Lucy's house around four a.m. Jake was still alive then, according to the pathologist, so had he been driving the car or had it been driven by someone else? If so, who? She didn't dare voice her thoughts. There was enough muddy water to traverse as it was. 'Any word on the movements of the car?'

'I'm working through traffic cams and whatever CCTV we can get our hands on, which isn't much,' McKeown said. 'So far, no luck.

'Another piece of the puzzle has been lobbed into the pot by Albert McAllister.' Lottie filled them in on the threat Lucy's father had received. 'Whoever sent the email said they would expose his clients for substance abuse and accused Albert of fight fixing. They demanded five hundred thousand euros and threatened to ruin his business, if it wasn't paid. The email is now with our technical department, and Gary tells me it's as sophisticated as Lucy's. Both email addresses were encrypted. Nothing to indicate they were sent by the same person, but it remains a possibility. Albert tells me the email was the reason they went to Malaga, because most of his business associates are located in Spain.'

'I can't understand why he'd leave his daughter at home with no protection,' Lynch said, 'after he received a threat like that.'

'Maybe he didn't see it as a threat against her, just against his business.'

'Or maybe he's just a greedy bollix,' McKeown said, 'who put his work before his family.'

'From what I've learned so far,' Lottie said, 'Albert adored his daughter, so to leave her at home like that, he must have been certain the threat was only against his business.'

'Terry Starr is his main client. What about him?' McKeown said.

'We need to trace his movements from the night of the murder until he got on his flight to Malaga. He most likely had nothing to do with the murder, but we need to eliminate him. Why did he go to Spain? Why did he come back? Where is he now? This all brings me to the boxing club where Jake trained.

'Ragmullin Goldstars is funded by Lucy's dad and Terry Starr. The coach is Barney Reynolds. He is Brontë Harrison's father. Brontë is married to Richie Harrison, the DJ.'

A few intakes of breath around the room.

Kirby said, 'Interesting connection.'

'Indeed. I want Barney Reynolds and the club investigated. Detective McKeown, please update us on the background checks on Noel Glennon, Richie Harrison, Cormac O'Flaherty and the cleaner, Sarah Robson.' Lottie tapped her finger on the desk.

'Erm, I'm working on them. I'll have a report to you later.'

'Sooner than that. I need to know more about Noel Glennon and the Harrisons in particular.'

'I also have to look at the traffic cams, shitty CCTV and dash-cam footage for Flood's car, but I'll do my best.'

'Do you want a medal?' Kirby said.

Lottie said, 'I need those background checks, yesterday.'

As the team dispersed, armed with their instructions, she wondered what could be the thread to link everything together. She glanced at the incident board. It was there in the midst of it all. She just had to find the thread and pull hard.

As Lynch approached her, Lottie's phone vibrated, skidding across the table.

Chloe.

'Boss,' Lynch said, 'I found a disturbing photo and I—'

'Let me take this, Maria. Bring in Ivy Jones and question her about Lucy's tattoo and the weekend away. Find Terry Starr. We need to know the reason for his quick trip over to Spain. I have to take this call.'

62

'What's up?' Lottie said to her daughter.

'Granny's in hospital. I had to call an ambulance. I'm with her in A&E.'

'Oh God, is she okay?'

'She's fine now. Giving orders to the nurses. They put her on a drip because she was dehydrated. They want to admit her for more tests but she's kicking off now.'

'She's on the mend so.'

'I didn't want to worry you, Mam, but Sean said to let you know.'

'Thanks, Chloe. I'll get there as soon as I can.'

'No need, it's fine. If there are any developments, I'll phone you. Okay?'

'Okay.'

After Lottie finished the call, she held her head in her hands. *How can I cope with my mother being ill?* Confusing emotions caused her chest to tighten. When everything was weighed up, good and bad, she knew she loved Rose, and Rose loved her. Boyd had made her see what had been in front of her nose, especially since Adam's death, when her resentment against her mother had festered. The lack of outward affection could have been terminal for their relationship if Boyd hadn't stepped in. She wanted to hear his voice.

Feeling better, she tapped his number. It went straight to voicemail. She hung up without leaving a message. She'd speak to him later.

First she had a murderer to catch.

There was still no sign of a solicitor for Cormac or Hannah, and Lynch had left the office, probably to find Ivy Jones, so Lottie was rereading the preliminary report on Jake Flood when Garda Lei knocked on the door.

Shifting like he had ants in his pants, he said, 'Sorry. Hello, Inspector.'

'Come in.'

'I've got a lead on where the lads on the bikes hang out. Do you want to come with me, or should I ask someone else? It's okay either way. Just thought I'd ask, you know, like. Sorry for disturbing you.'

'Is it in town?' Lottie scratched her head, unravelling the message couched somewhere in his words.

'Yes, it is.'

She plucked her bag from the floor. 'Come on, let's go.'

'Do you want me to follow on my bike? They mightn't even be there, but I just thought, you know ...'

'I'll drive. Let's go.'

Garda Lei talked so much, Lottie felt woozy as she drove into the army barracks. A direct provision centre had once been located on the premises until Lottie and her team had uncovered a gruesome human and organ trafficking operation, in part helped by Boyd's ex-wife, the elusive Jackie.

She pulled up in front of the old officers' quarters. She'd often been in the NCOs' mess with Adam, but never in the officers'. Rank, and all that.

'The kids use this as their base,' Garda Lei said when they'd exited the car.

'How did you find out?' The air had cooled since yesterday and she was sorry she'd left her jacket in the office.

'The bicycle shop owner said he'd overheard one of them mention it. I thought we might get lucky and kill three birds with one stone. You know what I mean?'

'I think so.'

She fetched her garda fleece jacket from the boot and stood beside Lei. She couldn't believe how derelict the buildings had become.

'How will we do this?' He shuffled from foot to foot and fluttered his hands about. Maybe he should have brought his bike to keep him from fidgeting, she thought.

'Stay in the car if you like.'

'Oh gosh, no. Not at all.'

'Follow me. And stop waving your hands. You're making me seasick.'

She had to give the lad a break. After all, he'd got the information, whether it turned out to be relevant or not.

The door pushed in easily, the lock busted a long time ago, evidenced by the amount of rust on the mechanism. She stepped inside, walking on top of debris. Bottles, cans, fast-food wrappers. A feeding ground for vermin. An involuntary shiver shook her spine and she tugged the sleeves of the fleece down over her hands.

Pressing forward, she glanced into the side rooms. A narrow staircase beckoned her upwards. Pausing at the bottom, she craned her neck to see around the bend halfway up and listened. Was that something skittering along the floorboards? Were there even floorboards left up there?

'If you want, I can go ahead of you,' Lei said.

She held a finger to her lips. 'No need to alert the world to our presence,' she whispered.

'Oh, sorry. I didn't think—'

'Shh, for God's sake.'

She ploughed on up the stairs. On the landing, she heard squeaking and stopped quickly. Her companion ploughed into her, almost knocking her off balance.

'What the ...?'

'Jesus, Inspector. I'm sorry. I didn't mean ... I'm sor—'

'Quit it.' Lottie glared at him over her shoulder.

Lei blushed and stumbled back. She grabbed his sleeve and he righted himself.

'And don't say sorry again.'

The landing was as narrow as the stairs and the accumulation of rubbish worse than in the hallway below.

'Stay here,' she instructed in a whisper. 'Keep an eye out for anyone arriving or leaving.'

The young guard nodded energetically. She escaped down the narrow corridor before his head flew off.

The doors had been removed from their hinges. In places, the walls had been stripped of paint and plaster, exposing wires and insulation. Plasterboard hung loose from ceilings; floorboards had been ripped up. She searched each room only to discover similar carnage.

At the end of the corridor she reached another flight of stairs. She mouthed at Lei to remain where he was and began her ascent.

The skittering and squeaking was louder now. It appeared to be coming from within the stripped walls. She pulled up her fleece hood, sheltering herself from anything that might drop from the exposed ceiling, then clamped her arms to her body, jacket cuffs down over her hands, and inched forward.

On this landing Lottie was met with a similar level of

neglect and dereliction, but one door remained on its hinges. She edged forward. The lock was damaged. A wire hanger in the slot where a handle should be. Pressing her shoulder to the door, she pushed it inwards.

A child's soft whimpering greeted her.

She quickly assessed the level of danger she might be walking into, but only the child was present.

'Sharon? Oh my God, are you okay?' She noticed a streak of blood on the girl's chin. 'What are you doing here?'

She reached out, but Sharon kept hugging her knees, her tear-stained face red from exertion. At first glance, Lottie couldn't see any obvious wounds, but what about those she could not see?

'Take my hand, Shaz,' she said. 'You're safe now. Come with me.'

'Go away. You're making it worse.'

Hunkering down to the girl's level, Lottie noticed a scattering of coins on the floor and a balled-up sweet bag.

'I know you miss Jake, and I want to find out what happened to him. I need you to help me, Sharon. I can help you too.'

'No one can help me.' Sharon refused to unlock her hands from her knees. 'Jake is dead.'

'Why are you here? Do you know what Jake was mixed up in? But listen, whatever it was, it wasn't his fault. He was grieving for your dad and grief sent him off in the wrong direction.'

'You don't know what you're talking about.' Sharon's breathing was strained, but she managed to scoff.

'Oh sweetie, I know a lot more than I'd ever admit.' Lottie rested a hand on top of Sharon's. The girl was trembling, her skin clammy. 'My husband Adam died a few years ago and I went off the rails big-time, a bit like Jake did. A good friend helped me, so I know I can help you. Will you let me be your friend?'

The little girl stared into her eyes as if searching her soul to see if she was speaking the truth. So pale and shivery. Lottie wondered if she was hiding an injury.

Sharon seemed to lose the fight then and rested her head on top of Lottie's hand. 'Jake talked about following his dream. He needed money. Dad used to pay the bills and stuff and now Mam hasn't a clue.' Her breath was expelled in a series of gasps as she struggled to utter the words.

Forcing a neutral expression, Lottie considered the best way to handle the child. She needed to get her out of here, but she didn't want to push her, to alienate her.

'You think Jake got involved with this gang to make money, and then he couldn't escape because he owed them?'

'He didn't know how dangerous they were.'

Expecting a deluge of tears, Lottie was surprised when Sharon raised her head and a hard glint spiked in her eyes. This child had learned to grow up way too fast.

'I need to get you out of here,' she urged.

Sharon shrugged off Lottie's hand and clutched her own tighter around her knees. 'Go away.'

'Who were you hoping to meet?'

'No one.' She released one hand and thrust her thumb in her mouth. To stop herself blurting out a name? Or reverting to a childhood habit? No, she was still a child.

'Is this their hideout? Do you know someone in the gang?'

'Stop asking questions.' Sharon bounced her head against her knees repeatedly. 'I can't talk to you. Please, leave me alone.'

'It can be our secret.'

She raised her head quickly, her face deathly pale. Through clenched teeth she hissed, 'I know it was drugs you took from Jake's room. Me and Mam will be killed if they don't get their drugs back. I wanted to pay them ...' Steely eyes, determined to win this battle. 'I tried.'

'You have to tell me who you hoped to find here,' Lottie begged, her ankles starting to creak.

'I heard Jake on his phone. He talked about this place. I swear there's no one here. Only you. Go away.' Defiance coated Sharon's words, but her breathing was worse.

Where was her injury?

'Who's in charge of the gang?'

A quick dart of bloodshot eyes around the room before she wilted and whispered, 'I only know one of them. He's the same age as Jake but Jake called him "the kid". I think he's evil.'

Lottie reckoned there was someone more senior pulling the strings than a kid, but she wanted Sharon to say a name in order to check if it was one of the three Garda Lei had discovered.

'Who are you talking about?'

'Oscar. Now go away.'

Lottie held out her hand. 'Come on, sweetheart. I'm taking you home to your mum.' She prayed that this time the girl would acquiesce, and sighed with relief when she did.

Sharon's hand was soft and sweaty. A child's hand. A little girl who carried her dead brother's burden like an anchor weighing her down. Fighting the urge to fold her into a hug, Lottie stood, legs numb with pins and needles. That was when she noticed the dampness on the girl's unzipped jeans and the bloodstain spreading across her abdomen.

'Oh dear God, Sharon, you're hurt.'

The child tottered before falling into her arms in a faint. Lottie lifted her dead weight to her chest and carried her out of the filthy, disgusting room.

'Lei! We need an ambulance. Radio. Now.' She was in a panic but couldn't help herself.

Lei climbed the stairs quickly and took Sharon from her arms, talking into his radio simultaneously. Sharon's pink runner with no laces fell off as he carried her down the stairs. Lottie slumped on the top step trying to make sense of what had happened. She prayed the injury wasn't serious. Prayed the little girl hadn't been abused. Shocked tears stung her eyes at this thought. No way. The gang were into drugs. That was all.

She heard Garda Lei soothing the child and silently thanked him for his gentleness. Sharon must have come out of her faint; Lottie heard her crying, the sobs disappearing as they went out of the door below.

The damaged and the damned. Coiled up in the bones of one so young.

Lottie picked up the lone shoe and wept.

63

Terry Starr pulled up outside the Goldstar boxing club. He was half afraid of leaving his new Range Rover in the back yard, in case some little bastard robbed it, but he wanted to punch someone and a punchbag would have to do. The door was locked but he had a key. This was where he had first learned to box, so it was like coming home.

He shouldered his kitbag and slipped inside the building. He was glad Barney wasn't around or he'd punch him too. He'd phoned Albert, asking for a meeting, but the grieving father hadn't turned up yet. They really needed to talk about Lucy.

He pulled his training gloves from the bag, slipped them on and fastened the Velcro. He would box to rid himself of the pent-up pressure. Only then would he be able to think of what he wanted to say to Albert.

———

Having composed herself, Lottie put Sharon's shoe in her pocket and was about to go down the stairs when she stopped.

Why had Sharon been up here? There was no one else around, was there?

Back in the room where she'd found the child, she looked upwards. Part of the ceiling had caved in and she couldn't see how anyone could gain access to the void above. Not from this room.

Moving next door, she was rewarded when she saw a ladder leading up to a loft. She thought she could smell weed. A guitar stood forlornly in a corner, two strings broken. As she climbed the ladder, she asked herself again why Jake Flood had been murdered.

At the top of the ladder she peered inside the cavern.

She'd found the gang's lair.

Sleeping bags and upturned crates. A box of Red Bull in the middle of the floor. A miniature fridge in one corner, which was strange as there didn't seem to be any electricity in the building. Or maybe she just assumed that because of the state of disrepair.

As she hauled herself into the space, a wave of claustro-phobia enveloped her. A shard of light streamed through a hole in the roof and her airways were quickly clogged from the insu-lation fibres floating in the air. Once she had balanced her knees on a wooden beam, she crept towards the nearest sleeping bag and reached out a hand. Before she could touch it, it moved.

Her body went rigid, hand poised in the air. Her vermin phobia paralysed every muscle and sinew. The sleeping bag was moving again, rising from the floor. A hand appeared from the folds of the nylon covering. It was attached to an arm inside a blue sweatshirt. Then the dazed face of a teenager was revealed as he emerged from his makeshift bed.

She fell backwards, almost tumbling through the hole, stop-ping herself just in time. The boy flung himself against the wall behind him. His face, initially masked in pale fear, was quickly replaced with a red-hot anger.

'How the fuck did you get up here?' he shouted.

'It's okay,' she said, struggling to regain control. 'I'm not here to hurt you.'

'You won't get a chance. I'll get you first.' His voice was high-pitched, as if it hadn't yet broken, but he looked about four-teen or fifteen. Was this the evil kid Sharon had mentioned? Oscar? In his hand he held a bicycle chain, and he began to wrap it around his fist, ready for attack.

'Put that down,' she said.

'Who's going to make me? You and whose army?' he sneered, not an ounce of fear in him. 'Fuck off.'

Lottie gambled on him being Oscar, the boy Sharon had mentioned. Had he hurt the little girl? She might just have struck lucky, because Jake's body had borne signs of having been beaten with a chain. Maybe this was the break she needed to wrap up his murder.

'It's cold up here,' she said. 'Why don't we have a chat downstairs?'

'Why don't you fuck off and leave me alone?'

'I can't do that, Oscar.'

'How do you know ...?'

'Listen, Oscar, I'm going back down the ladder, and you're to follow me.'

He remained silent. Good sign? Maybe not. Feck it.

She eased backwards towards the opening in the floor. Her feet found the ladder and she climbed down into the room below and stood beside a window with a broken pane of glass.

She inhaled air from outside. Garda Lei was standing beside the car and she hoped Sharon was safely inside. Where was the ambulance?

The ladder creaked and she whirled round on the balls of her feet. A pair of legs in a grey tracksuit and expensive-looking high-top trainers climbed down with ease.

Moving to the doorway to block the boy's escape, Lottie was

surprised when he stood staring at her, the chain wrapped tight on his hand, thumping his thigh.

'I didn't touch Jake. None of us did.'

'I never said that.'

'A pig was snooping around asking about us.'

'That was Garda Lei. We'd like a chat with you. Come on, Oscar.'

'Did Shaz tell you my name?'

'We found out about you ourselves.' So he knew the girl.

'Bet it was the cop on the bike. He's always trying to catch us. We're too fast for him.'

Why had Sharon called him evil? He was nothing more than a cocky teenager. Still, he had the bicycle chain in his hand. She had to play it cool.

'Come on, I'll buy you a McDonald's. I bet you're starving.'

He licked his lips, his face a mask of indecision. 'Okay, but you go first.'

'Fine,' she said. 'Don't disappear when my back is turned.'

She moved out of the room to the landing and cast a look over her shoulder to make sure he was following. She had gone down four steps when the clink of the chain alerted her to what was coming. Rookie mistake. The whack to the back of her head sent her stumbling downwards. She yelled, or at least she thought she did, as first her head cracked against the wall, then her spine, and down she tumbled into the detritus on the ground floor.

She didn't even see stars as the black curtain fell heavily on her world.

———

Everything is spiralling out of control. My feathers come loose and flutter away on the whim of a breeze.

The shiny things I've coveted are now corroded and poisonous.

Youthful innocence is no longer sufficient for me.

I flounder around in circles like never before.

I am in trouble.

I need to clear out my nest, put my affairs in order, gather my associates close and my enemies closer.

It is time for the magpie to find a new nest.

64

Garda Lei was standing over her when Lottie opened her eyes. A relieved smile broke across his youthful face.

'Don't move, Inspector, I've called another ambulance.'

Pain spiked as she groaned. 'You what? Cancel it. Don't need it.'

She attempted to stand on the filthy floor, but her legs wobbled in sync with her throbbing head and she gave up the attempt. She felt under her hair, surprised when her fingers came away bloody.

'That little shit.'

'Don't worry. I took him by surprise when he came sprinting out the door.'

'You caught him?'

'I sure did. He's handcuffed to a post. He's not happy at all.'

'I'd say that's an understatement. Help me up, please.'

She took his outstretched hand and stood gingerly. Outside, she inhaled deep breaths, trying to clear her lungs of the filaments of insulation she was sure she'd swallowed.

Barney Reynolds, in a navy Adidas tracksuit, was standing

by her car, while Oscar was angrily attempting to free himself from the post, chafing his wrists on the ties.

'What are you doing with Oscar?' Barney Reynolds came towards her.

The siren of the approaching ambulance shattered the air. Lottie pushed past Reynolds, momentarily wondering why he was there, and peered into the car. Sharon was curled up on the seat, a garda jacket wrapped around her. She looked like death.

'Oh Sharon, what did he do to you?' Lottie felt her own pain pale to insignificance as she took in the girl's fearful eyes and laboured breathing. Sharon remained mute. 'Ambulance is here. They'll take good care of you.'

'Don't tell M-Mam.' Her lips were as white as her face.

'I have to tell her, sweetheart.'

Behind them, the ambulance parked up and the siren died. As a paramedic leaned in to check Sharon, Lottie backed away and zeroed in on the boxing coach.

'What are you doing here? Do you know Oscar?' she asked.

Reynolds ignored her first question, flapping his hands, flustered. 'I don't *know* him as such. He joined the club a while back, but he didn't like it. Why is he tied up like a turkey?'

'He's about to be charged with assault.'

'Assault? Who did he assault?'

She turned around so he could see the streak of blood matting her hair. 'Me for starters. Why are you here, Mr Reynolds?'

He shifted from foot to foot. 'I have a storage unit for gym equipment in that building over there.' He turned and pointed to a block behind him. 'Needed to pick up a punchbag, not that I have to explain myself to you. Saw the lad struggling with that guard.' He backed away. 'You seem to have it all in hand, so if you don't mind, I'm in a hurry. I only came over to see if I could help.'

I'm sure you did, Lottie thought as he rushed off across the courtyard. She turned to see Sharon being lifted onto a trolley. She squeezed the soft flesh of her hand in reassurance.

'You're going to be fine, Shaz.'

Sharon closed her eyes slowly, as if the effort of keeping them open was too much for her.

'Will she be okay?' Lottie asked the paramedic – Louise, according to her name badge.

'Blood pressure is dangerously low.'

Before she pulled the restraining strap across Sharon's waist, the paramedic lifted the girl's top to check where the blood was coming from. That was when the full extent of her wound became clear.

'Good Lord.' Lottie's hand flew to her mouth, a reflexive action. 'That's deep.'

Louise called over the second paramedic and they worked quickly to staunch the blood with a dressing. When they were satisfied, they speedily set up an IV before raising the strap further up the girl's chest and drawing a blanket to her chin. Then they wheeled the trolley onto the hydraulic lift.

As the vehicle drove off, blue lights flashing and siren blaring, Lottie silently prayed that Sharon would be okay. She couldn't imagine visiting Liz to tell her that her last remaining child hadn't made it.

Another shriek of sirens alerted her to the approach of a second ambulance. 'Ah no!'

She looked around for her colleague. 'Garda Lei? I told you to cancel that ambulance.'

'Too late,' he said. 'You need to be checked by a medic. You might have concussion and you'll need stitches.'

'Not happy with the superhero antics, now you're a doctor too?' She wondered from where he'd suddenly acquired his assertiveness. She liked the nervy Lei better.

The ambulance was followed in by two squad cars.

Shit, he'd called out the cavalry.

65

Cormac O'Flaherty was still stewing, or maybe by now he was simmering. Let him, Lottie thought as she felt the growing bump on her head. His father had been contacted and was organising a solicitor. She really needed to spur on the interviews. Hannah Byrne was waiting too. God, she couldn't even form a cohesive thought; how would she be able to conduct critical interviews? She tapped her keyboard, the sound echoing in her head.

She'd escaped from the medics with five Steri-Strips knitting her head wound, which stubbornly refused to cease bleeding. She'd been told to attend A&E if she felt worse later on. Not a chance in hell. The mention of A&E led her to think of Rose, and she was about to phone Chloe for an update when Garda Lei appeared.

'That young lad Oscar is in the interview room. You got a right bump, didn't you?'

'Just find his parents for me.'

Two more of the gang members had been rounded up. All pleading innocence. The little bastards. Hearsay wasn't evidence, so they'd had to be released. But she still had the tight-lipped Oscar. She needed leverage to get him to open his mouth, but was unable to think straight with pain pounding a sharp beat in her head.

She headed down to the interview room, still wary of bumping into Superintendent Farrell. At this stage their avoidance appeared to be mutual.

'Where's my McDonald's?' The sullen boy glared at her, his expression twisting his youthful features into an ugly scowl. Where were the kids who feared and respected authority?

'That was before you tried to decapitate me with a bicycle chain.'

'You got in my way.'

'If you hit me with the same chain you used on Jake Flood, we'll match it forensically. Big trouble for you.'

'It's not the same one,' he mumbled.

She kept her surprise nailed down tight and went on the offensive. 'Why did you kill Jake?'

'What? Are you high, missus?'

'Did he steal from you?'

No reply.

'Talk to me.'

A wheeze of his breath into the silence.

'If you didn't do it, who did?'

Still nothing.

'Did you witness Jake being killed?'

Leaning back in his chair, staring at the ceiling now. He wasn't talking. This was useless.

'Why did you attack Sharon?'

He moved so quickly the chair tottered forward. 'I never touched her.'

'You must have, because she has a very nasty injury. She's been brought to the hospital. She might die.' God, Lottie hated herself at times, but needs must.

'I didn't touch her, I swear.' Fear replaced his earlier cockiness.

Who was the boy afraid of?

'You can talk to me, Oscar. You saw something. Tell me what you witnessed.'

A sneer returned to his face. 'No comment, pig.'

She shoved back her chair, a wave of agony shooting through her sore bones.

'I'm leaving you here to fry in the heat until your parents arrive. And mark my words, kid, I will charge you with assault and lock you up.' She felt a twinge of guilt for threatening him, but feck it, nothing else was working.

He shrugged a shoulder and forced a smirk. 'I'll be out in a few hours anyhow.'

And the annoying thing about it was that he was right.

'Don't bank on it. I know a judge who can't stand brats like you.'

'I didn't do anything.'

'The evidence will tell me a different story.'

'What evidence?' He sat up straighter.

'From the stash we found in Jake's house.'

'The scummy bastard. He *did* fleece us.'

At last, she'd cracked him. 'You admit to knowing about the drugs?'

His mouth hung open. He realised he'd made a mistake. Then a shake of his head. 'Don't know what you're talking about.'

'You do.'

'It's not me you should have in here.'

'Who, then?'

He chewed the inside of his cheek, childlike again, but she wasn't about to fall for that ruse.

'I can't tell you or I'll end up like Jake. Swear to God.'

'Give me something, Oscar. You owe me for this.' She twisted round and pointed to her head wound.

'Nah, you were in my way.'

Her turn to play the silent game.

Eventually he spoke, fingers fidgeting, clasping and unclasping his hands. 'It's all Jake's fault. That's all I'm telling you. I'm done.'

She racked her brain. Jake had had drugs hidden in his room. He had been a good kid but had fallen in with the wrong crowd after his father's death. He was a junior boxer getting ready for a big fight. And Barney Reynolds, the coach, had been hanging round the army barracks.

'Is someone connected with boxing involved in all this?'

Oscar's eyes widened, his jaw slackened and he bit his thumbnail. Then the glimmer of fear that had flashed across his face vanished.

'You're full of shit, cop-face.'

She left him sitting in the heat. She needed paracetamol, or codeine, or a shot of vodka. As the last was out of bounds, she'd have to settle for the pills.

66

Superintendent Farrell was talking to McKeown at the end of the corridor. Ducking her head, Lottie swung into the incident room. The exertion floored her. Every inch of her body ached.

Lynch, arms folded, was studying a new set of photos pinned to the board. 'You look like shit, boss.'

'Got any Solpadeine?'

She rooted in her tote bag and came up with a blister pack. 'Paracetamol okay?'

'They'll have to do.' Lottie dry-swallowed three Panadol and indicated the board. 'What's all this?'

'I tried to tell you earlier.'

Moving closer, Lottie studied the photos along the bottom. 'Let's see so. That's Lucy and Ivy. And isn't that Richie Harrison and Noel Glennon? Where did you get these from?'

'Gary got me into Terry Starr's Finsta.' Lynch tapped the photo pinned above the others.

'Fuck!' Lottie leaned back against the table and tried to make sense of what she was looking at. 'I don't understand.' She shook her head, relieved that the pills seemed to be working already. 'Did you locate Terry?'

'He's not at his Dublin apartment. I reckon he could be in Ragmullin. I don't know where, though. I've put a trace on his car and requested a check on the M4 toll booth cameras.'

'Did you ask Albert about Terry?'

'I tried but the McAllisters aren't at the Brook Hotel.'

'What? They can't go back to their home yet, so where are they?'

'No idea. Sorry.'

'This is a bloody disaster.' Lottie forced herself to calm down when she caught Lynch eyeing her intensely. 'Where could they be?'

'Albert isn't at his office and they haven't left the country. I checked. Maybe they went out for dinner somewhere.'

'Maybe Terry met with them and ... what? Something happened between them?' Lottie's brain was smothered with questions. Shit, this was bad.

'If Albert thought Terry had something to do with Lucy's death ...' Lynch paced a small circle. 'If he killed their daughter, maybe ...'

'But why would Terry bite the hand that feeds him? It makes no sense. No motive.'

Lynch tapped a page pinned to the board. 'Gary finally came up trumps with the email on Lucy's laptop. It was sent from an address in Ranelagh.'

'That's where Terry Starr lives.'

'Yep. He was clever, but obviously not as clever as Gary.' Lynch looked triumphant.

Lottie read the email with renewed interest. *Meet at Lagh Café, 19.00, Saturday. Bring a sexy nightie.* 'And we're sure there's no such a café in Ranelagh?'

'Yes, it could be code.'

'If Terry sent this email to Lucy, there had to be something going on between them. "Bring a sexy nightie." Fuck.'

'Will I organise a warrant to search his home address?'

Lottie pulled over a chair and sat directly in front of the incident board. 'Yes, but let's think this through first. Terry and Lucy had a dirty weekend away somewhere. Her house was free, but it mustn't have felt safe for them there.'

'He's thirty isn't he? Lucy was seventeen. Whatever they were up to, they were keeping it secret. Something's not right; besides the fact that if he had sex with her, she was barely the legal age of consent.'

'I get all that, but if they were in a relationship, what reason did he have to kill her?'

'Lovers' tiff?'

'I've had tiffs but I don't leave a trail of blood behind me. There's something else going on.'

'What?'

'If I knew that, I wouldn't be here brainstorming. Any luck on the tattoo?'

'Not yet, but maybe the initials were TS for Terry Starr.'

'Do you have proof?'

'No.'

Lottie leaned forward and unpinned one of the photos. 'Shit, Lynch is that ...?'

'Yes, it is. I tried to tell you.'

The photo shook in her hand. She couldn't quite understand what she was looking at, but it was making her sick to her stomach. 'Where was it taken?'

'At first I thought it might be a nightclub. It's shrouded in half-light, but look closely at the leather and stitching. I think it was taken in a car. A biggish one at that.'

Lottie examined the photograph carefully. 'An SUV of some sort?'

'Possibly.'

'Sweet Jesus. When was it taken?'

'No idea. It was posted on Terry's Finsta page a week ago, but it could have been taken any time.'

The two women fell into silence. Eventually Lottie voiced her thoughts, hoping Lynch would have a logical explanation.

'What was Sharon Flood doing sitting on Terry Starr's knee in a car?'

'I don't know, but the answer to your question might lift the lid off this secret world.'

She indicated the photo of Noel Glennon and Richie Harrison. 'Glennon said he didn't know Richie. A lie. So are they all in this together? Whatever *this* is. Any evidence of Hannah or Cormac in the photos?'

'Not that I've seen so far.'

'Keep digging, and find Starr and the McAllisters.'

'Sure, boss.'

'Have you spoken to Ivy Jones about these photos?'

'Not yet.'

'Can I keep your Panadol?'

'As long as you don't take them all at once.'

'I'd need something stronger to get rid of the rotten taste this is leaving in my mouth. And Maria, good work.'

In the canteen, Lottie fetched herself a full-sugar Coke. She'd read somewhere that it was good for migraines. She'd need a crate of it if she was to shift the carousel of confusion whirling out of control inside her head. On her way back to the office, she bumped into Garda Lei.

'I had a one-way chat with Oscar,' she said. 'Have you managed to contact anyone from his family?'

'That's why I was looking for you. His sister is in reception. She's a bit lippy.'

'I'll have a word with her.'

'Sure. Great. Thanks. That's fine, Inspector. Good.'

As she walked away, she pinged the tab on the Coke and gulped down half the can. Lei was still talking. Something about Oscar's address and his sister. She kept going, her head spinning.

In the reception area, she came face to face with a livid Ivy Jones.

'Ivy? What can I do for you?'

'You can release my delinquent brother, that's what.'

'Brother?' This was getting worse by the minute. Was this what Lei had been trying to tell her? Shit.

'Oscar Jones, my brother, the stupid prick. Mum will explode if she finds out you have him here.'

Failing to make sense of this revelation, Lottie said, 'Ivy, do you know why I had to bring him in?'

'No, and I don't care. He's always in trouble. Whatever you say, it won't shock me.'

'He hit me with a bicycle chain and knocked me down a flight of stairs. And I suspect he attacked a ten-year-old girl.'

Ivy rolled her eyes. 'Shit, he's out of control. He can stay here. I'll let Mum come to take him home. She'll flay him alive and—'

'It's time we had another chat, Ivy.'

A flutter of uncertainty flashed across the girl's eyes. 'I ... I can't. Sorry. I'm late already.'

'Something more important than your brother?'

'I've a ... a manicure appointment and I'll be late if I don't leave now.'

'On a Sunday? I won't keep you long. This way.' Lottie led the reluctant girl through to the interview room.

'Is he in there?' Ivy said.

'Yes.' Lottie opened the door.

Ivy marched in and stood, hands on hips. 'Oscar, I swear to God, you are impossible.'

'Piss off.'

'I can't believe you attacked a detective and a little girl. There's no hope for you.'

'Sit down, Ivy,' Lottie said forcefully. She needed to push on. She still had to contact the hospital to check on Sharon's status. Interview Hannah and Cormac. Locate Terry Starr and the McAllisters. Plus she had to visit her mother. And her entire body ached.

To her surprise, Ivy pulled out a chair and sat. She was even more surprised when Oscar began to sniff. Fake tears? She needed to measure the dynamic between brother and sister.

'Shut up, for God's sake,' Ivy snarled at her brother. 'You're making a show of me.'

Ivy was certainly the boss of this relationship, Lottie thought.

'Ivy, what do you know about Jake Flood?'

'Never heard of him.'

'He was at Lucy's party, working the bar.'

'Oh, that Jake.'

'Yes, that Jake. Why was he there?'

A shrug and pout. 'She must have asked him.'

'Lucy was your best friend. I'm sure you know more.' Leaning her hands on the table, Lottie stared into the girl's eyes.

'Be careful, Ivy,' Oscar said. 'She'll make you say stuff you don't want to say.'

'Shut up, you eejit,' Ivy said.

'Fuck off,' Oscar replied, but without conviction.

The boy was afraid of his sister.

Lottie quickly formulated her approach. Ivy's brother was involved with the same gang as Jake, and Ivy was the murdered girl's best friend. She'd have to launch an attack based on her suspicions and sprinkle it with a touch of the truth.

'Ivy, I believe you knew Jake Flood. You told Lucy he'd work the bar, isn't that right? Why did you want him there? To sell drugs to your friends? To kill Lucy? To drug Hannah? Get her to take the blame when she couldn't remember?'

'Are you for real?' Ivy made to stand.

'Sit down!'

'You can't make me. Oscar, we're leaving.'

'You two are going nowhere until you tell me about your roles in two murders.'

'What are you talking about?' Ivy sat, rolled up her sleeves and folded her arms. 'Are you on something?'

Her expression chilled Lottie. For a second she wished she actually was on something stronger than bloody paracetamol.

'Ivy, you knew Jake Flood was involved in your brother's gang. Kids riding around on bikes, accosting other kids and handing out colourful pills like they were M&Ms. Enticing them, hooking them, turning them into addicts while someone, perhaps you, got rich. I'm talking about children, Ivy. Do you see yourself as some sort of Fagin?'

Ivy turned up her nose, her mouth curved in an ugly sneer. 'You're nuts.'

'Who is your supplier?'

'Supplier? I have nothing to do with anything concerning Jake Flood or this twat beside me.'

'Bitch,' Oscar muttered.

Ivy thumped him on the arm. 'Shut your face.'

Now that she had both of them unsettled, Lottie changed the direction of her questions.

'Oscar, it could be your bicycle chain that was used to harm Jake. Did you kill him?'

The boy's mouth flatlined as his sister pulled him close and whispered in his ear. A cold smirk appeared on Ivy's upturned lips. 'We're saying nothing else to you.'

A trail of black spots danced in front of Lottie's eyes. She really should have someone in with her to formally interview these two. She needed their parents.

'I'll be back.'

She rushed out of the room and leaned against the closed door. Her body shuddered as she tried to shake off the feeling that there was something malevolent in the interview room. Was it coming from one of the Jones kids?

Or both?

Garda Lei agreed to sit in with the two teenagers while Lottie told Garda Brennan to find their parents. There was no point in discussing anything further with them without an adult present. It'd mean solicitors, but she could handle that. Better to have all the t's crossed.

She was about to fetch her keys for a quick trip to the hospital to visit Sharon and check on Rose when Gary called her upstairs to his workstation.

'Looks like you've been entertaining an army with soft drinks and fast food, Gary.'

'You're a slave-driver. I only have time to eat at my desk.' He was smiling, so that was okay.

'What have you got for me?'

'The threatening email that was sent to Albert McAllister; you mentioned it was about drugs in the sport, didn't you?'

'That's what he implied.'

Gary turned the screen, but she couldn't get close with the takeout boxes stacked haphazardly on the floor around the desk. The man was working in a pigsty.

'Can you print it for me?'

'Sure.'

She snapped the page out of the printer almost before it was done and flattened it out on a nearby desk.

Albert,

You have three weeks to declare your dishonesty. You fix fights and your clients take drugs. Your deceit can no longer continue. Within three weeks, you must reveal your role in

fight fixing. If you refuse, your family will suffer the conse-
quences. I also want half a million euros.

Both requests have to be met or I go public. Once you
make the revelation, I will contact you with instructions for
the payment.

Three weeks before the shit hits the fan.

Kind regards,

Your guilty conscience

Lottie stared at the words in front of her. 'What is this? It
clearly states his family will suffer. He fecked off to Spain and
left his daughter to fend for herself. Jesus!'

'Doesn't look good.'

'And there's no mention of him having to expose the
substance abuse. Albert lied to me. Can you trace the email
address, Gary?'

'It's cleverly encrypted, similar to the one on Lucy's laptop.
I eventually cracked that one.'

'You're a genius. Let me know, day or night, when you crack
the address on Albert's. Day or night.'

'Certainly, Inspector.'

She waved the printout. 'Someone is not telling the truth.'

67

Back in the office, Lottie picked up her phone to call Chloe for an update on Rose but instead found herself ringing Boyd.

Without giving him time to speak, she launched into the recent developments about Jake's death and the burned-out car, plus Sharon's injury. She omitted telling him about her own tumble down the old stairs.

'Terry Starr must be involved somehow. Haven't figured out how or why yet. He had a connection to Jake via the boxing. He could have been using the kids to push drugs for him.'

Boyd said, 'You have no proof and I doubt he'd ruin his reputation like that. Don't forget he was here in Malaga yesterday, so how could he have killed Jake Flood?'

'We don't have an exact time of death for the boy yet, but he was definitely killed some hours after Lucy. That would rule out Terry, but he could have had time to kill Lucy and make his early-morning flight.'

'What's his motive, though?'

'I don't know, but we've cracked an encrypted email address on Lucy's laptop. It came from a location in Ranelagh. That's where Terry lives. Probably thought it was safer than phone or text. They planned to meet up last week-end. It's got a coded location, some café. I'm waiting for Terry to be found to interview him. Albert got a threatening email too. Boyd, I need you to find out what you can about him over there.'

'I've no authority here, but I have kind of a link to the Spanish police and—'

'Great. I want to know what Terry Starr and the McAllisters were up to in Spain. There has to be something more going on for Albert and Mary to be there for three weeks leaving their daughter on her own. Why would they do that with a threat hanging over the family? It makes no sense.'

'Let me think.' He was silent so long, his breathing lulled Lottie into a sort of calm. 'Are you certain the email threat was authentic?' he said eventually. 'You need to grill Albert.'

'If I could find him. The McAllisters are not at the hotel and they have no access to their home. It's still a crime scene. Terry Starr is currently nowhere to be found. But I will track them down. In the meantime, see what you can find out. Please?'

'I'm heading home tomorrow. I've Sergio here and packing to do and—'

'Please, Boyd, can't someone watch Sergio for a few hours? I'm desperate.'

'Leave it with me. I'll do my best.'

'Thank you. I've another call coming in. Have to go. Love you.'

'Hey, Lottie, wait. I need to tell—'

She hung up and answered the other call.

'Inspector, can you come out to the McAllisters' place?'

'Gosh, Gráinne, I'm at the pin of my collar here. Just tell me.'

'Okay. We're finishing up with the garden cabin. We found a used condom and its wrapper stuffed down behind the cushions on one of the rattan couches. Hopefully the DNA in the semen will match one of your suspects.'

'Jane also recovered a trace sample from Lucy's leg. Fast-track what you found, please.'

'I will.'

'Thanks, Gráinne.' Lottie went to end the call, but the SOCO was still talking.

'You might not thank me in a minute. There's another reason why I'm calling you.'

She braced herself for whatever was about to be revealed. She wasn't sure how much more she could handle. 'Go on.'

'Thing is, I suspect the condom we found in the cabin is similar to the brand I found in your son's jacket pocket. His pack had one missing.'

'How can you be sure it came from Sean's pack?' Lottie closed her eyes. Dear God, please let it be a mistake, she silently implored.

'I can't be certain,' Gráinne said, 'but if it's not, then it's a very odd coincidence.'

Lottie hated coincidences.

She hung up and put her head on her desk, her ears ringing with bells of confusion. What the hell had Sean landed himself in?

Garda Brennan still hadn't returned with Oscar and Ivy's parents. Lottie wanted to talk to Sharon and see her mother, but first she had to find Sean. She grabbed her keys and fled the station. She had to look her son in the eye when she posed the question.

Outside her house, she gulped a few quick breaths. Silence greeted her as she made her way down the cold hallway. A good thing, or something to make her suspicious? At this stage she was too wired to care.

'Sean?' She leaned her head against the stair post.

No reply. Probably had earphones glued to his head.

After glancing into the kitchen to find a mess of bowls and a pot in the sink, she opened the living room door. The couch was still made up with her sheets, pillows and duvet.

Upstairs, she slammed into Sean's room. He was sitting with his back to the door. Some car race was playing on one of his computer screens, his headphones blocking out exterior sound. Swiping them off his head, she swivelled him around to face her.

'What the hell?' Alarm skittered across his face, his hand flying to his heart. 'Mam! You scared me. I thought it was Lucy's killer coming for me.'

'*I'm* coming for you, Sean Parker, and that should frighten you more.'

'What did I do now?'

Releasing the chair, she folded her arms and straightened her aching shoulders, ready for attack.

'The condoms found in your jacket pocket; one is missing from the box. When did you use it?'

His face blushed purple. 'I haven't had the ... erm, the opportunity to use ... Mam, this is so embarrassing.'

'One condom is missing from your box. And get this, my brilliant forensic team found it. Used. Shoved down behind a cushion in Lucy's garden cabin. Isn't that strange? I need an explanation.'

'What?'

'You heard me.'

'I ... Let me think. I bought the pack a while ago. Stuffed it into my pocket in case I met someone and ...'

She shook her head. 'And did you?'

'No.' His face was bright red.

'Why is one condom missing?'

He lowered his head and twirled the controller in his hand. 'Someone asked me if I had any spare.'

'Who asked you?'

'Ah Mam, can't you leave it at that? I don't want to get anyone into trouble.'

Lottie grabbed his hand to stop his incessant fiddling.

'Listen, Sean, you're the one in trouble. You have to tell me the truth.' She let go of his hand and paced his untidy room, despairing at the mess of dirty clothing and smelly runners. How could other kids wash their own clothes and her son couldn't? Then again, maybe the others were trying to hide something and he wasn't.

'I gave it to someone at the party. I'm not saying who ... I don't want to be a snitch.'

'For fuck's sake! This is a crucial piece of evidence. I won't be able to keep your name out of it if you don't tell me who you gave it to.'

'I felt sorry for her.'

The reality that he hadn't given it to another boy clicked. 'Ah shit. Do you know who Lucy intended to sleep with?'

'Lucy? You've got it wrong, Mam. It wasn't Lucy.'

Lottie stared at her son. 'Who then?'

'I gave the condom to Hannah Byrne.'

68

There was no time to digest or analyse Sean's revelation because she heard the front door open. As she raced back down the stairs, hoping her mother was home, she met Katie carrying a Tesco bag in each hand.

Her grandson held aloft an action figure still in its box. 'Look, Nana Lottie, I got Batman.'

'Later, Louis, I promise.' She smiled at her little grandson before turning to her daughter.

'I thought you were having Outback takeaway?'

'Chloe's got your credit card and she's still with Gran at the hospital. I'll throw on the chicken and chips that I bought with my own money.'

Lottie wasn't in the humour to argue, so she kissed her grandson and raced out to her car.

Before she interviewed Hannah again, she had to get to the hospital.

At the emergency department, Lottie found Rose asleep in a wheelchair in the corridor. An IV ran to a stand attached to the back of the chair. She hijacked a nurse to fill her in because there was no sign of Chloe.

'Your mother is dehydrated,' the nurse said. 'I've set up an IV to get fluids into her quickly. The doctor assessed her condition and wants to admit her.'

'Is it the summer flu?' Lottie asked helplessly.

'Her temperature is high and she has a UTI. When the fluids are finished, we'll do more tests. As soon as a bed is freed up, she'll be admitted.'

'My daughter was supposed to be here. I'll wait.'

'There's nothing you can do at the moment. I'll arrange for someone to give you a call once we get her settled on a ward. You might want to bring in nightclothes and toiletries.'

'Certainly. Thank you.' As Lottie turned away, she spied Chloe coming towards her, a coffee and sandwich in her hands.

'I was only gone five minutes,' she said defensively.

'Just take care of Gran. Call me when she gets a bed. Okay?'

'Sure.' Chloe set the coffee on the ground, leaned over and kissed her granny on the forehead. Then she sat on the floor and opened the plastic wrapper on her sandwich.

She noticed Lottie staring at her. 'Want half?'

'You're a life-saver,' Lottie said, taking the sandwich. Before she left, she bent and kissed the top of Chloe's head.

'What's that for?'

'To show you I care.'

'Go on, Mam. I'll call you.'

A porter told her where to find Sharon Flood. She took the lift to level three and walked along the sterile hospital corridor. Liz Flood was sitting on a chair outside the ICU, nursing a takeout beverage.

Lottie sat beside her. 'How is she?'

Liz bit her lip for a few seconds, then sipped her drink. The aroma reminded Lottie that she could do with a good shot of caffeine. She should have taken Chloe's.

'She said she was going to her friend's house. I thought that was where she was. She's seriously ill. She's being operated on.' Twisting on the chair, she looked at Lottie. 'They say she was stabbed. Possibly ruptured her spleen. They don't know what else was damaged, that's why they have to operate. Please tell me she'll be okay. I can't lose Shaz like I lost Jake and their daddy. I wouldn't survive it. Honestly, how could I go on?'

'I'm so sorry. It's a terribly worrying time for you. A colleague of mine was stabbed a few years ago and there's not a bother on him. He's out in Spain now, sunning himself. The doctors will do everything to help Sharon recover to full health.'

'Did you find the bastard responsible for hurting my little girl?'

'We have someone in for questioning.'

'Is it the same bastard who killed my Jake?'

'It's early in our investigations. I'm sorry, Liz, I can't tell you anything else at the moment.'

'Don't be bloody sorry, just do your job and charge him.'

'I will, I promise.'

Liz turned away and stared at the wall in front of her.

Lottie swallowed her awkwardness and decided to be bold. 'Can I ask you a question?'

'Sure.'

'Where were you the night Jake took your car to go to the McAllister party?'

'Okay, you got me. I wasn't at work. I was with someone. Met him two months ago and kept the relationship secret. I didn't want to upset my children.' Liz's face was streaked with tears. 'Now it looks like I might be about to lose them one after the other. This is what I get for moving on too soon after their daddy died. I was lonely. I needed a shoulder to cry on. And he isn't even here now. I should have spent my time with Jake and

Shaz and maybe they'd still be okay. I'm being punished for my selfishness.'

'No you're not, Liz. You're entitled to live your own life. Don't feel guilty. I promise Sharon will be fine.'

The swing doors opened and a woman dressed in blue scrubs approached.

'Mrs Flood?'

Liz put down her cup and stood quickly. 'That's me.'

'I'm Dr Rasheed. I was assisting on your daughter's operation. Can I have a word in private?'

'Please just tell me she's okay.'

The doctor pulled down her face mask and Lottie saw that the sadness in her eyes went all the way to her mouth. God, no, she prayed.

'Sit down for a minute, Mrs Flood,' Dr Rasheed said.

'It's Liz.' She sat, her frame rigid on the chair.

'Will I leave?' Lottie asked.

Liz shook her head, put out her hand. Lottie held it. 'Please stay.'

Dr Rasheed sat on the chair on the other side of Liz. 'The operation was very complex. Your daughter had suffered internal injuries. She lost a lot of blood ...'

Lottie closed her eyes. She knew what was coming next and she pitied the young doctor having to deliver the bad news. Her heart broke into a million pieces for Liz.

'Is she in recovery?' Liz asked. 'Can I see her?'

'I'm so very sorry. There's no easy way to say this ... Your little girl died a few minutes ago on the operating table. She went into cardiac arrest. We were unable to revive her. I really am very sorry.'

Liz's hand tightened on Lottie's.

Stealing a glance at the bereft woman, Lottie saw tears rolling slowly down her face, one after the other, like a death march.

The doctor continued. 'Once we complete the required protocol, you can see your daughter's body.' She stood, pressed Liz's shoulder and disappeared back through the double doors.

'What's happening?' Liz cried. 'I don't understand.'

'Is there someone I can call to come and be with you?' Lottie asked.

'I have no one. No one in the world.'

'What about your friend? Can I call him for you?'

'Don't. No. If I hadn't been with him, my children might still be alive. You can go now. I want to be alone. Please. Just leave me alone.'

Lottie didn't want to abandon the distressed woman, but now she had another murder to investigate. She stood and looked around, distracted. What was she to do?

'Just go,' Liz cried. 'And don't ever make promises you can't keep.'

69

The garage across the road from the hospital had a forecourt sign advertising coffee. In a daze, Lottie crossed the road to the shop. Once she found the coffee machine, she poured the black liquid into a disposable cup. Her hands shook terribly and she couldn't fix the plastic lid on properly.

The assistant looked bored as he lifted the cup and wiped the counter with a cloth. 'Wrong-size lid. Large lid for a large coffee.'

Like she was stupid!

'It's fine,' she said, searching her bag for her bank card and then remembering it was in her jeans pocket. As she tapped it against the machine, her eye was drawn to the cigarette dispenser unit behind the counter. 'I'll take twenty Silk Cut as well.'

'You could have told me that before I put the sale through for the coffee.'

'Just give me the damn cigarettes.' Her hands were jittery and she thought she was about to thump him or burst out crying. She couldn't get Sharon's death out of her head.

'No need to get your knickers in a ...' He must have caught

the anguished look on her face. 'Sorry, bad day all round, I think.'

'You can say that again.' She wouldn't have put it past him to repeat it and was thankful when he didn't, because she was liable to drench him with the coffee.

'Silver, blue, purple?'

'Pardon?'

He rolled his eyes and blew out a bored sigh. 'Light or strong cigarettes?'

'Strong.' She might as well be hung for a sheep as a lamb. The saying was one of Rose's. She should be with her mother, shouldn't she? No, Rose was better off with Chloe, who had more patience.

With the purple-branded cigarettes on the counter, she went to tap her card again and noticed the price on the tiny screen.

'I think you made a mistake,' she said.

'No mistake.' He smiled crookedly. 'Missus, how long is it since you smoked?'

She tapped her bank card without answer and didn't dare look at the restless queue behind her as she rushed out.

Back in the car, she dropped the window and lit up. She inhaled the nicotine before convulsing in a cough. Undeterred, she forced another drag. It did nothing to ease her despair. Cigarettes were useless as a salve on a wound. And in truth, she felt personally wounded.

She should have realised sooner that Sharon was badly injured and rushed her to hospital. Instead, she'd talked and talked, trying to extract information from the little girl. Though Sharon's death hadn't been caused by her directly, she knew she bore some responsibility. Her lack of action was akin to handing Superintendent Farrell another stick with which to beat her. The least of her problems.

Hands shaking with anger at her own ineptitude, she reached towards the cup holder for her coffee.

'Fuck's sake!'

She'd left it on the shop counter.

She flung the cigarette out the window and started the engine.

Wallowing in self-pity wasn't going to find the killer, or killers. She needed to bury herself in work.

The incident room dipped into silence before erupting in horrified questions when Lottie broke the news of Sharon Flood's death. She hurriedly dished out new tasks and called in SOCOs to examine the location where the child had been attacked.

Pausing to catch her breath, she decided to chance the canteen to see if she could salvage a late lunch and another coffee.

She caught sight of Superintendent Farrell storming along the corridor, so she scooted up the back stairs. With a feeling of being followed, she whirled around. Kirby was climbing the stairs behind her, wheezing.

'God, boss, I need to join a gym.'

She despaired for her rotund, perspiring detective. 'Kirby, you and I both know that's never going to happen.'

'I suppose you're right there.'

His breath smelled of cigars and she longed for another cigarette.

'What's up, anyhow?' she said.

'Cormac O'Flaherty's just finished a meeting with his solicitor. Are you okay to interview him?'

'The interview room is as good a place as any for me to hide.'

70

She entered the sweltering room, her hands shaking from the rush of nicotine and lack of coffee. Though she was heartbroken, she couldn't allow her guilt over the little girl's death to derail the entire investigation.

The solicitor, Brian Scally, a rake of a man with no hair, sat beside Cormac O'Flaherty. Scally had a wizened face like a prune. His starched shirt collar was eating into his scrawny neck. Sixty if he was a day. His navy suit, shiny from wear, rippled on his bones as he tapped a leather-covered A4 notepad with a silver pen. It could be an expensive Montblanc, but judging by the man's attire, Lottie concluded – unfairly or not – that it was more likely a cheap imitation. That observation helped her relax.

As Kirby dealt with the formalities for the recording, Lottie studied Cormac. The lad was trying to look like he hadn't a care in the world, sitting with one foot up on the chair, hugging his knee with both arms. He'd got rid of the zipped-up hoodie and she could see he was dressed in a short-sleeved plain black T-shirt to complement the custom-ripped jeans.

'I'm ready to begin if you are,' she said. 'We're entering a significant phase in our investigations, so I think it's time you told me the truth.'

'Told you all I know.'

'Did you, though? I believe you peppered your account with untruths and left gaps in your recollection of events. The fact is, Cormac, we now have a third murder on our hands.'

'A third?' Scally's eyes protruded like golf balls in his hungry-looking face.

'A young girl was stabbed earlier today. She died on the operating table …' Lottie paused to keep her emotions in check. She glanced at the clock on the wall, but she knew to the minute how long Sharon had been dead.

'Can't blame me for that. I was banged up in here.'

The solicitor nudged his client with his elbow and Cormac clamped his lips tight.

'Do you want to know who died?'

'Who?'

'Just answer "no comment",' Scally said.

Lottie ignored him. 'Cormac, Sharon Flood was murdered.'

He countered the flash of recognition that darted across his eyes by saying, 'Don't know her. No comment. That's it. No comment.' He dropped his leg to the floor and sat on his hands. Lottie saw a vein in his neck pulsing. The liar.

'Sharon was Jake Flood's little sister. Ten years old.'

She thought the solicitor paled, but the light was shite in the room so it was hard to get a proper read on him. Cormac's face had unmistakably turned to chalk.

'I … I don't know who you're talking about.'

'You knew her brother. Jake. He's the kid who sold you drugs at Lucy's party. You know who I'm talking about now?'

'So? I didn't do anything wrong. Recreational use.'

'We also suspect Hannah was slipped GHB. Date. Rape. Drug.'

'News to me.' He appeared blasé. Lottie wasn't buying his charade, though; his hands were trembling.

'Did you and Hannah have sex that night?'

'That's a no comment, son,' the solicitor said.

Cormac picked at a spot on his forehead, causing it to bleed. 'No comment.'

Lottie leaned in further. 'Listen to me, Cormac. Sharon Flood was assaulted in a room at the old army barracks. Stabbed. She'd gone there to talk to whoever had engaged Jake in drug pushing. She wanted to help her mother because she believed those people would come after them next.' Lottie gulped down her sorrow and stared at Cormac until he returned her gaze. 'Sharon was a brave little girl. Do you think you can be as brave as her? Can you emulate her by telling the truth? Or are you a bloody coward?'

'That's uncalled for,' Scally said, striking the table with his pen.

Returning her gaze to the mute Cormac, she said, 'Are you a cowardly rapist? Is that why you're scared to talk to me?'

'A r-rapist?' He shook his head vehemently.

'I'll be interviewing Hannah Byrne shortly. I believe her memory has returned.' White lie, but what the heck. 'I'm sure she'll tell me the truth when she hears a little girl has been murdered.'

Lottie grabbed the file, giving the impression the interview was over, and stood.

'Hold on. Wait,' Cormac said, his voice at an unnaturally high pitch. 'You've got it all wrong. Hannah wanted it. She dragged me out to the garden and down to the cabin, not the other way around, and we had … you know … It was consensual.'

'How can a girl who has been drugged with GHB give her consent?'

'I didn't know that, and she had a condom.'

'I'm sure many girls carry condoms. Doesn't mean they want to have sex with every waster they meet.'

'Is there a question there, Inspector?' Scally said.

'No comment,' Cormac said.

'Too late for that line,' Lottie said and sat. 'Tell me what really happened at Lucy McAllister's party.'

Without looking at his solicitor for a prompt, the lad launched into a jumble of words.

'Look, I'm nothing. I have nothing. I do a bit of gardening at the school and at Lucy's house and brand it landscaping to earn more money. That's all. I ... I panicked when you turned up yesterday morning asking questions. Twisted the truth a little. I was terrified.'

His solicitor put down his pen and folded his arms as if to say, it's your funeral, son.

'Go on,' Lottie urged.

'You have to believe me, no matter what Hannah says, I did not force her, but I didn't realise how out of it she was. Not then. Afterwards, we both fell asleep in the cabin. Something woke me. I thought it was a car engine, like an old car with a bad exhaust. Anyway, I shook Hannah. She was groggy and couldn't string two words together. I tried to dress her and pulled on my jeans and found my shirt. I just wanted to go home and have a proper sleep.'

'But you didn't go straight home, did you?'

'No.'

'What did you do?' Lottie hoped he was about to admit to the murder of Lucy McAllister. She kept her fingers crossed under the table.

'The party seemed to be over, even though there were lights on everywhere. I got Hannah into my car, but she started freaking out. Shouting about leaving her rucksack behind and how her mother would go ape when she saw the clothes she was wearing. She was totally ... What's the word?'

'Irrational?' Lottie offered.

'Yeah. She started thumping me. That was when I got most of the scratches, because I still had my shirt off. I pulled it on fast, I can tell you.'

'What did you do next?'

'You have to understand what Hannah was like at the time. You'd think she had a million euros in her fucking bag. Nothing I said could make her stop crying or leave without it. So we went back into the house. She came with me because I hadn't a clue what her bag looked like or where she'd left it. She was mumbling pure shite, but I figured out she'd left it upstairs, so we went up there. Found it in a room and went back down again. That's ... that's when we noticed the blood in the living room. The smashed patio door. Jesus.'

'Take a drink of water.'

He shook his head. His solicitor moved to whisper in his ear, but Cormac shrugged him off.

'I knew something bad had happened. There was no sign of Lucy. I said we should look for her in case she was injured or maybe someone else was. I dropped Hannah's bag on the couch and we went back upstairs. That's when ... we found Lucy.' He took the cup of water then and drained it.

Lottie had questions, but they could wait.

He squashed the cup between his fingers. 'She was covered in blood. She was dead. It was awful. I've never seen a dead person before and I was sure I'd throw up. We didn't kill her, that's the truth. Hannah freaked out again. Started to bawl. She nearly fell over on top of the body. I pulled her away, but her hands had blood on them and then I got the blood on me too.'

Shit, he was about to cry. Lottie could see the tears gathering along the rims of his eyes. *Not yet, lad.* She needed to get the full story before he fell apart. 'You're doing great, Cormac. What happened then?'

'I got Hannah down the stairs again, talking to her all the

time, struggling to calm her and trying not to leave blood anywhere. I pushed her into the living room to fetch her bag from where I'd dropped it. I wanted to get the hell out of that house. She screeched at me to wash the blood off her hands. We went into the bathroom downstairs and I scrubbed us both as fast I could. The towel was bloody, so I stuffed it in her bag and then we left.'

'Did you hear or see anyone else?'

'I think we were the only ones there, but I don't know.'

Lottie sucked in a relieved breath. Sean was in the clear. 'Why did you lie about finding Lucy's body?'

'I was terrified. We didn't make a pact or anything. I just think Hannah really doesn't remember. I took the same drug as her and I was fine, so maybe someone spiked her drink. I wouldn't put it past that Jake. He was watching her all night.' He paused. 'Can I go home now?'

Scally, the solicitor, found his tongue. 'My client is prepared to sign a statement confirming what he has told you. He has not committed any crime, so I ask that you release him.'

'If what he says turns out to be true, he—'

'It *is* true, all of it,' Cormac cried.

Lottie kept her gaze on the solicitor. 'He tampered with a crime scene. He left said scene. He failed to report a crime and the discovery of a body. He perverted the course of justice.' She cringed, thinking how Sean was guilty of the exact same crimes.

'Those are minor infringements that do not warrant his continued incarceration at this time.'

'Once I have his signed statement, Superintendent Farrell will make that call.'

'His father is frantically working with the army to be allowed home on compassionate grounds.'

'Cormac isn't dead.' Lottie couldn't help herself.

The lad flopped back in his chair. 'Ah man, if my dad has to come home, I'll be as good as.'

'Your dad is worried about you, Cormac,' Scally said. 'I've made arrangements for you to ring him once you're out of here.'

'He'll kill me for sure.'

'That'd be hard, seeing as he's still in Syria,' Lottie said.

'That's not even funny,' Cormac retorted. 'What have I to sign?'

71

Hannah Byrne was seated in the older interview room with her solicitor. It was a tight squeeze, but Lottie just wanted to get it over with.

'Where is Babs?' she asked.

'Hannah's mother has a two-year-old son to care for. Can I ask why my client is being kept in custody?' The solicitor looked almost as young as Hannah. Hair swept up in a bun, two curls trimmed over her ears, and foundation that rendered her face smooth as wax. Her eyes were as bright as the baby-blue jacket she wore over a cream silk blouse.

Lottie glanced down at her own faded T-shirt and grubby jeans. She needed a shower and change of clothes. There was probably still blood on her neck. To counter her embarrassment over her appearance, she scanned the single sheet of paper Kirby had handed her before they entered the room, searching for the solicitor's name. Cassie Ballesty.

'Ms Ballesty, I'm working around the clock on three murder investigations. I was ready to interview Hannah earlier, but her mother wanted a solicitor. Now that you're here, what has Hannah to say for herself?'

As Ballesty whispered in Hannah's ear, Lottie's head pounded. She needed more painkillers to help her concentrate and see the bigger picture. If Hannah and Cormac were innocent of Lucy's murder, which of the other suspects had a motive? Was she looking for more than one killer? She had three victims and no arrests. Easing her phone from her jeans she checked to see if Boyd had called. Nothing from him, but a text from Lynch. Superintendent Farrell was on the warpath.

'My client has nothing further to say to you.'

'Was the sex with Cormac consensual, Hannah?' Lottie barged in, ignoring the gasp from Ballesty.

'What?' Hannah gulped.

'What has that to do with a murder?' Ballesty said. She nudged Hannah. 'Reply no comment.'

'No, no,' Hannah cried, leaning towards Lottie, her palms outstretched in a plea. 'What are you talking about?'

Lottie inclined her head to one side, donning a sympathetic expression. 'Hannah, we know you had a sexual encounter with Cormac O'Flaherty at the fateful party. I'm asking you, was it consensual?'

'I don't understand.' Hannah swung round to her solicitor. 'What's she saying? I never had sex with anyone.'

'What did you drink at the party?' Lottie asked.

'Coke, I think. I still don't under—'

'Who served you?'

'The boy you asked about before. Jake. Please, did Cormac have sex with me?'

Lottie pressed on. 'Did you know Jake Flood before that night?'

'No. I never saw him before.'

'Did you know Sharon Flood?'

'Who?'

'Jake's little sister.'

'You have to believe me, I never heard of them.'

'When did you fetch your rucksack?'

'What? You're confusing me.'

'It's a simple question. When did you get your rucksack from Lucy McAllister's house?' She couldn't be any clearer.

Hannah shook her head. 'I can't remember.'

'Cormac says you woke up together in the garden cabin and he took you to his car to drive you home but you got hysterical, shouting for your bag. Do you recall any of that?'

'No. I swear.'

Lottie tended to believe her. 'Why do you think Lucy circulated that half-naked photo of you?'

Ballesty interjected. 'Inspector, I've been briefed about your interviews to date. I believe that issue has been sufficiently covered.'

'You might *believe* that, Ms Ballesty, but I *know* it hasn't been resolved sufficiently.'

'What's the point of your question?'

'The photo is a motive for Lucy's murder.'

Hannah slapped the table, tears streaming down her face. 'Why would I murder Lucy over *that* photo? It's not the first time she's done that to me.'

Lottie glanced at Kirby and back again at Hannah. 'Why didn't you tell me?'

'I don't like thinking about it. It was awful, but I'd never murder anyone over a stupid photo.'

'Where were these other photos taken?'

'Mainly in the locker rooms at school and in the showers at the athletic ground.'

'Are you sure Lucy took them?'

'I assumed it was her because she sent them around to absolutely everyone.'

'But you went to her party. Why?'

Hannah paused. 'I suppose I wanted to be accepted by her group. Maybe I was fed up being a loner. Maybe I just wanted a night out. How do I know why I went? But I'm sorry I ever set foot in her house.'

'Had you ever been there before Friday night?'

'No.'

'You sure?'

'I'm sure.'

'How well did you know Cormac O'Flaherty?' Lottie hoped the quick-fire questions and change in direction would cause Hannah to slip up.

'Just to see him around.'

'And still you had sex with him.'

'I didn't. If I did, I don't remember.'

'You brought a condom with you to the cabin.'

'I did not! No way.'

Shit, now she'd have to implicate Sean. Careful, she warned herself. 'I have a witness who claims you asked him for a condom and he gave you one.'

'I never ... Who are you talking about?'

Ballesty got in on the game. 'That's right, Inspector, who is this witness?'

'It doesn't matter for now, but I believe the person who told me.'

Hannah was shaking her head slowly, her fingers probing her temple. 'I ... I think I did, you know.'

'Did what?' Lottie asked.

'I was mad at Lucy and I think I asked a guy if he had any condoms.' Hannah scrunched her eyes shut, as if visualising a memory. 'He gave me one and I slipped it into my skirt pocket.' She looked up then and eyed Lottie. 'I remember now. Sean Parker gave it to me. Your son.'

Lottie squirmed on the chair. 'How come you can remember that and nothing else?'

'I don't know, but my drink must have been spiked afterwards. That's why I can't remember anything later on.'

Ballesty straightened her shoulders. 'Inspector, if your son is involved in this investigation, we have a clear conflict of interest. You must remove yourself from this investigation. I request a meeting with Superintendent Farrell. Immediately!'

'Oh, get a life,' Lottie muttered.

'I beg your pardon?'

'I have no conflict of interest. My son has made his statement. Cormac O'Flaherty has made a statement. I just need Hannah's. I have evidence that ties her to Lucy's murder.'

'What evidence?' Ballesty was now like a Rottweiler with bared teeth, having shed her prim image.

Lottie explained about the blood on Hannah's hands and the bloodied towel in her rucksack. She was well aware that if Cormac was telling the truth, this evidence was useless, but she kept that to herself.

'Does not prove murder.'

Lottie ignored the solicitor. 'Hannah, why do you think Lucy picked on you with those photos?'

'Because she could.'

'Are you sure it was Lucy? Do you think anyone else might have been involved?'

'I could never prove it was her. When she accidentally shared that photo with me at the party, it was obvious she was behind the others. But you have to believe me, I didn't kill her, no matter what evidence you have.'

'I honestly don't think you did, Hannah,' Lottie admitted softly. 'But I need your help to understand who had a motive. You mentioned that some photos were taken in the athletics shower room. Why would Lucy have been there?'

'She was always hanging around with Ivy, and Ivy had a crush on Mr Glennon, my athletics coach.'

Ivy! Lottie thought. Was she the key to unlocking this mystery? She quickly considered what she had so far.

Ivy's brother Oscar had been at the same location as Sharon

Flood when the girl was found stabbed. Jake Flood had been reportedly pushing drugs with Oscar's gang. Terry Starr and Lucy's father funded the club that Jake had belonged to. His coach, Barney Reynolds, had turned up at the barracks. Had he been there earlier, when Sharon was stabbed? Could he have killed the little girl? Barney's daughter, Brontë, was married to Richie Harrison, the DJ at Lucy's party.

What was she missing? What was the motive for the murders? Who were the puppets, and who was the puppet master pulling the strings?

'Inspector?' Ballesty prompted. 'What else do you need from my client before you release her?'

Lottie shook herself out of her musings. 'Hannah, I believe you were drugged for a reason. I need your help to understand why, and who was behind it.'

'But I can't remember anything.'

'Was Lucy in a relationship?'

'Maybe. I know she was away last weekend.'

'How do you know that?' Lottie sat up straight. At last she had someone who could shed light on Lucy's mystery weekend.

'She was late for Monday morning's exam. I heard her tell the supervisor that she'd missed the early-morning train from Dublin. I assumed she was away for the weekend.'

'Do you know Terry Starr?'

'The boxer?'

'Yes.'

'Heard of him.'

'Did Lucy ever talk about him?'

'I wasn't in her inner circle. Ask Ivy.'

'I will. Lucy had a tattoo. Did you ever see it?'

'No.'

Lottie scratched the back of her head, thinking. 'Ouch!'

'Are you okay?' Kirby said, lifting his head from his note-taking. Or had he been asleep?

'Sorry, scratched it. Now it's bleeding.' She stood, eased around the table and went to the door. 'Give me a minute.'

'Don't take too long,' Ballesty said. 'If you're not charging my client, I'm taking her out of here.'

Without answering, Lottie left to the sound of Kirby announcing her departure for the recording.

72

After patching up the cut on her head with a handful of plasters, Lottie discussed Cormac and Hannah's interviews with Kirby, and decided to let them go until they had evidence that couldn't be discredited by a savvy defence solicitor. The more she thought about it, the more she felt they were innocent of murder. Had they been set up?

She nabbed Lynch. 'Where is Oscar Jones?'

'We let him go. We don't have any evidence yet to confirm he stabbed Sharon Flood. Unless his DNA is on her body or we find the murder weapon. SOCOs are at the scene.'

'He assaulted me!' Lottie tried to stem her growing frustration. Everything in this case was sending her in increasingly dizzying circles.

'You need to make an official statement. Oscar is a minor. We have to be careful how we handle it.'

'Right.' Lottie exhaled loudly. 'He had a bicycle chain. Is it with forensics? It might have been used to beat Jake.'

'It's been sent for examination.'

'Okay. I want to interview both Oscar and Ivy again. Check

that they're at home, then bring the car round the front. Any sign of Terry Starr or the McAllisters?'

'Starr's Range Rover went through the toll bridge earlier today. I checked with the Brook Hotel manager, and their CCTV shows both McAllisters leaving with a man who fits Starr's description. McKeown is looking for them on whatever CCTV he can get his hands on.'

'Ragmullin is a town, not a city. Find them.'

'The CCTV is rubbish, though. Did you know your wound is still bleeding? It might need stitches.'

'I'll wear a hat.'

'Sure you will.' Lynch laughed as she walked off.

Downstairs, Lottie found a T-shirt balled up on the floor of her locker. It didn't smell too bad. At least there was no blood on it. She cleaned the wound as best she could with water from a dripping tap, screeching as it stung like hell, then flicked out the T-shirt, tugged it over her head and blazed up the stairs. She flew straight into the superintendent. *Oh shite!*

'Ah, Superintendent Farrell, there you are. I was looking everywhere for you.'

'Here I am is right. You've been avoiding me?'

'Not at all, just busy. Actually, I'm on my way out to interview a suspect. I'll call into your office later.' She made to sidestep, but the superintendent grabbed her arm.

'Not so fast. I requested a full report into your son's involvement in the McAllister murder case. I told you if you couldn't give me a genuine response you'd be off the case.'

'Did you? Gosh, I—'

'Don't act all innocent. That ploy might have worked with my predecessors, but it doesn't wash with me. My office.'

'Please, give me half an hour. I've the murders almost solved.' Lottie hoped the lie didn't show on her face. She had no idea how long she needed, but Farrell might buy half an hour.

And she'd already broken one promise today; another wouldn't make much difference.

'You have no notion of being in my office in thirty minutes. I want ... Is that blood?'

'Shit, yeah. I got belted with a bicycle chain. I'd better go to A&E and get stitches before I faint.'

Farrell shook her head in defeat. 'Do that, then my office.'

'Sure thing. Thanks.'

Lottie scooted around the super and took the stairs two at a time, almost falling over her feet in her haste. This was her last chance to come good. She had to make it count.

Just as she was making her escape, McKeown called her back.

'Hit bingo on the CCTV. We checked the footage for the night of Lucy's murder around the homes of some of our main players. You'll want to see this.'

Lottie took the image from him and smiled. At last!

'You're a star. Thanks.'

Outside, Lynch had the engine idling.

'You have the address?' Lottie flung herself into the passenger seat.

'Yeah, but you forgot your hat.'

'Just drive the fucking car, Lynch.'

Lottie thought the phrase 'keeping up with the Joneses' didn't appear to have been adopted by the neighbours. The Jones house stood out from the others as if it had been dropped from the sky and landed among ordinary residences. The tightly manicured lawn was bordered by a shingle driveway with a BMW SUV parked crossways in front of the steps. Lynch parked up behind it.

Palatial white pillars stood sentry at the red door, and the monstrous bay window to the right compounded the excessive grandeur. Lottie wondered if the interior decor was a match; if so, she'd need sunglasses to protect her vision when she went in.

'Each to their own,' Lynch said.

'They can keep it.' Lottie's bones ached as she got out of the car. 'Listen, if tea and biscuits are offered, we take hand and all. I'm bloody starving.'

'Sure thing.' Lynch looked puzzled. 'Where's the bell?'

'Bang on the door.'

Lynch obliged. After thirty seconds, it opened.

'What do you want now?' Ivy Jones had a cupcake in one hand and a bottle of nail polish in the other. She wore a pair of white denim cut-offs and a long red shirt at least two sizes too big. Her feet were bare; only one had red polished toes.

'We'd like a word.' Lottie stepped in past the teenager. 'This is some place.'

'It's gross,' Ivy said, 'but Mum loves it. Why are you barging in uninvited?'

'We'd like to have a chat with you and your brother, with your parents present.'

'We have nothing to say to you. Dad isn't here. You should leave.'

'You still have plenty to tell us, Ivy. And your brother is about to be charged with assault of a senior member of An Garda Síochána. We'll wait here while you fetch your mother.'

'Mum!' Ivy stomped off, her bare feet flapping on the marble floor. She disappeared through the doorway at the end of the hall, banging it shut behind her.

'She doesn't seem too pleased to see us,' Lynch said.

Lottie was staring at the floor. 'Is this marble?'

'Cold enough, anyway.'

Glancing around the hall, Lottie felt it exuded a faux-wealthy vibe. Were the Joneses trying to be something they were not? The wide staircase led up to a landing, or maybe she should call it a mezzanine. A crystal chandelier, which might even have been plastic, hung low, casting distorted rainbows on pink-wallpapered walls.

The door at the end of the hallway opened and a short woman with a plump smile walked towards them wiping her hands on a towel. She wore a pair of football shorts and a maroon jersey sporting a local club crest. Her feet were shod in a pair of UGG slippers.

'Rita Jones, Inspector.' Her hand was soft, still damp as she shook Lottie's. 'Sorry I couldn't get to the station yesterday morning with Ivy. Couldn't let the teams down. I'm a qualified referee, for my sins.'

'Is there somewhere we can talk, Rita?' Lottie was totally wrong-footed by this small, pleasant woman. 'We'd like a word with Ivy and Oscar.'

'What has he done this time? Come in here.'

She led them into the room with the obtrusive bay window. It had a clutter of furniture and a marble-tiled floor.

'I swear to God,' she lifted a throw from the couch, folding it over her arm, 'that boy will be the death of me. I do everything in my power to keep him on the straight and narrow, but I don't have eyes in the back of my head, do I?'

Lottie was about to agree, but Rita was on a roll.

'Isn't it sad about poor Lucy? Ivy was joined to her at the hip. Awful tragedy. What is the world coming to? Sit down and I'll make tea. Or would you like coffee? Jim, my husband, installed all the mod cons, but I say you can't beat a kettle, a tea bag and a large mug.'

Sitting on one of the red leather chairs, Lottie felt exhausted by Rita's chatter. If the tea was to be a drama, she'd do without.

'We're fine, thanks. Is your husband around?'

'He was here earlier, but he's gone to train the under sixteens hurling. We're both sport mad. But our two … enough said.'

'Can you get them?'

'No problem at all.' Rita trod over to the door and yelled into the hall. 'Ivy! Oscar! Get in here.' She marched back into the room. 'Have you got kids, Inspector?'

'Three.'

'It's a huge responsibility, isn't it?' She turned to Lynch. 'You look too young to have any.'

Lynch was saved by the door swinging inwards, thumping against the wall.

A sullen-faced Oscar stomped in, followed by Ivy still holding her nail polish but without the cupcake. They plonked themselves on the couch. Ivy folded her arms.

Lottie watched the boy as he picked at the skin around his left thumb. Where Ivy was full of bravado, her brother appeared nervous.

'Oscar, you know you will be charged with assaulting me?' Lottie touched the back of her head, unsurprised to see blood on her fingers.

Standing with her back to the fireplace, Rita seemed to grow taller with indignation. 'You mean ... the blood ... your head? No way. My boy may be a bit of a troublemaker, but he'd never do that.'

'A bit?' Ivy snorted.

'The fact is,' Lottie said, 'I was assaulted by your son earlier today.'

A stern mask fell over Rita's happy face. 'What proof do you have?'

'I was there. He was there. A colleague of mine was also present.'

'He was outside,' Oscar muttered. 'Look at my wrists. He had no right to tie me up.'

Rita's eyes turned cold, her body rigid. 'This conversation is over.'

'We also need to talk to Ivy about Lucy,' Lynch said softly. 'There's nothing to be concerned about.'

'On condition you don't accuse my girl of anything.' Rita squeezed onto the couch beside her progeny.

Lottie took the CCTV image from her bag. 'Ivy, we checked the CCTV in this area. It shows you exiting a van at 4.35 on Saturday morning. The driver also got out.' She was thankful for McKeown's expertise.

Ivy grew rigid and silent.

'Ivy, how do you know Richie Harrison?'

'I don't know him as such. Just that he's a DJ.' Ivy looked like a rabbit in the headlights.

'That's enough,' Rita said.

Lottie ignored her and turned her attention to Oscar. 'Do *you* know Richie Harrison?'

He dipped his head with a shake.

Ignoring an increasingly agitated Rita, she said, 'Oscar, I need you to tell me exactly what happened today at your hideout in the army barracks.'

'Nothing happened.'

'Did you stab Sharon Flood?'

'I never touched her,' he insisted, still not looking at her.

Rita's jaw dropped. Lottie hurried on.

'Do you know who did?'

'No.'

'Why were you hiding at the barracks?'

'Wasn't hiding. I went there to collect ... something. I was wrecked and must have fallen asleep. I never knew Sharon was there.'

Lottie reckoned he'd smoked weed and conked out. Otherwise why not hole up in his own bedroom?

'That's enough,' Rita said.

'Yeah, enough,' Ivy said.

'Shut up, Ivy.' Oscar thumped her on the arm and the nail polish bottle fell from her hand and smashed on the tiles.

'Now look what you've done. Fucking moron,' Ivy screamed.

'Stop it. The two of you are a disgrace,' Rita said before quickly calming down. 'Don't worry about it. Sarah can mop it up.'

'Do you mean Sarah Robson?' Lottie asked.

'Yes,' Rita said. 'She comes in once a week. Mary McAllister recommended her and she's a good worker. Says little. Just my kind of woman.'

'She never said.' Lottie tried to figure out if there was any significance to this revelation. She didn't like coincidences. She'd have to talk to Sarah again.

Ivy stood and stepped over the remnants of her nail polish bottle, hands on hips, her tone mocking her mother. 'Huh! Anything the McAllisters have, we must have it too. Including their cleaner.'

'Young lady, sit down.' Rita's cheeks reddened.

Ivy sat and folded her arms grumpily.

Parking the information about Sarah, Lottie turned to Oscar. 'Sharon is dead, Oscar. She was stabbed while you were in that building. What were you really doing there?'

'Oh for heaven's sake,' Rita said. 'Oscar?'

'I ... I ...'

'You're such a baby,' Ivy said.

'I'm braver than you.'

'What's that supposed to mean?'

'I was there at Lucy's after you left.' His lips curled into a sneer.

'Don't know what you're talking about.' Ivy attempted casualness, but her eyes grew wider. Lottie wondered if she was sending a silent message to her brother.

'You know right well,' he said. 'This is all your fault. And Lucy's.'

'Now *I* want to know what you're talking about,' Rita said, leaning forward.

'I was doing what I was told. Watch and report back. That's all.'

'Watch who?' Lottie said.

'Jake. Then the next day, you and whoever you were after.'

'I don't understand.' Lottie glanced at Lynch, who shrugged a shoulder.

Oscar crossed one arm over his chest while he chewed a nail on his other hand.

She couldn't lose him now. 'Why were you watching Jake?'

'He stole drugs from a special stash hidden at the barracks. I was told to find out where he had them. But then he was attacked at the party and everything went to shit.'

'Who attacked him?'

'Don't know. I was way back in the trees. Just heard the patio door smashing, then saw Jake lying there on his back.'

'What happened then?'

'I texted it in. Like I was told to do. Reporting it. That was my job.'

'Texted who?'

He shrugged and slipped a hand into his pocket. Taking out his phone, he tapped the screen. 'I have the number.'

'I'll have to take your phone into evidence to be checked,' Lottie said. She suspected Oscar's contact used a burner.

'You're in big trouble,' Ivy hissed at her brother.

'Shut it, Ivy,' Rita warned, her face flushed from her son's revelations. 'I have no idea what's going on.'

That makes two of us, Lottie thought.

'You're not meant to know,' Oscar said to his mother.

'You'd better speak up about it now, before this gets out of hand,' Rita told him.

'It's already out of hand,' Lottie said. 'Three young people have lost their lives since Friday night. Oscar, this is your chance to explain. I want to find this murderer.' She was going to add *before he or she gets you*, but the boy seemed traumatised enough.

'You already know about our gang,' he said. 'The drugs are always stashed in the attic where you found me. We pick up the pills there and sell them. Jake joined us after his dad died. Said he was doing it for his little sister.'

'Go on,' Lottie said. Time enough for analysis later.

'Thing is, he was greedy. Stole some of the drugs we aren't allowed to touch. I don't think they were for him. He didn't use, not like ...' He glanced up at his mother before dropping his head quickly. Lottie could see Rita almost frothing at the mouth.

Oscar continued. 'I don't know who the boss is because we only communicate by text. I was told to watch Jake, to find out where he hid the drugs and if he sold them.'

'How did Jake come to be working at Lucy's party?'

'I presume he got a text to go there. I got a text to watch him.'

'What else did you see that night?'

'Not much. I was hiding in the trees. Didn't want anyone to see me.' He glared at Ivy. 'I thought Jake was dead, but then he got up and crawled back inside on his hands and knees. After that, I saw his car leaving and I followed it, but I was on my bike, so I lost it.'

'When you reported this to whoever you were texting, what were you told?'

'To watch the guards.'

'When did you find out Jake was dead?'

'Got a text to go to the canal last night. Saw you there and the body on the ground.'

'Who killed Jake?'

'I don't know.'

'Where was he killed?'

'Don't know.'

'Who burned his car?'

Oscar shook his head. 'I really don't know.'

'What do you know about Lucy's death?'

The boy shrugged.

'Come on, Oscar. You have to tell me what you saw at the house.'

'He has to tell you fuck all!' Ivy roared.

'Ivy Jones! Your father will ground you for a month if you don't lose that mouth.'

'This is ridiculous.' Ivy got up and moved to the door. She pointed at her brother. 'You don't know the half of it, Mum. He's stoned off his face most of the time. How can he even know what he saw? Might be hallucinations. A figment of his warped imagination.'

'You're the one with the warped imagination!' Oscar cried. 'You and that DJ bollix, screwing in his van. Now who's ridiculous?'

Ivy leapt across the room, grabbed her brother's T-shirt and spat into his face. Lottie and Rita reached them at the same time, each taking one teenager, successfully separating the screaming pair.

Lottie's phone rang, its shrill tone splitting the noise. Caller ID – Boyd.

She left Lynch to calm the teenagers, and as she answered the call, the room slipped into an uneasy silence.

73

In the garish hallway with its faux chandelier, Lottie sat heavily on the bottom step of the stairs. Slipping her tired feet out of her shoes, she found the cold tiles strangely therapeutic.

'What's up, Boyd? Did you talk to your police contact over there?'

'I tried to tell you earlier, but you hung up. Then I had to get food for Sergio. It's about Jackie.'

'Has she reappeared to stop you taking Sergio with you?'

'You're half right. Mind-reader.'

She didn't hear the usual laugh in his voice. 'Oh shit, Boyd, what are you going to do?'

'I'll figure something out, but that's not why I'm ringing you.'

'I'm listening.'

'This is hard to believe, but I think it's true. Jackie's been working as an informant with the Spanish police, snitching on her drug pals. This is relevant to your investigation. She'd been infiltrating the world of Albert McAllister and Terry Starr for some time.'

'Albert is a drug dealer?'

'That's what they thought originally. But Jackie stumbled on something much more sinister. She felt she might lose her cover and once Sergio was safe with me, she went into hiding, trusting I'd keep him safe. I had no idea what she was involved in, and her police handlers had no idea where she'd gone.'

'Go on.'

'Jackie discovered that there's drug smuggling via Spain to Ireland, but it's small-time. A bit of coke here and there. GHB and pills.'

'So that might be why Albert hightailed it to Spain when he was threatened. What's the sinister news?'

'Terry Starr. She uncovered something about him that really scared her. And believe me, it takes a lot to scare Jackie.'

'Something to do with underage girls?'

'Yes. The slimy bastard is all over the dark web selling photographs and videos.'

'We found some photos of him with a young girl who was murdered this morning. It was buried in a fake Instagram account. I hoped it couldn't be linked to anything this disturbing. Shit, Boyd, I need to get my head around this. Can Jackie provide proof?'

'She's with her handler at the moment and said she'll fill me in when she gets back. I just wanted to give you the heads-up.'

'Thanks a million.' She grabbed her shoes and put them on, anxious to get working on this angle.

'You still there, Lottie?'

'I have a problem. The McAllisters and Starr have disappeared.'

'You think the parents are involved in their daughter's murder?'

'At this stage, I'd believe anything. Mary didn't get on with Lucy, but Albert seemingly adored her. Keep your ear to the ground in case they turn up in Spain. I'll alert airports and ports.'

'There's nothing stopping them hopping on a private plane,' Boyd said.

'I'll request private airstrip monitoring.'

'If they are behind all this, Lottie, you need to find them before someone else dies.'

'I'm working flat out to discover the links that join up the circle. What about you and Sergio? Will you get home tomorrow?'

'I'll work on Jackie. You just solve your murder cases. And Lottie?'

'Yeah.'

'Be careful.'

She cut the call and assessed this new information. Was Terry Starr Oscar's mystery boss? If Terry had suspected Jake was stealing from him, he'd had time to beat the boy up at Lucy's, but he was on a plane leaving the country fairly soon afterwards. Forty-five minutes, or less, to get to the airport at that hour of the morning. A dash through security and a sprint to the boarding gate – an hour and a half at most. But he wouldn't have been able to dump Jake's body or dispose of the car. Someone else had to be involved.

Had Terry killed Lucy? There had been no mention of him being at the party, and anyway, why would he kill her? Was he grooming underage girls? How did he get access to them? What was the missing puzzle piece?

She reached the same conclusion as a moment ago.

Someone else had to be involved. Or more than one person.

Her head was spinning by the time she returned to Lynch and the Joneses.

'So, Ivy, is it true about you and Richie?' Lottie said.

'What if it is? I'm eighteen next week.'

'Richie Harrison is thirty years old, married, and his wife is expecting a baby in a few weeks.'

'That's his problem.' The girl was belligerent, an ugly pout on her face.

'There's more to the relationship, isn't there?' Lottie persisted. She noticed Rita had her back to the room as she stared out of the bay window, and her shoulders were heaving.

Oscar piped up. 'You may as well tell them. They're going to find out anyhow.'

'We sure are,' Lynch said, her feet apart, arms by her sides, ready in case another row broke out.

Ivy twirled towards her, pushing her face close. 'I'm not doing your job for you. You can find out on your own. I'm sick of it all.'

Before either Lottie or Lynch could stop her, she ran from the room.

Rita turned round, her eyes leaking tears. 'Here was me thinking I had one delinquent in the family when I actually have two. I'm ringing Jim to come home.'

She sounded a little self-pitying, and Lottie couldn't blame her. She'd had a lot to take in over the last half-hour.

'Rita, I need you to convince Ivy to be honest with us. Keep them at home while I make further enquiries. Can you do that?'

The woman shook her head. 'I can't promise anything. They rule the roost here. I lose myself in my sports to escape the torment. I'm sorry.'

'I'll stay, Mum,' Oscar said. 'I'm sorry for the trouble I've caused.'

Lottie didn't believe him for a minute. He was used to doing whatever he liked, and if Ivy was correct, he took drugs himself. Even though she'd taken his phone, she knew he would be putting out warnings before they had the car down the drive.

'Detective Lynch, request two or three officers to guard this house and the occupants. A precaution, in case your family is in danger, Rita.'

'Oh, I hadn't thought of that. Do you think we might be?'

'Anything is possible. Oscar, I have your phone and I don't want you using anyone else's or a computer to make contact. You hear me?'

'No problem.'

She still didn't believe him. He would be arrested for his part in the drug dealing, but she had other fish to hook and reel in, so she had no option but to move on.

74

Everyone at the station was still stunned by the death of ten-year-old Sharon Flood, and Lottie couldn't get the image of a broken Liz out of her mind. She put Sharon's laceless runner on her desk to remind her of the senselessness of the little girl's death. The only way to stay sane was to nail the bastard who'd killed her. She owed it to Liz to find out why her two children had been brutally murdered, and who had done it.

Sam McKeown burst into her office. 'Those background checks you asked for. I made a start.' He spread his shoulders, trying to make himself the dominant one in the room. Well, he could fuck right off. Lottie planted her hands on the desk and leaned towards him.

'Tell me you've found the McAllisters and Terry Starr.'

'So far there's nothing to indicate where they are. The cameras around town are shite, as you know, but we're on it. I started the background checks. Sarah Robson, the woman who found Lucy's body, is interesting. I read through the report of your interview with her. I then talked to the school principal, and her version doesn't match with some of the things Sarah told you.'

Sitting down, Lottie had a feeling she knew what was coming. 'Is this to do with why she left the school?'

'Exactly.'

'You'd better tell me.'

Sarah Robson opened the door to Lottie and Garda Brennan.

The cat scampered from the back of the couch to the window ledge when they sat down.

'I find it hard to believe Lucy is dead.' Sarah had washed her hair since Lottie had last seen her, and it shone copper in the light coming through the small window. The band holding back her fringe revealed a gaunt face with black rings circling her eyes. Her jeans looked too big on her tiny frame and her pale pink sweater accentuated the greyness of her skin.

Lottie dived in. 'What was your role in her murder, Sarah?'

'How can you think I had anything to do with it?'

'The fact is, you lied when I interviewed you yesterday. When I asked myself why you would do that, I suspected you were hiding something from me. That something must be your involvement in Lucy's murder. And Jake Flood's, for that matter.'

The woman's throat wobbled as she swallowed half a dozen times before speaking.

'Who is Jake Flood?'

'Doesn't wash with me, Sarah,' Lottie said.

'I don't know him. What do you want from me?'

'The truth.'

Sarah kept shaking her head.

Lottie said, 'We know the reason you left the school. You quit in disgrace and not because of anything Noel Glennon did. I am giving you the opportunity to tell the truth.' And if she didn't, Lottie was so wired she was in danger of shaking her to death.

'Wh-what do you think you know?'

'If that's the way you want to play it, I will gladly spell it out for you.'

Lottie held out her hands, then brought them together in a loud clap, making Sarah jump in the armchair.

'Sarah Robson, you took photos of the girls in the showers. Noel confronted you with a statement from one of the girls. He went to the principal about you and she dismissed you. She should have brought us in; might have saved a few lives. But I don't blame her. The blame lies squarely on your shoulders. Now, are you ready to talk?'

Sarah stood and went to the window. She took the cat in her arms and rubbed him. Her mouth hardened, a nerve in her neck twitched and her eyes narrowed.

'You have it all wrong, Inspector. It was a misunderstanding. I didn't tell you lies at all. I just—'

'Twisted the truth?'

'This is ridiculous,' she snapped. 'Noel Glennon is a creep. He hung me out to dry in order to save his own sorry arse.'

'I still haven't heard an explanation. Have you, Garda Brennan?' Lottie glanced at the young garda, pleased to see she was busy taking notes.

'No, boss.'

When Martina spoke, the cat jumped from Sarah's arms, catching Lottie off guard. Had she actually thrown the animal at her? Leaning back, fearing it was about to attack, she relaxed as it walked along the arm of the couch to lie down on the back cushion again.

Sarah sat, eyes still wary. 'You seem to know the truth about my dismissal. What else can I tell you?'

'Why did you take those photos?'

A shrug. 'Because I could. Then Ivy Jones caught me and threw a wobbly. Told Glennon. I'm convinced he was already up to something with her and others.'

'Were you taking the photos for someone else?'

'Only for my personal perusal.'

'Likely story.'

Sarah flinched, then sat like a weary statue.

Lottie continued. 'Do you like young girls? In particular, naked girls taking showers?'

Silence.

'Why did you tell us Lucy was a bully?'

'It was the truth.'

'Then you said she was sad, only acting the prima donna. Why?'

'I believed she wasn't being true to herself.'

'What do you mean by that?'

Sarah sighed. 'I thought she was hiding something. It was like she put up protective armour. But she hadn't always been sad. Something had to have happened to change her.'

'How do you come to that conclusion?'

'She acted differently in public to what I saw at her home.'

Lottie reckoned all teenagers did that. 'Was she taking drugs?'

'Wouldn't surprise me.'

'How was her relationship with Ivy Jones?'

'Best friends. Always hanging out with each other.'

'Do you think Ivy could have been jealous of Lucy?'

'For sure. Anything Lucy turned up with, Ivy arrived with something similar the next day. Be it a phone, an iPad or a jacket. Lucy got what she wanted because her father spoiled her. Ivy got what Lucy had because she was jealous.'

'Was Lucy dating anyone?'

'I heard he had a lucky escape to Australia. But before him, and afterwards, there was definitely someone. She was secretive about it, though.'

'Then how would you know about it?'

'I've worked with young girls and teenagers for a good few years. I know the signs,' Sarah said smugly.

'Any names?' Lottie was lulling the woman into a sense of comfort, biding her time to pounce again about the photos.

'Noel thought he was clever at hiding it, but he was with her a lot at the athletics ground. Lucy had no interest in running, so what other reason had she to be there? He was probably shagging her for years. Had to be something in it for him.'

'She was underage. Why didn't you report it?'

'I couldn't once Noel found out about my photos. He held that over me until finally he did the dirty on me and reported me to the principal. By that stage I was ready to leave. I'd had enough of the shit that went on in that school.'

'Was Noel Glennon involved with Hannah Byrne?'

A shrug. 'I wouldn't put it past him. Hannah's sweet but easily taken advantage of. Lucy and Ivy treated her like shit. And the poor girl stood around and took it.'

'What about Cormac O'Flaherty?'

'The gardener? He was always hanging about. Bit of a loner really.'

'Ever see him with any of the girls? Lucy or Ivy, even Hannah?'

'Not that I recall. He did some gardening for the McAllisters too. He'd have known Lucy.'

'Did you ever see Cormac with Noel Glennon?'

Sarah shook her head.

'Who were the photos for, Sarah?'

'I didn't mean any harm.'

'It's child abuse,' Lottie said angrily, 'no matter how you choose to look at it.'

Sarah stood, hitched up her jeans at the waist and dug her hands into her pockets. 'I'm truly ashamed about what I did. You need to understand, I was always short of cash, even then. He paid good money for the photos.'

'Who did?'

'At first I didn't know who he was. I didn't recognise him. I saw him in the school car park one day, sitting in a flashy car. Noel was leaning in the window talking to him. Then when Noel headed off, the guy called me over. That's when I realised who he was. He made me a proposition and I agreed.'

'You agreed to give photos of girls in your care to a guy you barely knew? I find it hard to believe.'

'I did know him. I went to school with him. He was an overweight lad back then, always getting into fights. I was small and miserable. Both of us were targets for bullies to pick on. For some reason, even at ten years old, he watched out for me. The more he fought, the better he got. He kept the bullies away from me. I hadn't seen him in years until that day at the school. That's when he cashed in his chips with me.'

'Cashed in his chips?' Martina asked.

Sarah sat. 'He called in the favour. I couldn't ... there was no way I could refuse.' She jiggled her knees, irritating the hell out of Lottie.

'A simple no would have sufficed,' she said. She kept her face as bland as she could and twisted her hands together in an effort to mask her anger. Sarah Robson had ultimately handed over innocent girls on a plate. For what? To be groomed and abused? 'Name of the guy in the flashy car. Now.'

'Terry ... erm ... Terry ...'

'Starr,' Lottie said, and flopped back on the couch. The cat grunted and moved over to the window again.

'Yes.'

This confirmed what she suspected, but she couldn't see how it had led to Lucy's death. Jake and Sharon's deaths had to be related to the drugs. But what about the photo of Terry with Sharon on his knee? God, no, she thought, and wished she had a clear head to work through everything she'd learned.

'You do realise what you've done, don't you?'

'It was just a few photographs.'

'Are you for real?' Lottie couldn't help repeating her kids' favourite saying. 'He was grooming and then abusing girls. Young girls, whose photos you supplied him with.'

'I never ... I can't have ... You have it wrong.'

'I have it right. You knew exactly what you were doing.'

'No, I—'

'I want the copies of the photographs you handed over to Terry Starr.'

'I destroyed the images.'

The cat hissed. Lottie glanced at it, then stood and leaned over the cowering woman. 'I know your type. There is no way you would bring yourself to destroy them. I want them. Now!'

'Okay, okay. Get away from me.' Sarah shrank behind her raised hands. 'This is ... it's harassment.'

'Harassment? Wait until you're incarcerated in the general prison population. Do you know what they do to child abusers?'

'I never in my life abused any child.'

'What you did, aiding and abetting, is child abuse.' Lottie wanted to arrest her there and then, but first she wanted possession of the images, because once arrested, Sarah would get a solicitor and ask for a plea deal in exchange for them. No way was she letting the leech get away with her disgusting crimes.

'Give me a minute.' Sarah fetched a slim laptop from a shelf on the bookcase behind her. 'What's your email address?'

Lottie handed over her card with the details and waited impatiently, watching over Sarah to make sure she didn't hit the delete key.

'They're in folders. Sending them to you now. I'm so sorry. I—'

'You can tell that to the judge.'

Lottie opened the email app on her phone and checked. A spread of folders appeared. She clicked on one and gasped. Images of girls in various stages of undress lit up the small screen. Such was her revulsion and rage, she wanted to lash out and punch Sarah Robson. She needed to rein in her fury for another few minutes at least.

'Is there an image of Lucy in here?'

'Erm, possibly.'

'The money incentive came later, so I still can't understand your motive for endangering the lives of these young girls by taking illicit photos. This is voyeurism. Did you desire them sexually? Were you jealous of their youth?'

'No!'

'You live alone and now you have to clean houses for a living. It might have culminated in greed, but I think it started out with jealousy.'

'Ivy Jones is the jealous one,' Sarah muttered. 'Never met a girl so twisted in all my life.'

'Ever look in the mirror?' Martina said quietly.

'That's uncalled for,' Sarah snarled.

Lottie said, 'Fetch your coat, Sarah. You're coming with us.'

'Why? I gave you what you wanted.'

'Believe me, this is just the beginning. Come on.'

'Who will mind my cat?'

Lottie was so enraged, she was seconds from losing control. 'You should have thought of your stupid cat before you crept into shower rooms and took photographs of young girls to sell to a man as warped as yourself.'

Silently Sarah fetched a jacket. Lottie grabbed her by the elbow and shunted her out of the door behind Garda Brennan.

As they walked to the car, she glanced up at the apartment window.

The black cat stared down at her. She'd have to make calls to get him looked after. She wasn't so furious as to leave the animal to fend for himself. But she was very fucking close to it.

75

With Sarah Robson in custody, Lottie dispatched a squad car to bring in Noel Glennon. Still no news on Terry Starr or the McAllisters. All the alerts were out and she wanted them found soon.

She steadied herself with deep breaths before she could bring herself to trawl through Sarah's photos. Tears gathered in her eyes and she fought to control her emotions; to remain professional despite the images breaking her heart.

This is my job, she reminded herself. I can make a difference. Suitably motivated, she continued.

The photos were date-stamped, going back six years. Most of the girls looked like they were first-year students, twelve- and thirteen-year-olds.

'Children just out of primary school groomed by depraved adults.' She spoke her thoughts aloud to ground herself. The images constituted child abuse, but how many of these girls had ended up in Terry Starr's clutches?

'Groomed and abused,' she reiterated.

There were a couple of hundred photos and she swiftly examined each one to see if she recognised any of the girls. She found a very young Ivy Jones, and then Lucy McAllister. Both naked in what looked like school showers.

As she scrolled on, she recognised another girl. Partially clothed, standing in a locker room. Flat-chested, long, lean legs. She was aged about thirteen in the photo. Hannah Byrne.

Lottie jumped up, knocking her chair against the wall, and paced around the tight space. This case was so much more than drug dealing. What to do next? Tell Farrell? Yes. But not yet.

Sitting down again, she made her decision and phoned the Garda National Protective Services Bureau, which specialised in sexual abuse crimes. She spoke to a sympathetic inspector, Fred Reilly, who was in charge of the online child exploitation unit, and forwarded the images to him.

'Rest assured,' he said, 'if even one of these images has been distributed electronically, my team will locate them. But it will take time.'

'Appreciated,' she said. 'Liaise with your colleagues in Spain. There's a possible connection to Malaga.' She recounted what she knew. 'I need the names of these girls, Fred, and of those involved in their exploitation and abuse. I have a few suspects who are genuine flight risks. I'm lacking airtight evidence to allow me to issue arrest warrants.'

'I'll put a team straight on it. Minute we find anything, you'll be the first to know.'

Thanking him, she hung up, powered off her computer and went to the incident room.

The fading light was dim outside the window, a dark and dreary summer evening. More like winter, with bulging clouds of rain on the horizon. Lottie had no idea of the time. Her stomach had given up growling in protest about lack of food. The thought of eating after seeing the images of those young girls filled her with nausea. She didn't want to think of how their photos had been used, or how many of the girls had ended up being groomed and sexually abused.

Kirby and McKeown sat at laptops at the end of the room, heads down, working away. Lynch was still at the Joneses' house awaiting someone to relieve her.

At the incident board, Lottie moved from one photo to the next, tapping each one with her finger. Victims, witnesses and suspects. All marked up in their relevant columns. She now knew that some witnesses were also victims, and at least one suspect was a victim too.

'You okay, boss?' Kirby joined her, stale cigar aroma hanging in the hot, airless room.

'I'm hungry, tired and wired. My mother is in hospital and I should call to see how she is. I'm missing Boyd and his wisdom, not to mention a hug.'

'I can give you a hug if you like.'

'Thanks, Kirby, I'll survive.' She pointed to the board. 'What or who connects it all?'

'We need to outline everything in a linear manner – stole that word from McKeown,' he panted. 'Then it will come together.'

'Is your optimism going for free?'

'Go home and rest, boss. Things are always clearer in the morning.'

She held up her hand, thumb and index finger almost touching. 'We are this close to unlocking it, Kirby.'

'Go home.'

She moved to the second board, recognising McKeown's writing. A series of bullet points, his attempt to bring clarity to the jumble of knowledge gained and evidence secured.

'Who first brought Hannah and Cormac to our attention?' she asked.

'Ivy Jones,' McKeown said, abandoning the laptop and approaching the boards clutching his iPad.

'And who first mentioned Ivy Jones?'

'Sarah Robson,' Lynch said, entering the room. She looked as wrecked as Lottie felt. 'Lei turned up eventually. He's stationed inside the house now, listening to Rita's tales of woe. A squad car is parked in the driveway.'

'Learn anything after I left?'

'Only that Rita Jones is one sorry cookie. She is spitting anger at her hubby for never being around when the shit hits the fan. Oozing with self-pity.'

'The sort who doesn't like her little world being upended?'

'Exactly.' Lynch pulled out a chair and sat facing the boards. 'Are we brainstorming?'

Lottie fetched a chair for herself. McKeown and Kirby followed suit. They sat in a semicircle.

'Can I light up?' Kirby chanced, rolling an unlit cigar between his fingers.

'Not on your life,' Lottie said. 'Anyone see the super around?'

'Gone home,' McKeown said. 'She held a half-hearted press conference. She was breathing fire with your name burning in it as she left.'

'Glad I missed her so.'

As Lottie told them about Sarah Robson, McKeown added more bullet points to the whiteboard.

'I can't believe we haven't found Terry Starr and the McAllisters yet,' she said.

'Not a sign of them.' Kirby shook his head.

'What are they up to?'

'Destroying evidence?' Lynch suggested.

'I hope not. I can't see the McAllisters being in cahoots with Terry over the abuse of young girls. But Albert could be involved in the drugs angle, based on what Boyd told me.'

'Is Boyd due home tomorrow?' Kirby said.

'Focus and concentrate, Kirby.'

McKeown said, 'Terry Starr is the only one who has avoided an interview with us thus far.'

'Boyd spoke with him,' Lottie said. 'It only confirms Starr was in the McAllisters' Malaga apartment yesterday.'

'Leaving the McAllisters aside for the moment,' Lynch said, 'Oscar Jones mentioned that his sister Ivy was, quote, "screwing", unquote, Richie Harrison the night of the party.'

'And he left her home. Go on,' Lottie prompted.

'Sarah told you Ivy was jealous of Lucy.'

'Not sure I'd believe much of what she said, but continue.' Lottie wondered where Lynch was going with this.

'If Terry Starr was involved in the child abuse, and Richie Harrison and Noel Glennon appear in some of the photos I discovered earlier, and Harrison was cheating on his wife with Ivy, is it logical to conclude that the three men and even Ivy are working together in a tight little web?'

'You can include Sarah Robson too,' Lottie noted. 'I found Ivy and Lucy in her photos. They were victims. I also discovered an image of Hannah.'

'Hannah Byrne? Shit.' Lynch rubbed her eyes. 'Maybe Ivy started out as a victim and was later groomed to work for the other side?'

'What about Sharon Flood?' Kirby said.

'She is too young to have been in Sarah's images, but she appears in a photo on Starr's fake Instagram thing. Come on, guys, what the hell is going on under our noses?'

McKeown tapped his iPad and paced. 'We have boxing, athletics, drugs, child pornography. Locations involved are the McAllister house, the boxing club and the army barracks. The girls' school and the athletic grounds. Plus Malaga.'

Lottie stood and stared at the names on the board. 'What about Cormac O'Flaherty? He worked at the school and Lucy's house.'

'So did Sarah Robson,' Lynch volunteered.

Lottie nodded. 'Barney Reynolds trained Jake Flood and he turned up at the army barracks after Oscar assaulted me. Was he there earlier? Could he have attacked Sharon? He's a link to Jake. We need to formally interview him. Noel Glennon told us he didn't know Richie Harrison, but both of them work at nightclubs and feature in one of the photos. Those two, plus Terry, are around the same age. Did they know each other years ago? Sarah said she knew Terry as a ten-year-old.'

'Sharon's age, the poor little creature,' Kirby said.

Lottie stopped in front of Sharon's photo and turned to McKeown. 'What did you find on Terry's background check?'

'He was born in Tullamore, schooled in Ragmullin.'

'He was an overweight kid. Bullied, according to Sarah, if that's even true,' Lottie said.

McKeown continued reading. 'It's true. His web page bio says he joined a gym, lost weight and started boxing. Barney Reynolds was his trainer until Barney suffered a head injury in a training session five years ago.'

'Terry might have known Brontë through Barney before she married Richie Harrison.'

'Bronte isn't relevant to this,' McKeown said.

'We don't know what's relevant or not,' Lottie said spikily. 'Boyd told me that his ex, Jackie, was working as a CI for the Spanish police investigating Albert McAllister and Terry Starr in relation to drug smuggling. Albert got a threatening email that sent him to Spain. Did Terry send it to get them out of the way. But why now? What changed?'

'Why did Terry head off to Malaga?' Kirby asked.

'Maybe he killed Lucy, then fled,' Lottie said. 'She might have been with him last weekend. She was one of the few followers he allowed on his fake Instagram account. Could she have posted the photo of him with Sharon without his knowledge, hoping someone would see it?'

'It's possible, but his Finsta has limited access and she'd need his passwords and stuff,' McKeown said.

'But if she did do it, maybe he found out and killed her.'

'Or Terry could have posted the photo himself,' Kirby countered. 'Why didn't Lucy report it to us, if she knew about it?'

Lottie said, 'She might have thought her father would be dragged into it as Terry's agent, and she only wanted to target Terry. That's if she even posted the photo.'

Lynch said, 'Ivy must know. We need her to talk.'

'I think a better bet is Hannah Byrne. She has been traumatised, abused, set up for murder and—'

'But like you asked a minute ago, where does Cormac O'Flaherty fit in?' McKeown powered off his iPad.

Lottie bit on her bottom lip. 'Suspect, witness or victim? All three?'

'A guy in the wrong place at the wrong time?' Kirby said.

Lottie glanced down at Lucy's full post-mortem report that McKeown had printed out. 'The pathologist confirms Lucy had defensive wounds. She got DNA from them. Not a match for Cormac or Jake, or anyone else we have interviewed so far.'

'Damn.' Kirby tapped his cigar shirt pocket idly. 'I still don't see how Jake Flood fits into this scenario.'

'Was he killed for stealing drugs?' Lottie said. 'Or did he discover the photo of Sharon with Terry and was working with Lucy to blow the lid off? He might even have witnessed Lucy's murder. Oh, I don't know.'

'The drugs he stole, that you found hidden in his house, might have been his attempt to draw people out,' Kirby suggested.

'This is all speculation. We need to ask who had the most to lose if the child pornography angle was exposed,' McKeown said.

'Depends on what was most important to them,' Lottie said. 'Reputation, career, money, or even a marriage.'

Silence ensued before she sent them home.

'Like Kirby said earlier, things are always clearer in the morning. Fingers crossed.'

————

My wings are clipped. My world flutters around me. I want to flee, but first I have to regroup and discover who knows what.

I concealed my identity and only revealed myself to a select few. But Lucy turned into a devious snitch and Jake was a thief. Bye bye, Lucy and Jake. Sharon was too cute for her own good, but I didn't mean to kill her. The knife slipped as I nicked at her clothing. If I'm caught, which I won't be, that will be my defence. Why couldn't she have been as compliant as the others when I first welcomed them to my nest? Their shining innocence took a while to wear off, but they remained faithful. Until it came to Sharon. She pushed Lucy over the edge. I know that now. I shouldn't have been so cocky, flapping my wings at what I knew would be a new treasure to add to my trove.

I've lost it all. But I can start again. A new nest. Ready to be lined with bright new things.

A magpie never gives up.

I will never give up.

I am ready to begin again.

76

Lottie had no recollection of driving home. Katie forced her to eat reheated food. Sated, she fell into bed without changing the sheets Rose had slept in the night before. In the midst of a nightmare, the incessant ringing of her phone dragged her awake.

'Mrs Parker, I really need you to come to the hospital now. It's your mother.'

'Oh God.' Lottie shot up in the bed. She swung her legs over the edge, trying to shake her brain into reality 'Is she ... She's not ... you know, is she ...?'

'Your mother is asking for you,' the tired voice continued. 'She has all the other patients in the ward awake. She's distressed and refuses to calm down until she speaks with you. Could you get here as soon as possible?'

'I'll be there in twenty minutes.'

Rose was sitting up in bed attempting to remove a cannula from her arm. A bedraggled nurse was struggling to stop her.

'You took your time,' Rose said as Lottie rushed to her bedside.

'Stop doing that, Mother. You'll bleed to death.'

Immediately Rose gave up her battle.

The nurse shot Lottie a weary smile. 'I'll leave you to sort things out.'

Sitting on the edge of the bed, Lottie said, 'You wanted to talk to me.'

'Yes, and you took your own good time. I want you to bring my bottle-green suit to the cleaners.'

Lottie sighed and moved to the chair beside the bed. 'It's after three o'clock in the morning and you drag me here about a green suit. I don't believe it.'

'It's the one I wore to Adam's funeral. It has a silver brooch on the lapel. Take that off or the cleaners will lose it. Do you know which suit I'm talking about?'

'Yes, but where do you think you're going to wear it?'

'I want to have it ready.' There was an edge to Rose's voice that Lottie couldn't decipher. Still in a nightmare, she concluded.

'Ready for what?'

Rose shrugged. 'For when I need it.'

'I've only seen you wear that suit once, so I don't see why it has to be cleaned.'

'I want to look good when all those old biddies are staring at me. Wouldn't give them the satisfaction of saying Rose Fitzpatrick's family couldn't be bothered.'

'I'm at loss to know what you're talking about.' Lottie wished she was back home in bed.

'I want to wear it in my coffin.'

'What? Don't be silly.'

'I can't be looking like a washed-up old crone. I have to be smart. Make sure the undertakers don't cake make-up on my face, and don't let them near me with red lipstick. I've seen some corpses in my lifetime that looked like they were straight out of a Stephen King novel.'

'Will you stop? This is daft talk.'

'I want Father Joe, but no singing. Just organ music.'

Deciding to play along, Lottie said, 'You fell out with the Catholic Church years ago. You hate all that rigmarole.'

'It would make a better impression to have a Catholic burial.' Rose leaned over and nudged her. 'Are you listening to me?'

'Of course I am.'

'What's his name?'

'Who?'

'I knew you weren't listening at all.'

Maybe Rose had convinced herself she was going to die, but Lottie wasn't so sure.

'I heard you, Mother. Suit to cleaners. Take off brooch. No lipstick. Father Joe. Organ music. No singing. Would you like me to organise soup and sandwiches or canapés for your wake?'

Rose sank back into the pillows. 'You aren't taking this seriously. You know my wishes now, but I'll write them down for you all the same.'

'That's fine,' Lottie said, rising. 'I'll send Chloe in tomorrow with paper and a pen.'

'It might be too late by then.'

'I don't think so.'

'Make sure to tell your father to wear his good suit.'

Lottie halted at the foot of the bed. Was her mother genuinely confused?

'Dad died a long time ago.'

Rose closed her eyes. 'He said he'd wait for me.'

Lottie moved towards the door in silence.

Sitting bolt upright, Rose said, 'What are you doing here, Lottie? Do you know what time it is?'

On her way down in the lift, Lottie considered her mother's mortality. She'd spent most of her life at loggerheads with the woman she called mother; the woman who had raised her as her own; who'd kept the truth of Lottie's birth hidden from her. Despite their differences, she couldn't envisage a time when Rose would no longer be a part of her life. Unbidden tears filled her eyes and she hastily swiped at them. It was just tiredness.

At least Boyd would be home soon. With his son. And then a horrible thought entered her head. Would his ex-wife arrive with them?

She headed for her car, no longer confident about tomorrow after all.

77

MONDAY

The first thing Lottie did when she arrived at the office the next morning was to send for Hannah and Cormac. She wanted to interview them together for the first time. For all she knew, they had spoken to each other to align their stories, but it was the only thing that made sense after a disturbed sleep. Following the visit to her mother, her night had been one of twists and turns, and dreams filled with little girls in garish make-up with mad red lips.

She felt on edge, cranky and irritable. God, but she'd love a Xanax or a vodka. She made do with a coffee.

They arrived without their respective legal reps, and Lottie was relieved. Hannah kept her eyes focused on the floor, while Cormac stared at a spot on the wall behind Lottie's head.

'The two of you have a lot to sort out between yourselves, but the reason I asked you here this morning was to pick your brains.'

'What do you mean?' Hannah said, looking up. Her face

was thinner, her hair a tangled mess falling over in a lopsided topknot.

'There is forensic evidence against you both, but I believe you are innocent of Lucy's murder. Hannah, it's possible you were set up, either intentionally or because the opportunity presented itself. I can't understand why Jake would slip you GHB. Are you sure you didn't know him, or his little sister Sharon?'

'I'm sure.'

'Who would want you drugged?'

'I don't know.'

'Any ideas, Cormac?'

'None.' He still refused to meet her eye.

'You're a gardener at the school and at Lucy's house. Were you ever friends with her?'

'She talked to me sometimes.'

'I thought she enjoyed insulting you?'

'She used to.'

'What do you mean?'

'She only kept it up so that Ivy wouldn't suspect.'

Lottie leaned forward. 'Suspect what?'

With one hand Cormac worried away at his acne. In the other he held his inhaler, tapping it infuriatingly on the table.

'Can you stop doing that?' Lottie tried not to screech at him.

'Sorry.' At last he brought his gaze in line with hers.

'You were telling me about Lucy ...'

'Yeah, well, she talked to me a lot recently. Studying for exams and with her parents away, I think she was glad of someone to confide in. She was scared.'

'Scared of what?' Lottie had to restrain herself from leaping across the table to shake him. Why was he only telling her this now?

'Not a what,' he mumbled, 'a who.'

'Who then?' Lottie glanced at Hannah, who had her head bowed again.

Cormac said, 'I'm ... Look, I can't say. Lucy said, "She terrifies me." That's all I know.'

'She?' Lottie exclaimed. 'Did she mean Ivy Jones?'

'I don't know.' He clamped his mouth shut and picked at a spot on his forehead. Lottie felt like jamming her nails into his other spots. Did these kids not realise what they'd been involved in?

She turned her attention to Hannah. 'What do you know about this?'

The girl shrugged one shoulder.

'We can protect you.'

'You couldn't protect Sharon Flood,' Cormac shot at her.

'Cormac, you really need to tell me what's going on before someone else gets hurt.'

Silence.

Lottie decided on a direct approach. 'Hannah, when were you first abused?'

Cormac shifted uncomfortably and took a puff from his inhaler. Hannah remained stock still, the only movement a single tear journeying a lonely track down her cheek. Lottie waited. Prayed the girl would open up to her.

Cormac nudged her. Hannah gave a gentle shake of her head, but he nodded and took her hand in his.

'You have to tell her,' he said.

'It's too late,' Hannah whispered.

Still Lottie waited, counting in her head. She'd reached twenty-five when Hannah spoke.

'I didn't know about them. The photos at school. I didn't know about them even when Mr Glennon started ... you know ... interfering with me.'

'He's a bastard,' Cormac said.

Lottie felt a lump form in her throat, preventing her from jumping in with questions. Glennon?

Hannah continued. 'He brought me to a party and the boxer guy, Terry, he started pawing me and telling me I was beautiful and my legs were gorgeous and that there were a lot of men who liked me when they saw my photograph. I hadn't a clue what he meant by that. I do now.'

'When did you find out the truth?'

'Lucy told me. She was up her own arse most of the time, but she'd been sexually abused herself, she told me, and she didn't really know who she was any more.' Hannah sobbed and Cormac placed his arm around her shoulders.

'Hannah, sweetheart, you have to tell me everything you know.' Lottie knew she was nearing the crux of the case.

'This is your chance to lose the guilt, Hannah,' Cormac said. He turned to Lottie. 'I had a long chat with Hannah last night and she thinks it's all her fault, what happened to her.'

'Oh sweetie,' Lottie said, 'none of this is your fault. Those people, they'll go to prison for what they did to you and countless other girls, but I need your help to put them away.'

'I'm so ashamed.'

'We can arrange counselling for you. It's good to talk it out.'

'I didn't know Lucy was going to send around that photo. I thought she was after lying to me and making fun of me. I lost my head and attacked her. But now I think I know why she did it.'

'Why?'

'To get attention. To make a fuss so people would ask questions. But I went for her and made it worse. And then … someone killed her.'

'Why didn't she come to us?'

'She didn't know who she could trust. She said she was hoping to make it public.'

Lottie digested Hannah's words, then turned towards Cormac. 'You didn't know Hannah before the party, did you?'

'No, but Lucy had mentioned her. I wanted to look out for her. We, me and Lucy, we never thought for a minute that anyone would get killed.'

'She got her publicity in the end but paid with her life,' Hannah said, sniffing back her sorrow. 'Why was I drugged?'

'I'm not sure. Do you think Jake knew what was going on?' Lottie wondered if Jake had been threatened and forced to drug Hannah. But why? She couldn't figure it out. She needed to find Terry fucking Starr.

The girl was shaking her head.

'Hannah, I've issued an arrest warrant for Noel Glennon and Terry Starr. Do you know where they would go to hide out?'

'No.'

'You could try the old army barracks,' Cormac said. 'That's where Sharon was killed, wasn't it?'

'Thanks, Cormac. I'll have it checked. You need to tell me who it was that Lucy was so scared of.'

He shook his head. 'I told you, I don't know.'

'Even after Hannah has bared her soul, you still refuse?'

Silence.

Lottie smiled sadly. 'As soon as you feel okay, you can both leave. Have a long, hard think, Cormac, because I need that name.'

She left them there, in each other's arms.

78

Garda Lei had fallen asleep, his head resting on his folded hands at the kitchen table. A scream woke him up sharply.

Rita ran into the room. 'Ivy's gone. I can't find her. You're useless, the lot of you. Where is she?'

Lei raced around the house. He found Oscar asleep in bed, shaking like a leaf. Withdrawal from whatever shit he'd taken, maybe. The boy groaned as he tugged at him. Lost cause.

Outside, he talked to the two guards in the squad car. They hadn't seen anyone leave. Around the back of the house he noticed a gate in the rear wall swinging open in the morning breeze. Beyond it a narrow lane. At the end of the lane, the main road. Easy for someone to pull up in a car and collect her. Shit!

He shook as he called it in. He knew Inspector Parker would be angry. And that was an understatement.

———

Lottie swore like a trooper after receiving Garda Lei's phone call. Bloody hell! One step forward and ten backwards. She rounded up the team in the incident room and reported on her interview with Hannah and Cormac.

'Do you believe them?' Kirby asked.

'For the moment, yes. Ivy Jones is missing from her home.'

'What?' Lynch exclaimed. 'Did Lei fall asleep on the job or what? Did the pair in the car not see anything?'

'Lei thinks Ivy might have left via the back gate. An oversight not to have it covered.'

'Yeah, but we didn't think she'd run,' Lynch said.

'She might've been taken,' Lottie pointed out.

'Damn it.' Lynch looked pissed off.

'Why haven't we found Terry Starr and the McAllisters? Are they hiding out somewhere?'

'Are they all in this together?' Kirby asked.

'I don't know.'

McKeown was furiously tapping his iPad. 'CCTV footage from the pub across the road from the army barracks shows what might be Terry Starr's Range Rover heading into the barracks late yesterday evening. It was too dark later to catch if, or when, the car left again.'

'Are SOCOs still there?'

'They finished up fairly quickly yesterday afternoon,' McKeown said.

'The barracks was used as a drug den. It's a remote possibility, but Terry might still be there. Kirby, you're with me. Lynch, with McKeown. Whoever is behind all this is well ahead of us and I'm sick of looking like a fool.'

'That wouldn't be hard for you, Inspector Parker.' Superintendent Farrell marched into the room, her tie askew and her skirt twisted like she'd rushed out the door. She was still spitting fire.

'I was going to update you,' Lottie said. 'We're about to close all three murder cases.'

'That's what you said yesterday.'

'I know, but now we're running out of time. I'll give you my report on my return.'

'Is that another crock of shit?' Farrell said.

'Ivy Jones is missing. She could be the next victim. We have to fly. Sorry.'

Lottie shooed the three detectives out the door. With her back straight, trying to appear more professional than she felt, she followed them without a backward glance. She didn't need to see the expression on Farrell's face. She could guess it was furious.

At the gate of the derelict barracks, Lottie issued orders to those she'd rounded up to help with the search. She checked they were all wearing Kevlar vests.

The area was vast. She ruled out the officers' quarters at the far end because SOCOs had been there yesterday. There was the large cookhouse and the NCOs' mess, as well as various office and housing blocks. Without adequate personnel because of the short notice, she had to be strategic in her approach.

Along with Kirby and a uniformed garda, she herself took the cookhouse. Changing her earlier plan, she now directed Lynch to go with Garda Lei to the NCOs' mess, while McKeown and Garda Brennan would take the neighbouring block.

'Proceed with caution,' she advised.

The cookhouse was directly inside the main gate. Any activity here wouldn't have been noticed by the SOCOs who had been working further down the complex. The building was the newest on the site and boasted floor-to-ceiling plate-glass windows, now boarded up. The lock on the side door was busted, and holding a finger to her lips, she stepped inside.

It was dull but not dark, a sliver of light penetrating the

boarded windows. Tables and chairs were stacked at the end wall, the space before her bare.

'Is that a light?' she whispered to Kirby, pointing to the swing doors leading to the kitchen. A fractured streak spilled out beneath them.

'Yeah,' he said.

She crept forward holding her gun.

She was expecting the doors to be stiff from lack of use, and was surprised when they opened easily. The stainless-steel appliances were black with soot, and there were the remains of a burned-out fire on the floor. The drug gang kids, she suspected. Beyond the appliances was what she assumed was a large pantry.

Beckoning the others to follow, she stealthily approached the pantry door. She had no idea what she would find inside.

The door creaked inwards and she stepped inside, weapon pointed. She recoiled at the strong odour of urine, and then she gasped.

Seated on the floor, back to back in their own mess, hands and feet bound, mouths gagged, were Albert and Mary McAllister.

Rushing forward, she pulled the gag from Mary's mouth while Kirby worked on Albert. Mary was unconscious. Lottie glanced at Albert. His eyes were open and bloodshot.

Kirby slit the ropes and caught Mary as she collapsed forward. The uniformed garda was on the radio calling for an ambulance.

Lottie hunkered down in front of Albert. 'Who did this to you?'

'T-Terry. I d-don't understand. I treated him like a son; why would he do this to us? Is Mary okay?'

'She's passed out. Might be dehydration. Ambulance is on its way. Did Terry say why he took you?'

'He said he wanted to talk in private. He drove around back

roads for ages, talking shite, and wouldn't tell me anything useful, but he knew his way around this place.'

She figured Terry coached the young gang of drug pushers within the barracks walls. Why else would Oscar Jones be camping out in the officers' quarters? Sharon Flood had come here too, to plead for her family.

'How did he overpower two of you?'

'He wasn't alone. Another man joined him.'

'Noel Glennon?'

'I don't know who he was.'

'Was there a woman with them? Or Ivy Jones?' Lottie remembered Cormac's reluctance to name the female Lucy had been so frightened of. And Ivy was still missing.

'Ivy? No. I miss my daughter. Did … did Terry kill her?'

'I don't know, but I'm going to find out.'

Lynch and Garda Lei arrived, followed by McKeown and Garda Brennan. The pantry was suddenly too tight for all of them.

'We found nothing,' Lynch said.

Sirens blared in the distance.

Lottie stood. 'Make room for the paramedics.'

'Inspector,' Albert said, 'find the bastards. I'll look after Mary.'

She had a mountain of questions for them, but he was right.

'Lei, you stay with them, and don't fall asleep. Accompany them to the hospital and stand guard.'

'Got it. I'm sorry, about Ivy. You know …'

'Later.' She holstered her gun, then stepped out of the pantry with her three detectives behind her.

'Where to now?' Kirby asked.

'The boxing club?' Lynch offered.

'Industrial estate is too public.' Lottie shook her head. 'Where is he?'

'What about Noel Glennon's house?' Kirby said.

'There was no one there when I sent uniforms yesterday after I'd talked to Sarah Robson.'

'What about Richie Harrison?' Lynch said. 'Ivy could have left home to go to him. Or maybe he took her? But he has a pregnant wife and—'

'Perfect cover for a couple of paedophiles,' McKeown said.

Lottie heard Albert's voice coming from the pantry.

'What is it, Albert?'

'Before he left us here, Terry said something about a safe house. He said the guards wouldn't suspect a pregnant woman.'

Lottie rejoined the others. 'Harrison's house it is.'

79

Brontë Harrison pressed her hand to the side of her bump. Still nothing. Her baby wasn't moving. She walked around the garden in her bare feet, trying to jolt the little fellow awake.

Richie poked his head around the patio door. 'Come in, Brontë. You're making me dizzy going round in circles.'

She glared at him. 'If anything happens to my baby, Richie Harrison, you will not live to regret it.'

Her father appeared at Richie's shoulder. He held up a mug. 'I've made you a cup of tea, Brontë.'

She marched up to the door.

'You disgust me,' she hissed. 'The pair of you fuck up everything you touch.' As she barged past them, Barney spilled the mug of tea over her shining floor. 'See? You're useless.'

'You need to calm down,' Noel said.

The creepy fucker was sitting at her table. She clenched her hands into fists. 'As for you, what shithole did you crawl out of?'

He shrugged his shoulders uselessly. 'Terry brought me here.'

She swore and moved into the sitting room. Banged the door behind her and flopped onto an armchair.

'What's your next bright idea, Terry?'

'If you'd shut up for half a minute, I might be able to think.'

'If the guards find any of those girls, they'll talk and we'll be fucked. What about my baby then?'

'Thought you couldn't feel it moving?'

'You're a shit.'

'We'll sort it out. We all just need to stay here for a couple of days, until the heat dies down. Then we can leave for Malaga. I'm organising a private flight.'

'You're a stupid cliché! Three kids are dead and you think the heat will clear?' She scoffed. 'Grow the fuck up. Why did you have to kill her anyway?'

'Lucy? She was going to talk. That photo of Hannah she sent around, it was part of her big plan to expose us. The bitch wanted to bring us all down. I'm sure she said something to Jake. He was acting weird.'

'You could've left him alone. He was too much into making money to be a nuisance.'

'He saw me at Lucy's when the party ended.'

'Why were you even there, you moron? How did he see you?'

'I watched Lucy all night from the trees in the field behind her house. When I thought everyone had left, the bitch accused me of raping her.'

'Don't tell me you had sex with her the night of the party? Why, for God's sake?'

'She came up to Dublin last weekend, gagging for it. I thought she'd want more.'

'Lucy was in your apartment? For fuck's sake. Did you watch her every second she was there?'

'No. Should I have?'

'I bet the sneaky little bitch accessed your computer. She probably copied your hard drive. Why else would she agree to meet you up there?'

'She liked me.'

'She despised you, like I despise you. I want the truth about what happened the night of the party. Now!' She couldn't help the screech in her voice. Her baby could be dead, and Terry was acting like a total fuckwit.

He leaned forward. 'You never understood me, Brontë. All you wanted was money. I was the one putting my head on the block for you.'

'If you don't tell me what went on after the party, I'll call the guards myself.'

'You're a bitch, you know that? Lucy liked me, and I couldn't understand why she'd changed. She resisted when I tried to kiss her and I hardly had the condom on when she started calling me a rapist. She started screaming that she was going to the guards, that she had—'

'Evidence?' God, but he was so stupid. 'And then you go and kill her in her own house! It's crawling with cops and forensics. Your DNA must be everywhere.'

'The bitch got away from me, yelling blue murder. I grabbed a knife and went for her in the living room. She fought like a demon. Bruised the shit out of me. I totally lost it then. It was like I was in a final round just seconds before the bell. I chased her up the back stairs and I ... I shut her up for good.'

'That was so fucking stupid. Even more stupid was killing Jake Flood. Why?'

'I found the little shit cowering behind the drinks table. He saw and heard everything. I went for him with the knife and he started to run. I was high on adrenaline, like I am in the ring, and I grabbed him and threw him across the room. He went through the patio door.'

'Then you had the bright idea to involve my father.' Her blood pressure was surely through the roof, but she couldn't calm down. 'For fuck's sake, Terry!'

'Where else was I to go with a half-dead teenager? I

bundled him into his car and drove him to Barney's. He had to help me because I've made you both so much money. He said he'd deal with Jake, and I hightailed it to the airport.'

'Why leave?'

'To give myself an alibi. If I was in Spain, I couldn't have killed anyone, could I?'

'You didn't think that other people might need an alibi, did you? Don't answer that.' She felt nauseous and still her baby was motionless. 'You shouldn't have come back.'

'I had to. What Lucy said about that little weasel Sharon ... I couldn't trust the kid. Plus there was Ivy with a mouth on her. They were threatening everything I'd built up.'

'You shouldn't have killed the kid.'

'If your dumbass father had got there before the guards they would never have found her.'

'I can't believe that Ivy turned up at my house.' Brontë shook her head angrily. 'The bitch my husband was fucking prances up to my front door and ... Oh fuck it, Terry, you're a dose, you know that? A bloody great dose.'

She dragged herself up from the armchair and walked around the room, tapping her tummy anxiously. Still no movement. She paused at the window and glanced out.

'Holy shit! Fuck!'

She sensed Terry moving to stand beside her. 'Is it the baby? Has the little bastard moved?'

'Look outside! It's the guards! They've brought the bloody army!'

As she turned to leave the room, the baby kicked and she sank to the floor with relief.

'It's over, Terry. The whole thing is over. Your stupidity has brought everything down around our ears. I hope you rot in a hole.'

'I never wanted you on board anyway,' he spat. 'Barney thought you could help us find more girls after Sarah got cold feet. Photos are old-school, he said. It's all video now, he said, and my Brontë is good at that. Your dear daddy. The money I was about to make from Sharon alone ... If I go down, rest assured, you and your old man are coming with me.'

A huge crash rang out from the hallway, and Brontë Harrison's world collapsed along with her front door.

80

Lottie found it a surprisingly subdued capture and arrest. It was like they knew the game was up. Brontë seemed delirious, going on about her baby. Barney Reynolds tended to his daughter, while Noel Glennon seemed relieved that the truth was out. Richie Harrison twisted his necklace into knots until it broke and coloured beads skittered across the floor. He was the only one who appeared mystified.

They found Ivy in an upstairs bedroom in floods of tears.

'I wanted him to save me. To go away with me.'

'Who?'

'Richie. I had it all planned out for him to leave her. When I ran from home this morning, I came straight here, but his bitch wife opened the door.'

'It's okay, Ivy. You'll have your chance to tell your story. But you need to go home to your mother.' Lottie didn't think there was anything to charge the girl with at the moment, and her evidence would prove crucial in the trial.

'I'm so stupid,' Ivy said.

'You were taken advantage of. What they did to you is

abuse, from the first illicit photograph back when you were twelve or thirteen. You'll need therapy.'

'I'd do anything to remove this shit from my head.' She burst into tears. 'I should have helped Lucy, but I don't think she trusted me the last few months. I was always jealous of her. I was a bad friend.'

'No, you weren't.'

Ivy sobbed. 'I honestly thought Richie could take away my pain. Is this agony I feel because of what those bastards did to me?'

'Probably.' Lottie thought that if Rita Jones had given as much attention to her kids as she did to her sports, then maybe her daughter and son might have been spared their anguish. 'Did you know what Oscar was into?'

'It was easier to turn a blind eye to him and his friends. I was in self-preservation mode and it was difficult to admit my brother was taking drugs and messing around with the wrong crowd. I never guessed Terry had Oscar in his claws as well as me.'

Lottie arranged for Ivy to be brought home, then turned her attention to Terry Starr. His attitude was in stark contrast to his evil associates. He was belligerent, prancing around like a turkey cock.

When Garda Lei snapped handcuffs on his wrists, Terry shouted, 'I am the magpie! I can plunder your nests. You'd better be careful, because I am watching you all. I will come for you.'

Two hours later, sitting with Kirby opposite Terry Starr, who was arrogant enough to believe he didn't need a solicitor, Lottie observed the boxer closely. Beneath his sleeked-back hair his eyes flashed with anger.

'You know who I am?' he said, his baritone voice making him sound a lot older than his thirty years.

'You are a murderer.'

'I'm the magpie. The glorious wings and—'

Enough of this shit, Lottie thought as she interrupted his flow. 'A witness places you at Lucy's house after her party. He saw you attack her.'

'Huh? No way he'd tell you anything.' A smirk streaked across his face. 'I found him hiding under a table. Gave him a good thump and landed him into next week.'

'You're talking about Jake Flood. The boy you put through a glass door?'

'He couldn't tell you anything because—' He slammed his lips shut, realising he'd walked himself into a trap.

Lottie smiled coldly. 'My witness is someone else. They saw what you did to Lucy. They saw you assault Jake then put him in the boot of his own car and drive off.'

Terry looked at her incredulously. 'If not Jake, then who?'

'You don't need to know.'

'Barney? He owes me too much to rat me out.'

'Enough to kill his most promising young boxer and dump his body in the canal?'

'If so, none of it was my doing.'

'I'll get back to Barney Reynolds but I want to know why you raped and murdered a seventeen-year-old girl?'

'I never raped her.'

Lottie quelled the urge to punch him in the face. 'We fast-tracked your DNA, Terry, and it's a match for that found on Lucy's defence wounds and for semen found on her body. Do you know what happens to rapists in prison?'

'I wore a condom, and anyhow, she was with me last weekend in my apartment. She didn't say no then.'

'She said no to you on Friday night, though, didn't she?'

'The bitch threatened me.'

'And you chased after her with a knife and didn't stop until she took her last breath.'

'She had it coming.' His smugness was so irritating, Lottie fought to control her disgust.

'Why do you think she was with you last weekend?'

'She wanted me. Plain and simple. But I knew something had changed with her, and I needed to keep her close. Thought I'd find out by having her in my nest ... my home. But now I suspect she either stole something from my computer or planted something on it.'

Lottie showed him the photo of Sharon sitting on his knee. 'This was on your fake Instagram account.'

'I never ... What is this?' His eyes narrowed, scrunching his face into an ugly scowl.

'It was posted to your account last Monday at four a.m.'

'Fucking Lucy!'

'Clever girl,' Lottie said, feeling a growing admiration for the teenager, who'd acted bravely even though she was too scared to go to the authorities. 'Why did you attack Sharon Flood?'

'I had to scare her. I wanted her for myself, though I knew she'd be good for business ... I mean ...' He paused, eyes closed.

Lottie forced down her abhorrence. 'You were grooming her, like so many others before her. A little girl who hadn't even a shoelace for her runners. You killed her. Why?'

He shrugged. 'She wouldn't stop going on about paying me back what her thieving brother owed me. As if a couple of euros from her fucking money box could ever account for the value of the drugs Jake stole. She got what she deserved.'

'She was ten years old!'

'Not my fault.'

Christ, but he was a narcissist of the highest order. 'How did you come to target her?'

'She was at the gym with Jake one day. Barney rang me to

come have a look at her. Scared as a rabbit she was, but I recognised her potential. Innocence and fear are good at online auctions.'

Inspector Reilly, of the online child exploitation unit, had mentioned these auctions. They hadn't discovered any images of Sharon online or on the dark web. That was something to be thankful for, she supposed.

'Tell me about Hannah Byrne.'

'Ah, sweet Hannah. She looks younger than she is. She can pass for thirteen. And those legs go on forever.' His expression turned salacious.

'You instructed Jake to drug her. Why?'

He laughed. 'Drug Hannah? No, he was supposed to slip it into Lucy's drink. The little prick couldn't even get that right. But it worked out okay for a while. You had her as your prime suspect.'

'You wanted Lucy drugged with GHB so you could do what you liked with her. Am I correct?'

'No comment.' He smirked.

'How many defenceless girls have you raped after slipping them GHB?'

'You're sick,' he said slyly.

'Why cut the tattoo from Lucy's body?' She was flying through her questions, dying to get away from his vile evil.

'It had my initials on it. She had it done a few months ago, to impress me. All proud like, thinking she was mine alone.'

'But then she discovered what you were really like.'

'Ivy has a big mouth.'

'You're saying this is Ivy's fault?'

'She's a leech. First she was into Noel Glennon and then Brontë's husband. So yeah, she is partly to blame.'

'How did you get Glennon involved in your scheme?'

'Easy. It started with Ivy. She told him about this teacher, Sarah Robson, who she suspected of taking secret photos of the girls in the showers. Noel told me about it and I realised I knew Sarah from years ago, so I got her on board. She gave me her back catalogue, so to speak. We had a great little number going until she got cold feet and Noel dibbed her to the principal. We didn't need her by then; he had access to youngsters at athletics.'

'Who did you sell the images to?'

'There's plenty of buyers. Supply of fresh meat is the main issue.' He grinned and her stomach churned. He was acting like he believed he was going to get away with his crimes.

'How did you get Brontë involved?'

'Barney was useless as a trainer after his accident. He had gambling debts and needed money. I put a proposal to him and he roped his daughter in. She has a good business head. Dollar signs are like diamonds to her. She's ruthless. Puts the fear of God into those who seem to be unwilling.'

'Did she put the fear of God into you too?'

'I'm able for Brontë. Noel has just discovered she's my right hand, and now he's scared shitless of her.'

'So you, Noel and Brontë ran the show, keeping Barney for the dirty work?'

'I tried to keep everyone separate. Noel didn't even know Brontë was involved until today.'

'Richie's part of this too?'

'Brontë didn't want her husband anywhere near young girls. She's raging over the fact that he hooked up with Ivy.' He laughed. 'She told me Noel turned up at her house yesterday looking for Richie, unaware of her involvement.'

'Richie wasn't afraid of being photographed with youngsters at nightclubs, though.'

'Part and parcel of his DJ gig. Noel was working on getting him more involved with me.'

'The thing is, Terry, Noel tells me that he was trying to get out and wanted Richie to help him escape your claws.'

'Claws? Good one, but that's a lie.'

'Brontë says you coerced her and her father to get involved.'

'Also a lie. Trying to save her own skin and that of her kid.'

'What were you planning to do if we hadn't discovered that you'd murdered Lucy, Sharon and Jake?'

'Barney finished Jake off, not me. Now I want to make that call to my solicitor to get me out of here.'

'You will be incarcerated for a very long time, Terry. No flying the coop on this.'

'I can spread my wings far and wide. You don't know who you are up against, Inspector.'

'Oh, I do. And Albert McAllister knows too. You've made one very powerful enemy.'

When Kirby finished up for the recording and switched off the machine, Lottie stood and leaned over the table towards Terry. 'Your wings are about to be clipped for good. And once the other prisoners are finished with you, I hope your sorry arse melts into the sewers of hell.'

She expected him to cower. Instead he stared back at her, a slow leer creasing his face. She believed in that moment that she had never seen a more terrifying sight in her life.

81

Albert McAllister was heartbroken all over again. His pain at the loss of his adored daughter was stronger than any anger he could muster. Lottie knew that would come later, and then Albert would be a force to be reckoned with.

He sat by his sleeping wife's bedside. Mary had been administered a strong sedative and a saline infusion for dehydration before being discharged from hospital.

'When can we go home?' His glazed eyes swept around the apartment bedroom.

'Tomorrow or the day after. SOCOs should be finishing up soon. Albert, I'd advise hiring in contract cleaners for your house. I don't think Mary will be able to handle the ... There's a lot of blood.'

'I want to see for myself what that bastard did.'

'Of course.' Lottie felt so weary she had no idea if it were day or night.

'Thank you, Inspector. You've worked tirelessly and quickly to catch my daughter's murderer. I'm still processing everything. I feel so foolish. I welcomed Terry Starr into my home. Introduced him to my wife and daughter. Put all my energy behind him to bring him success. And all the time he was smuggling drugs and targeting my little girl to fuel his perversions. He abused her. Raped her. Murdered her ...'

Tears flowed unchecked down his leathery cheeks. 'I can't forgive myself for falling for the threatening email he sent. I left my girl alone and he ... he ...'

'His plan was to get you out of the way while extorting money from you. It was hatched in conjunction with Brontë Harrison. Because Brontë was pregnant, Terry was preparing to set up his vile business elsewhere. I think he had become suspicious of Lucy.'

'Why? What did she know?'

'It's possible she realised the scale of their depravity once Sharon Flood became Terry's target.' Lottie showed him a photo of the little girl. 'Do you recognise her?'

Through blinding tears Albert studied the image. 'No.'

'If you remember anything, let me know.'

As she left the room, Albert was holding his wife's hand, his tears endless.

THREE WEEKS PREVIOUSLY

Sharon looked up as Lucy McAllister came and sat beside her.

'Hi, pipsqueak, what's with the sad face?'

'Oh, hi.' Sharon tugged down the legs of her too short jeans and groaned at her dirty socks and her pink runner with no lace. Lucy was a rich girl and Sharon was so embarrassed, she didn't know where to look.

'Come on outside for some fresh air. The sweaty smell in here is making me sick.'

Outside the gym, Lucy leaned against the wall, her face turned to the watery sun. Sharon copied her.

'Shaz?' Lucy said. 'That's what your friends call you, isn't it?'

'Yeah.'

'I want to be your friend.'

'Cool.'

'I saw you with Terry Starr. You know him? The boxer.'

'Yeah. He sometimes watches Jake training. He told me I was cute. He said he wanted to bring me for a drive in his car.'

'What did your brother say to that?'

Sharon felt her cheeks flare. 'I didn't tell him.'

'Didn't he wonder where you'd gone?'

'It was only for an hour, and he was training for two hours. Please don't tell him.' The conversation was making Sharon uncomfortable. She couldn't help staring at Lucy's silver trainers. They were fab. And expensive.

'Shaz, you need to stay away from Terry.'

'Why?'

'I don't like the way he was acting with you.'

'What do you mean?' Sharon felt awkward and scuffed at pebbles with the toe of her runner. She really needed to get new laces.

'I saw you in his car. He had you on his knee.'

Feeling sick to her stomach, she jumped when Lucy stood in front of her and grabbed her by the elbows. Her long black hair was wild, like a witch's, and Sharon was suddenly afraid of her.

'Don't be scared, Shaz, I'm your friend. But remember this, Terry is not your friend. Do you hear me? You have to stay away from him.'

Sharon wondered if Lucy was jealous. 'He was nice to me. He bought me an ice cream.'

'I'm sure he did.' Lucy paced.

When she turned around, she leaned down and was so close their noses were almost touching. Sharon had to stifle a giggle.

'This is serious, Shaz. I want you to tell me everything he did, no matter how bad he made you feel.'

After biting her lip for a few seconds, Sharon said, 'Is he a toxic man?'

'What makes you say that?'

'Jake warned me to stay away from toxic people and you're telling me to stay away from Terry ...'

'Honey, Terry is so toxic he will poison you to death.'

The shiver that took hold of Sharon was so fierce it made her cry. 'I didn't want to do anything wrong. I'm a good girl. He made me.'

She felt Lucy's arms wrap around her, and the smell of her jumper was like the lilies on her dad's grave the day he was buried.

Between sobs, she told Lucy what Terry had done to her.

And then Lucy cried too.

'Don't worry, petal,' she said. 'I'll make Terry Starr regret the day he ever laid a hand on you.'

'What are you going to do?'

Lucy was silent.

And Shaz was suddenly scared of the darkness that filled Lucy's eyes.

82

Lottie had spent ages in the shower and had lashed on a bit of make-up to hide the bags under her eyes. After pulling on a clean pair of black jeans, she found a white T-shirt that somehow had made it out of the wash unscathed. She wasn't sure if it was Boyd she wanted to look good for, or whether she wanted to make an impression on Sergio. But first she had an audience with her boss.

The sound of the superintendent's shoes stomping back and forth was driving her nuts. Her head would spin right off and hit Farrell in the face if the woman didn't sit down soon.

'Any hope of getting DNA from the knife found in the canal?' Farrell said.

'Gráinne believes they might get something. Anyway, Terry Starr's DNA is a match for that found on Lucy. She fought hard for her life.'

'Did he rape her?'

'Consensual according to him. He's obnoxious. I'm sure Brontë Harrison knows the full story.'

'Will she talk?'

'She will if she wants to spend any quality time with her baby before he reaches adulthood.'

'They were all in on it?'

'Terry was the ringleader. He fell on his feet when Noel Glennon told him Sarah Robson's secret. Ivy thought she was doing the right thing telling Glennon, but the poor girl walked straight into a vipers' nest. Terry brought Brontë and Barney into his scheme. Such a band of fuckers.'

'Was Richie involved?' Farrell didn't even flinch at Lottie's profanity. 'Didn't Glennon say they met at a nightclub?'

'Yeah. But I think Richie was only interested in having teenagers for himself. I don't believe he realised the full scale of what was going on under his nose. Glennon claims he had no idea that Brontë was involved, as he only dealt with Terry. But he was friends with Richie and they were both photographed in a nightclub with girls. Time will tell who rats out who first.'

'I think I understand most of it.' Farrell eventually sat behind her desk and Lottie breathed out a sigh of relief. 'But how did Terry Starr come to know Sharon Flood?'

'Jake sometimes brought her to his training sessions, when their mother was at work. Once Terry Starr laid eyes on the child's innocence, she became a target.'

'And that was the catalyst for Lucy to take action?'

'I think seeing Terry pawing the little girl brought her to her senses. She wanted to stop it all, but she went about it the wrong way. It's likely Sharon told her what was going on and Lucy decided to handle it herself.'

'Have any photos or videos of Sharon surfaced?'

'Inspector Reilly says his team hasn't found any images of her so far. He's liaising with the Spanish police.'

'These cases can take years,' Farrell said dejectedly.

'Ivy and Oscar Jones are willing to give evidence. Oscar claims he never knew who he reported to via text, but I reckon it was Brontë. Gary is working on it.'

'How is young Hannah doing?' Farrell said.

'She'll need therapy, and she has to work things out with Cormac over the sex they had. He didn't spike her drink, so it's unclear if charges should be brought against him.'

'If Cormac didn't drug her, who did?'

'Terry said Jake was supposed to drug Lucy, but I feel Lucy may have spoken with Jake earlier that night about Sharon. He either drugged Hannah on Lucy's say so, or someone else did. Cormac mentioned that Richie gave Hannah a drink after her argument with Lucy. But if Richie wasn't part of the evil gang, then it's hard to know what really happened.'

'We have Terry for Lucy and Sharon's murder and Barney Reynolds for Jake's?'

'The bike chain Reynolds used to beat Jake with was found in a filing cabinet in the boxing club. He owns a boat moored a few miles up the canal and that's how he transported Jake's body to where it was discovered. Everything is being examined by SOCOs.'

'I still find it difficult to understand how Reynolds could actually beat the boy to death, then tie him up and dump his broken body in the canal. A kid he had worked with and coached for months.' Farrell shook her head wearily and loosened her tie. 'Cruel and heartless.'

'Barney Reynolds is a greedy bastard who saw his gravy train running dry. He played a blinder with me when I spoke with him the day after the party.'

'How are the McAllisters?'

'Bereft. Spanish police now believe the drug smuggling was all Terry's doing. The only thing the McAllisters are guilty of is not recognising the signs of abuse in their daughter.'

'It's been a tough few days. I suppose you don't want to do the press conference for me?'

'You suppose correctly. I've somewhere I need to be in less than an hour.' Lottie made her way to the door.

'I've to call to Liz Flood,' Farrell said.

Lottie gulped back tears as she placed Sharon's pink runner with no lace on the superintendent's desk. 'I was keeping this to remind me how I failed to protect Shaz. I think her mother might like to have it.'

She headed for the door.

'Inspector Parker?'

'Yes?'

'I take back what I said. You're nobody's fool. You're a bloody good detective.'

83

Lottie hated the airport. Vertigo always hit her when she had to drive to the upper level of the short-term car park.

As the evening closed in around her, she crossed the road to the arrivals hall. Late.

She saw them before they saw her. Standing to the right of the barrier. Father and son. No ex-wife in sight, thank God.

Pausing at a pillar, her eyes welled up. Sergio was the spitting image of his father. She studied Boyd. His skin was lightly tanned and healthy-looking. His hand rested on his son's shoulder, two suitcases at their feet. She wanted to run over and hug him forever, but she had to be careful around the boy. She wasn't his mother, and he'd only recently been introduced to his father, so she struggled to grasp how he'd react to her.

As she stood there, unable to move, Boyd caught sight of her, and his face lit up with a smile. She watched as Sergio shouldered his rucksack and Boyd picked up the two cases.

'You've no idea how good it is to see you.' He leaned over and kissed her cheek.

'You're a sight for sore eyes,' she said, before turning to the boy. 'You must be Sergio.' She held out her hand. 'I'm Lottie.'

'Are you Papá's boss?'

'I am.'

'Does it rain here all the time?'

'Not today. The sun was shining earlier. Almost as warm as Malaga.'

'Papá says he'll have to buy me warm clothes.' He turned to look up at Boyd. 'When is Mamá joining us?'

Lottie noticed Boyd's face flush. Ah no. Shit.

'Not for a while,' he said awkwardly. 'She has things to sort out.'

'Not for a good while, I hope?' Lottie whispered into his ear.

'It's complicated,' he said, and kissed her cheek again.

'I'm no stranger to complicated. Let me carry one of those. Care to drive us home?'

'Oh yes, I've missed driving.' Before they moved off, Boyd took a jiffy bag from the rucksack. 'I think you will find this of benefit in your case against Terry Starr.'

'What is it?'

'Detective Lopez gave it to me before I left. A small package was delivered to the McAllister apartment this morning. The police confiscated it. This is a copy of the USB that was in the package.'

'Lucy.' Lottie's breath caught in her throat. 'She managed to copy Terry's hard drive. She was a brave girl.'

'Small comfort to her parents, though.' Boyd straightened. 'Now, what planet did you park the car on?'

'By the way, my mother is out of hospital and living with me for a while.'

'Seems like you have a lot to tell me.'

'I sure have.' Lottie linked her free arm through Boyd's and felt whole again. 'Hey, Sergio, do you like McDonald's?'

'Yes.'

'There's a drive-thru not far from the airport. My treat.'

The boy gave her a gleaming smile. 'Can I, Papá?'

'Lottie is my boss and she must be obeyed at all times.' Boyd winked at her.

As they reached the car, Lottie's phone rang.

'It's Sean,' she said. 'Any bets it's about my mother?'

Boyd smiled. 'You better answer it.'

'Whoever said life was plain sailing didn't have a hole in their boat.'

Sergio's eyes lit up. 'I didn't know you have a boat. That's so cool.'

She turned away with a smile and answered the call as they loaded the cases into the boot.

'Mam, where are you? Gran is wrecking the house.'

'What's up with her?'

'She insisted I call you. She's looking for a green suit.'

'Tell her it's at the dry cleaner's.'

'She's frantic. She'll end up back in hospital if she doesn't calm down. She keeps calling me Peter.'

'That's your dead grandad.'

Sean groaned. 'Will you be home soon?'

'Put your granny on.' Lottie waved the phone at Boyd with an eye roll. He smiled and pulled Sergio close.

'Lottie,' Rose shouted. 'Peter won't look for my suit. The green—'

'It's fine, Mother. I'll pick it up from the dry cleaner's tomorrow,' Lottie fibbed. 'I'm bringing Boyd home.'

'Oh, that lovely man with the big ears. He might know where you put my suit.'

'I'll be there in an hour.' She cut the call. 'Sorry.'

Boyd winked at her. 'I've missed the chaos you create, Lottie Parker.'

'Get in the car, Boyd.'

'I'm hungry,' Sergio said.

Lottie sat in. 'You and me both, kiddo.'

Boyd grinned and started the engine.

Leaning back into the seat, Lottie closed her eyes, thinking that a little chaos was fine. She had never lived any other way, and she wasn't going to change now.

'I'm glad you're home, Mark,' she said. 'I've missed you.'

A LETTER FROM PATRICIA

Hello, dear reader,

I am delighted that you have read *The Guilty Girl*. If you enjoyed it and want to keep up to date with all my latest releases, just sign up at the following link. Your email address will never be shared, and you can unsubscribe at any time.

www.bookouture.com/patricia-gibney

Thank you for sharing your time with Lottie, her family, Boyd and the team in this the eleventh book in the series. I hope you enjoyed *The Guilty Girl* and I'd be thrilled if you could post a review on Amazon or on the site where you purchased the e-book, paperback or audiobook. It would mean the world to me. Thank you so much for the reviews received so far.

To those of you who have already read the other ten Lottie Parker books, *The Missing Ones*, *The Stolen Girls*, *The Lost Child*, *No Safe Place*, *Tell Nobody*, *Final Betrayal*, *Broken Souls*, *Buried Angels*, *Silent Voices* and *Little Bones*, I thank you for your support and reviews. If *The Guilty Girl* is your first encounter with Lottie, you should enjoy the previous ten books in the series.

You can connect with me on my Facebook author page, Instagram and Twitter. I also have a website, which I try to keep up to date.

Thanks again for reading *The Guilty Girl*.

I hope you will join me for book twelve in the series.

Love,

Patricia

www.patriciagibney.com

 facebook.com/trisha460

 twitter.com/trisha460

 instagram.com/patricia_gibney_author

ACKNOWLEDGEMENTS

We are living through difficult times, and I find writing comforts me. I wrote *The Guilty Girl* towards the end of 2021 as Covid was still a fear across the world. I edited it as war broke out in Ukraine. Life is fragile, no more so than now, but I hope you find reading allows you a peaceful escape. Thank you for reading *The Guilty Girl* and for travelling Lottie's journey with me.

There are many people involved in bringing this book to you. I wish to take this opportunity to thank them. My agent Ger Nicol of The Book Bureau has been with me from day one and I value her advice and friendship.

I am grateful to Lydia Vassar-Smith for her editorial expertise. She continues to extract the best from me!

Publicity is so important for writers, and I'm thankful to Kim Nash, head of publicity at Bookouture, for her friendship and tireless work on my behalf. Also to Sarah Hardy, Noelle Holten, and Jess Readett for the promotional work on my books, and thanks to Mark Walsh of Plunkett PR in conjunction with Hachette Ireland.

Special thanks to those who work directly on my books at Bookouture: Alex Holmes (production), Alex Crow, Melanie Price and Occy Carr (marketing). Thanks to Tom Feltham for proofreading. I'm forever grateful to Jane Selley for her excellent copyediting skills. My sister Marie Brennan is the first reader of my manuscripts, including *The Guilty Girl*, and I'm grateful for her assistance with proofreading.

Sphere Books and Hachette Ireland publish my books in paperback, and I'm grateful for their support. Thanks to Hannah Whitaker of The Rights People and to my foreign translation publishers for producing my books in their native languages.

Michele Moran is the fantastic voice on the English-language audio format of *The Guilty Girl* and indeed all the Lottie Parker books to date. Thanks to Michele and the team at The Audiobook Producers.

Bookshops have been hard hit over the last few years, and I am grateful that they continue to bring books to readers. Thank you too to librarians everywhere.

I am grateful to readers who post reviews and also, a huge thank you to the hard-working book bloggers and reviewers who take the time to read and review my books.

Special thanks to Niamh Brennan and Kevin Monaghan, who helped with some of the technical details in *The Guilty Girl*. I'm grateful to John Kenny of Kenny's Cycles, Mullingar, for allowing me to use his name and shop in the novel.

My family is everything to me. My children, Aisling, Orla and Cathal, are the strongest, most hard-working and sensible young people I know. You and my grandchildren make me whole.

I dedicate this book to my long-term friends, Jo Kelly and Antoinette Hegarty. Thank you both for your friendship and support. You are true friends, through the good times and the not so good.

On a final note, as a reader you make my writing worthwhile. I'm currently writing the next book in the series (book twelve), so you shouldn't have too long to wait to see what chaos Lottie and Boyd create next!

Sincere thanks for accompanying me on this journey.

Note: I fictionalise a lot of the police procedures to add pace to the story. Inaccuracies are all my own.

Printed in Great Britain
by Amazon